I0666279

COWGIRL EDUCATION

A Camden Ranch Novel

JILLIAN NEAL

Edited by
CHASITY JENKINS-PATRICK
Cover Design by
THE KILLION GROUP, INC.

Written by Jillian Neal

Copyright © 2019 Jillian Neal

Published by Realm Press

ISBN: 978-1-940174-37-2

Library of Congress Control Number: 2016950918

First Edition

First Printing – October 2016

CONTENTS

To Nick and Mel

- for all of the Brit-splaining, the Twitter chats, the musical aid, and all of the help you provided that allowed me give the world Dec and Holly.

I could never thank you enough.

CHAPTER ONE

Declan St. James had spent the last hour and a half sitting at a corner table in Duffy's Tavern watching the woman seated alone near the bar swat them away like flies one after another, adding more surly snark with each and every brutal takedown.

As the cover band droned on injecting noise into the painted splashes of neon light and the smoky air, all of the classically painful pick-up lines had been surreptitiously executed with a lash of her merciless tongue, incinerating her would-be drink buyers into piles of ash. Declan was genuinely enjoying her responses. Not quite as much as he was enjoying the way her gorgeous lips pursed in indignation or how the fire in her emerald eyes roared as she took out her opponents, however. His eyes lingered on her slender figure complimented by the cleavage-revealing dress she was wearing. The curved barbell pierced through the head of his cock stirred anxiously. Damn, he was too old to be sporting a semi in a smoky bar from simply staring at a woman. What was she doing to him?

Helpless to resist, his eyes traveled up and down her tender curves once more. Her fight was fierce. Her quick rebuttals vicious, but her weary eyes told another story entirely.

"That dress is sexy as hell, baby. It'd look so good on my bedroom floor," spewed stupidly from a young man living high on the cheap beers he'd consumed. Safe bet his blood alcohol level was equal to that of his IQ.

"Know where I think it would look fabulous?" she snarled.

"Where's that?"

"Jammed in your windpipe, which is where it's going to be if you don't leave. . .now."

"Hey, at least that means I got you out of it." The idiot wasn't going down easily.

The woman narrowed those gorgeous eyes and leaned in. "Never, ever underestimate my ability to hit a moving target, douche bag."

Declan drew another long sip of his Newcastle Brown to keep from laughing out loud. He set the beer back on his table wishing he'd gone with laughter instead. Damn American bartender had chilled the beer past the point of recognition as a decent British ale, and laughing might've been nice, certainly not something he'd done in a while.

Declan's eyes returned to what had to be the most beautiful woman he'd seen since he'd set foot in the country, and that was saying something. The dress in question was a deep crimson and showed off all of her many assets to perfection. Lady in red generally wanted to be noticed. Something had obviously gone wrong. She was getting plenty of attention, but none she wanted. And if he wasn't mistaken, rejection — or maybe it was frustration — was penned in those gorgeous green eyes.

Calling himself a dumbass, Declan stood as if each man in the bar was being forced to take on the siren at table seven. He'd never been any good at turning down pain anyway. Hell, he had a reputation to uphold in his family as the brother always addicted to the wrong things. Besides, if he got anywhere at all, it might bolster his ego enough to make it worth his while. Potential pulsed in his veins as his eyes memorized the sway of her long, silken brunette hair as she brushed it behind her shoulders, readying herself for another opponent. If he got anywhere at all, it would be one hell of a night.

"May I, love?" He gestured to the seat opposite her at the small table. He worked his British accent hard. It seemed to have some kind of proper superpower over American women. Not something he understood, but he wasn't above using it to his advantage.

"Why not?" she huffed. The flicker of intrigue in her eyes said it was indeed his accent that had secured him the seat.

"Declan St. James, reformed douche bag at your service. And you might be?"

"Impressed, if that's actually true. They have some kind of rehab for that I'm unaware of?"

"Oh, don't kid yourself, love. Rehab's for quitters, isn't it?" He would certainly know.

Try though she might, a hint of a smile played on those full pink lips that had enchanted him for most of the evening. A half-second later she cracked and offered him a slight chuckle. "That reformed douchebag line ever work for you?"

"First time I've tried it. Suppose I'll tell you in the morning. I guess I could've gone with, *'Please allow me to introduce myself. I'm a man of wealth and taste. I've been around for a long, long year.'*"

And there it was. The volatile fire in her eyes cooled to a far more pleasant temperature. If she wasn't careful, she was going to give away one of what had to be a rarely-given, coveted grin. "The Stones. Very nice. Figured you for a Beatles fan with that accent."

"The accent means a lot of things, darling, but it definitely does not mean I have no taste in music."

"A Brit who doesn't like the Beatles and is a reformed douchebag. Interesting."

"Have you had some terrible experience with Beatle-loving Brits still in their douchebag state, my love?" He craved a real laugh from her like he used to long for a hit of something strong enough to numb the world around him. When she supplied a sweet giggle, his breath tangled in his lungs. Damn, but a woman like her could be the most dangerous drug in existence. Beautiful angel face with enough devil in her eyes to swell his long-ignored cock right along with his bruised ego.

"No, I guess I haven't, but I'm more opposed to douchebags than the Beatle-lovers."

"Well, we do have to give them, 'The End,' don't we?

"Do you always speak in song title, Declan the reformed douche bag?"

"You don't have to use my full title. Declan will do, and I try to as often as I can."

"Musician, I take it?"

"If you're taking, I'm giving, but which name shall I groan out between the sheets tonight when I'm reminding myself of you after I strike out as well?"

Heat climbed in seductive streaks out of the low cut of her dress, slightly swelling her breasts and settling high in her cheeks. "Who says you're striking out? Fair warning though, *the path to heaven runs through miles of clouded hell.*"

A low hungry groan wrenched itself up from Declan's gut. This woman was clearly an angel sent to rescue him from his shitty existence. It remained to be discovered if she was an agent of heaven or hell, however. "A beautiful woman that knows Stones and Dragons lyrics. If I had a heart, pretty sure I'd willingly hand it over right about now."

"And I'm pretty sure it's the thing holding up your rib cage, pumping blood through your body."

"Doctor?"

"Cowgirl. . .for now."

"Interesting. Not a lot of farms, or ranches as you call them, here in Lincoln. What brought you out here?"

"You first."

"I gave up my name and infinitely better song lyrics than you. Careful, sweetheart, even reformed douchebags know when they're unwanted."

"My name's Holly Camden, and you're not unwanted. And don't slam Imagine Dragons. Somebody has to be this generation's Stones."

"Agreed, but how I got here is a tremendously long, boring story that you don't want to hear tonight. What time was he supposed to be here anyway?"

"Is it that obvious I got stood up?" She shrank back into her chair before his very eyes. Until that moment, he'd been convinced his heart had been shattered too many times to ever really exist again, but just then it ached for the pain his reminder brought to her eyes.

"Only thing obvious to me is you're a stunningly beautiful woman with excellent taste in music, and if some tosser skipped out on you, he's a bastard of epic proportion. A fool you shouldn't waste any time worrying over. Especially when this band is perhaps only *mildly* shitty, and you could be dancing with me. It is so rare that those of us who are reformed get to benefit from the non-reformed's idiotic mistakes. You could give hope to thousands of nice guys sitting at home wishing women like you would give them a mere moment to stand in your sunlight."

"Is that so?"

"Absolutely." Declan stood and offered her a hand, rather proud that he still had a few moves that worked. Maybe America wasn't going to be a total loss like the rest of his bloody life.

"You know, Nirvana used to play here," she informed him as she took his offered hand and let him guide her towards the dance floor.

Turning back towards her, he gently pressed his index finger over her perfect cupid's bow and those alluring lips. He'd wanted to touch them all evening, preferably with his own mouth, but his finger would do.

"Shh, darling, speaking the sacred name might summon Kurt's attention from Heaven, and he'll hear how badly the lead guitarist is off key this evening. He suffered enough here on earth. There's a distinct chance the knowledge that bands like this would one day be covering 'About a Girl' is what finally drove him over. Best not to remind him of it now."

In the gentle caress of his finger over her lips, he learned more than she would ever care to admit after just one conversation. Her guess was partially correct. He was a musician in his off-time. He'd been playing guitar since he was eleven. Had formed his first band, back in Buckinghamshire, at the ripe old age of thirteen. Eventually, they'd tasted a little success, but he'd chosen his vices over music.

His friends still occasionally got together to play pubs outside of London, but he'd come to Lincoln, Nebraska, a place he'd only even heard of a year ago, desperate for a job that he'd secured through an old university buddy. Still looking to make up for all he'd taken away, he'd joined the prestigious Lifespan Psychological Counseling Center as their lead sex therapist. He'd lost it all and had somehow managed to recreate his life once again.

He knew sex, and he knew women. In fact, he'd always loved both. When he was certain his life was over, the only thing that made sense to him had been to desperately try to save humans from themselves. Trying to keep other fools from making his mistakes wasn't easy, but the knowledge he'd gained came in handy on occasion.

The very slight dilation of Ms. Camden's eyes and the quickening of her breath said she craved his touch and sensed his desire. Curiosity and hunger were pinned in the gentle furrow of her brow. So many things she deserved to learn and discover. So many things he could help her explore. He started to envy the man who would ultimately teach her, but then remembered that the majority of women never encountered anyone who could — or would — unlock the things about themselves that they would never admit out loud. Not that his ability to do so had ever gotten him anywhere worth being.

He guided her gently into his arms and tried desperately to convince himself that her curves and her warmth didn't soothe him more than anything he'd yet experienced since he'd gotten clean. She fit perfectly in his arms, the cheeky girl with rosy lips and a fiery soul who'd had no time for anyone in the crowded bar. . .anyone but him.

Declan shot several predatory glares to the men still admiring her. She certainly wasn't his, but something about her triggered protective instincts he hadn't felt in a decade. He was far from worthy, and there would inevitably come a time when he'd screw something else up, and she'd need to be protected from him.

A twinge of guilt over telling her he was a musician twisted in his gut, still full of frigid beer, but one did not introduce themselves as a sex therapist ever. The inevitable questions, expectations, and incumbent hell that came from that wasn't worth it. It was the kind of thing you confessed on some drunken night eight months down the road when there was precious little in the relationship worth saving.

Besides, this was just a dance, maybe a night of making each other forget everything wrong with the world, and then they would both move on without him managing to ruin her life as well. He could show off his knowledge and skill, give her a night she'd remember when she settled down with some *farmer* he supposed. She'd said she was a cowgirl, after all. *You used to be a farmer yourself.* Remembrances of his youth intruded on the longing in his mind. He shut them down with relative ease as he swayed Holly in time to the music. This was nothing more than a one-night stand.

When she tucked her face against his shoulder, his entire body responded. Protecting her took an ever-so-slight precedence over fucking her. She wanted a place to hide. The world had been too much that day. He knew the feeling only too well. And damn it all to hell if he wasn't going to be the man to make her night infinitely better than her day.

Unable to help herself, Holly cuddled closer to Declan's well-defined chest. She felt her breathing steady and her frayed nerves soothe. Her mind instantly recalled the vast ink work that peeked out from his rolled-up sleeves and continued all the way down to the knuckles on his left hand that she'd tried to discreetly study while they'd been sitting at the table. She'd wanted to ask him about them, but somehow, that seemed too intimate for their current setting. Why did she feel so close to him so quickly? They'd certainly never met before. She would've remembered meeting a man whose name and body dripped with rampant sex appeal and quiet confidence. Her night had been infuriating. Why did she suddenly feel safe in his arms? If she was the kind of girl who believed in fairytales, she might guess she'd known him in another life, but she was definitely not one of those kind of girls.

Okay, what the hell happened? Mentally reversing the course of her night she tried to remember that she was supposed to meet that asslicker, Trevor Singleton, for drinks. She'd only agreed because Singleton was the latest offspring in the Singleton family — the ones who had three buildings, a performing arts center, and a parking lot named after them at Nebraska-Lincoln.

She and Trevor had competed in every single thing since the moment they'd both set foot on campus six years ago. Now, they were both up for the coveted spot to have Dr. Richard Newsome be their PhD supervisor. Trevor had called her to explain that his father had heard that Dr. Newsome was taking two students this year, and perhaps they could discuss the possibility of working together to be those students. She'd swallowed the whole damn story hook, line, and sinker. Trevor had texted her a picture of him and his parents at Dr. Newsome's backyard barbecue an hour ago. She planned to gut him like a trout at their next encounter.

When Declan cradled her closer, she inhaled the mix of cologne, soap, and some potent musk all his own emanating from him, and she couldn't quite find it in herself to care about her degree, or Trevor, or anything else. A tatted-up, brow-pierced, British, badass musician with an accent that had already thoroughly melted her panties was definitely not a bad way to forget all about the Singletons and every other thing she'd been obsessing over for the last week.

And he was most definitely not a cowboy. Her number one rule for dating. Boots, spurs, calloused hands, bossy, demanding, arrogant, foul-mouthed, and shit-covered were not for her. She had three older brothers that fit all of those bills and had grown up with dozens upon dozens of others. Nope. She would always be a cowgirl at heart, but cow*boys* were not allowed to darken her doorsteps for dates *ever*. Declan, on the other hand, was more than welcome to keep distracting her from her shitty evening.

The song wound towards the end, and Holly's heart sped right along with the crescendo. She didn't want this dance to be over. It had been far too long since someone had held her close and stirred the longing she kept tucked inside. She was sick to death of the *boys* in her classes. They were psych majors, just like her. All they wanted to do was analyze her and then fuck her. Not that she could blame them. She wanted to analyze them as well, right along with the rest of her life.

Before she'd given them up for good, the cowboys back home weren't any better. No analyzation there, but no exploration, either. First and foremost, she longed for a *man*, not some college kid, that might attempt to have sex with her soul; a man who could unravel the riddles of her with every touch of his fingertips and every brush of his tongue. She wanted someone to answer her questions without judgment. Someone who would explore with her. Somehow, Declan seemed like he could do all of that and so much more. Something in the assuredness of his arms around her, the cool confidence that exuded from him, and that barbell through his eyebrow spoke to the desperate desires residing deep within her body.

She'd never asked a guy to come back to her apartment after one dance. She'd never been the one-night stand type. Something about it irked her. There was so much she'd never done, but that was all about to end. . .maybe. If only the searing pain in the center of her back would let up. A kiss from Declan would surely make it better.

The band bled *About a Girl* into *Pour Some Sugar on Me* rather well in her non-expert opinion, but Holly had no desire to dance to a faster song. She lifted her head and licked her lips, hoping that would be invitation enough.

She swore his dark chuckle penetrated her skin and gripped her soul. "The band clearly took the ever popular *'greatest cover hits every band should know'* quite literally, and you, my love, really shouldn't give me looks like that."

"Why not?"

"Because you are awfully, awfully tempting, and I've never been all that good with restraint."

"Who's asking you to restrain yourself?"

"I am. You don't strike me as the kind of woman who snogs a guy she just met."

She bit back her giggle at his British phrasing. She really should get out more. There just weren't that many ex-pats in the middle of Nebraskan cattle country. "We'll add that to the lengthy list of things you don't know about me. I've done my fair share of *snogging.*"

"Trying to make me jealous, love?"

"Is it working?"

"Too damn well."

He threaded his fingers in her hair and guided her mouth towards his own. She had no idea where the anguished noise of pure need she made came from. She took it as a clear indicator that her recently self-imposed celibacy should come to an end.

His pained grunt of approval had her melting into his body. The moment their mouths met, she opened for him like a woman starved, desperate to taste more of the craving on his tongue. His lips were the perfect mix of soft heat and demanding pressure. A heady combination of greed and desire filled her mouth. He tasted like expensive beer and liquid sin.

His hand caressed along the center of her back and then latched onto her right ass cheek with a seductive squeeze.

"Dammit! Ouch!" she tensed in pain.

"I'm sorry. I didn't mean. . . ." he jerked his hand away. Confusion broadcast from every chiseled plane of his face. "Are you all right? I'm sorry I got carried away. You seemed like. . . ." He bit off the inevitable ending, '*you were into it.*'

And she had been. Dear God, she'd been more than into it. "I was," Holly squeezed her eyes shut and called herself an idiot. "Trust me, I was very, very into it. You didn't do anything wrong. It's just. . . uh. . . . " She was certain Declan, who sported an infinite number of tattoos, was going to laugh at her outright no matter how polite he'd been thus far.

"Are you hurt, darling? The guy who was supposed to meet you. . . ? He didn't?"

"Oh, no. I'm sorry. It's got nothing to do with him, and I'm not dating him or anything. He's not even a friend of mine. I actually hate him." She glanced down at the dress she'd decided on just for the satisfaction of making Trevor's tongue hang out of his mouth like the horn-dog he was and understood that her actions had to be speaking louder than her words.

The caring concern that weighted Declan's perfect gray eyes drew the confession from her. "I got a tattoo yesterday. It's. . .kind of big, and like an idiot, it never occurred to me that I can't really reach all of it to put the lotion and ointment on it. Kind of hurts like hell."

"I see." He tried to hide his smirk, but humor had replaced the concern in his eyes. "I'm terribly sorry you're in pain, darling, but tonight is apparently my lucky night. If you'll allow it, I do happen to know a little bit about taking care of tats."

Holly's eyes widened as he edged his shirt cuff further up his arm revealing a full sleeve of intricate ink work. Her heart flew as she watched him unbutton one single button at the top of his shirt to show her his left shoulder and a peek of his chest. The longing to order him to show off more of his credentials formed on her tongue, but she bit back the request.

"Yeah, I noticed those. Just kind of an odd thing to ask about since we just met."

"Like I said, this is clearly my lucky night. Now, Miss Holly Camden, may I escort you home and see about this new ink?" He held up his right hand. "You have my word, certified by the Queen herself, that I will be a perfect gent, unless, of course, you'd like me to be something other than completely civilized."

"The Queen, huh?" Holly rolled her eyes, but the rapidly drying skin had worried her all day. Now it burned and felt swollen. Her entire body was confused. Declan had floored the accelerator on her sex drive, which had dampened the pain to non-existent until he'd squeezed the wrong places. She had no hope of convincing herself that she wasn't also desperate to know just how uncivilized Declan St. James could be and what else he might do with his skillful hands.

Besides, she didn't really have anyone else to ask to help. All of her friends from the last few years had finished their Masters and moved on. She had no one to call to help her and driving home would have hurt like hell. Not to mention her parents' reaction to her tattoos. It was distinctly odd to be in a city she'd known her whole life, the place where she'd managed to become something other than "little Holly Camden," and to suddenly know no one. Concessions had never come easily for her, but tonight she was willing to make one.

"I'll take you up on that perfect gentleman thing tonight, if you're really willing, but I'd be very interested to discover just how *uncivilized* you can be when my back doesn't feel like someone set it on fire."

"Tempting as hell, love. My God, how would I ever turn you down on anything? But you're breaking my heart. I wish you'd said something earlier. I understand why you didn't, but pain is not something you should ever have."

"Thought you didn't have a heart."

"You, my dear, have a wicked tongue, a killer body, and kisses so sweet I may never recover, and I am not a man known for my patience. You've been killing me slowly for hours. That kiss bloody damn near made me embarrass myself. Come show me this tat and finish me off for the evening."

CHAPTER TWO

"What the hell, bitch? What he got that I ain't?" The stumbling, slurring, piss-poor excuse for a man blocking Declan and Holly from the exit door clearly liked a hefty dose of pain with his booze. He was also the idiot Holly had already threatened with lodging her dress in his windpipe.

Rage rocketed up Declan's spine and sizzled outward to his fists. His biceps flexed ominously. He'd been in more bar fights than he cared to recall, but never before had he wanted to remove his opponent's sac and then shove it down his throat.

Something about Holly, her tender strength, the way she must've been trying to drink off the pain of the tattoo, the way she obviously leapt before she looked, the sinful looks she gave him coupled with her sweet kisses, it all spoke to places in his soul he thought long dead and buried back in that tiny graveyard not two miles from his father's farm in the Chilterns.

"Pardon me, darling." He slid Holly to the side and had the punk pinned against the nearby wall by the strength of his shoulder in the punk's throat. Using his other hand, he shoved the guy's head into the wall, giving him nowhere to look but in Declan's infuriated eyes. "To answer your question, you incomprehensible jizztrumpet, I possess the ability to speak without sounding like I've spent the better part of my life under a stone. I also know how to handle a woman of her caliber, which you haven't a clue in hell as to how to do. On top of that, do you feel how I'm allowing you to continue breathing?" He leaned in, shutting off his airway for a moment to make his point. The asshole managed a nod. "Yes, well, as you can clearly feel, I also have the ability to make breathing far more difficult for you. Not only that, but I can shove that beer bottle you're clinging to so far up your arse you drown in it. Stay the hell away from her, and if I ever, *ever* hear of her so much as crossing your pre-pubescent mind again, I won't hesitate to expand on all that I *have* that you do not, and all that I can *do* that you cannot."

With a hard hip check into the idiot's groin, Declan let him slink to the ground in pain and quickly escorted Holly to the parking lot. Poor thing was shaking.

"Uh. . .thank you," she finally managed. If she worried that bottom lip anymore she was going to draw blood, and she stumbled, trying to follow him while keeping her eyes on the door to the bar.

"Come here, love." In the middle of the tavern parking lot, he gently wrapped her back up in his arms. "I need to see this tat so I know where I can hold you." No laughter. She just buried her face against him. That same hollow place in his chest he'd noticed, when he'd asked her about the guy who'd stood her up, ached. If he ever had the chance to meet the wanker who'd blown her off, he'd buy the guy a nice scotch for not showing up. "Deep breath for me, okay? All's well."

"I'm sorry. This night has been. . . ." She squeezed her eyes shut and edged out of his embrace.

"Shitty? Yeah. Mine too, until I saw this gorgeous woman with brilliant comebacks take on every Y chromosome in the bar and beat them badly. Now, it's looking to be one hell of a night. Let's get you home and see if we can't get you out of pain."

"Thanks for everything, Declan. Maybe I should just go. . .alone. I'm not up for much else."

A disturbing sense of panic twisted in Dec's gut. She couldn't go. Not yet. There was more to her and him, more to them. Much more to be discovered. Wasn't there?

He forced what he hoped was a cocky smirk. "Can't let you go yet, love. I swore to the Queen I'd take care of you, remember? And I'm not asking for anything other than to ease what ails you. Ten minutes, fifteen tops. Tomorrow morning, I'll come back to your place, after having slept completely, sadly alone in my own bed, apply more ointment, and see if you might let me take you out for breakfast. That is all I'm asking for."

"I know. Thank you. I'd love to have breakfast with you. It's just. . . don't you think I've gotten you in enough trouble?" She gestured back to the tavern.

Declan couldn't help but laugh. She thought *that* was trouble? Dear God in Heaven, she was more naïve than he'd originally guessed. She was also more caring, tender, and sweet, and probably had no business getting involved with a guy like him. With a deep breath he reminded himself that he wasn't that guy anymore. That was why he was in America, wasn't it? To start over.

"That was no trouble, love. Trust me. You okay to drive? I can give you a ride." He gestured to his latest purchase — a decidedly American Harley Fat Boy Softail.

"Wow." Her eyes ran the length of the bike. "Of course you drive a motorcycle. Should have guessed that." She mumbled to herself.

Declan chuckled. "I normally despise clichés, but the bike was too much to resist. It completes the fucked up musician picture, don't you think?"

"Trust me, it's not at all a bad picture, but I can drive. Do you just want to follow me?"

"Lead the way." He followed her to a rather large, siren red, Chevy Silverado with mud splatters on the body, and offered her his hand as she stepped up. "Of course you drive a truck big enough to intimidate the shit out of most anyone. Should have guessed that."

And there it was, her beautiful smile and an honest-to-God laugh. "It's big enough to haul horse trailers, tractors, and cattle. Told you I was a cowgirl."

"I must impress upon you how hard I am trying to avoid asking just how well you *ride*." With that, he offered her a wink and returned to his bike.

When the customary metallic rattle of the powerful machine ripped through the air, Declan gripped the handlebars and tried to sort through his evening. He'd been in Duffy's to study the crowds before his band, *Original Sinners*, played on Wednesday night. Not a particularly original name in his opinion, but he was still earning his place in a band that had been around for ten years before he'd arrived on the scene. He'd met his one and only friend, Kade Griffith, at a Narcotics Anon meeting right after he'd moved to Lincoln. Kade had recruited him to be their front man when their original lead had moved to Arizona to be near his wife's family.

Holly had kept him too distracted to really discover much about the bar. The band wasn't half bad. They weren't half good either, though. The crowd hadn't seemed to mind either way.

Holly. His mind had little room for anything else. What was it about her that drew him in like a moth to a flame? She turned down a road near the University. He followed as his thoughts churned over the girl who had him so thoroughly distracted. His propensity for obsession coupled with the confection of the kiss they'd shared and created a Molotov cocktail in his mind. As they turned into a mundane apartment complex, he'd redirected enough blood flow from the head in his jeans to the one on his shoulders for the warning bells to sound off.

Declan had the untoward and unwanted gift of being a one hit wonder. He'd nicked a smoke from his older brother when he was fourteen and had taken to stealing them from Mr. Kapoor down at the Village Store for the next several years. He'd tried taking a couple of his old man's painkillers and had craved something stronger by the weekend. Searching for any variation of hash he could score, he'd landed on Molly, then he'd crashed and burned in a fiery explosion of cocaine, shrooms, acid, and painkillers. It had all taken him only one hit to make him want more, and it had all come from bedding Evie Taylor on his sixteenth birthday. One and only time in bed with her and he'd been addicted to the girl that would ultimately ruin his life.

When the roar of Holly's truck motor silenced, Declan shut down his bike and reminded himself that Holly was most certainly not a junkie. She was vibrant with life itself. Warm and sweet and alive. But he knew he must constantly remind himself that addiction invariably clawed beneath his skin. He'd been clean for almost eleven years, and he'd fought for it every second of every hour of every day. He couldn't become addicted to her, and she was so utterly tempting. He couldn't ruin her life the way he'd ruined his own.

Holly's cringe as she slid out of the driver's seat of her massive truck prodded that hollow space in his chest once again.

"The dress stuck to it," she whimpered. Arching her back to try to loosen the fabric from the tattoo made an alluring presentation of her gorgeous cleavage to his starving eyes. His mouth went drier than the Mojave and his palms burned to touch her skin. He ordered away the urgency that swamped his blood. She was in pain. He had no business getting involved with her anyway.

"Come on, love. Let's get you taken care of."

He followed her past the elevators in her building and up the stairs. "Elevators haven't worked in three years according to my landlord."

An invitation to come back to his expansive lakefront home formed on his tongue. The need to care for her overwhelmed him once again. He longed to tuck her up in the lap of luxury. His position at the counseling center boasted a sizeable salary, and he suddenly wanted to spoil her. He told himself that was good. Addiction was ultimately a selfish thing. Caring for her, instead of seeing what he could get her to do for him, was a good sign. The soft swish of the silky fabric over her delectable ass as she climbed the steps reminded him he was far from a saint, however.

Her apartment wasn't any nicer than the building that housed it. He could see the tiny kitchen and small bedroom from the living room where they were standing. Declan suspected that his cowgirl had taken it without having a job. She'd gotten a tattoo without anyone to help her care for it, after all. She'd also trusted some shit-licker to meet her at a bar, and he hadn't shown, and she'd had no hesitation about daring him to kiss her. Yep, Miss Holly Camden definitely leapt before she looked. Damn, if that didn't make him like her all the more.

"Here, darling." Gently, he settled his hands on her shoulders to steady her then slowly eased the fabric away from the center of her back. She shivered under his caress. His previously missing heart roared to life with nothing more than a tender quiver of her body.

"Thanks." She turned to stare him down. That sassy tongue darted over her lips again. Was she trying to kill him? Did she have any bloody idea how hard it was for him to turn down things that *wanted* to kill him? "Uh. . .I'll just go change into something. . .looser." Longing set up in those emerald eyes. Such a rarity to find a brunette with eyes like that. She seemed to be suffering from desire almost as much as he was, but that wasn't even a remote possibility.

"I'll wait right here."

"No. I mean, make yourself at home." She gestured around the fairly barren apartment. A small pile of unpacked boxes was stacked along the sliding glass doors that led to the diminutive balcony overlooking the dumpsters. There was a well-worn sofa on one wall in front of a particle board entertainment center where a television stood sideways, vomiting its own wires out of the gaping hole in the center.

"Couldn't fit my DVD player in the truck when I moved in. I'll get it next time I'm home," she explained as she noted where he was staring.

He wanted to ask her where exactly home was, but he had no real desire to share anything about London or his life before that moment, so he nodded his understanding instead. An uncomfortable silence extended between them. He hated it. He needed her to be comfortable with him. Always. "Go get changed, love. I want to take care of you."

That addictive smile spread the width of her face and warmth flooded her cheeks. "Be right back."

When he heard the bedroom door lock turn, Declan drew a deep breath, desperate to regain a little equilibrium. She'd lived there long enough to perfume the air, however. The scents of spicy orange blossoms coupled with sweetened vanilla and took up residence in his lungs. He swore the essence of her wrapped itself around his cock and squeezed. Adjusting himself quickly, he studied a few framed photographs, stacked on an end table, of his cowgirl flying on horseback across an expansive pasture. There were others of her taking jumps of the sort he'd never hope to make in this lifetime or the next. He'd ridden horses most of his life, but he'd never ridden like that.

Fierce determination broadcast from her body, laid low over the horse's shoulder and crest, masterfully holding the reins, and braced for wherever the jump might've landed her. Graceful and ready, poised to succeed. No fear. The photographs definitely matched Holly, or at least what he knew of her.

Holly gripped her dresser and ordered her heart to stop pounding in her chest. *What the actual hell?* He'd barely touched her shoulders. They'd had one mind-blowing kiss. How was she suddenly desperate for Declan to strip her out of the dress himself? She wanted those hands all over her fevered skin. She wanted him naked in her bed. She wanted to study all of that intricate tattoo work on his chest and arms. She wanted to know what it might be like to tame a bad boy. And more than anything, she longed for him to fill the emptiness that pervaded both her pussy and her soul.

Remembering his purpose in coming over was to help her with the tattoo, she tried to carefully ease the dress over her head without making the burning sensations worse. *He probably thinks you are a huge baby and an airhead for not knowing that the tat would have to be moisturized.* Not only that, but she'd been running hot and cold on him ever since he'd taken the seat at her table.

She'd had no idea why she continued to sit there after she realized Trevor had played her for a fool. She'd told herself it was to take out her spiteful temper on all of the assholes that kept hitting on her, but that wasn't it. She'd felt rooted to that seat like she was there for a higher purpose. Being able to have breakfast and possibly fuck a British bad boy with the body of a god probably didn't qualify as a higher purpose, but who was she to question the universe?

Working quickly, she located her brother Luke's old Carhartt sweatshirt and eased it over her shoulders. It was her favorite. Since her big brother was almost a foot taller than her and built like a cowboy it was huge on her petite frame, and best of all it smelled like home. Adding a cute and rather skimpy pair of Nebraska University sweatshorts, she summoned courage and checked herself in the mirror. The sweatshirt almost covered the hem of the shorts. Perfect.

Her cheeks were already flushed pink from the chemical explosion that occurred every time Declan's hand touched her skin. There was no need to pinch them. She rubbed a little cherry flavored Chapstick across her lips, hoping for another kiss before he left, grabbed the tube of Aquaphor the tattoo artist had given her, and headed back into the living room.

The quick lick of Dylan's tongue over his bottom lip as he stared at her like he wanted nothing more than to take a bite was highly satisfying, but when their eyes met she lost a little of her bravado. She should hate him for making her feel needy in his presence, but my God, she needed him desperately.

"This shirt is really big, so you should be able to touch all of me. . .uh, I mean. . .all of me. . .no, it. The tattoo. All of the tattoo. With the ointment. I mean. It won't take you long. Not that if it did that would be a bad thing." *Shut up Holly!* She expected him to laugh at her outright, but his eyes darkened seductively and his brow furrowed.

"Sweetheart, has some bastard given you the impression that touching you would be some kind of chore?"

To keep all of the potential stupidity locked up inside of her, she simply shook her head to avoid another verbal suicide mission.

"I think we should wash it first, get any dress fibers off of it so you don't get an infection. That okay with you?"

"Uh, sure. Thank you." Holly tried to remember what state she'd left her bathroom in before she led Declan through her bedroom. As soon as she flipped on the light, her eyes landed on her favorite vibrator, a small, neon pink number with a butterfly clit massager, laying on the side of the bathtub. She shoved it in a nearby towel and tried to hide it in the hamper, but she wasn't quick enough.

Another one of those seductively dark chuckles sounded from Declan. "Very interesting indeed," was his only comment.

The mirror confirmed that Holly was the precise shade of an overly ripened raspberry. "Sorry."

"For what?" He looked genuinely confused.

Having no control over her own eyes, her gaze landed back on the hamper. "Uh. . .it's such a mess in here. I'm not usually a slob. Just haven't unpacked everything yet."

"Only the most important things then." He made no effort to hide his smirk.

"Funny." Her scowl dampened his laughter.

"This soap good?" He lifted a bottle from the counter.

She nodded as he eased the sweatshirt up her back. His heated breath whispered over her shoulder blades, igniting the nerve endings there. He studied the tattoo before turning on the sink to let the water warm.

"I didn't mean to offend you. Trust me, the only thoughts running around in my head are those of supreme intrigue and the orders not to beg you to let me watch you use that tonight just before I take it in my hands and allow you to relax while I bring you pleasure."

Holly's mouth hung open long enough to dry out her tongue. *Holy fucking hell.* "Little forward, don't you think?"

Just then Declan lathered his hands with the soap and gently massaged the largest part of the tattoo in the center of her back. Her entire body shook with hunger. "Was it? I find myself having little to no ability to act properly when I'm looking at your gorgeous body. I'm sorry, dear. I'll try harder."

"Well. . .don't try too hard."

A low growl sounded in her ear. "So damn tempting. I may not survive this, but can you pull those shorts down just a little so I can get to the ends of the strands?"

Holly eased the shorts down, revealing the hollow at the base of her spine and the top of her ass.

"You are so damn beautiful." The words seemed to have been wrenched up from his gut. His eyes were dark and craving. She should have been frightened, or at least cautious. No one knew where she was or who she'd brought home, but she could locate no fear in her body, only pure, unadulterated lust.

"Since I've effectively become your tattoo doctor, do I get to know what it means to you? I take it this isn't your first. Had to hurt like hell to get it there over your ribs. That was the worst, wasn't it?"

"It did hurt like hell. I broke my wrist last summer when I got thrown on a horse I was helping broke. I had a few of the pain killers left over, so I took that before I went in. They helped."

Declan's entire expression darkened dramatically. "That's a terrible idea. Never do that again. Do you understand me?"

The abject torment residing in the depths of his eyes kept Holly from informing him that she'd do whatever the hell she wanted whenever she wanted to do it. "I do have a few others," she supplied instead.

She lifted the bottom hem of the shorts to reveal a small garland of roses she'd had tattooed on her right hip.

"Sweet baby Jesus are you trying to kill me?" he panted, but at least he'd loosened back up a little. Grinning at that, she pulled down the front of her shorts and panties just enough to reveal the heart-shaped Latin quote, *Libera te, Qui in te unt, Honoremus te,* positioned between her mound and hipbone.

"I find myself utterly devastated that I didn't get to tend those as well." He shook his head as he gently dried the tattoo on her back.

"It means. . . ."

"Free yourself. Be who you are. Honor yourself."

"You know Latin?" Okay, that was definitely not something she expected from a musician with a brow piercing and a motorcycle. She called herself on being judgmental.

"A little. Had to take it at university."

"The one on my back is sort of the same thing, actually. It's a Native American dream catcher. Normally they have webbing in the circle, but I did the moon and the sun there instead, and the feathers and five tendrils represent parts of myself that I want to remember to honor."

"It's beautiful. A few days from now when it's not so red I want to study it closely." Before Holly could respond, Declan began tenderly rubbing the ointment over the moon and sun portion. "What do the moon and sun mean to you?"

"Uh. . . ." Holly lost herself in the heat of his touch. She couldn't recall the pain she'd been in just moments before. His fingertips held seeds of magic.

"Love?"

Shivering from his tender care, she tried to remember what he'd asked her. "The moon. Right, I kind of always feel like there were two distinctive parts of myself. I guess my cowgirl side and my other side. I can't ever seem to get them to exist together. I thought the tat might help. I like how they're right on top of each other like that. That sounds crazy though, right?"

"Most definitely not. Most all of mine mean exactly the same. I'll show you sometime."

"That feels really good," Holly gushed, unable to stop herself.

Declan's grin said he liked that. "Americans have it all so wrong. Touch was never meant to be a luxury. Never supposed to be forbidden or taboo. It's not something meant to be regulated or predicated on something else. It's a validation of life, a necessary human need as long as the contact is wanted."

Holly managed a nod. She'd written something like that in her thesis. She couldn't quite recall the title as Declan rubbed the ointment along the top of her ass. She was certain that whatever she'd written about touch, it hadn't sounded as seductive and discerning as it did coming from Declan's lips. That accent was going to be her undoing. Liquid heat soaked the crotch of her panties. She longed to beg him to leave the tattoo and tend to her other needs.

When his hands left her back, the unwanted vacancy stung far worse than the tattoo.

A harsh swallow tensed his neck. His Adam's apple contracted seductively. "Perhaps just leave the shirt off after I go. Let it get some air. Try to sleep on your stomach."

Too far gone to have ever stopped herself, she whipped off the old sweatshirt and spun to face him. Her breasts swayed from the motion. Her nipples stood in stiff, painful points of desperate need.

"Holly," he moaned her name. "Darling, you are vastly overestimating my ability to maintain my control."

"Good." She traced her fingertips over her collarbone and then spun them around her own nipples.

"Holly." This time her name was a warning.

"Declan," she challenged.

She could almost see the moment he lost all hope of denying himself in his voracious eyes.

His hands landed on her hips and jerked her closer. He latched his lips onto her neck like a man possessed.

"Yes," gasped from her as she ground against the rock hard bulge in his jeans. His right hand tangled in her hair and a low, agonized groan echoed off the bathroom tile. His lips blazed a fiery trail from the hollow of her collarbone to her right breast.

"They hurt, don't they, love? They ache. I know. So needy for me, aren't they?" His expert tongue bathed over her right nipple. She dug her fingernails into his shoulders, pressing her breast further into the heat of his mouth. He cupped her left breast in the strength of his hand, kneading her flesh until she felt raw.

When he'd sucked until she was certain she was going to come from this alone, he left her aching, brushed a kiss between her breasts, and lifted his head. "I could bring you like this, sweet girl. I know what you crave. Someday I'll show you, but not tonight."

"Why?" she whimpered.

"Your back is still healing. We just met. We've both been drinking, and I need to get my head straight so I can be the lover you deserve. If I stripped right now, I'm likely to unload all over your sink."

Fevered embarrassment flooded her cheeks. "Yeah. I guess you're right. Sorry."

"I'm not sorry at all. Sweetest confection I've had in my mouth in far too long. Please don't think that wasn't the most difficult thing I've ever turned down, and you have no idea just how significant that is."

What does that mean? She eased back into Luke's sweatshirt and willed her face to return to its normal shade. "You were gonna show me your tats." Yes, there, that was better. Not throwing herself at a guy she'd just met in a bar. She started to congratulate herself on her resolve, but then realized she'd just effectively asked him to take his clothes off. Her entire body craved him like a drug. When it came to him, she had zero self-control. Her heart couldn't locate a steady rhythm, and she was still gasping for breath.

"Later. Tomorrow maybe. I think it best if I remain fully clothed. If you put your hands on me, we're very likely to do something we might later regret."

Burning up with both passion and embarrassment, Holly rolled her eyes. "I can control myself." That was probably a lie, but she was going with it.

"It's not you I'm worried about. I desperately want to get to know you better, and we clearly have enough chemistry to see where this might lead. If you still want me to, I'll pick you up in the morning for breakfast. What time does a cowgirl eat?"

Your cowgirl, she mentally corrected, and then wondered where on earth that had come from. "I like to sleep in when I'm not working the ranch, but whatever time is fine."

He lifted her hand to his lips and brushed a tender kiss along her knuckles. Her body responded like he'd just pressed his tongue between the folds of her pussy. Her stomach clenched and her nipples throbbed anxiously.

"I could name a time or I could tell you that I'll call when I'm on my way over, which would get me your phone number."

"Very smooth." She laughed despite the disappointment whipping through her veins.

"I thought so."

She couldn't help but appreciate his humor coupled with the devastation in his eyes. He seemed worried he'd hurt her feelings. That at least made her feel a little better.

CHAPTER THREE

Declan spent several long minutes leaning up against the cold brick wall outside of Holly's apartment building, desperately seeking some semblance of control. He gulped in the cool Nebraskan evening air, though it did nothing to douse the fire ignited by the addiction of her lips. The image of her teasing her own nipples would be forever emblazoned in his mind. He'd indulged himself in far more goodnight kisses than were really required given the amount of time they'd known one another. They were both playing with fire, but he suspected only he knew it.

God, she was irresistible. She stirred feelings in him he'd pushed away for far too long, throughout the entire debauchery of his marriage, through months of rehab and then university, for what felt like forever. He craved her more than he'd ever craved another hit. Had he not been damming his own demons for the last decade, he wouldn't have had the strength to walk away that night. Taking another deep breath of non-Holly scented air, he reminded himself that he could indulge in her without fear of killing himself or anyone else.

The way she'd whipped off that sweatshirt. The confidence that resided within the very marrow of her bones coupled seductively with an innocence that said she didn't have much experience. The succulent heat of her mouth made him overly eager to taste her nectar. He'd been able to feel the wet heat of her crotch when she'd pressed herself against his raging erection. He hated the desperation and frantic desire she summoned from him. Red flags of addiction if ever there were any. The problem was he'd always been dangerously attracted to red flags.

He stared at the door she'd begrudgingly closed when he insisted that it was time for him to go. Every cell in his body longed to demand she open herself for him. Open her door, open her mouth, open her legs, open the drenched lips of her pussy, open her mind, open her heart, open her deepest darkest fantasies, and let him own it all.

She'd been more than willing, but he didn't want her to have any regrets. He also didn't want to fuck her senseless against her bathroom counter and then go through the awkward fallout of inevitable explosions of passion.

He didn't want to rush any part of being with her. What a tremendous waste that would be. He wanted to linger in each kiss, breathe life into her soul, show her how she was meant to be worshipped. Fulfill her every fantasy. Spend hours making her desperate for him to soothe the burn he ignited.

In that moment, as his cock finally figured out that it wasn't getting any attention that didn't come from his own hand and retreated, he knew he could spend years showing her what sex was supposed to be, owning her satisfaction, discovering what Holly Camden required to come completely undone, to be entirely freed of the expectations the world dumped on women's sexuality. The flavors of her release on his tongue, every silky ripple of her channel, the shade of her nipples when deeply aroused, the pucker of her backside, the flush of her soft skin under his touch or the perfectly timed strike of his hand, the knowledge he'd desired an hour ago had quickly become a requirement. He desperately needed to unfold the complicated delicate truths of her with his own body.

Far too hyper to ever have slept, Holly debated. It wasn't *that* late. There was a decent chance Cheyenne was still awake. Having never possessed the ability to talk herself out of anything at all, she touched her best friend's name on her phone.

"Oh my God, why do you hate me?" was Cheyenne's sleepy response.

"Sorry," Holly whispered as if that would make her call more tolerable.

"S'ok. What's wrong?"

"Nothing. It's fine. Go back to sleep."

"Well, I'm up now so spill it. You never call me this late. This has to be good."

"I met this guy."

"They do make up half of the human population, Holl, so get to the more interesting parts of this convo, or I'm going back to sleep."

"A guy I really, really like, but I just met him."

"Now, we're getting somewhere. Keep going. What's this guy's name?"

"Declan St. James."

"If he's as sexy as his name, please tell me he's nekkid between your sheets, and you're calling me from the bathroom to ask my advice on how to best secure him to your bed. Scarves and neckties are your friends here. Anything else can get dicey and leave marks."

"Cheyenne, focus. We didn't sleep together. I all but threw myself at him, and he left."

"Bastard!"

"No, he's not. He's really sweet, but also definitely has a bad boy vibe that is supremely sexy. I'm choosing to believe that he really was being a gentleman and that he didn't leave because he's not into me."

"How is he a gentleman and a bad boy?"

"He just is. You'll have to trust me on this."

"Uh, not that you're not a kickass girl, but I'm pretty sure there aren't gentlemen anymore. They're just all assholes."

"I know, but I swear he is a gentleman. A badass gentleman with a motorcycle and fucking awesome tattoos. And he's British. You should hear him talk."

"Oh Holl, babe, you sound like you're already all the way in. That could be bad. It took Ron seven books to even kiss Hermione."

"Cheyenne. He is not a wizard. We will not communicate via owls. This is not a children's book. This is my life. Could you just shut up and listen for a minute?"

A deep yawn extended via the phone two hundred miles east from Pleasant Glen to Lincoln. "Shutting up and listening, but I will say Hermione should have *accio-ed* herself some Ron-cock one of the times she was staying at The Burrow. Or when they were staying at Sirius' house."

"Cheyenne!"

"Sorry. Listening."

"Thank you. You know how my dad and brothers are always talking about how they knew my mom, and Summer, and Indie were the ones as soon as they saw them?"

"Uh, yeah, I know the story, but a couple of months ago you told me it was all bullshit they told their wives because it sounded good. Remember? You said it wasn't true. I need it not to be true, Holl, because the first time Grant saw me I was twelve, and it was that summer that I had braces and headgear, and I'd let my aunt perm my hair so I looked like I'd wired my headgear up to an electrical socket or something. He couldn't have fallen in love with me like that, and that means I broke the Camden legacy, which is really bad because Grant needs to fall in love with me."

Holly rolled her eyes. Just like every conversation she ever had with Cheyenne it turned into talking about her brother Grant. "You did not break the legacy. Grant is just an idiot. I have no clue why you're so into him. Could we, just for a moment, wonder if maybe it isn't just something my dad and brothers say? What if it is true? There is a highly supported psychological belief that human beings actually fall in love in one-fifth of a second. Because you fall in love with your brain not your heart. I'm telling you, something about Declan and me, it was weird. I've never felt like this before, and I just met him. I've never been so attracted to someone, but it was more than that even. When we kissed. . .it was just different."

"Are you asking me if the Camden guys *and* the Camden girls fall in love at first glance?"

"Yeah. Maybe."

"Maybe Grant just needs to see me more, or maybe we need to kiss."

Holly sighed. Cheyenne was her best friend. Every now and then her advice was a little less self-centered.

"Why don't you ask your mom? She'd know better than me, right?"

"Yeah, that's a good idea. Not sure when I would do that, but maybe."

"K, can I go back to sleep now?"

"Yeah, sorry I woke you."

"No problem. I'm here for all of your British badass-slash-Harry Potter needs."

"You're the best. Love ya!"

Holly ended the call and stared around her tiny apartment. A student stipend didn't afford her much in the way of abodes, but she loved that the space was her own. At least this year she didn't have a roommate.

Staring up at the star strewn night outside her bedroom window, she couldn't help but miss the ranch. The stars were always brighter there outside of the city lights. She missed the low bellows of the cows and the soft neighs of her horses. She even missed the scent of sweet corn and manure on the constant Nebraskan breeze.

Determination quickly swept through her mind, whisking away the longing to go home. She wasn't giving up now. She'd figure out some way to be Dr. Holly Camden DMFT, doctor of marriage and family therapy with a specialty in sex therapy, and to be Holly Camden, youngest daughter of Ev and Jessie Camden, kickass horse rider, expert cattle roper, down and dirty cowgirl, and partial owner of the legendary Camden Ranch.

As for Declan. . . with a sly grin, she retrieved her favorite vibrator from the hamper and went to bed.

Right-forward, right-down, left-forward, left-down, over and over and over, Declan let the rapid-swiveled squeak and soft swish of leather against his fists from the speed-bag soothe him. Dammit, why had he looked at the date on his phone that morning? Why couldn't he have just continued to tell himself it was sometime in late August? His plan this year had been to let sometime in late August blend into the middle of September so he didn't have to remember the ending date stamped on the tombstone. Today's date eleven years in the past.

It was nearing ten in the morning. He should have left over an hour ago to pick up Holly. It killed him to think her tattoo might be hurting again, but terror kept him standing squarely at the bag, pounding out his frustration and his desperate need.

He'd already run six miles and had performed enough chest presses to make his muscles weep in agony. Sweat raced down his chest, pooling along the waistband of his shorts.

With one final blow from his right fist, he cursed himself and the entire universe to hell. This wasn't working. He needed to see her again, needed to feel her silky skin in his hands, needed to draw her candy-sweet nipples in his mouth, needed to know everything there was to know about Holly Camden.

You'll never be good enough for her. That damned tombstone slammed into his chest with all of the weight of its marble and stone fixtures. *You've been good for so long. You can't have a girl like her. You deserve something to ease this pain.* The incessant demon call was louder that morning.

I'm not giving up eleven years. I've fought for too long. I won't give up ever.

His mind was a house divided. Or perhaps his mind was set on self-preservation, his demons were hell bent on bringing about his demise, and the head on his cock was staging the revolt.

"Holly is an amazing, beautiful, brilliant woman. She's not a substance and she is sure as hell isn't Evie," he growled at the still-swinging speed-bag as if it had presented the argument.

Sex is so much sexier when it has a little help. His cravings continued to send vicious troops into battle, but he was stronger now. He could have her without getting addicted to her or using again. He'd learned his lessons, and maybe now was the time to prove it. *'Never get cocky about your addiction. Never think you've outsmarted it.'* Dozens of counselors' advice rang clearly in his mind.

Before he could convince himself to stand Holly up for her own good and his, he grabbed a towel to wipe his sweaty hands, and texted

Holly to apologize and say he was on his way. There. No turning back now. Gall-driven determination armored itself in his drive as he headed for the shower. If nothing else, he would take care of her until the tattoo was healed, and maybe it was time he proved to himself that he could have a healthy relationship. Proving to his addiction that he was stronger was how he'd survived the last eleven years. Damn it all to hell. He could do this.

CHAPTER FOUR

So, he isn't coming. Holly glared at the clock, furious that she'd actually believed Declan was a gentleman. She'd stupidly convinced herself that he was different, that he cared. She'd gone as far as to phone her best friend to drone on about him being the one. *Idiot!* Disgust roiled in her gut. She'd gotten up early to shower, shave, and attempt the coveted *I woke up like this* look to impress him. *Asshole.*

If he was going to stand her up, why didn't he just sleep with her the night before? She'd all but demanded it. The only obvious explanation for bolting after she'd whipped off her shirt was that he wasn't into her. Well, his loss.

The scorching blister of his kisses were still branded in her mind, serving as both a cruel reminder of what he'd done to her fully clothed and a nudging concern that maybe something had happened to him. He'd been into her. She'd felt it. Cowgirls always lived by their gut, and she was a psych student. She could read people quite well. He wasn't going to stand her up, so where the hell was he?

Her phone buzzed on the bathroom counter. Had anyone seen the speed at which she leapt for it, she would have been thoroughly embarrassed.

So sorry I'm late, sweetheart. Had to work through a few things. One doesn't turn down a night with a woman like you and not have to suffer the regret. I'll be there in a half hour. Promise. – Dec

Holly stared at the text for the better part of a full minute. The humility of signing it, meaning he honestly didn't believe she'd immediately entered him in as a contact as soon as he'd given her his number, coupled with curiosity as to just how he'd suffered through his regret and brought a broad grin to her face.

There were two distinctive sides to Declan St. James, or Dec, apparently. How did one man possess such skill, bravado, and confidence when he was twisting her libido into coils of desperation and still not believe that she could possibly be into him? She had no idea, but she couldn't wait to find out.

Determined to prove to him that she really wasn't a slob, she'd spent the time between getting ready and his appearance unpacking and cleaning her new apartment. She'd deposited her collection of vibrating sex toys in her bedside table drawer so he wouldn't encounter anymore unless they were mutually looking for one. Thoughts of him wielding a vibrator sped her heart and brought a fresh rush of liquid heat to her crotch. She definitely needed to make that particular fantasy come to life, if he was really willing. Trying to turn her thoughts from sex with Declan to anything else proved difficult, but she persevered.

The apartment was getting there. It was a long way from offering her the cozy comfort that always came from walking in her mama's kitchen or from saddling up Aurora Belle for a ride, but maybe someday she'd figure out how to make Lincoln a place she really felt at home. After she graduated with this final degree, there would be no more calling Camden Ranch her home. She knew she could always go back, but she'd have to work in Lincoln if she was going to be a sex therapist. It was the closest city with a counseling center.

A wicked thought brought another mischievous grin to her face. The look on her big brothers' faces if she were to show up at the ranch with Declan. A badass, tattooed, brow-pierced, musician would be sure to get the Camden cowboys up in arms. She lost a little of her glee when she tried to imagine introducing him to her parents, however. They'd never denied her a single thing that it had been in their power to give her. She was the baby through and through, but she doubted her daddy would approve of a musician as her boyfriend. Not that they were anywhere near giving each other titles or parental introductions.

Drawing a deep breath as she stood at her back door watching for his bike to pull up, she ordered herself to grow up. They hadn't even been on an official date. They were country miles away from a relationship. Why did she always leap fifteen steps ahead of where she was? Because once she set her sights on something she refused to take no for an answer. She was going to make Declan St. James hers, come hell or high water — or both.

"Bloody hell." Dec couldn't help but offer her a cocky grin. "I was sincerely hoping my memory of you from last night had somehow been improved by the alcohol or my dreams, but it turns out they didn't do you justice at all." His eyes raced up and down her slender frame. From the swells of her breasts, to the inward slope of her waist, to her soft, feminine hips, perfect for gripping while he drove himself inside of her, down the length of her legs, and then on a slow, reverse track to those eyes.

Those seductively-sweet eyes that were the novels of her soul said she'd been worrying and doubting. Another round of lambasting began in his mind. She'd thought he wasn't going to show. If she'd inked that on her skin instead of the insanely enticing tattoos she already had, it couldn't have been any easier to read.

"I'm sorry I'm so late. I, uh, just had. . . ."

"To work through your regret," she challenged with a wicked grin. Despite her attempt at vexing him, a seductive rose of heat bloomed across her cheeks at his compliment. This girl. Fucking hell. She was just too much.

"Something like that. Had to work through what might happen if I found out something terrible about you. You know, like you have Nickelback, or worse, Coldplay on your playlists, or that you play *Wonderwall* on repeat or something dreadful like that. I decided I could deal with it and just educate you on good music."

"I see. Well, relax, I don't have either of those 'bands' on my phone." Even her finger quotes were cute. "I will readily admit to having Taylor Swift, however."

"Yes, well, I suppose I can work with that. I might even have *Bad Blood* somewhere, not on my phone of course, but in some other music storage facility."

"Right." Holly was still trying not to smile. He wasn't forgiven yet, but they were getting closer.

"Shall we?" He gestured back to her bathroom, stupidly hoping he might stumble upon another vibrator. The revelation of her sexual preferences drove him almost as much as the quest for her smiles and the sound of her laughter.

Her brow knitted in confusion, and he almost rejoiced aloud. The tattoo clearly wasn't bothering her enough to be at the forefront of her mind, and she'd all but forgotten the original reason for his coming over.

She'd clearly gotten ready for their breakfast date and had hopefully been looking forward to it. Up until she'd decided he wasn't coming. Probably about the time he'd extended his run yet another mile. Reminding himself that he owed her much better, he took her hand in his. "All I've been able to think about is having my hands on you. The tattoo is the perfect excuse. I've never been granted such a gift. It allows me to continue to tell myself that I'm being a gent and taking care of you while I'm really indulging my baser nature."

"Anyone every told you you're a very smooth talker, Declan St. James?" Her jaw clenched, and her eyes turned wary in a split second.

He sighed inwardly. Yeah. He'd heard that a time or three dozen. For some unfathomable reason, he didn't want to just be a smooth talking one-night stand, a terrible-at-actually-having-any-kind-of-relationship type of man with her. Showing up late after turning her down when she'd offered him such a stunning invitation to her gorgeous body relegated him to the very kind of asshole he was trying desperately to keep from being.

"I'm pretty sure it's just the accent. We Brits can be vomiting lines of complete shit, and for some reason people believe it. But you, my beautiful Holly, I mean every word I say to you. I am truly sorry I'm so late."

"Yeah, I can tell. Probably be safer for me to believe it when I see it, though. Actually, I kind of forgot you were coming over for the tattoo. Why were you really so late?"

Her mind was clearly wired with hesitation and misgivings. He owed her an explanation, just not one that contained any of the harrowing reasons he'd really been late. Wanting to prove himself waged war with the desperation to hide his entire past from her. She may have whipped off her top the evening before, but innocence was penned firmly in every single one of her curves that served to drive him insane with need. So many sides to Miss Holly Camden. He longed to know each and every one. From her naughtiest thoughts to her most mundane activities, something about her made him want to intimately know every single facet.

"Shall we take care of your new ink before I begin proving myself, or would you like me to throw myself on the ground at your feet and beg your forgiveness for my tardiness?"

Another round of heat pinked her cheeks and the wariness vacated her eyes. He hadn't meant to embarrass her, but if that kept her from prying into his reasoning too much, he wouldn't regret it. "Sorry. I guess. . . . I just kind of thought maybe I was being stood up. It's not like you even said what time you'd be here. Forget I said anything about it."

"It's nearing eleven. I'm late for breakfast. You had every right to call me on it." He stared directly into her eyes, needing her to believe what he was about to tell her. "I meant what I said last night. I had to get my head straight. I'm telling you up front I didn't used to make the best decisions in my life. I've been in jail and in rehab for drug abuse. That was years ago, and I've been clean every moment of every day since. Now, I never do anything without a great deal of thought about the consequences. That's how I've stayed clean. Thoughts about you kept me up most of the night."

"Declan, we barely know each other. You don't have to tell me this."

"I know, but I wanted to. I owe you an explanation for being late, and I find myself wanting to see where this might go, even if we do barely know each other."

The abject delight that lit through those eyes sparked life anew within him. "I feel that way, too."

"Then let's see what kind of disaster we can create together, shall we?"

Holly led him back to her bathroom. Disappointment that she'd straightened and unpacked quelled his elation over being able to tell her a little about himself.

He'd managed honesty, left out the most gruesome details, and she still wanted to see where this led. So far, this day, this date that had only ever held haunting memories, was rapidly improving.

He'd enjoyed the mess her room had been in the evening before. There were so many more details in a messy room, more to study, so much more to be learned. He had no interest in the facade she showed other people. He wanted her raw, open, exposed, and vulnerable only to him. Long way to go before he could earn that kind of trust.

She spun in her bathroom, gave him another one of those impish grins, and unbuttoned her blouse. Desire surged from the head of his cock outward to his limbs. Once again, his little vixen was clearly trying to kill him, and this time he was more than ready to take her on.

The cotton candy pink bra blended readily in with her pale skin. He swallowed harshly, unable to order his eyes from her lush tits. She spun, offering him her back. Every cell in his body ached for her touch, for her heat. His tongue thirsted for her taste. His lungs begged to know the scent of her arousal. His brain had been right — he was never going to survive her. In her presence, he no longer cared. He'd figure this out. She was worth him discovering how to be a human being again.

Using the dexterity that could only come from decades of guitar playing, he had the bra unhooked in a half second. "So bloody tempting. I feel the need to insist upon the one-week rule."

"Would that be the '*we can fuck each other senseless but not until we've been dating one-week*' rule?"

"Precisely. Breakfast this morning can be date one. Dinner tonight can be date two, I'll come over every night you'll allow me this week. Take you out, stay in, whatever you want, and then my band is playing back at *our* bar Friday night. That night, darling, you're mine."

Intrigue, desire, and a playfulness that was going to be his undoing paraded through her eyes. "I've never been asked out on an entire week of dates all at once before." The melody of her laughter tightened like a vise around his cock.

"Clearly American men are imbeciles and completely incapable of knowing what to do when they are in the presence of a beautiful seductress such as yourself."

"Okay, you are totally forgiven for being a smooth-talker, as long as you keep saying stuff like that."

As Declan began administering the ointment to her tattoo, he let his breathy chuckle slip over her shoulder. He wanted to watch her body respond to his breath. She didn't disappoint.

"You haven't officially agreed to the aforementioned dates."

"Maybe I planned to string you along," she sassed.

"Cruel and unusual punishment. Have to up my game." Wrapping one arm around her waist, he strategically positioned her sexy little ass, caught up in a pair of Wrangler blue jeans, against the bulge in his trousers. "You'll find I can be as persuasive as you need."

With one quick wiggle of her backside, blood surged through his stiffening cock. "So can I."

"Clearly," he half-moaned against the torturous friction she was creating with every sexy sway.

"I take it Duffy's is *our* bar?"

"Naturally."

"It's really cool you're playing there. You must be pretty good."

Indulging himself in a quick grind of his pelvis against her, he chuckled. "Trust me, my love, I am very, very good."

CHAPTER FIVE

"Are we going to Trace?" Holly was astonished as Declan's Honda Pilot made the turn off of 16th. Given the approximate value of both of his modes of transportation he was clearly a very successful musician, though she'd never heard of him.

"You know about Trace?" Declan seemed equally as shocked.

"Yes, I love Trace. It's my place, but you can't know about it because if people start knowing about it they'll see its complete awesomeness and go there, and I won't be able to get a table whenever I need it."

Declan's addictively sexy chuckle stirred her heart and sent spirals of lust on a southbound course directly between her legs. "See, I was just thinking how amazing it was that we both know and love Trace, and that perhaps we could share a table there often, as long as I vow never to tell another soul about the best tea shop in Nebraska."

"It's technically a coffee shop, but I might still be willing to share my table with you."

"Americans and your coffee shops. Have you ever noticed that most of them are ridiculously banal, so crowded and loud all creativity is choked out at the door, and that they serve far more whipped sugar in an infinite number of varieties than coffee?"

"I *have* noticed that, and that is what makes Trace so perfect."

"Wrong. Their outstanding ability to make non-tampon tea with the correct splash of milk, not cream, and the Tombow pencils are what makes Trace an example of tea shop excellence."

"Agreed on the pencils completely, but did you just out and out say I was wrong? Because I am not wrong. And dare I ask what tampon tea might be?"

"Ha. So, my sexy little cowgirl does not like to be told she's wrong. Noted. Tampon tea is tea made with a stringed teabag. Why do you Americans like your tea and everything else with strings?"

Holly couldn't seem to stop giggling. There were a million questions brewing in her mind, but she was currently enjoying the fact that Declan seemed to know a great deal about most any topic and had his own personal twist on everything they'd shared so far. She was dying to ask what exactly he'd been arrested for. He'd been drinking in Duffy's the night before, but was vehement that he'd been clean for years. Alcohol clearly wasn't his vice.

Grinning up at him as he navigated the roads to the historic district of Lincoln, she went on with a confession, hoping he'd share a little more about his past. "Last year for Christmas I might've bought myself a massive pack of the HB Writer Tombows."

Declan turned to stare at her like she'd suddenly sprouted an additional head. "The HB writers are by far the best pencil in existence, but I'm desperately curious, what does a cowgirl do with that many pencils?"

"I'm not only a cowgirl. Remember, I have a whole other side."

"And when do I get to learn more about this other side?"

"Feel like I should be asking you the very same thing."

"Ah, I see. You are aware that you already know more about me than I've told most anyone ever?"

"I don't feel like I know anything."

"Well, then pardon me, a song title I've always felt aptly applied to my life, upon my arrival there, was *Anarchy in the UK*."

"Sex Pistols. I love them."

"You are good, darling. Perhaps far too good." He put the Pilot in park and made it to her side of the car to open the door for her. Declan St. James, song master and a complete enigma.

Declan stopped her just inside the door of her favorite *coffee* shop. "Breathe, my love. Take a deep breath. Life doesn't offer nearly enough breaths like the first inhale of a tea shop."

Holly's grin expanded the width of her face. "Agreed." She let her eyes close and filled her lungs with the intoxicating aromas of coffee, tea, the books that lined the four exterior walls of Trace, and best of all, the subtle scent of graphite. "I always try to memorize the scent before I leave here, so I can take it with me out into the world."

"Me too." He winked at her and then guided her to the humble drink counter. Trace didn't serve mocha-cinos-macciato-latte-with a twist of anything. Nope. Trace served coffee, light, medium, or dark roast, or tea, English Breakfast, Earl and Lady Grey, hot chocolate, and colas in bottles along with old fashioned donuts, and that was it.

Housed inside a one hundred-year-old, two-story colonial revival, Holly adored all of Trace's nooks and crannies, where you could find a tiny table and get lost for as long as you like, or until closing time at ten every evening.

"And what would my love like this morning?" Declan's whiskey-smooth voice brought Holly back to their date.

"Holly?" Trace, the owner, gave her a broad grin. "Holl always gets a dark roast with room for extra cream and two donuts." He winked at her.

"Guilty as charged. Clearly, I come in here too often."

"Nah, my regulars keep me in business. And Dec always gets Earl Grey with a splash of milk and a donut, then he complains that I don't serve crumpets, even though I've told him I can't get the damn things in, and I don't have time to learn to make them."

"Are you seriously giving Trace problems, dear?" Holly mocked.

"It is a bloody shame to have tea this good without a proper British treat. That's all I'm saying."

"So far I've heard him call you love and you just called him dear. Not sure when you two got together, but now that I'm seeing it, I should've introduced you two ages ago, if I'd thought of it. You both come in here and take up a table for hours, but you always remember to return my pencils to me."

"Stealing another man's Tombow should be a felony offense," Declan vowed. Holly felt another little piece of her doubt slip away. There was still so much to figure out about Declan, but that suited her just fine. She loved figuring things out. Her determination never faltered, even with his confession that he was an addict. They were on their way to something worth having, even if she couldn't quite decide what that might be exactly.

Trace set their orders down in front of them. "Round booth upstairs is open if you hurry." He gestured to a crowd of people heading through the front doors.

"Brilliant." Declan carried their tray upstairs and settled in the back of the semi-private booth that overlooked the garden. A massive mug of Tombow pencils sat in the center of every table, stacked on top of a half-dozen yellow notepads with a few of their pages torn out. Holly grabbed for a pencil and ran it under her nose until she caught a whiff of wood and lead.

A sexy half-grin played on Declan's lips. "While I agree that pencils are the single most important invention of humanity, I'm beginning to wish you'd inhale me like you do those pencils."

Laughing, Holly leaned closer to him and breathed in his scent from the collar of his shirt. "Mmm, you smell even better than the pencils."

"That so?"

Holly nodded before downing a large sip of the best coffee in town. "If I ask what you do for hours at one of Trace's tables, are you going to give me another song title?"

"Actually I'm going to give you dozens of them since I generally come here to write music."

There. Now they were getting somewhere. "And will I get to hear any Declan originals when I come hear you play at Duffy's?"

"Maybe. We play mostly covers, though. Kind of greases the wheel, to use an American expression. You warm the crowd up with songs they know, then you can slip in a few of yours and see how they respond. Since there are at least four dozen questions aggravating your spectacularly beautiful eyes, my love, shall we go quid pro quo?"

"How many song titles will become answers?"

"Depends on the questions."

He was being honest. She didn't guess she could ask for more than that. "Fine. I just asked one, so it's your turn."

"The question is the same. What does my cowgirl come in here to do other than drink coffee and huff pencils?"

He kept her laughing, and his question for question game was certainly one way to learn more about him. "Trust me, I've never huffed anything stronger than coffee and pencils."

Declan's grunt was yet another mystery. Could a grunt be laced with regret? Definitely sounded like it was. "Truthfully, I always come in here intending to read or study, but I end up staring out the windows and drawing pictures of my horse with the pencils. Sadly, all of my doodles still look exactly the way they did when I was seven." Holly cringed, certain she shouldn't have admitted that to a musician who probably had more creativity in his little finger than she had in her entire body.

Another one of his seductive chuckles quaked through her soul. "I think you may be the most dangerous creature in existence."

"Unless I'm in full-on cowgirl mode, I'm not terribly dangerous. Why did you say that?"

"You're dangerous because you're honest. No one is brave enough to be honest."

"I like to be honest, and I know what I want. I wonder if you might be dangerous because you don't know what you want."

"I know exactly what I want, love." Lust darkened and then sheened those deep gray eyes, a salt and pepper mix of seduction.

"And what might that be?"

"One, to figure out exactly what song I could sing or play that might speak to your soul. Two, to learn your most hidden desires and see that I cater to each and every one of them. Three, to know you, spend time with you, and maybe let you get to know me." He gently traced from her thumb to her index finger. How the hell did one tender caress from him keep her so thoroughly on edge? She shifted against the wet heat that had pooled in her panties from just sitting so close to him.

Holly's heartbeat raced into overdrive. Her nipples throbbed against the lace of her bra. The way he looked at her. The way he touched her so innocently yet so provocatively. There was still so much she wanted to ask, but she didn't want answers as badly as she wanted this.

Licking her lips, she leaned in. His intent focus zeroed in on her mouth. "Need something, sweetheart?"

She managed a quick nod.

"Tell me what you want."

Holly eased back. She'd never actually been asked that by a man. The daunting question hung in the coffee-infused air between them.

"I was hoping for a kiss," she admitted, irked he'd made her verbalize that.

"That's all you're needing?"

"For now."

With that, he slanted his mouth over hers, taking what he wanted and giving her what she required before he softened his exploration and dipped his tongue between her lips, tasting her. A hungry moan escaped her. He consumed it to keep it from belonging to anyone but him.

Unable to help himself, Declan rubbed his hand up Holly's thigh, extending the kiss that would have him hard up from now until he finally got her to his home Friday night. Dear God, the sweet addiction of her mouth, the way she suckled at his tongue with her gorgeous lips that he couldn't wait to see wrapped around his cock.

His thumb grazed the crotch of her jeans and her entire body rolled against him, so needy for his touch. A rumbled groan of approval vaulted from his mouth. "Mmm maybe you're not so honest. I think you're lying to me, love," he managed before he turned back to consume more of her. "I think you need so much more than a kiss."

"Yes," gasped from her as her hand landed on his zipper line. "Oh God," she groaned softly as she kneaded his fierce rigidity.

"Indeed." Declan finally ordered himself to pull away, lest he stick his hands down her jeans to discover just how wet he'd made her. He wrapped his arms around her, thankful for the expansive and relatively secluded booth. She burrowed in his chest once again. That was almost as satisfying as kissing her. That feeling that she needed him to be her harbor, to dam back the world, needed him to hold her close was far more fulfilling that he should ever have allowed it to be, but there was no going back.

The sum of your vices will always remain the same. Every addiction counselor worth their salt knew that. The trick of it was to trade vices that sought your death for those that didn't mind you remaining alive. Perhaps she could be one of his. His addictive nature would always remain, but maybe being addicted to her might not be so bad.

She gently ran her thumb down his trouser-trapped cock once more, but kept her face hidden in him.

Grinning at that, he caressed her cheek warmed from their passion. "I love the way you feel in my arms," he admitted.

A full minute later, she lifted her head. "Really?" Her eyes were volatile storms of need once again, but there in the emerald depths resided a hearty dose of embarrassment.

"God's honest truth."

"It's my turn to ask you a question," she insisted. That impish grin was just one thing on a very lengthy list of items he adored about Miss Holly Camden.

"It is. Technically I asked you three, so the next three belong to you."

"How did you ask me three?" Skepticism replaced the embarrassment in her eyes. He was pleased to see it go.

Leaning in to whisper in her ear, he kept her cradled gently to him. "I asked you what it was you needed, if that was all you needed, and also instructed you to tell me exactly what it was you wanted. I see that as three, and I always play fair. I do want you to get very used to the idea of telling me precisely what you'd like for me to do to you when we're together. Understood?"

Her hesitant nod spoke volumes. His all-too-innocent cowgirl had clearly never been with a real man. Declan had no doubt that she'd had sex, but she'd never been worshipped, never been seduced, taken, and owned the way he planned to own her.

He waited patiently for her questions, not in any hurry to begin confessing much of anything and rather enjoying the fact that one of his kisses had scrambled her so thoroughly.

"Uh," she took a quick inventory of his face, from what he could tell. "Did it hurt to have your brow piercing done?"

He drew a sip of tea to keep from laughing at her outright. Of all the things he'd alluded to, from a slight sense of submission that he sought from her in the bedroom to the fact that he'd been arrested, and that's what she'd come up with. She was completely adorable. When he'd regained his composure, he set down his teacup and stared her down. With the lift of his pierced eyebrow, he smirked. "Not nearly as bad as my other piercing."

One, two, thr. . . and there it was. She was infinitely quicker than most. Realization lit her entire face. Her mouth was actually hanging open. This time he couldn't hide his chuckle.

"So, you have your. . .I mean. . .it's pierced?"

"Does this count as your second question, love?"

"Sure. Why not?"

"Because I'd really rather discuss all of that Friday at my house if it's all the same to you."

"Oh."

Dec watched her glance flit around the coffee shop. There were enough other patrons tucked away at the scattered tables nearby to keep her from demanding he tell her more now, but he had no doubt she longed to hear more about his Apadravya piercing.

"Uh, okay, how about would you rather I call you Dec, like Trace does?"

She was digging deeper. A low level sense of panic rose in his gut, a tidal wave of fear. Desperate to keep things light, he forced another grin. "You can call me anything you want, angel. Declan, Dec, daddy, sex god, master, whatever makes you smile, or better yet moan."

"Funny. I won't ever be calling anyone master, just make sure you remember that. Think I'll stick to Declan or Dec until you prove yourself a sex god, then we'll see about that." Her body language was once again loud and clear. The gentle brush of her right breast with her inner arm and the intrigue in her eyes said she was curious about the master business despite her adamant verbal objections.

"Can't wait to prove myself." Certain he did in fact sound like a surly Dom, he debated. Nothing sounded more appealing than allowing Holly to explore her latent submissive fantasies with him as her guide. Instead of leaping head first into that extremely interesting rabbit hole, he braced for the next question.

This time the narrowing of her eyes complimented the hard cock of her jaw. "All right, how about: what were you arrested for?"

And there it was. His heart thudded out a frantic beat urging him to flee, but he was determined to do this right.

Drawing a deep breath, he nodded his head to his own destruction. "I believe the actual charges were reduced from possession of a Class A controlled drug, possession with intent to supply, and premises I occupied being used for the consumption of controlled substances, down to simply possession with the agreement that I spend a lengthy amount of time in Betel Rehab in London in their highly acclaimed program."

"Wow."

Dec swore she nodded for the better part of the next five minutes.

"So, is Class A in Britain the same as Class A here? Cocaine, ecstasy, heroin, stuff like that?"

Yes. "Holly, I swear I've been clean for years. I hated myself then, and I still hate myself because I'm sitting here in my favorite tea shop with a beautiful woman and having to tell her this."

"Hey." To his shock, she scooted back into his arms hugging him fiercely. "Don't do that. Addiction isn't something you should hate yourself for, ever. You wouldn't hate a cancer patient for having cancer would you? You know you have it. You manage it every single day, I'm sure. Don't be so hard on yourself, especially for me. I'm glad you told me. Thank you for being real finally."

She thought he was being real with her? The stabbing pain of that gutted him. There was so much more to the sordid tale. He'd told her nothing but the bitter end, and had no intention of ever telling her the beginning, or the horrendous middle portions. There was only so much he could ask of himself, and she didn't deserve to have to bear the weight of his failures.

"It's your turn to ask me a question," she reminded him sweetly.

He searched her for ridicule or judgment. It had to be in there somewhere. You didn't confess to owning and selling drugs and get away without retribution from the listener, but he couldn't find anything in those all-telling eyes that said she was either afraid or ashamed of him.

Declan had no idea how to respond to that. He'd alluded to his addiction back at her apartment as a last ditch effort to scare her away. He'd elaborated to push her further, and she'd responded by coming closer.

Evie had overdosed that day eleven years ago, and never once since that moment that had fractured and divided his entire life had Dec ever admitted his weaknesses and had anyone respond by reaching out to him. Everyone he'd ever loved had pushed him away. That was what he deserved.

"Where would you like to have dinner with me tonight?" He landed on a question he did want the answer to, far too confused to ask her something deeper or more meaningful. "Remember, I'm basically awful at dating. I haven't ever really done it, certainly not since my divorce."

Completely powerless to shut himself up, he detonated another bomb, unable to believe that she could want more of him after learning about a few of his more horrendous moments.

Her responding smirk was definitely unexpected. "If I didn't know better, I'd say you were trying to scare me off. Now, allow me a song title, *I'm Not Afraid.*"

"Damn it all to hell, woman, you up and pulled Eminem on me. That's not fair. One cannot argue with Eminem."

"Yeah, I'm pretty proud of that one." Another one of her sweet giggles lit through him, warming the frigid darkness housed in his soul.

"I never loved her." He continued to spew forth the insanity of his life. He downed another gulp of tea, desperate to dam back any further confessions.

"Seems like Trace's proper English tea is some kind of truth serum. Definitely have to remember that. I'm sorry you were in an unsuccessful and unloving marriage, but last time I checked, we were living right now not in your past."

"I'm definitely being bested in the healthy relationship knowledge department, which makes me disappointed in myself."

"Don't be too hard on yourself, I really like to win." She waggled her eyebrows.

"Oh, darling, I promise I will make it my mission to make certain that you win over and over and over again." And he would. He'd just met this woman, who'd somehow accepted him via a song title like the God he'd refused to believe in had forged her specifically for him. If she would allow it, he would teach her how to exist in pure ecstasy whenever she was in his bed. He owed her that and so much more. What else could he ever hope to give her?

One question remained, where did he go from here? He'd shown her the results of the most gruesome parts of his life, and she was currently nuzzling her head against his neck while she sipped her coffee. How was she really able to exist in the present and not in the past? Who was truly capable of such a thing? His little cowgirl should up and decide to become a psychologist. She'd make a spectacular one. Dear Lord, he'd lay on her couch for hours letting her soothe his every regret if she'd allow it, then he'd lay her down on that same sofa and show her the one thing he'd always excelled at.

"Hey, did you know there's a podcast about pencils?" She announced, still remaining true to not being shaken by his divorce. He was beginning to wonder if he was somehow caught up in a febrile dream. That was the only logical explanation to any of this.

"Erasable. I know. I listen to it when I run. It's bloody brilliant."

"It's my favorite. They did that one Extra Dark episode but. . . ."

"It just wasn't as good. My God, woman, what are you doing to me?"

She lifted her head and gave him a delighted grin that he swore could light a thousand distant planets. "Hopefully, seducing you so well you'll agree to amending your one-week rule."

Declan arched his pierced eyebrow once again. "Seduction by pencil conversation. Tempting as sin and twice as lethal, but anticipation is the second most potent thing in our reality, darling." He returned his right hand to her thigh, gauging her reactions to the strength of his grasp as he kneaded her pliant flesh. Her legs spread ever so slightly and her wicked tongue swept back over her lips. So many things one could learn when they paid attention.

"What's the most potent?"

"*Desire* is the most potent, most powerful, most persuasive emotion there could ever be. By the time we leave the bar Friday after our sets, I'll have worked you into a frenzy of anticipation and desire. After I've accomplished that, we'll explore just how well my cowgirl rides and what she requires to come completely undone in my arms."

A harsh swallow. Heat settled high in her cheeks. Her legs eased further apart. Oh, they were definitely getting somewhere.

"You sound pretty sure of yourself."

"Sex god, remember?"

"If I tried chattering on about other writing instrumentation, would that work?"

Shaking his head at her, certain she was going to be his undoing, he leaned in and brushed a kiss below her earlobe, reveling in the seductive shiver he'd caused. "As if anything could ever be more seductive than pencils."

CHAPTER SIX

After going by Holly's apartment Monday morning to tend her tattoo, which was healing up nicely, Dec hung his sport coat on the back of his office chair and mentally reviewed his clients for the day.

There was a new couple in for their first session that morning, a referral from one of the marriage counselors at Lifespan. Then the Dickersons. She wanted to be dominated. He thought she should confess her sins to their priest to get over this particular '*condition*' as he called it. Dec sighed. Then the Carters. Some of his favorite clients. His depression meds had robbed him of any sexual desire or drive. His wife was desperate to help and also desperate for the missing connection, and they were getting somewhere. Couples like the Carters were the reasons he'd specialized in sexual therapy. After the Carters came Matthew, sexual abuse victim trying to restore his life. Dec's heart ached for them all, and he reminded himself of all he owed the world. Helping his patients was how he paid for his sins.

After the full round of patients, he planned to show up at Holly's apartment with pizza and a copy of *To Have and Have Not*, her favorite Bogie and Bacall movie. Her entertainment preferences were all over the map. He hadn't quite been able to decipher her age as of yet. Her music knowledge said she had to be nearing his age, though she looked a decade younger. She was stunningly beautiful, and sweet, and her innocence coupled with her intelligence was seductive as hell.

He took great pains to remind himself that tonight was only to stir the anticipation and multiply the desire. Friday he could have her. Friday night after his last set, approximately one hundred thirty-five hours, thirty minutes, and the few seconds it would cost him to strip her out of whatever she wore to hear him play. He stopped short of setting a countdown on his phone.

"Dude, you trying to get fired?" Scott Evans strolled into Dec's office and gestured to his shirtsleeves. They were still rolled up his forearms, revealing the intricate tattoo work on his left arm.

Rolling his eyes, Dec rectified the sleeve situation.

"You know Gibbons can't stand the tats or the eyebrow. He just knows better than to push it too hard, or he'll have HR breathing down his neck."

"I've been working here an entire year and the man hasn't let one day go by that he hasn't reminded me that my visa is tied to me keeping this job, or that he believes sexual therapy is some kind of perverted pseudoscience. He's all but come right out and asked me if I'm sleeping with my female patients. Keeping my brow piercing in is my one and only source of rebellion. It's bloody keeping me alive."

"He can't stand that you've only been here a year and have already gained a reputation as being a therapist that actually gets results."

"How dare I? God knows we should all have subpar performances so that our client reviews suck more than his."

Scott's chuckle accompanied the slight furrow of his brow. "Something's different about you."

This was the problem with hanging out with psychologists. They never missed anything, and Dec had no desire to share much with his colleagues, even if Scott had gotten him the interview at Lifespan.

"I ate questionable Chinese leftovers for breakfast. You could be seeing the beginnings of death. Never know."

"Funny, but it's not something you ate. Who is she?"

"She?"

"Yep, I have four psychology degrees, loser. I know lust when I see it."

"What makes you think I haven't developed a deep physical attraction to you? We've been friends since you came to London to obtain yet another one of your degrees. I've been trying to suppress these urges for a while but. . . ." Declan smirked.

"You're so full of shit. I'll figure out who she is. Just give me time." Thankfully, Scott headed back towards the door. "Sherry from accounting?"

"Sherry is fifty-seven years old, and vastly more important than that, she is happily married, and has something like eight grandchildren. Perhaps you should forfeit one of your degrees for that imbecilic guess on whom I'm seeing."

Scott stuck the tip of his tongue between his front teeth, looking entirely too proud of himself. "Don't have to give up one of my degrees. I knew all of that, but I just got you to admit that you are seeing someone."

"Get out," Dec demanded.

"I'm gone. Maybe you could bring her over for dinner sometime. You know Claire worries about you."

"Claire is a darling girl who had the dreadfully unfortunate luck of marrying you. I worry about her."

Annoyance needled along Declan's spine. Introducing Holly to his colleagues would mean confessing what he actually did for a living. Something deep within his soul needed to know her intimately, know her preferences, earn her laughter and her smiles before he exposed her to that information. The assumptions about a sex therapist were inevitable. He didn't want her to feel any pressure when it came to their sexual relationship.

Panic replaced the annoyance. Maybe that wasn't a good sign. Hiding things was never a good sign. My God, how long had he been able to hide his addiction from anyone who might've been able to save him before he threw himself head first into the deepest well?

She is a person not a drug became his mantra for the morning.

Holly checked her reflection in the mirror once more. Somewhat conservative dress. Check. Hair up in a professional twist. Got it.

Favorite cowgirl boots. Oh yeah, she was ready. Trevor Singleton might've taken round one, but Holly was going to win the whole damn rodeo. He could suck up her dust while he kissed her ass. Today, at the Welcome Back luncheon for PhD students, alumni, and faculty, he was going down.

I shouldn't. She couldn't help the wicked grin that spread across her face when she pulled into the Psychological Sciences parking lot. *Oh, but I'm so going to.* Temptingly, Trevor's ridiculously stupid, bright yellow Scion was parked horizontally across two spaces in the front corner of the lot. Checking to make certain no one was close enough to see this in the expansive lot, she expertly guided her Silverado over the curb and into the mud left over from the storm. Stomping the brakes and flooring the accelerator, the tires spun and rather effectively and efficiently peppered his windshield and hood with huge splatters of mud.

A minute later she parked on the other side of the lot and headed inside. *Never mess with a cowgirl, Singleton. I have thin line reins thicker than your cock.*

Wiping her smirk off of her face, she straightened her dress, and headed towards the banquet area. There he was, chatting with his father and grandfather, and Dr. Newsome. Trevor was a vile, smarmy shitstack if ever there was one.

Narrowing her eyes, she stomped towards them, almost plowing over Beth Kinders in her stride.

"Beth? What are you doing here? I thought you were going to Berkley."

"Holly, I'm so glad you're here. I thought you might've given up the ranch and moved to Boston after all. I thought I was going to Berkley too, and you are the only person who will understand this and not think I'm insane, but I just couldn't leave Sangster and Nash. I just couldn't. I walked out to the barn to attempt to tell them goodbye, and I cried for three hours. Guess it's just me, you, and Singleton from last year, though. I've never seen most of these people."

"I'll never ever give up the ranch, girl, and I completely understand about your horses. I'm UN-L all the way, and we can show the newbies who's gonna ride circles around the Psych department this year."

Beth laughed. "Guess you can take the girls off the ranch, but you can't take the ranch out of the girls, huh?"

"You know it."

Beth's family had a large corn farm near Broken Bow. She and Holly had worked on their thesis research together. Holly had even taken Beth out to Camden Ranch for Thanksgiving the year before when her entire family headed south to vacation once the harvest was in. Just knowing that Beth was going to be with her and that she wouldn't be forced to face Singleton alone made Holly feel hopeful. Between Beth and Declan, this year was definitely looking up.

Setting their sights back on Dr. Newsome, they headed towards the gathering crowd surrounding him. Trevor's father, Dr. Singleton Sr., was soaking it up like a pig in mud. He wasn't letting Newsome get more than five centimeters out of his reach.

"Oh good, the cowgirls have ridden in. Hope you didn't park your horses near my Scion, ladies." Trevor tried for a joke and achieved a few uncomfortable chuckles.

To Holly's delight, Dr. Newsome shot Trevor a warning glance before turning to her with a warm smile. "Ms. Camden, how are you, dear?"

"I'm great. Excited to be here and to get classes started."

"I was reviewing your thesis again last week. Very impressive work. Your points on healthy sexuality being negatively affected by politics and pornography approached through the lens of sociobiology were absolutely outstanding. I swear I've been doing this since the earth cooled, and it's rare I'm so taken with a master's thesis work. UN is very lucky you've decided to continue your research here."

Certain she was going to burst from pride, Holly beamed. "Thank you, sir. That means so much to me."

"And Ms. Kinders, how are you?" Newsome smiled at Beth.

While they exchanged pleasantries, Holly offered Trevor a gotcha grin. *Take that, Singleton.* His mouth was twisted up like he'd just been instructed to lick Holly's boots. Laughing at that, Holly narrowed her eyes. "So nice to see you again, Trevor, and of course you wouldn't attend a campus gathering without your father. Dr. Singleton, how are you, sir?" She offered her hand while watching Trevor try to decide if he'd just been insulted.

"Ms. Camden." Dr. Singleton was worse than his son. He and his wife both held positions on the board, which they readily used to get their way on most everything.

"I personally found Ms. Camden's thesis to be tiresome and contrite. She offered no real solutions to anything," Dr. Singleton took a stab. "Trevor's work was far more compelling."

How stupid did you have to be to understand that publicly disagreeing with your boss might not be the best idea?

"I couldn't disagree with you more, Dr. Singleton. Ms. Camden's assertion that most of today's sexual health problems resulted from lack of viable, pertinent, non-politically motivated sexual education was spot on," Dr. Newsome came to her rescue.

Dr. Singleton offered no rebuttal.

"Have fun at the barbecue, Trev?" Holly cornered him by the refreshment table with a gloating grin. "Maybe Dr. Newsome will let you grill his corn for him or something. I'm pretty sure we just saw that he's going to become my supervisor."

"Why don't you go back to your one room schoolhouse out on your beloved little ranch and leave the actual degrees to the men who deserve them. You are nothing more than a stubborn, whiny, ridiculous excuse for a psychology student. Besides all of that, if Newsome takes you on, I highly suspect it has more to do with what's in your pants than what's in your head."

"You know, no matter how many times I try to be nice you just always manage to flip my cowgirl switch by being a complete douche. Listen up." Holly leaned in for the kill. "Dr. Newsome is going to be my advisor. Don't think for one second that the entire department doesn't know that your daddy's money paid for the piece of expensive carpeting you're standin' on. What'cha gonna do when your daddy's money can't buy you into whatever you want, Trevy? Life's gonna suck then, isn't it? Poor thing never learned to piss without daddy holdin' your hand. Stand back and watch me, asswipe. Things are about to get real, real interesting." With the quick flip of her hand, the contents of Trevor's punch cup were pouring down his designer shirt and puddling on the toes of his ridiculous loafers. "Whoops."

CHAPTER SEVEN

"Dr. St. James, might I join you for lunch?" Disdain dripped from Dr. Elliot Gibbons' lunch invitation. It always did.

Dec took great care to remember that Dr. Gibbons was capable of completely ruining his life with one swipe of his pen. Being fired from this job meant a one-way trip back to London. Back to the incessant drinking culture. Back to the farm where he could prove his father's predictions correct — that he really didn't deserve to live. Back to facing Victoria's father's practice and Victoria herself, though Dec highly suspected she'd already moved on to another unsuspecting bloke she could take advantage of. He didn't care if he had to personally wipe Dr. Gibbons' ass on a daily basis. He was keeping this job and never going back to the London he'd known.

"Certainly, sir. Where shall we dine?"

"Anywhere is fine. You choose."

Anywhere was certainly not fine. Holly had been right. Too many stuffy imbeciles in Trace, and it would lose all of its rampant appeal. Plus, it would be a cold day in hell when Dec showed his boss where to find him when he was out of the office.

Normally, he jogged the ten blocks to Banhwich Café for outstanding curry to go or a sandwich, then jogged back to Trace, got tea, and hid himself away for the two hour lunch afforded doctors at Lifespan. Trace encouraged all of his customers to bring lunch there. He wasn't going to serve it, but people paid readily for tea and coffee and then dessert to go with. The business plan meant Trace was pulling in more cash at lunch than most places downtown ever hoped to.

But none of that would be happening today. Unfortunately, Dec had already changed into his running shorts, something Gibbons had voiced his disapproval of in the past.

"Don't suppose we could get into the Longbranch with you dressed like that," Gibbons commented as if he'd known precisely what Dec was thinking.

"Give me just a minute. I'll change back into my suit. No problem, sir."

Edgy from not getting his run in and not having any tea, Dec shifted against the stiff cushion at his back in the corner booth of the stuffiest steakhouse in Lincoln. It had to be eighty degrees in there, and Gibbons literally had him up against the wall. He seemed to have planned it that way with their seating location.

He listened to Gibbons drone on about some problem with the students from Nebraska-Lincoln doing clinicals at Lifespan this semester while he attempted to chew the brisket Gibbons had insisted he order. It largely resembled something manufactured from the local Goodyear plant. Some kind of unforgivable John Denver Muzak was being piped through a sound system that sounded as if it was on life support and going down for the third time. Hell couldn't possibly have been much worse than this. Satan himself wouldn't listen to John Denver, surely.

"I'll tell you, Docklan, it's just not the same as when we started the firm. Insurance nightmares. Drug reps. Every other commercial on television is for a new, better medicine. Patients who think they know more about their issues than we do. Interns with opinions. Longer hours. Lawsuits. If it weren't for the bottom line, I'd drink more." His uproarious laughter accompanied several pieces of half-chewed brisket that landed on the table. Dec fought not to gag.

"It's Declan, sir, and I rather respect that my patients are more educated on medications and their own feelings and symptoms. Taking charge of their own health is a positive sign for our industry, is it not?" Try though he might, he couldn't help but argue.

"Just gotta remember that mental health is a two-way street," Gibbons huffed once he'd regained his composure.

"Between the doctor and the patient, you mean?"

"No. We have to make certain we keep enough patients coming back to keep us in business. We can't have them reach wherever it is you think they should go too quickly. You've only been here a year, and you've already released a dozen patients. That's not good for our bottom line."

"Ah, I see. Be good at my job but not too good because preparing clients to handle their life without our aid makes us less money."

"Exactly. Now you're seeing it the right way."

Rage Against the Machine's *Killing in the Name* had already played in his head three times. Normally, he didn't care for the repetition in the song, but he currently found the phrase '*Fuck you*' over and over again rather soothing. Most importantly it drowned out Gibbons and John Denver. Who could really ask for more than that?

When Gibbons began complaining about his wife, *Rage Against the Machine* no longer seemed to work. Agitation twisted in Dec's gut. The lyrics were more difficult to access with every word Gibbons whined.

"I'd let her go, but you know how it is. Psychologists in family practice aren't allowed to get divorced. I mean, God knows you know," Gibbons laughed.

The hot breath of the ridiculous laughter incensed Dec. He sank his teeth into his tongue. No, if you were stupid enough to marry a woman you were absolutely certain you would never get addicted to because you couldn't stand her, in exchange for a job at London's premiere psychotherapy foundation that happened to be headed up by her father, you most certainly could not get divorced. Too bad he hadn't figured that out a little earlier in life.

"Wouldn't mind trading her in on a younger model, two twenties are better than one forty." His wink made Declan want to vomit, or perhaps it was the brisket. "I'm sure you understand." Gibbons continued on with his repugnant laughter.

Dec closed his eyes, trying to force himself to appear unaffected.

The hazy swirl of his life, or the parts he remembered, spun rapidly in his mind and churned in his gut. Deep breaths. He knew how to keep his temper in check. He had to learn that when he learned to stop seeking out drugs to dull the searing pain of life.

Holly. Suddenly, when he'd been seeking another lyric, another song, something else to concentrate on to soothe him, Holly's beautiful smile planted firmly in his mind. His breaths came easier. He'd been fantasizing about her since he'd walked out of her apartment after she'd whipped off that ridiculous sweatshirt that was so large on her frame it had to have belonged to some male figure Dec had instantly hated.

With every breath he took to keep from telling Gibbons exactly what he thought of him, more of Holly's clothing disappeared. Last night, in his dreams she'd been wearing black leather and lace. Sexy as hell, but it hadn't quite suited her. No, his little cowgirl's perfected seduction came in that once in a lifetime combination of deliciously naughty innocence. An angel in public, a seductress behind closed doors. He had every intention of drawing out her seductively wicked side in bed Friday night. He'd slowly coax it every night this week if he was allowed.

For the purposes of shutting out his boss's stupidity, he pictured her wearing nothing but those alluring cowgirl boots she wore so well and a pair of white lace boyshort panties, complete with a pink bow and a hidden open crotch.

His mouth on her heated skin. The rough scrape of his morning beard inside her tender thighs. Slowly, gently, drawing her sweet little pearl into his mouth while he drew her deepest desires from her soul. Her musk and her arousal fresh on his tongue. *Friday night.*

"St. James, your phone's ringing." Gibbons' annoyed chirp ripped Dec from the fantasy.

"Sorry, sir, I. . .was so caught up in your story." He gambled. Gibbons' grin said he won. He'd pay homage to the universe later for that one.

Holly's name glowed on his phone screen, and all of the annoyance and tension bled from his psyche.

"I need to take this, sir." He stood, threw down thirty dollars, and headed outside. "You have absolutely impeccable timing, my love. I was just about to lose my mind."

"So, I saved you from a life of mindlessness? Seems I should be rewarded a king's ransom for such a thing."

Dec had no trouble envisioning dozens of ways to reward her. "A king's ransom, huh? And how would my cowgirl like to receive her spoils?"

"Preferably naked in bed."

Dec tried to turn his low rumbled groan into something of a cough when three people in the parking lot turned to glare at him.

"Listen, I don't have long. Trace called me. All of his waitresses skipped out on him again. I told him I'd come help out. I thought maybe if you don't have practice today, you might want to come help, too. Then I could see you."

Oh, the assumptions one could make when they didn't want to probe deeper. Surely she didn't really believe he made enough money playing guitar in bars to survive on. She was far too perceptive and quick to think such a thing. Most human beings liked nothing more than to be right. The most intriguing humans wanted to understand and be understood.

Dec's mind negotiated with itself. He didn't want to tell her about his day job. He also didn't want to lie to her. She clearly didn't want to ask because she'd already made assumptions that he was busy during the day with band practice. All of that most likely meant she didn't want him asking too much about how a cowgirl living in an apartment with no land to speak of made money at all. Interesting, and given the current complexities of his job, somehow also comforting. He wondered how often she filled in at the tea shop and then decided it didn't matter. There was so much more to the two of them than their professions anyway.

"Practice. Yes. Um, not tonight. I'm a little busy for the rest of the day, but I could pull the dinner shift with you if Trace needs the help."

"I'll ask him when I get there, and let you know."

"We still on for *To Have and Have Not* after your shift?"

"Definitely. See you later."

Throughout the rest of his afternoon, Dec kept a timer running in his mind. Holly had texted to say that Trace's sister had agreed to fill in for the other barista. He'd been instructed to meet her at her apartment later with his DVD player. He'd agreed simply because inviting her to his home would make everything far too easy.

He had precious little resolve when it came to her anyway. His expansive bed, his hot tub, his couches — hell, the countertops in his kitchen, they were all far too available for him to put her off. He could keep his head straighter at her place. Friday night, he'd take her home, wrap her up in a little bit of comfortable luxury, spoil her thoroughly, and make her fly higher than she'd ever flown with another lover.

He shook himself when Matthew Hutchins knocked on his office door just before easing inside and setting down his battered guitar case. Dec always arranged it so Matt was his last patient of the day. Once their session was over, he'd been helping Matt learn to play guitar.

Dec stood and smiled. He shook Matt's hand and was genuinely thrilled to see broad grin on his patient's face.

"Something must be going well."

"You always know stuff like that don't you, Dr. St. James?"

"It's kind of my job. Tell me what made your day." Dec settled on his couch while Matt took his favorite chair. Matt had never cared for sitting on the sofa. According to him, the clichés were just too much. Dec had assured him he understood.

"More like made my month. I asked that girl Megan out for Friday night. She's the one I was telling you about that I met at group sessions at the Center. She said yes."

The thrill of accomplishment and pride for just how far Matt had come warmed Dec's entire being. "Congratulations. She's a very lucky girl."

Matt turned serious a moment later. "Well, I mean, she isn't though, Doc. Obviously, you know why we both go to those group sessions. Lucky kids don't end up in sessions for all of that shit. We're both fucked up, I guess. Her stepdad." Matt shuddered, so did Dec.

"I am very sorry for her, but I'm terribly proud of you. And we're all fucked up. Don't let anyone tell you differently. Finding a person that wants to hang out with us despite whatever our particular brand of fucked-uppery is a tremendously great part of this world."

Matt laughed, another thing Dec wasn't certain he was ever going to get to hear eight months ago when he'd taken him on as a patient. He'd been seeing him three times a week, every week. Asking a girl out was a massive step for Matt.

"Yeah, I guess maybe you're right."

"Maybe." Dec chuckled. "Little nervous about this date?"

"Are you some kind of mind-reader or something? How do you do that?"

If you rub your hand against the knee of your jeans any harder you're going to wear in a hole. You've shifted in your seat about a dozen times in the last two minutes, and there's a dew on your forehead. Of course, Dec would never point any of those things out, so he just smiled. "Honestly, I have a date myself Friday night, and I'm a little nervous. I was hoping it wasn't just me."

"You're not nervous. You're just saying that. Liar." Matt withdrew. He almost always did. He'd lived through hell, and he trusted no one. Not that he should. Dec didn't see this as a failing. Teaching Matt new boundaries and how to enforce them was his job. Teaching him that some authority figures were trustworthy would come years and years down the road, if he ever got there at all. Matt was seeing other counselors to help him deal with all that his uncle had done. His mother had hoped Dec might help him navigate some kind of normal sexuality balance for a nineteen-year-old kid.

"I told you months ago I would never lie to one of my patients. I'm not lying to you. I just met this girl, and she's got my head spinning day and night. I am nervous. I want to impress her."

"Really?" Matt slid closer and narrowed his eyes.

"Really."

"You're way too cool to get nervous, Dr. St. James. You probably know how to do everything the right way."

"Trust me, no one knows how to do everything, and there is no one right way to do anything at all. Have you decided where you're taking Megan Friday?"

"Well, she's in the county home, so she has to get special permission and everything. She did that, but I don't want to take her anywhere that might make her uncomfortable. I don't want to do anything wrong. Sometimes. . .she can have. . .uh. . .what do you call the things that make you think you're back in a bad place when you aren't?"

"A triggered panic attack or a flashback. Those are very common. You can show her how to calm herself down the same way I taught you if you'd like to."

"Yeah, I taught her the song lyric one. That one works the best for me. She likes the counting one. But I want this to be perfect. I don't want her to have to sit there rocking back and forth counting and me to sit there with my eyes closed remembering the lyrics to Goo Goo Dolls, ya know?"

"I do know, but might be best to deal with where both of you are instead of wishing you were someone else. Might also mean a great deal to her if you show her how much you understand what she's going through. And the Goo Goo Dolls, come on, their lyrics are outstanding examples of humanity." Dec had discovered that wrapping wisdom within the heart of lightness, in this case the Goo Goo Dolls, eased Matt and helped the pill go down a little easier.

"Yeah, I know. I'd just like to give her one night where she doesn't have to remember any of that."

Gutted. His job absolutely gutted him on a daily basis, and he'd never give it up. He deserved it, and more than anything else he needed to help these people. Helping them kept the constant cravings at bay.

"A more than worthy goal, but might be asking a lot of the universe. Not saying it's impossible, just saying let's take it moment by moment, and take some of the pressure off."

"Moment by moment. Yeah, I get that. If you add up enough moments it could be a pretty great night."

"Indeed."

"How do I know if. . .you know. . .she wants me to do something I'm not doing, or stop doing something I am doing?" Panic set in quickly. Kid was nineteen years old. What had been inflicted upon him had stunted his development. It always did. It stunted it, but nothing could stop it. Matt wasn't even sure what he was trying to ask. He just knew there were things his hormones desperately wanted that his mind had no idea how to go about obtaining in a healthy way, or what to do with it if he should actually get it.

"You remember when I taught you to play the intro to Slide?"

"Yeah, I can do it perfect now."

Dec grinned at that. "You can, but do you remember my advice when you kept tripping over the arpeggios?"

"Yeah, you said take a deep breath, relax my shoulders, and go really, really slow until I had it just right. And if I messed up to stop immediately and slow down again until I got it right."

"And why is it important to slow down when you realized you might've played it incorrectly?"

"Because you can get really good at playing it the wrong way."

"All excellent advice for your first date as well, my friend."

Matt's smile returned. "You also told me too much of my pick was sticking out. That won't be happening on this date." He laughed.

"There is a reason you're one of my favorite patients." Dec chuckled.

"Bet you say that to everyone. Any other advice? I really want Megan to have a good time."

"Well, what does Megan like to do?"

"Read. A lot. And also she draws these amazing pictures of like fairy things and stuff. They're incredible. They look real."

Dec shouldn't have gotten so attached to Matthew. He'd already broken a half dozen arbitrary doctor-client privilege rules. He'd met Matt in a parking lot on the rougher side of town two months ago when he was grappling with all that he'd been through. Three weeks before that he'd gone back to his aunt's home, desperate for closure that he would never receive. When he'd finally figured that out, he'd snapped. The cops had come. So had Dec. He'd managed to talk the officers out of an arrest and had sat with Matt on the cold sidewalk for hours, talking him through things as best as he could.

Psychotherapy didn't always fit neatly inside a one hour, three days a week box. Life just didn't work that way. Sometimes it was more than one could bear, inconveniently and often arbitrarily. Dec didn't believe in only being available for his patients during business hours. Any psychologist worth their salt knew it was the night time phone calls, the gut-wrenching screams when the light of day had abandoned them to darkness was when it really mattered.

"I can't think about anything but how bad I want to hug her, and maybe kiss her if she wants me to, and it wouldn't trigger anything. I don't know where to take her. I haven't been able to think straight since she agreed to go out with me."

This was precisely why Dec was quite certain he didn't really have a heart anymore. It had been utterly decimated far too many times.

"Deep breath. Relaxed shoulders. Nice and slow."

Matt gave him a begrudged nod. "I kept kinda thinking maybe I could take her somewhere to dance. You know, then I could kind of be near her, just hold her close or whatever, but not make her think of anything else."

"How old is Megan?"

"Nineteen, same as me. Her birthday is May 17th and mine's April 17th. She thinks that's cool. Girls think the weirdest shit is cool."

Dec couldn't help but chuckle. "There's an entire pseudo-science based on the belief that there is a relationship between numbers and coinciding events. Her thinking that's cool isn't so weird."

"She's way smarter than me, too. She probably knows about what you just said. What do you think about the dancing idea?"

"Sounds like a solid plan to me. Neither of you are old enough for bars, but there have to be a few places you could take her where you only have to be eighteen to party. No drinking, though. Understand?"

"No drinking. I know, Doc. I don't know why you care so much. No one else ever has."

"That isn't true. Your mother cares very much, not that you give her credit there. You are worth being cared about, Matt. That's why I care. And I still say Megan is an incredibly lucky girl to have you to care about her."

CHAPTER EIGHT

Holly grinned as soon as she saw Dec's bike pull into the lot at Trace's. By the time he made his way inside, every cell in her body felt like it had been strung on a livewire. She'd never had such a strong physical reaction to anyone. His low-cut, v-neck, grey t-shirt showed off a peek of the tattoos on his chest and his left arm along with his impressive biceps and pecs. He was wearing a leather necklace with some kind of silver pendant she hadn't noticed before. His low-slung tattered jeans were rubbed in all of the perfect places, all of the places Holly desperately wanted to rub. They pulled at his substantial thighs and hugged his enviable ass. God, she couldn't wait to run her hands over every chiseled plain. Her mouth went dry, and her palms began to sweat. She quickly sat the carafe of coffee she was carrying on the counter.

Declan offered her a sexy-as-sin grin while he performed his customary deep breath after entering the coffee shop.

"The view here has certainly improved, Trace. You should see if you can keep her around." He winked at Holly behind the counter.

"I've tried to hire her every semester but she's too. . . . " Trace explained and Holly promptly panicked.

"I'm a terrible waitress. I've already spilled coffee on one lady's white pants. I'm so glad you stopped by."

"Couldn't keep myself away. I needed to see you."

Holly's stomach flipped in elation at that while she prayed Dec hadn't picked up on the word *semester*. "I'll leave it to Trace in about an hour when the evening crowd dies down. Tea, I'm guessing?"

The furrow of Dec's brow said he'd noted her forced interruption. Trace also looked thoroughly confused. Thankfully, he said nothing else.

"I'll take most anything you're serving, love."

"I'll bring it over."

When Dec found a table by the back windows, Holly turned to Trace. "I don't want him to know I'm a student yet."

"Yeah, I got that. Dec won't care that you're younger than him, sweetheart. My wife was eight years younger than me."

"That's not it. Wait. How old is he?"

"And if he asks me the same thing about you, am I allowed to tell him?"

"No."

"Then leave me out of this. I'm not sure anyway. I just know he's a good bit older than you."

"Age is not the problem. I just want him to get to know me slowly. I want him to trust me."

"You want him to trust you, but you don't want him to know anything real about you? You're smarter than that, Holly."

"Yeah, well, this is complicated."

"That's what they all say," Trace sighed as he went about wiping down the marble countertop.

Holly fixed Dec's tea, complete with a splash of milk that she hoped wasn't too much.

"I could definitely get used to the sight of you in an apron, love," he goaded as she approached.

"Oh yeah?" She set the tea down on his table, stepped back and swayed her hips, making the skirt portion of her dress tied up under a black waist apron swish seductively. "And what might you do with me in an apron, Mr. St. James?"

A quick confused grin creased Declan's face before he rearranged his features and cocked his pierced eyebrow up. "So many things. How are you with a feather duster?"

Holly couldn't help but giggle. "Fantasy of yours, I take it?"

"I keep telling you, if you're giving I'm taking."

"Seems like the strings of an apron would make great tie-ups, too." Holly watched closely to see what he did with that.

"Fantasy of yours, I take it?" He tugged gently on the strings of her apron, teasing her, stirring the need swimming in her veins. "One I'd be more than happy to take care of."

"I'm hoping."

"Oh, honey, I doubt you even want to know the decidedly dirty things I've fantasized about doing with you all damn day. I plan to spend my evening watching the sexiest barista in the Midwest serve coffee. Instead of writing music, I'll be conjuring all kinds of deliciously scandalous things I long to do with you."

Holly swore every time he spoke her entire body vibrated to the tune of his bravado and hunger. She wasn't going to survive until Friday. She simply couldn't make it that long without having his hands on her, inside of her, touching her, marking her, owning her. Whatever kinds of scandalous things he wanted to do, she was all for it.

Trace insisted he could close up on his own and shooed Dec and Holly out the door at 9:00.

"You really don't have to watch Bogie and Bacall with me," Holly offered.

"Why wouldn't I want to watch it with you?"

Because there are about a million far more interesting things we could be doing. "I don't know. Guys usually don't like old movies."

"I like being with you. The rest is just icing on the cake, darling. Did you ask Trace if you could keep the apron?"

"Didn't figure we'd need it tonight since you're hung up on the one-week rule."

"I'm not hung up on anything, except maybe you. Patience, anticipation, desire, remember?"

"Oh, I remember," Holly vowed as she unlocked her apartment door. Dec was loaded down with his DVD player and the movie he'd sweetly purchased.

While he set up the DVD player, she poured two glasses of wine, popped a bag of popcorn in her microwave, and settled on the sofa, wondering what to talk about since her morning was out. Trace was right. She eventually needed to tell him she was a psych student, but he was an addict. What if he thought she was only dating him to analyze him?

Besides, her current preoccupation about how exactly she might be able to go down on him while he wore his piercing had her deciding she could tell him next week. Or the week after that. Or any time after Friday night.

He joined her on the sofa with a smirk. "Just so you know, this little dress you're wearing is driving me to distraction. Can't seem to think about anything but getting my hands under that skirt."

"Then that definitely tops the list of things I love about this dress. Don't stop yourself on my account."

She watched his eyes darken dramatically. He licked his lips. She loved the look in his eyes that said it was taking everything he had to keep from stripping her bare and taking her so hard she could feel it for days to come. Since coming was definitely what she was after she scooted closer, hoping to amp his desire.

"Holly, darling, you are just absolutely irresistible."

"Then don't resist." She whispered the words across his lips as she leaned in. He captured her breaths and her mouth with his own. A tortured moan reverberated against her tongue as he began to suck gently. His hands threaded in her hair, guiding her closer still. She touched his face, memorizing the feel of the stubble on his jawline.

Without thought, she climbed over him, feeling his cock harden against her as she began to grind.

"Fucking hell," he groaned as his head fell back, and she moved faster.

He lifted his head. His dark grey eyes were greedy with lust. His hands slid up her thighs, kneading a path towards her ass. His touch was electric against her skin. She leaned in for another kiss.

His wanton little cowgirl loved to be kissed. Dec already knew this. He just couldn't fathom how each and every kiss slipped down his throat and wrapped itself around his cock. She pressed that sweet little snatch against him, rocking up and down, wrecking him thoroughly.

His control slipped with every motion, with every sexy sound she made. The kiss ignited into a wild, frenzied feast.

"Gonna ride me, cowgirl? Gonna ride me and show me how sweet you come?"

Pressing his hands higher under her skirt he located her delicious ass, completely exposed in the thong she was wearing. She cried out for him, rocking faster. Oh, hell yeah. "You like that, don't you?" Gripping her firmly, he pressed her to his hard on, rocking against her, meeting her grind for grind. "Did you wear those naughty panties, so I could grab your sweet little ass? I think you did. You like my hands right here, don't you?"

She moaned something unintelligible. Always a good sign. Any man that vowed that he knew how to make any woman come or knew everything they desired was a conceited asshole with less than half a brain. Oh, but you could learn. Those addictively sexy sounds and gasps, the way they moved, what you might get them to admit once you'd created a safe space for their desires, where the heat settled in their bodies, those were the cipher to the complicated truths of a woman. Ever changing, ever needing, always variant, but constantly there if one just listened and paid very close attention.

Gauging her as he plied her ass and bit at her lips, he began to unfold the complicated, intricate details of Holly. Given the way she threw her hair back and rode him with wild abandon he knew she liked being watched, which worked out perfectly because he desperately wanted to view. She also deeply enjoyed him verbalizing precisely what she wanted. Understanding meant something to her, and Declan understood every sign.

"I want to see, darling. Let me see how wet you get for me." Using his right hand, he gathered the flowy material of her dress and pulled it upward to reveal her wet satin panties. The sight wrenched a low guttural growl up from his gut. She pressed in with more vigor, clawing at his shirt, trying to cling to her sanity. Her restraint long gone, just the way he wanted her.

His cock was an iron spike against her. Her wild cries said his piercing was hitting just the right satin-covered spot. "That's it, isn't it? Right there. Gonna feel so good deep inside of you, too. Ride me, cowgirl. Hard. I want to watch you come for me." Dec was going to lose it. What the hell was she doing to him? How could he possibly be so close still fully clothed? He gripped her ass with one hand and moved the other to her right breast, squeezing her lace-covered nipple between his thumb and index finger. His cowgirl liked it rough. He was more than happy to provide.

"Oh God, oh God, Dec, yes," blended into a symphony of indecipherable carnality. The rest was pure noise as she began to tremble.

Heat streaked her face. Her musk perfumed the air and flooded his lungs in his rapid breaths. He wanted to drown in it, to be fully consumed by her orgasm.

"Give it to me, sweetheart. Let me have it. It's all for me. All mine."

His commanding thrum had the desired effect. Her entire body tensed with a gasped scream of pure pleasure that erupted from her core. Collapsing against him, she buried her face against his neck. He wrapped her up in his arms, making her a sanctuary in him, a place to feel that level of pleasure without any judgment.

God, she'd come so damn hard fully clothed. He'd never seen anything like it. Whatever was going on between them was explosive and more powerful than anything he'd ever experienced. What if he never got enough of watching her do that at his command?

"That was the most beautiful thing I have ever seen, sweetheart. I'm going to want to watch you come undone every single day. That okay with you?"

When she finally lifted her head, her hair was mussed, her eyes half-opened, her lips kiss-swollen and ripe, and the heat coursing through her body settled high in her cheeks. She looked good and fucked, and Dec amended his decree. Her climax was most beautiful sunrise in existence, but the look of his sweet little sex-kitten thoroughly satisfied had to be the most stunning of sunsets.

"Little embarrassed. I didn't even make it through the annoying previews."

Chuckling as he kept her cradled safely in his arms, he shook his head. "Don't be. You come so sweet, love. It's spectacular. There are so many ways I want to make you do that over and over again."

"Yeah, I want that, too. I can't seem to think about anything other than the things I want to do with you."

"You name them, one by one, we'll explore them all. I want to know the things you're afraid to admit to anyone, the things you think of when it's just you and that adorable little butterfly vibrator."

Another round of that seductive heat blossomed across her features. "And why should I trust you with my darkest fantasies, Declan St. James?"

"Because, my beautiful Holly, I can make them all come true."

CHAPTER NINE

Holly had been busy most of the week; doing just *what* Dec hadn't managed to get her to confess as of yet. He hadn't pressed seeing as how he'd been busy with patients all week and hadn't wanted to discuss that.

As they'd both quickly discovered when he'd been over to care for her tattoo or to simply enjoy being in her presence, words weren't necessary. They connected on a soul level they reached through physical contact. It had taken Herculean levels of willpower to put her off until tonight.

Thus far, he'd picked up on Trace's comment about hiring her every semester, and another slip about an advisor she'd made the night before on the phone with him when the late hour had robbed her of her guard. The few clues he'd managed led him to believe she was possibly a graduate student. Nothing wrong with that, but he desperately longed to know what she was studying.

He'd asked her to spend the entire weekend with him. His fantasies of Holly Camden came by the dozens; one night simply wasn't going to be enough. If Dec were being honest with himself, he would admit that he was damned proud that he'd managed to keep his cock out of her delectably tight little snatch until they'd met his one-week rule. His addictions weren't running the show this time, and he'd just proven it. He deserved a reward, and an entire weekend with Holly would allow him to really get to know her, to ravish her in every imaginable way, and to indulge her in the finer points of love making. There was no better reward than that, but first, he had to put on one hell of a show at Duffy's Tavern and see just how Holly reacted to his rock star persona.

Holly wedged her cell phone between her shoulder and cheek while she skillfully applied eyeliner to her right eye. If grad school had taught her anything, it was to multitask.

"Please tell me you went with your Corral boots with that short, strappy, hunter green dress that cuts down low to show off your girls, with your denim short jacket. I want to know you made whoever this guy is absolutely drool tonight," was Cheyenne's greeting when she answered. Holly had texted her pictures of three outfits. They'd been debating most of the afternoon.

"Drooling is always a good thing, and I did go with that, but I can't wear a bra with this shirt. My girls aren't at their best."

"I don't see what the problem is. Save you a little time once you get back to his place."

"Well, yeah but there are saggage issues, and I want to sort of play a little bit hard to get."

"Um, the way you've been talking about him for the last week, I think we're way beyond hard to get."

"We are. I know. I swear, the things he does to me. Most of the time I think I'm dreaming. No guy has ever made me feel the way he does."

"I am aware of this, and I am also tremendously jealous. Why do you always get the guys you want, and I never get anything I want? I need details of this weekend. I plan to live vicariously through you."

"No dice, babe. You know I love you, but this weekend is all for me. I kind of hate myself for being nervous, though. He's just a guy. What's wrong with me?"

"First off, he doesn't sound like just a guy. He sounds like some kind of orgasm deity, and you're nervous because we already know he's freaking good in bed and because we still don't know exactly how much older than you he is."

"Being older than me is probably how he got so good in bed, so they're kind of one and the same."

"Maybe, but I think some guys just have really good mojo, ya know? Guys like your big brother."

Holly rolled her eyes. "I do not want to think about Grant's mojo, thank you very much." Dec's knock on her door injected her with another round of nerves. "That's him. Wish me luck."

"Wait, do you know if Grant's going to Saddleback's tonight?"

"I have no idea, Chey."

"Could you find out?"

"I can't. I gotta go." Holly ended the call, rushed to the door, and then forced herself to pause and count to ten. She made it to six before she wrenched the door open.

Dec was leaning against the door frame looking every bit the sex god. His jet black hair was slightly messier than he normally kept it. He was wearing a grungy, white v-neck t-shirt with a pair of ripped blue jeans and a well-worn black leather jacket. The leather necklace was back around his neck. It all gave him a wild edge that Holly found absolutely irresistible.

"Jesus Christ, darling, you have any idea how bloody difficult it is to play the guitar while you're harder than a steel pipe?" He ran his index finger softly from the hollow of her throat to the low dip of her blouse that ended just above her navel. The move effectively left her breathless.

"You look pretty hot yourself."

"Oh yeah?" He stepped inside. His presence sent shockwaves of awareness throughout her. "I'm glad you think so. Right now I'm worried I should've packed a few extra guitars for the night?"

"Do you play more than one at a gig?"

"Sometimes, but that's not why I need them. I never understood the smashing the axe thing that used to be popular among the more obnoxious rockers until I saw you dressed like that and remembered that there will be at least a hundred assholes there tonight near you, and I'll be on stage and unable to remind each and every one of them who you're going home with tonight."

The electricity between them was palpable as he dragged his darkened gaze from her boots up her legs, to the skin exposed between her breasts, along her neck, and finally to her eyes.

A shiver shook through her. The look that said he was going to fuck her senseless all night long was back in those cryptic grey eyes. There were secrets there, she knew. Beyond his addictions and beyond his rehab. There was so much more to Declan St. James. She just hadn't yet managed to get him to confess anything else. That was her goal this weekend. To take them deeper. To learn. To become more with him. To see if this relationship was going to be all she knew it could be. Somehow, even though there was still so much that hadn't been verbalized between them, she knew there was more. More than she'd ever fathomed maybe. More than she ever believed possible.

He'd invited her to his home for the entire weekend. If that wasn't a sign of trust from an addict, she didn't know what was, and she would prove herself trustworthy for him at any cost. She was ready for him, all of him.

"This all you need for the weekend, love?" He already had her duffle bag and toiletry kit gathered up in his strong arms. Holly had never wanted to be luggage more in her life.

"Yeah, unless we're going out somewhere I need to dress up for. I don't usually wear a lot of make-up or anything."

"Yet another thing I find myself falling hard for, and I don't plan on us leaving my house all weekend. I'm hoping to get you to forgo clothing altogether." His winks at her always elicited a physical response. Every cell in her body responded to his very breath. The simplest gestures made her feel exposed to him, and she didn't mind at all. "You look a little needy, love."

"I am. It's all I can do not to beg you to throw me on the couch."

"A little something for the road, so to speak."

Reckless desire pulsed through her blood. "Please."

He dropped her bags. "Lean against your kitchen counter with your gorgeous arse high in the air. Shake it for me."

"Are you serious?"

"I never joke about touching you, darling, and I've also told you repeatedly that I'm not a man known for my patience. You aren't the only one who's needy. I've thought about nothing but burying myself inside of you all week. I have so many plans for you once I get you back to my place. Lean over, arch your back, and spread your legs."

"Oh my God." Breathless and spinning, Holly complied, not certain what he was about to do, but desperate to find out. His hands roved over her ass. The silky fabric of the dress swayed to the rhythm of his fingers, taunting her. A breathy moan shook from her lungs.

"Such a sweet girl for me." His low groan washed over her skin, priming her for more. With his index fingers he traced up her thighs and drew the loose fitting dress upward to expose her ass. He brushed a kiss on each of her cheeks before his fingers centered along the satin crotch of her thong, and she was certain she was going to combust. "So wet."

"Dec. Please." She managed in a pant.

"Please what?"

"Touch me. Bring me. Please." Wriggling back and forth against his touch, she ached for more.

"That's what I need, love. I need to hear you beg."

"Please," she whimpered desperately.

"Good girl. I intend to hear that all weekend. You understand me?"

"Oh, hell yeah."

Expertly, he traced his fingers under the slip of satin and then up and down her slit, gathering her dew, making her raw with need. Her body jerked when he tempted her clit, circling and learning her at the same time. Before she could beg for more, he dipped two fingers deep within her channel, pressing, exploring, possessing her.

She groaned out his name and gripped the cheap countertop, pressing back against his roaming fingers.

"So fucking tight. So fucking perfect. God, I'm gonna fill you so full. Over and over until you ache, and the only thing that makes it better is more of me."

"Yes!"

Out and in, he fucked her thoroughly with his fingers, making her desperate for his cock.

"Right here, isn't it darling? That sweetest little spot. It's right there. I know. I always know what you need."

Holly shook as he strummed her g-spot perfectly. The tell-tale rhythmic spasms came fast and furiously. Her body begged for more, tensing against his masterful fingers.

"It's right there, isn't it? You come so good for me. So ready for it, aren't you? So needy. I can't wait until you come on my cock and then on my tongue, love. Over and over again, dripping down my legs and then down my face while I devour you. I dream about your flavors. I want to know them. I want them to be all mine."

"*OhYesDec,*" blended in a single word as her back arched and heat sizzled at the base of her spine. Pleasure rocketed upwards and then her body gave itself over completely to his touch. She shook with the orgasm that overwhelmed her in frantic waves as she clawed at the counter and collapsed.

When she steadied her breath, she stood. The dress whispered down her legs, covering her and taunting her overly-sensitized skin. Her gaze met his. Wild craving stormed in his greedy eyes.

"Watch me." He brought his fingers to his mouth and sucked her nectar from them. Another aftershock from her climax shook through her. His eyes closed as he sucked harder, like he'd never tasted anything better. Something inside of her snapped. The barriers of propriety she kept erected shattered into a million unrecognizable pieces. She couldn't build them back. She didn't want to.

"What. . .what does it taste like?" Her breath stammered as if it couldn't believe she'd verbalized that particular question.

Keeping his covetous eyes locked on hers, he pulled his fingers from his mouth, caressed her lips, and leaned in. "Taste."

Copying his movements, she hesitantly licked his fingers. A mix of her release and his saliva filled her mouth, spicy heat and liquid sin. She took more, until he replaced his fingers with his tongue, making another exchange of flavors.

When he finally broke the kiss, his eyes closed in an extended blink. "I have to play tonight, but sweet baby Jesus, I'd love to pack you up, take you home, and get to so much more of that."

Delighted to hear that, Holly beamed. "We have all weekend to do more of that, and I'm hoping we have months after that to keep going."

"Months, huh? I haven't scared you off properly then?"

"Do I need to quote Eminem again?"

"No, darling, and I have no intention of doing anything that might make you change your mind on those next few months, but right now, we need to head on. I want to take you to dinner before the gig, but I do have to be there to finish setting up. Garrick and Kade have been there most of the afternoon running lines."

"Garrick and Kade are. . . ?"

"Drums and bass. Both back up vocalists."

"To your. . . ?"

"Lead guitar and vocals, of course." Another wink that spoke directly to her soul.

"I assumed. I just thought I'd ask. Are there any other band members I should know about since we just agreed to a few months?" She couldn't help but remind him. She wanted to make certain she hadn't dreamed that up in some kind of post-orgasmic bliss state.

"I'll introduce you to everyone tonight. Brett Packston plays keyboard and Andy Campo plays rhythm. They'll love you, and they'll love harassing me about you."

"Sounds like we'll get along just fine."

"I have no doubt. As long as no one calls you Yoko you have nothing to worry about."

"Not funny, St. James. I will get you back for that."

"So much to look forward to." With that, he scooped up her bags once again and guided her out to his Pilot.

CHAPTER TEN

With every step he advanced on the way back to his SUV, Dec mentally lambasted himself. Downfall of every fool was pride. He'd been so pleased to have been able to resist Holly all week, proving to his addictions that he was stronger, he'd blown all restraint straight to hell as soon as he'd walked in her door. *What the fuck, St. James?* She was completely irresistible. He'd fought for so long. Pushed her away for a week trying to navigate the endless road between fighting his addictions and wanting desperately to make love with her.

Shaking his head, he opened the back, added Holly's bags to the load of guitars and equipment stowed there, and opened the passenger side door for her.

"Did you always want to be a rock star?"

"I'm far from a rock star, darling, but at one time I definitely wanted to be one legitimately. That's pretty much all I thought about from the time I got a second-hand Epiphone when I was eleven. I was gonna play Wembley. Become some kind of sexy mix of Eddie Vedder, Chris Cornell, and Dave Grohl. I finally figured out being a rock star wasn't so good for me." Yes, this was good. He needed to let her in slowly.

"I'm sorry." A slight case of nerves seemed to have overtaken her.

She was fussing with the hem of her dress and staring out the passenger side window like the star-strewn night was out to do her in.

"You okay, love?"

"Oh, yeah, just doubting I'm cool enough to pull off lead guitarist's girl. I've always loved the lyrics to music. I love to think about what made the songwriter write them just that certain way. How do they know how to arrange the words so they speak to the masses? But I also have zero clue as to how to even hold a guitar the right way. I don't even know what an Epiphone is."

"Hey." Dec reached and took her hand to keep her from pulling at her dress anymore. "You told me you didn't want me to be ashamed of being an addict; well, I never want you to be ashamed of what you don't know. An Epiphone is a kind of guitar. Mine is particularly crappy, but it happened to be my first, meaning I can never get rid of it because that just isn't done, but I also never play it. I'm the one playing tonight, sweetheart. You don't have to know how to hold a guitar. I'm just happy you're holding my hand. You're also the only thing I want in my arms tonight. It means a lot to me you're coming to hear me play."

That earned him a genuine half-smile. "This is just weird," she sighed.

"Me and you, or going to this gig?"

"Me and you. Everything is different. I've never felt this way before." She shifted away from him. He could see the hot glow of her cheeks flash repeatedly in the lights of the oncoming cars, and he saw something in her eyes he'd never seen before — fear.

Signaling to change lanes, Dec immediately pulled into the empty parking lot of an abandoned grocery store. "Look at me." He waited until she'd lifted those beautiful eyes, every possible shade of green known to man and a few he was certain hadn't yet been named, to his. "Afraid of me or afraid of what happens between us?"

"I told you I'm not afraid of anything."

Gently, he tipped her chin upwards, drawing her closer. "But you are, love. Maybe not of me, but of this."

"On one hand, I feel so different when I'm with you. I feel closer to you than I ever have anyone, and then on the other hand I feel like I don't even know you, not really. I know there's stuff we still haven't told each other. Maybe it's not even really important stuff, but it's stuff. And on the *other* other hand, I know we've only been hanging out for a week, and I'm always getting ahead of myself when I should just let things take their own time. I'm no good at not going after what I want full force."

Dec couldn't help but grin at her less-than-eloquent definition of the things left unspoken between them. "I had no idea you had three hands, but I cannot wait to see what that might be like in bed." She slugged him in the shoulder rather hard. "Totally deserved that, but now I may not be able to play at all tonight," he teased as he rubbed his injury.

She tried unsuccessfully to twist her grin into a glare.

"I feel different with you too, Holly. Honestly, you completely overwhelm me. You occupy my every thought. What we just did back at your apartment, I should never have done that with so little time. That's not how this is supposed to work. I obviously left you feeling insecure. I took what I wanted and clearly didn't give back. I just can't seem to physically resist you any longer, but that does not mean that I don't also want to connect with you emotionally if that's what you want. I am also aware that I've fucked up a lot of things in my life, and I've fucked up a lot of other people's lives because they had the unfortunate luck of being near me. I don't want to do that with you. I'd love to have a healthy relationship, but you might have to teach me how. You okay taking this one day at a time? We can talk about all of the *stuff* as it comes. That sound good?"

"Yeah, that sounds good. Sorry I brought all of that up now. I loved what we did back at my apartment, and I'm definitely not sorry you're having a hard time keeping your hands off me. Not sure where all of that came from. Been a weird week I guess."

"You can bring up anything you want anytime you want. We ready for dinner?"

"Are we eating in the old Sun Mart parking lot?"

"Not unless you packed some kind of sustenance in that bag. I pulled in here so we could talk. I may suck at relationships, but I am aware of how important talking is. I was thinking we'd go get pizza at Isles. That sound good to you?"

"Sure. I love their Leaning Tower."

"Like I keep saying, girl after my non-existent heart."

"Your heart is right where it should be. I'm going to prove that to you. I'm also going to keep asking you questions."

"I'll consider myself warned." *I'll also ignore the fact that I really wish you wouldn't.*

"You said you figured out being a rock star might not be so great. What made you decide that?"

Evie happened. His mind supplied the answer but his lips refused it, and damn it all to hell if his cowgirl wasn't digging deep this time.

He stared at her for far too long, weighing his options. "It was the drugs." *It wasn't just the drugs and you know it.* Dec steadfastly ignored his own mind trying to get him to make a real confession. "Every pound I made playing financed my own death."

"I read somewhere that addicts often feel like they're dying their entire life." Realization weighted her words. She was getting it.

"It wasn't just me that was dying. I did damage to everyone involved."

For the fourth time in the last ten minutes, Holly ordered her mind to ease up. He was confessing more, maybe. Even if he was still dancing around his truth, so was she. She had no right to take any more than she was giving, and she was far from giving him the truth.

He kept one arm around her and managed his guitar and a gig stand in the other hand while he guided her inside a back entrance of Duffy's. There was still equipment in his SUV, but he'd refused to let her help carry it. She knew part of it was his desire to care for her and to be a gentleman. She suspected another part was that he didn't want anyone touching his gear.

Nervous energy surged through her veins. The weight of this night sat heavily on her chest constricting her breath. Something about Declan, something about the two of them felt inevitable. There was no turning back from this, and she already knew it. She wondered if he felt it, too.

Every kiss they shared was more powerful than any orgasm she'd ever had with another man. There was nothing fleeting about Dec. In one week's time, he'd managed to become a permanence in her life, the life she'd told him precious little about.

He was a requirement. His touch, his laugh, that smirk that said he was telling her half-truths but wished he could somehow confess more, his voice graveled and deep — they had become as necessary as her breath. How was that even possible? They hadn't even slept together yet. Her buzzing mind offered her no substantial answers. All she knew was she wasn't going to be able to walk away unaffected this time. This time, she might not be able to walk away at all, and that should have scared her into running, but her boots were planted firmly on the floor of Duffy's bar, clinging to Dec's hand.

"Holly, baby, this is Garrick Meyers, Kade Griffith, Andy Campo, and Brett Packston. They're all basically a bunch of muppets whom you should waste no time worrying over. Since you are my. . . ." Declan leaned in, gently tucked her hair behind her right ear, and whispered, "We good with girlfriend?"

Holly's heart dislodged itself from her chest, performed a high-flying kick routine, and then settled somewhere in the vicinity of her throat. She managed a frantic nod. Holy shit. Girlfriend. Already. Clearly, dating men her own age had been a massive mistake. She didn't give a damn how old Dec was, this was how real men behaved in a relationship. This was precisely what she wanted.

"Good." Dec brushed a kiss along the shell of her ear, sending a quick shiver through her body. Dear Lord, she had to get it together. She wanted his band members to like her, not think she was some kind of nympho only after Dec for his body or his bad boy ways or whatever. "Like I was saying, since you are my girlfriend, they should bow down at your feet, grovel, buy you drinks, defend your honor even if it costs them their own arse, and naturally behave as something other than the bell-ends they are."

Jesse, Garrick, and Brett all stared dumbfounded at Holly as if she might be some kind of hallucinated dream. Kade looked delighted.

"Um, bell-ends?" Holly inquired.

"Sorry, love, pretty sure dickhead would be the closest English to English translation."

"You're shitting us, right? She's like your little sister or something," Andy declared.

"Don't have any sisters, and why would I be shitting you?" Irritation riffed heavily in Dec's tone. Holly tucked herself closer to him.

"He's just joking," she whispered.

"Not joking, honey. Can't quite figure out why a stunning angel like yourself would want to be Doc's girl." Andy was quick to correct her.

Doc? Holly hung on his nickname. Did he mean Dec? Sizing Andy up didn't take a terribly long time. He was shorter than her with decidedly Italian features, right down to the surly scowl. She narrowed her eyes. "Well, you know what they say about lead guitarists. The way they finger those strings. It does something to a girl. You just play backup though, right? I guess you wouldn't know."

Dec doubled over laughing. He was quickly joined by the rest of his band members. Andy tried to pretend he was unaffected. He laughed along, but Holly knew she'd shut him up for good.

"And that should clear up any question about us at all," Dec gloated. "As Andy pointed out she's stunningly beautiful, and as you just witnessed has a wicked tongue and a wicked mind to go with. I am but her humble string-playing fuck toy. We like it this way."

Holly shook her head at him, but was thrilled he seemed to enjoy having her there.

"Ignore them both, Holly. It's nice to meet you, and nice Dec's actually smiling. You watching the show from here or you want me to have Scott reserve you a table near the stage?" Kade lifted her hand to his mouth and brushed a kiss between her knuckles. This kiss had no effect. When Dec did that, she swore she could feel the brush of his lips all the way to her core.

"I'd rather watch from the front if that's okay."

"It's fine, sweetheart." Dec guided her back out to the SUV to finish unloading it.

"Scared of what they'll say to me if you're not in there?" She called him on the move as soon as they were in the parking lot.

"Obviously. Everyone but Andy is great. He's got a chip on his shoulder so large his strap hangs over his ear."

"Was this band a band before you moved here?"

"It was." Dec grinned at her. "Keep going. I love watching your mind work."

"I'm betting Andy was trying to fill in as lead and was sucking at it, and all of a sudden you show up and now you're getting gigs at the biggest bar in Lincoln and he's pissed."

"Bloody brilliant and hot as hell. I have absolutely no hope of ever surviving this." He planted another kiss on top of her head.

"I guess the question is are you okay with that?" Holly stared him down. He felt it, too. He felt their inevitability, their permanence. She knew.

"More and more so with every passing moment. Right now my only concern is how to get this concert over with as quickly as possible, so I can get you home and indulge myself in you."

"That might piss Andy off." Holly swallowed down raw need, trying to lessen the effect of his words unsuccessfully.

"Andy can fuck the hell off."

Seated at a table less than five feet from the brick stage area at Duffy's, Holly tried to take another sip of the drink Brett insisted she would like. The fishbowl's syrupy sweetness curled on her tongue. Dec pulled his hand away mid-strum, sat his custom Stratocaster down, and leapt off of the stage.

"Let me get you something decent to drink. That shit Scott likes is not how I want your toes to curl this evening."

Delighted with his adept perception and precision, she brushed a kiss on his chiseled jawline. "And how did you want them to curl tonight?"

With every lift of that pierced brow, she swore she fell harder for him. He guided her up to the bar and was immediately waved to the front of the line by the bartenders. He ordered her a Cabernet. When he offered to pay, they refused his money. Apparently, there were perks to being with the band.

While they were pouring her wine, he wrapped her up in his arms, cradling her against the crowded bar. "My sweet little cowgirl likes it when I tell her all the decidedly naughty things I plan to do to her, doesn't she?" He roved his hands over her back and discreetly grabbed her ass.

Holly nodded against him. The way he understood the things she longed for but could never manage to fully verbalize flooded her with heated need. She knew he would indeed make her fantasies come true. He seemed able to understand the ones even she didn't fully comprehend.

With a gentle shift of his hips, he settled his rigid erection against her soft abdomen. "Do you feel what you do to me, darling?"

Winding her arms around his neck, she nodded into that perfect cradle where his substantial shoulder met his tensed neck. She pulled him closer, desperate to feel more.

"We're standing in a bar full of people and when I hold you, Holly, everything else disappears. Nothing else matters. I want to make you feel things no one else could ever hope to make you feel. I intend to own every single thing I coax from your gorgeous body tonight. Every moan, every scream, every kiss, every mark, every single climax. All for you. All *from* me."

"Oh, God." Had Dec not been holding her up with ease, she was certain she would have melted into the concrete floor.

"Be a sweet girl for me for a little while. Be patient. But when I get you home, love, the very last thing I want is for you to be my sweet girl. I want you loud. I want you dirty. I want you demanding. Then I want you begging, aching, and naughty. All for me."

"Here you go, Dec." The bartender slid Holly's wine towards them and effectively ripped her out of the thick, erotic haze of words Dec had painted around them. When he eased back from her to retrieve her drink, the unwanted sting of abandonment stabbed through her.

"Come on, sweetheart. Just a few more hours." Another wink. Another flutter of her heart. Holly didn't want any more of his agonizing teasing. She didn't want to be patient for a few more hours. She wanted to be owned.

"I do need to know one quick thing before I go do my thing."

"What's that?" Holly barely recognized her own voice. It was distant and breathy. She sounded needy. That wasn't something she ever wanted to be.

"What's my cowgirl's favorite song?"

"I don't have just one favorite. It depends on my mood."

"Naturally. So, what favorite are you in the mood for tonight?"

"You'll make fun of me."

"I will do no such thing." He looked pained she'd even suggested that.

"Okay, well, I guess *I Need You* by Tim McGraw. The one Faith sings with him. It's so sexy. Makes me think about you," she admitted.

"Why would I have made fun? That's a brilliant song."

"I just figured you didn't like Country."

"Not a fan of anything involving a lyric about a beer can, but there are Country songs that capture life better than any other genre. Perhaps I'll manage to capture your heart as well as Mr. McGraw captured his *Mississippi Girl's*."

CHAPTER ELEVEN

"We good with the new setlists? I need to add one more after the last." Dec tried to discreetly adjust his ridiculously eager hard-on as he made his way backstage. It was a quarter after nine. They were due to start within the hour. If there was an encore, they wouldn't be able to leave before one, and there was always an encore. Dammit, he wasn't going to last that long.

Brett's smirk said he'd noticed Dec's rearranging. "New sets look great. Can't imagine why you picked *those* songs." He laughed. "Let me guess, we're adding her favorite song to the end."

"*I Need You* by Tim and Faith. We've played that before. It'll be fine."

"You're lucky we already know that one," Brett chided.

Garrick slapped Dec on the back as he joined them. "We're starting with *American Girl*, man. Little desperate don't you think?"

"Who says I'm not desperate?" Dec had no defense. He didn't even want one. All he wanted was Holly.

"Yeah, let's change up the whole damn list for Dec's jailbait." Andy's sneer tore through what little remained of Dec's resolve. Rage shattered the heated blood coursing through his veins. In two quick moves, he had Andy caged up against the brick wall of Duffy's staging area.

"I don't know what the hell your problem is, asshole, but if you ever refer to her as such again, I can guarantee I'll bury that shit guitar so far up your arse, you'll never locate it. Think you can get that through your thick skull?"

"Andy, come on, lay off. What's up with you anyway?" Garrick and Brett made an unsuccessful attempt to pry Dec away from his intended target.

Begrudgingly, Dec stepped back. His muscles flexed, eager to drive his fist through Andy's face.

"You denying she's barely legal?" Andy continued to tempt his own fate.

"She's more than legal. Just shut the fuck up. He'll kill you. I don't even think it would tax him to do so." Garrick gestured to Dec's biceps.

"Whatever." Andy grabbed a pack of cigarettes and headed out the back door.

Kade joined everyone in the back room. With a quick study of everyone's faces, he shook his head. "What'd he say about her? Wait. No. Don't even tell me. I'm so sick of his shit, and we gotta get warmed up."

"We were waiting on you. Where you been?" Brett asked.

"He was buying the guy at the table near Dec's new girl a drink. You invite him or did he just show up?"

"Name's Wyatt. I invited him, but I didn't think he'd show. We met a week ago at Panic. Fucking gorgeous, isn't he?" Kade all but sighed.

Dec's fury at Andy was quickly replaced by hope at Kade's obvious infatuation. Kade had it rough. His parents kicked him out when he was fifteen and attempting to come out. He'd gotten caught in a few rough spots and had ended up hooked, something Dec understood only too well. But he'd gotten cleaned up, and he was making his own way now. His family hadn't spoken to him in almost twenty years. The band was his family, and Dec would never let Kade down.

Peeking out at the large crowd, he watched Holly invite Wyatt to sit at the table upfront with her. Damn this woman. If he'd bottled perfection and poured it out, it couldn't have been any better than her.

She caught him staring from backstage and offered him that sweet grin and a quick wave. He blew her a kiss and wished the fans, the performance, everything but her away.

The broad, beaming smile and delighted laughter he earned from her when he strummed out the first few chords of *American Girl* made opening with Petty one of the best decisions he'd ever made.

The neon lights bathed the crowd. Dec couldn't make out many faces, but the energy in the bar sizzled around them. They'd packed the house. Hundreds of bodies crowded the tables surrounding the stage, a few of them calling his name.

The heady sense of fulfillment eased his soul. The electricity and thrill of the connection of humanity through music made him believe this life was worth living. It always did. You could sing any lyric to most any song and a thousand different people would sing it right along with you. What so few understood — those thousand people all had a thousand different reasons for singing that one song, but in that moment they were united by the lyrics and somehow agreed to allow Dec to lead them home. It was a responsibility he never took lightly. And tonight, Holly was in the crowd singing back to him. Few things could top that. He knew.

Wyatt sang with them all. Dec prayed Kade could see that. He prayed Kade felt the acceptance he was being offered.

Kade and Dec moved back to back, bracing against each other as they played their hearts out for no one other than the two people at the front table.

The buzz of the crowd swelled in Holly's chest. When they played the opening to *Should've Been a Cowboy* by Toby Keith, she knew he'd done the entire arrangement all for her. Never before in her entire life had she even imagined having a rock star sing just for her.

All she wanted was to figure out how to make this moment last. Anything that hadn't yet been spoken between her and Dec didn't matter. She shook her head when he proclaimed that he should have been a cowboy.

He chuckled onstage at her vehemence. "No?" he managed while the rest of the band sang on.

"No," she shouted over the crowd.

"That's my girl," he declared as he picked up the chorus and fell back to join Andy and Kade.

They played a few newer songs, but the crowd became a dancing mass of delirium when they played the classics. Somehow Dec's addictive accent disappeared when he sang. Holly found herself missing it.

"Hey, Dec, what's she gonna say tonight," bellowed from Garrick as he kept a steady beat on the snare.

Kade and Declan both laughed as Dec edged back to the front of the stage with the opening line to *Rebel Yell*.

If Holly's cheeks weren't already ablaze from the heat of the surrounding crowd and being so near the stage lights, they certainly were as soon as he set his guitar down and leapt to her side in a move she'd only ever seen on YouTube videos, he dipped her back and kissed her and then made it back onstage like this was something he did all the time.

She wondered just how close he'd gotten to being a full-fledged rock star before he'd succumbed to the drugs. She hated that his addictions had robbed the world of his music, but just then she was thankful he was hers for the time being.

"He's smitten, darlin'. I hope you're wanting to ride as bad as he's wantin' to be ridden," Wyatt elbowed her when the bartender sat down the pitcher of water Dec must've had sent to their table while they took a quick break.

"I definitely am," Holly admitted. "Are you friends with Dec or just Kade?"

"Just met Kade last week. Not even friends with him yet, but I know a good thing when I see it."

Holly wasn't certain if Wyatt was referring to Kade or to her and Dec, and she couldn't shake the feeling that she'd seen him somewhere before. "Hey, where are you from?"

"Little town nobody's ever heard of."

"Oh, yeah? Me too. Try me."

"Gothenburg."

"Are you serious? I'm from Pleasant Glen. We played Gothenburg in football every year."

"You mean you *beat* Gothenburg every year. What did you say your last name was?"

"Camden," Holly stated cautiously.

"Sweet baby Jesus in a basket, you ain't Austin's baby sister, are ya? I tried to break into the rodeo circuit a few years back. Austin helped me out. Ridin' broncs never really got me anywhere but the emergency room. Bulls didn't like me much either, but your brother's a real nice guy. You all own that big ranch on the west end of Lincoln county. You got several older brothers, don'tcha?"

Holly sighed. Yep. She was Austin's *baby* sister, and partial owner of the legendary Camden Ranch, and she did have three big brothers. She just wished she could lose that *baby* part and figure out how exactly to explain all of that to Declan. "Yeah, Austin's my brother. He won the PBR buckle a couple of years ago."

"Yeah, I heard he won and then dropped out."

"He got married. Has two kids now."

"You don't say. Tell him Wyatt said hello next time you see him."

"I will."

Suddenly a mischievous grin creased Wyatt's rugged features. "Austin don't know about you and Dec, does he?"

Holly shook her head. "We really haven't been together very long."

"Don't figure you'll mention it when you have. I have three little sisters. Guys like him get big brothers all up in arms. We can't help it, and I don't know anybody who'd want to take on your big brothers."

"Yeah. Me either." The pent up excitement and magic of the evening deflated slightly. At some point she had to tell Declan about her family, her ranch, the fact that she was a psychology student, and that despite all of that she still desperately wanted to prove that there was something between them that she'd never experienced before. There was a plan for them. Something substantial. That sense of permanence settled her. He was and would always be an addict. Nothing about that frightened her. For the first time in a long time she felt a purpose in her quest to become a psychologist. The purpose somehow united the two sides of herself that were almost always at war.

When Dec returned to the stage after their break, her libido shifted into overdrive once again. That was all it took. He set a small cup of water near his mic stand and shrugged his guitar strap back over his shoulder while blowing her another kiss. He was entirely too cool, and she was entirely head over heels for him. *Don't act like some kind of idiotic schoolgirl. If you're going to date an older man, you should probably at least act your age.* She offered him a slight smirk and returned the blown kiss.

CHAPTER TWELVE

Girlfriend. I said the word girlfriend. My God, St. James, are you ever not a selfish bastard? So much for ridding himself of his one hit wonder status. She'd offered him a little. He'd immediately asked for more.

"Come on, let's see if Doc can really play it, or if he's as full of shit as I know he is," Andy taunted quietly as the rest of the band returned to the stage.

Dec rolled his eyes. How like Campo to start something onstage in front of 897 people. Duffy's was turning people away at the door. They'd hit the limit for their maximum occupancy. Nothing as cowardly as hiding behind a crowd.

"If he wants to play it, let's do it."

Campo needed to learn that Dec never took a gamble he wouldn't win. He'd learned that decades ago. Even high, getting your ass beaten by your supplier when you decide to blow what you were supposed to sell will teach you something. Surely there were more pleasant ways to learn to keep your word, but that was how Dec had learned. Horrible decisions would occasionally teach you the right things, but it was almost always an extremely painful lesson.

"You seriously think you can play it?" The delight on Campo's face was ridiculous. If a grown man needed to best some guy he'd been playing in a band with for almost a year, something very serious was wrong.

"I know I can play it. What I can't figure is why you need me to."

"Just play," Campo sneered. With one forceful strum down the strings of his lackluster guitar, he had the crowd's attention.

Dec turned to check with Garrick who looked a little queasy. "Man, Alex Van Halen strung four basses together for this. I have two," he pled to Andy.

"You'll be fine," Andy scoffed.

Everyone else on stage shook their head. If Andy's asinine insistence that they do this cost them another gig at Duffy's, he was out, and he knew it.

Garrick tapped his sticks together, took a gulp of the smoke infused air, and made the sticks fly. He laid it all out on the bass drums he had.

With a nod, Dec played fast and furiously as the lead guitar must do when playing Van Halen's *Hot for Teacher*. Andy sang and Dec stole a quick glance at Holly during the solo. Her mouth was hanging open as she watched his fingers fly. Well, maybe Andy wasn't a total cum-trumpet.

This was easily one of the most difficult songs to play. Dec doubted even Eddie Van Halen played it the same way twice. If it impressed Holly, maybe it was worth it. If he lost all feeling in his fingertips, however, he'd kill Campo twice. Nothing was going to keep him from feeling Holly's soft, supple skin that night. Not Campo. Not his own selfishness. Tonight, he was going to give her everything she was seeking. He would take nothing for himself, nothing but her pleasure. He'd prove his power over his addictive behavior if it was the last thing he ever did.

Gritting his teeth, certain his fingers were going to shatter as they danced frantically along the strings, he managed the end of *Hot for Teacher* and fell into a bow out of sheer exhaustion.

Holly, and the entire rest of the bar, was screaming his name collectively, jumping up and down, and looking genuinely impressed. Dec decided to only kill Andy once.

The owner of Duffy's was standing with two of the bouncers. Their look of collective amazement probably meant Dec and Garrick had just scored them a regular spot at Duffy's Tavern.

Andy, however, looked like the sheep back on St. James' farm right after a shearing, ornery and misunderstood. Like something was missing, but they didn't dare look at themselves to figure out what.

Dec's eyes sought Holly. He needed to see her smile at him. Needed to feel her presence in that room with hundreds of people calling his name. And there she was.

"That was amazing," she mouthed as soon as their gazes locked.

No. That was nothing. *She* was amazing. He just had to show her that.

If Andy could fuck with the set lists, *his* set lists, so could he. "We're playing that one I've been working on," he informed his bandmates at large, not caring if anyone heard him. He could play this on his own.

He worked through the first few chords slowly letting Garrick figure out a steady beat, and Brett joined him on rhythm as he drawled,

I want to dance in your light
Affect the chemistry of my longest night
Vanquish the darkness in the heat of your sun
Let your touch give me sight

"Oh my gosh," Holly choked over the rock-like enclosure in her throat, denying her air. She'd never heard this song. Neither had anyone else in the bar. They were swaying along, listening intently, but no one knew it, and no one knew it because he'd never sung it publicly before. Something in the raw tender strain of his voice told her he'd never sung it before because he'd written it for her.

'You could give hope to thousands of nice guys sitting at home wishing women like you would give them a mere moment to stand in your sunlight.'

"I can't believe he did this." She shook her head in disbelief as Dec handed her a piece of his soul in front of what had to be a thousand people. Focusing on the lyrics, memorizing them, understanding that they were nothing but his absolute truth, she knew there were moments in everyone's life where time was fractured. In one brief second, the person you were before was a distant stranger because a moment occurred that forever altered everything you'd ever known about yourself. This was one of those moments.

The rest of the set was a blend of Aerosmith, Pearl Jam, some current chart toppers, and a few Country hits. They did indeed play *I Need You* for their final encore, but Holly could barely hear it over the lyrics she repeated in her head over and over. Her lyrics that he'd written. Tim McGraw had nothing on Declan St. James.

"You ready to go, love?" Dec brought her back to reality with the graveled clearing of his throat. Last call had been an hour before. Everyone was clearing out now that the show was over. She shook herself and threw her arms around him.

"That was amazing, Dec. I'm serious. I can't believe you did all of that."

His throaty chuckle wrapped tightly around her heart. "Well, I'm glad you enjoyed it." He nodded his appreciation to one of the bartenders who handed him a steaming mug.

"Is your throat sore?" Holly brushed a kiss along his neck, more than ready to get to the next part of their evening.

Dec downed a long swallow of what must've been hot tea. His throat contracted under her lips. She spun her tongue near the hollow of his collarbone, greedy for the tang of his sweat. She longed for his flavors to saturate her every sense.

A low greedy groan sounded in her ear. "You are once again vastly overestimating my ability to remain in control."

"If I didn't want you in control, what would we do?" she purred as she nuzzled her head against his chest.

"You really want to know that?"

"I wouldn't have asked if I didn't want to know." She lifted her head, staring into his darkening eyes. The shades of grey blended into a black storm of pure heat and irresistible desire.

"I'd take you out to my car. . ." He bit off the end of his explanation. Was he really afraid he'd scare her off? Holly almost laughed at that.

"You'd take me out to your car and do what?" She watched his muscles tense and his jaw tighten as she breathed the words over his chest. "Tell me. I want to know."

He swayed against her, fighting with himself unnecessarily.

"Tell me," she whispered again. "God, it turns me on so much when you tell me what you're fantasizing about doing with me."

The clunk of the mug of tea on the table echoed against the vibrations of her entire body. He wrapped his arms around her tight. His left hand kneaded her ass, jerking her forward until she collided with his potent erection. His right threaded through her hair. "You feel how I have your hair right now?"

Holly managed a nod. His grip on her hair tightened. Every nerve-ending on her scalp responded. *More.*

"I'd push your head down to my lap, wrap those gorgeous lips around my cock, and make you suck me off. Not let you stop until you swallowed me all. I'd fuck your pretty mouth hard. Fill it full. Watch you swallow me whole. Teach you how to relax and take me deep, let me feel your throat contract around me. But we're not doing that right now. Not tonight. Tonight is all about you."

Holly heard the concession in his voice.

"Do something for me," she commanded.

"Anything."

"Never assume that having your cock in my mouth wouldn't be exactly what I want, or that you teaching me things wouldn't be the thing that turned me on more than anything I've ever done with anyone else. Never assume that asking for what you want isn't exactly what I need. By my count, I'm a half-dozen orgasms ahead of you since you've brought me in one way or another most every night this week but have refused to even take off your pants. Our love life is never going to be a one-sided venture. You got that, St. James? It's for both of us. Every single thing we share has to be all me and all you. Never ever just me. What I want more than anything is to explore with you."

He captured her lips like a man possessed. His fingers pressed into her hips with enough power to leave marks she hoped she could see the next morning. "You want to explore, love? God, you want to know what I want? I'll sure as hell show you. I'll teach you anything you want to know. You gonna be a good girl and do as I say?"

Her responsive, "Yes," was nothing more than a choked breath stolen with his mouth as the hand that had been tangled in her hair gripped her neck and pressed along her throat.

A full minute later, Dec broke the kiss, startling her. He shook himself. His breaths were as quick and shallow as hers. He leaned his forehead against hers. "You want me to tell you what I want?"

"Yes, more than anything."

"Stand right there, love, until I can walk you out of here without embarrassing myself. Then I'm taking you home. I hope you're ready, baby. I really do. Because it's going to be daylight before I've had enough of you to even sleep. I'm gonna fuck you raw. Keep you wrapped up in my bed all fucking weekend because you won't be able to walk without feeling how much of you I owned. You understand that? You understand that's what you're asking me for? You understand that's what I want? I take things I shouldn't, Holly, things that shouldn't belong to me, and I just keep wanting more. I try so damn hard not to be that person, but that's who I am."

"But don't you see, taking what you want is exactly what I need. I need you, the parts I don't know yet, the parts I do, whoever you are right now, and whoever you're going to be tomorrow."

His jaw worked frantically as he searched her eyes; for what she had no idea. "I don't deserve that." His voice was haggard and laced with a piercing regret. Holly doubted it was from singing for the last few hours.

"*We* deserve that."

CHAPTER THIRTEEN

Dec searched her eyes. She couldn't actually believe what she'd just said. She couldn't actually want him to take everything he wanted from her. There was curiosity, hunger, lust, maybe even greed in her gaze, but nothing to indicate she hadn't meant every word.

She stood solidly on those sinfully sexy boots, staring him down. The heat of her arousal stained her cheeks. Her eyes were bright and fervent with her wants, as if her desire was penned in the pools of emerald ink. Her intoxicating cleavage beckoned him from the low cut of her blouse. He could have her naked in one minute's time. See her sweet juices sheened on the lips of her pussy. Touch her. Make her quiver with need. See his fingerprints on the curves of her delectable ass. Take what he so desperately wanted. Then take more. Mark her in places no one had ever kissed.

She was right there asking for those very things. She was utterly irresistible. He reached for her hand and decided to turn the red flags warning him off into what they were most commonly used for— a blindfold.

He helped her step up into his car, intent on giving her exactly what she asked for.

"I have a new favorite song." She gave a sly grin.

Declan's heart thundered out its approval. Damn thing refused to quit, apparently. She'd figured out the song was about her, not that he'd had any doubt she would. "Oh yeah?"

"Yeah. It's beautiful. Way better than *I Need You*."

"Well, Cowboy McGraw is pretty good. 'Least the record labels seem to think so."

"When did you write it?"

"Started it last Saturday night. I sensed I'd found a new muse, one that wouldn't kill me."

"Muse, huh? That sounds very sexy."

God, what was she doing to him? How did she make everything okay just by sitting there flirting with him? He was all over the place. He had to get it together. His constantly slipping control scared the shit out of him. Control was the key to survival.

"She is *very*, very sexy."

"Do you wish you hadn't quit? Music, I mean."

"No. Honestly, I don't. If nothing else, quitting got me here, and for some reason I may never understand I finally feel like I'm right where I need to be."

"Yeah, I feel that way, too. Pretty sure that's what freaked me out earlier, actually."

Dec turned to study her as he drove further outside the heart of Lincoln. "We'll figure this out, sweetheart. Whatever it is. I just needed to tell you how I work. I want you to walk away now if my personality flaws scare you. God, I don't ever want to frighten you, love, I just need you to understand that I will fight as hard as I possibly can against my truest nature. I just don't know if that will be enough. Sometimes it isn't enough, and I push too hard." There. She wanted the truth. He would do his damnedest to give it.

"I don't want you to fight it. You can't push too hard with me. I don't want you going back to drugs, obviously, but I kind of think you've spent a long time fighting the tides. Sometimes the universe gives you a life raft. You just have to take hold of it."

"Oh, honey, believe me, it's all I can do to keep my hands on this steering wheel. I plan to take firm hold and not let go. I just sincerely hope we both don't drown."

"You'll find I'm an outstanding swimmer, and I'm still singing Eminem. *I'm not afraid.*"

"But you should be."

Holly rolled her eyes and didn't care that he saw. She reminded herself that he had no idea that she knew a great deal about addictive behaviors. She'd counseled addicts at the drug centers in Lincoln and Omaha before she completed her Masters. She could help him if he'd let her.

The city lights were slowly fading away as he drove them further South. As he turned towards the golf course at Wilderness Ridge, her curiosity magnified. She wondered what else he did besides play gigs at bars. That certainly wouldn't pay for lakefront property near the nicest golf course in Lincoln.

"I didn't know you lived out here. I don't know anyone who lives out here," she confessed.

He turned that penetrating stare on her once again as he slowed to take the tighter turns past the ridge.

"I'm going for dual citizenship. It looks better to Immigration Services if you purchase land, or a house, or whatever as long as you can do it in cash. Your banks aren't terribly forthcoming with loans to foreign nationals. I'm not a huge fan of the pretentious neighborhood, but the water is soothing and you can't even see my closest neighbor's house from my decks. In London, everyone lives right on top of one another. There's more people than the country can contain. It's suffocating. Drove me mad. When I got here, I'd never seen anything so flat or open. I decided to take advantage of it."

Holly grinned. If he wanted wide open spaces with no one around for miles, he should see Camden Ranch. "I get that. I'm actually from a massive ranch out in the middle of nowhere. Lincoln gets to me. I can't breathe for all of the people. Most of the time I'm here I just want to go home."

"Am I allowed to ask where exactly the middle of nowhere is, love? Or should I wait for tomorrow for anymore reveals."

"The ranch is about an hour and a half due West if I'm driving. Two hours if someone else is driving."

"Out in cattle country, I take it."

"Yep. Told you I was a cowgirl."

"You also told me in the middle of a song that you didn't want me to be a cowboy. How does that work?"

"Tomorrow."

CHAPTER FOURTEEN

Dec hated himself for wishing that tomorrow would never come. If he could just extend the darkness of the night, just make this part of the two of them last eternally, explanations would never have to be made. That idea was highly appealing. She'd just put a date on their confessions. He was going to have to tell her more. You couldn't wish away the sunlight, no matter how much darkness you carried. She was quickly becoming his own personal sun, just like the lyrics in the song he'd written for her. He just had to keep his darkness away and let her light their path.

When he turned down his long driveway, he watched Holly take it all in. Low tree limbs swept over the windshield as they neared the house. He wondered if this might frighten her, being so far away from civilization with a man she'd only known a week. The way she eased forward in her seat to see more said she was more eager than fearful. Apparently nothing much frightened his cowgirl.

Maybe growing up on *the ranch* as she'd reverently referred to it had better prepared her for life than his father's sheep farm had readied him. God, he hoped so.

He parked in the left side of the double bay garage. His bike was in the single bay beside it.

"Wow," was her only comment as he retrieved her bags and guided her up the steps to the kitchen.

She ran her hand along the steely-black granite countertops, the former owner's choice, not his, before she headed to the home's best feature — the wall of windows that constructed the back and showed off Waterford Lake in all of its man-made, boulder-encrusted glory.

Dropping her bags on the leather sectional in the living room, he wrapped his arms around her waist, pressing her back to his chest while she gazed out at the moonlit view.

"Does wow mean you approve?"

"Dec, your home is stunning. Dying to ask how a musician without a record label affords this, but I suspect the answer will be. . . ."

"Tomorrow."

She turned in his arms and nuzzled her sweet face against his neck. "Tomorrow's good." She traced the v-neck of his t-shirt with her fingertip, taunting him.

"Already on ragged edge, sweetheart. Every time you touch me, I lose a little more control." He brushed a tender kiss on top of her head.

"Good," she half moaned as she jerked the shirt upwards. He helped her lift it over his head. She was playing with fire, and this time, he was certain she knew. Her palms pressed over his pecs as she ran them down his chest, pausing to spin her thumbs over his nipples.

A grunt of appreciation escaped the tight lock of his jaw. His muscles flexed, so anxious for more.

"Am I allowed to ask what the dragon eating his own tail on your necklace means, tonight?" She lifted the weighty amulet that hung around his neck.

"Reminds me of exactly what I was doing every single time I got high."

"Take it off. We're not getting high tonight. We're making love."

"Making love with you will be the highest I've ever flown, love. I have no doubt. You are so damned addictive, and you have no idea." He unclasped the leather necklace and tossed it on the couch. He was rewarded with her mouth, and what a reward it was. She nibbled and licked her way across his collarbone. His cock throbbed so fiercely she felt its prod against her midsection.

Her sweet little curves shuddered against him. It was more than he could stand. He peeled the jacket she was wearing off of her and tossed it away. Running his hands up her arms, watching chill bumps scatter under his fingertips, he jerked the sleeves of her blouse down, revealing her naked breasts.

His growl of pleasure echoed around the room. "Very naughty, Miss Camden. I wanted to strip you myself. What shall I do with you showing up uncovered to one of my shows? Makes me want to unload my cock all over your sexy tits, baby. Remind you just who you belong to. I told you I take. It's all I know, and you volunteered to become mine."

"So do it," she dared.

"Also makes me want to turn you over my knee and see how many strikes it takes to turn your sweet little bottom as pink as your pussy after I've fucked you raw."

"Oh my God. Yes!" she cried out for him.

Dec almost convinced himself that he was saying these things because he knew that was what she wanted to hear. Almost.

No. He had to stop. This wasn't going to happen this way. Not with her. Not tonight.

"Holly, shh, come here to me." Gently he pulled her back into his arms. "We have to talk before this goes any further. I've got to get control of myself."

Disappointment ravaged her eyes, but she allowed him to tuck her to his shoulder and begin to sway. "Listen to me, love. I want this to last all damn night, but we have to talk first."

"Okay, so talk."

Impatient little thing. She had so much to learn, and he was her willing instructor in every capacity.

"Have you ever been with a man that had a piercing?"

She shook her head against him and wrapped her arms tighter around his chest. That feeling of her needing him to protect her from the world washed over him once again. He wanted to protect her innocence while simultaneously taking it all for himself. Contentment coursed through his veins. It fought for dominance over the longing to possess her. *Both*. He needed to be her protector and her possessor.

"It's fine, love. I won't wear it if you don't want me to. I can take it out at any moment, but if you want me to keep it in, I can't wear a condom. It can tear them. I'm clean, honey, I swear to you. I was tested as soon as my divorce was final, and I haven't been with anyone since I moved here. I'd sworn off women for good until I saw you sitting at that table in Duffy's. You blew my resolve all to hell. You always do." He brushed another kiss on top of her head.

That earned him a grin as she lifted her head.

"I can pull out or I can take it out and wear a condom. Don't be afraid to tell me what you want. All I want is to be with you."

"I'm not afraid, Dec. How many times do you need to hear me say that? And I have an Implanon implant." She pointed to her arm. "I have no intention of getting pregnant any time soon. I'm clean too. There. . .haven't been. . .all that many guys. . .and it's been a while."

"Good. You're all for me." He couldn't help himself. His demons howled out a victory call. She was his. There would be no others.

"What does it feel like? The piercing, I mean," she asked.

"For me or for you?"

"For me."

"Lets me hit all the perfect spots, sweetheart. All those tender places that need to be tended. Lets me love you the way you need to be loved. Make you come harder than you ever have with anyone. We're gonna take it nice and slow at first. If you don't like it, I can always take it out."

"Pretty sure I'm gonna like it." Her decree was breathless, reckless, and desperate. Dec's blood sang for her. It had been too damn long since anything had wrecked him so thoroughly, and it was all her. All Holly. And she was all his.

"I'm pretty sure you are, too."

"I don't want you to pull out." A harsh swallow constricted her throat.

"You sure, baby girl? You sure you want my cum soaking down your sweet pussy? You want my seed dripping down your thighs when I'm done taking you over and over again?"

"God, yes," she whimpered out her desire.

"Done." With that, he lifted her up into his arms. Her dress hung off of her oddly as he carried her upstairs to the master bedroom at the end of the hall.

Gently he settled her in his bed. He'd taken care to fix the sheets before leaving to pick her up. He'd wanted everything to be perfect for her. It was a fruitless negotiation he'd gone on with despite its stupidity. Typical addict behavior. The same way he used to keep his guitars absolutely pristine, his vinyl collection perfectly organized, and his motorcycle in top-notch condition while he snorted death into his own body.

He knew he could never be good enough for her. He was tainted and she deserved better, but he'd cleaned his home to show her he would try to be closer to the man she deserved.

"I've watched you come for me all week. Most beautiful thing I've ever seen, but every night I got back here and dreamed about watching you come completely undone, naked in my bed. I want to see all of you, Holly. I want to touch all of you. I'm fucking tired of coming alone in this bed, grinding against this mattress, dreaming of you."

"Please." She writhed against his white cotton sheets. "Now, please. Take everything you want. Then take more."

She had to stop saying that. How did she not understand that he would? He would take everything he wanted and would feel no remorse.

He made quick work of her boots and socks, discarding them before he traced his callused fingertips up her legs, revealing her to his craving eyes. Trembling, she sat up as he lifted the dress off of her, leaving her in nothing but a slight pair of purple lace thong panties. There was a cutout in the fabric exposing her bare mound. She'd waxed that day, if he had to guess. He'd noticed it earlier in her kitchen, but had been too intent on getting his fingers inside of her to comment. Two evenings before he'd brought her with his hands down her jeans. Then she'd been natural. He'd reveled in the wet heat gathered in her curls all for him.

He was once again torn. It was sinfully sexy. Jesus Christ, he wanted to spend hours with his mouth covering every centimeter of her silky flesh that she'd altered just for him, but sex wasn't about Brazilian wax jobs or scripted moans. It wasn't an anesthetized act the world copied from some overdramatized television show. And by God, *that* was something he could give her. He could teach her that sex was about release. It wasn't a performance, and it was never meant to be.

His beautiful cowgirl needed to be freed of any kind of restraint to achieve the sweet release she longed for. She needed to understand the power she wielded simply by letting go. He could rid her of the bounds the world had heaped on female sexuality. She needed to feel raw abandon without the pressure of social mores. He would shatter the chains with the might of his hands, the force of his friction, and the commands of his lips.

He spun his tongue in the cut of fabric, nursing at her mound with the heat of his mouth. "Did you do this for me, sweetheart?"

A quick nod accompanied another roll of her body as he blew cool breath over the skin he'd just suckled.

"And did you do this because it makes you feel as deliciously sexy as you are, or did you think you *had* to do this for me?"

She lifted her head. Irritation twisted her features. "Are we seriously talking about this right now?"

Dec chuckled. "We're going to talk all night, love. Talking leads to great sex, and that is the only kind we'll be having. Tell me."

"I did it because I thought you would like it."

He continued to kiss the tiny patch of skin her panties exposed, dying to work his way up her body. Impatience to have her nipples, the perfect shade of ripened raspberries, in his mouth churned through his veins.

"I do like it, but don't ever do this again unless it's all for you. You understand me?"

The furrow of her brow said she didn't fully understand. Clearly, the few men she had been with were selfish bastards, hell-bent on having her the way they wanted with no worry about her fulfillment. *Typical.*

If a man couldn't get his head out of his ass long enough to navigate a woman's deepest desires, to make her understand her own beauty and the beauty of her sexuality, and make her feel rapturous and worshipped every time they were together, he ought to get the fuck out of the bedroom, not that he'd ever state that to his patients.

He dropped several kisses over the satin fabric of her panties priming her. "You smell so damn good. I can't wait to taste your sweet little honey pot."

Her breath caught deliciously as he began his ascent up her body. He spun his tongue over the heart-shaped tattoo of Latin words, intent on uniting each and every side of his cowgirl.

"So fucking beautiful. Your tits drive me wild." And they did. Petite, with nipples that tipped upwards, beckoning his mouth in undeniable invitation. "All mine, and I want everyone to know who you belong to." He warned before he left marks from her collarbone to her left breast.

He scooped his hands under the lush cheeks of her backside bringing her to his denim-covered erection as he latched his mouth onto her left nipple.

"Oh, yesssss," she all but hissed as she began to grind against him to the rhythm he set with his tongue. He gauged her, drawing harder to see her response. Just as he'd suspected, his cowgirl liked it rough. He nipped at her nipple and then eased his draws juxtaposing the sensations. She thrust hard against him. Her fingernails bit into his back. The pain registered instantly as undeniable pleasure.

"You like that, don't you, sweetheart? But you don't just feel it here, do you? When I suck your tits you feel it tighten right about here, don't you?" He eased off of her and spun his index finger back in the opening over her mound as he nipped her again.

"God, yes, mmm," she panted. "Don't stop."

"Had no intention of stopping." He moved to her right breast, nipping and sucking, unleashing unrelenting devastation there until she was a quivering mass of need.

"Please, Dec, please," another whimper perforated with desperation.

"Tell me what you want."

"You know. . . . Just please."

"Tell me, Holly. Say it."

"Make me come."

"That's my girl." With another few draws, he was certain he could have given her an orgasm like this, but he was fighting his own impatience as well as hers. He dipped his right hand into her panties, groaning over the wet heat coating her fevered, satin skin. "So wet for me. Your beautiful little body already knows how to beg for me, doesn't it, angel?"

"Yes." The words came easier now as he slowly deconstructed the barriers surrounding her sexuality. He slicked his fingers with her honey and tempted the hood of her clitoris. Her hips shot upwards off of the bed, spreading her legs wider, making him have to turn to hide his grin.

"Feels so good when I touch you right here. I know, love. I always know."

Several unintelligible and devastatingly sexy noises mewled from her. *Oh, hell yeah.* He could live on nothing but her, bringing her pleasure, but there was still so much to learn. Returning his mouth to her nipple, he suckled softly, adding to the pressure with every rotation of his fingers over her hood. He slipped his ring and middle finger deep within her satin channel and groaned from the sensation, tight and rippling for him.

"Do you feel that? God, do you feel your pussy pulling me in, sweetheart? You're so hungry for it, aren't you?"

Another whimpered cry of need was her only answer. Gently he eased his thumb under her hood, revealing that sweet little pink pearl. He desperately wanted to suck her here, but he had to know how sensitive she might be. "That feel good? Does it hurt if I touch you here, baby? Is it too much?"

Her thighs clamped over his forearm as she began to fuck his hand in earnest.

"It feels so good. Please, Dec. Bring me."

"Spread your legs for me. You don't get to hide from me. Not in my bed. Never." He eased her thighs back apart. "Open yourself all for me. Let me see. Let me make it better." With one more drag of her left nipple and rotation of his thumb, she shattered with a frantic cry of his name. He could definitely get used to that.

She came in tensed waves that racked through her body. He wasted no time easing off the bed and ridding her of the panties, exposing her, making her vulnerable to him. Gently, he settled her legs over his shoulders and dragged his tongue up and down her slit, sucking the nectar of her climax into his mouth. Sweetest addiction he'd ever tasted. "I want you to come for me again, on my tongue. Relax and let me get you there. That was only the beginning."

Holly was already drunk on the aftershocks of the orgasm he'd just orchestrated to perfection. His talented tongue dipped deep within her channel and then spun up over her clit. She could feel herself pulse against his lips as she began to grind against the slight stubble on his jaw. The contrast of the soft heat of his mouth and the abrasion on her thighs made her quake.

His every touch was masterful. Sex god indeed. His tongue gently coaxed at her swollen clit. She shook. He drew the tender bud into his mouth and began to suck. Every cell in her body rejoiced. She thrust hard against him, losing all control over herself.

"Be still for me." His command was laced with greed. He fixed his forearms over her thighs, pinning her to the mattress with his strength, and used his thumbs to further separate her lips. His tongue returned to her clit with torturous ministrations as he held her open.

"Oh God, yes." She tensed, trying to obey him but needing more. She was so close. Her entire body honed in on the strokes of his tongue.

He lapped at her, alternating between drawing her fully into his mouth and bathing her as her body bloomed all for him. "That's it. It's right there, isn't it, love? Gonna come on my tongue for me?"

Holly managed a half-strangled cry. Her hands clawed at his sheets, trying desperately to cling to something as he deconstructed her entire world. Then he took her orgasm hostage, holding it just out of reach.

She whimpered and begged constantly as his teeth nibbled at her inner thigh while her clit pleaded for him to return. He taunted her mound with his tongue and she was certain she was going to lose her mind.

In a world-altering form of hostile negotiations, he dragged his teeth along her soaking wet folds. She thrust hard in his face, pushing against the strength of his arms.

"I said be still," he rasped as he affixed her to the mattress once again, not allowing her any more movement. "Now, ask me like a sweet girl to let you come. Let me hear you beg. You're all mine. This is all for me. You understand that?"

Something inside of her unhinged. He unleashed her own sex goddess with the power of his body and the tender caresses of his tongue. *Master.* How had he known? How had she allowed him to discover her darkest desires? It was as if he'd popped the locked clasp of a diary in her soul, one even she was occasionally terrified to read. The elaborate fantasies she allowed to play out in the darkness and conveniently forgot about in the light blended in the reality of him.

He'd been holding back. She understood suddenly. Something about her thrust in his face and her flavors had freed the beast he housed behind that wall of muscle and reserve.

She gave herself over to his control. The thing she wanted most. Clearly, the thing they both wanted. "Please, please let me come."

"That's a good girl. If you can convince me you'll behave, I'll give you what you want. It's all for me. Say you understand, sweetheart. You understand that you asked me to take what I wanted. I want all of you to belong to me. I want to own you and your pleasure. Every release is all mine. Only for me, and only when I say."

"Oh, God, yes."

"And only when you're a good girl for me."

"Yes," she cried out in relief that he understood exactly what she craved.

Slowly, he forged a path with his tongue back to her clit and circled it, refusing her still.

"Please," she cried.

"Tell me who you belong to."

"You. Please."

"Say my name, love. Say my name, and I'll give you what you want."

"Dec," flew from her lips in a keening plea as he drew her fully bloomed clitoris into his mouth and suckled gently.

Her entire world spiraled out from that one tiny spot of supreme pleasure. She lost everything she'd ever been. It all spilled out onto his tongue, and he drank her like a parched man finally offered water.

Clawing at his shoulders and gripping his thick black hair, she pressed his face to her as she rode the waves of ecstasy he orchestrated. Convulsive aftershocks shook through her, and he finally lifted his head.

The moment it took him to rid himself of his jeans made her feel raw and exposed. She needed him. Needed to be naked in his arms where for some unfathomable reason she felt safe.

He returned to her as understanding settled her soul. This was indeed more than she'd ever experienced before. This relationship, Dec, her, it was more than she'd ever fathomed. It might just have been everything.

Cradling her in his arms and tucking her head to his shoulder, his hands drifted down her side, settling her as he rubbed her ass. A half hour ago she would have worried that he probably noticed that her rear end was substantially larger than her breasts, but the way he held her close, the way he massaged as if he'd never felt anything so good erased any doubts she might ever have had about most anything.

"There's so much I want you to experience with me, sweetheart. God, I'm trying so hard not to just take, but I want to devour you. I can't help it. I need more. I need another hit of you. I'll never get enough." His voice strangled with emotion.

Shocked, Holly lifted her head and stared him down. He refused her gaze. Holding his face in his hands she forced his dark grey eyes, still sheened with need, to her own.

"Look at me and listen to me, Dec. I am not a drug. You are not getting high with me. We're making love, and no one has ever made me feel the way you just made me feel. No one has ever understood the things I'm afraid to even say out loud."

"Never be afraid, darling. Never. There should never be any shame in your desires. Please, I want to hear them all."

"Fine, but you have to promise me that you understand that there is a difference in what we're doing and using."

"Have you ever been high, Holly?"

"No." Somehow that felt like the wrong answer, but she wasn't going to lie to him, not about this.

"Never even weed? Nothing?"

"No. I. . .just. . .never did."

Fully aware of him, she watched the harsh contraction of his Adam's apple when he swallowed down that bit of information. His musk filled her lungs. His long eyelashes barely blinked. If she'd leaned in slightly to kiss him, she knew she would taste herself on his tongue. Her heart flew at the thought.

"Being high used to feel better than the most powerful orgasm you could ever imagine times a dozen. There is a reason people use. No one understands that. They paint it out to be this dark world of lost souls, and when you come 'round, it is, but in that moment, the feeling is otherworldly. I've never felt that way about anything else until I laid down in this bed with you and took that climax from you, and I haven't even gotten off yet. You may not be a drug that's out for my death, love, but sweet Jesus, you are more addictive than anything I have ever experienced, and right now, I'm going to indulge myself."

He thrust against the slick dew still covering her pussy. His long, thick cock glided along her folds, instantly robbing her of breath. He burned like a hot brand against her tender skin.

"Touch me, sweetheart. Put your hands on me. Feel me before I take all of you. I'm going to fit your tight little snatch to me and make you all mine."

A low purr of approval avulsed from Holly's lungs as she wrapped her right hand around his cock. "God, you're so big." She mapped every ridge and vein with her hand, spun her fingers around his crown and eased down in the bed to lick the pearly beads of pre-cum seeping under the barbell piercing through the head of his cock.

"That's right. I am, love. And I don't have enough restraint left in me to be gentle, so if you're not ready, tell me now." His command was a low, graveled growl. His eyes closed as she wrapped her hand back around him and gave a tug.

"I'm more than ready, but you taste so good." Once again, any inhibitions she'd ever possessed were gone. The Declan effect, apparently. She lowered her head to suck him fully.

"Fuck," he growled. "It does taste good, doesn't it, baby? I'm gonna fill you so full of it. Take more. Then let me see my cum on your lips."

Clearly voicing his desires wasn't something he struggled with. Only too happy to comply, she ran the head of his cock along her closed mouth, reveled in the feel of the heated metal on his tightened flesh, and channeled her inner bad girl, indulging him in several voracious sucks. Lifting her head, she locked her eyes on his and slowly dragged her tongue over her lips, indulging herself in his flavors. "Fuck me," she ordered.

CHAPTER FIFTEEN

Dammit all to hell and back, his would-be submissive, if only in his bed, just turned the tides once again. So, now she wanted to be the one giving orders, did she? He sure as hell would fuck her. Fuck her so hard she couldn't walk. God, she was tighter than any woman he'd ever been with. And he was going to take her higher than she'd ever flown. She didn't think sex was a drug. He'd prove her otherwise.

Pinning her to the mattress, he clasped her hands and held them over her head. "I'll fuck you when I'm damn good and ready, darling. That's how this works."

"Mmm, yes." Relief played in her eyes. She didn't want to be the one giving orders. Not really. Clearly in charge of her own orgasms for far too long, she hadn't grasped that he was now her willing servant, a slave to her desires under his commands. She didn't yet understand the power of giving him control. The yin and the yang. He would show her. He would teach her.

Keeping her hands clasped in one of his own, he gripped his cock and ran it along her folds, letting her feel the apa piercing as it tempted her slit. "It's gonna feel so good. Tell me you're ready for me."

"So ready. Please, Dec."

He would never tire of hearing her beg. He swore he could get off just listening to her asking for him. Slowly, he eased his head just inside of her. Her pussy throbbed, desperate for more.

"You feel that, love? You feel yourself milking me? So hungry aren't you?"

"Please," came out in a breathless plea.

"You feel my piercing?"

"God, yes."

A dark chuckle shook Dec's body, easing him further inside of her. "You're gonna feel it all the way up, honey. Take me." With that, he gave a full thrust, and his entire world tilted off of its axis. Everything he'd ever understood dissolved in the silky heat consuming him.

He'd tasted hell far too many times not to know when he was tasting heaven. "Jesus Christ, you feel incredible. So tight. So fucking beautiful." He tried to explain what she was doing to him, but there were no words. There was only her. Only her body accepting his own, accepting his failures, accepting him.

Frantic for redemption, he baptized himself in her over and over, in and out blending together in a heavenly oblivion. He took and tried desperately to give back.

"Oh God, oh God, that feels so good. So. . .so good." She barely managed the words. He captured her lips with his own, stealing her moans of pleasure as well. They were his. All his.

She shook in his arms.

Some part of his schooling and experience came back to him. Reaching down, he angled her legs higher over his back. "Right there. Cross your ankles over me."

She obeyed. Her thighs tightened against his sides, allowing his piercing to slide back and forth along her g-spot, and his cock to fill her to overflowing. With the clench of his jaw, he damned back his own release, ridiculously anxious to leave his body to claim hers.

"It does feel good, doesn't it? Feels good when I take what I want."

"Dec. . .yes. . mmm." Her head shook back and forth as she met his every thrust.

His entire body drew taut. Not yet. Fucking hell, he hadn't had this problem ever. What was she doing to him? That warm tidal pool of atonement he found in her arms drew him in and wouldn't let him go.

It felt too good. For the first time in his entire life, he felt complete. "Look at me, Holly," he commanded.

Her eyes managed half-mast, and he swore he could see all the way to her soul in those dark, hungry depths. Every part of her wanted all of him. He didn't understand it, but he had no power with which to deny her anything at all.

"Come on, sweetheart. Come for me. Let me feel you. Let me hear you screaming my name." With another thrust, she trembled against his girth. He took more. Faster. Greedy. Selfish. Precisely the way he'd sought every hit he'd ever scored. Only this was so much more. He desired the lustration more than the drugs. He'd never wanted anything more than for her to heal him.

He pounded in harder and drew the orgasm from the depths of her soul. She did indeed scream his name and writhe wildly as her pussy spasmed around his cock, obliterating him.

He seized, gripping her hips and forcing himself deep. His release barreled through his veins, decimating any resolve he ever hoped to have. His muscles tensed. His jaw went slack. She was too much. He spilled himself inside of her and then quickly pulled out so the next spurt of cum christened her pussy, swollen ripe from his love.

"All mine," he growled out his own pleasure.

When he managed breath, he collapsed beside her on the sheets, tucking her close. She started to turn in his arms, but he blocked her path, keeping her on her back. "Let me look at you like this, sweetheart. So damn beautiful." Her body was painted in a dozen shades of rosy pinks from their passion. Like a sunset all for him. Her heavy eyes sought his. Her lips were bruised. Tender love bites resided along her neck and at the top of her left breast. Notes of his fingerprints were on her hips from his dominance and his need. Her pussy covered in his cum. His claims of ownership all over her. All his.

The muscles in Holly's body were the approximate consistency of a jellyfish. Exhaustion tugged at her eyelids. She should have been anxious, frantic even. No one had ever made her feel the way Declan did, and she didn't even know what he did for a living, not really.

All the many things she'd wanted to ask seemed too far to reach at the moment. The mattress lowered under his weight as he returned from the bathroom. She trembled when he tenderly rid her of his cum with a warm wet washcloth. The contrast of his power when that's what she required and his tender touch when that was what she wanted was intoxicating. Maybe sex *was* a drug. All she knew was she did indeed feel better than she'd ever felt before times a dozen, just like he'd said.

"Sleepy, baby?" he chuckled as he aimed and tossed the washcloth back on the tile floor of the bathroom all the way across the room. He eased them under the soft sheets and down comforter and cossetted her to his chest.

"There was so much other stuff I wanted to do," she yawned.

"Oh yeah?" Though she was too tired to open her eyes, she could hear the smile in his soft tone.

"I wanted to touch all of your tattoos."

"Tomorrow, and the next day, and the next."

"Promise?"

"Promise."

"And I wanted to know," another yawn robbed her of breath, "why you got your cock pierced."

"Pretty sure you just felt why, love."

"Yeah. That was incredible, but I don't think it was the piercing. I don't know. . .it was just. . .different. I think." She tried to explain but couldn't quite hit the mark. Words eluded her.

"It was different. I felt it, too. Go to sleep. We'll talk about it in the morning."

"Promise?"

"Promise." He brushed a kiss on her forehead and turned off the lamp. The last thing Holly remembered feeling was the pillow of firm muscle under her cheek, and the last thing she remembered thinking was that she sincerely hoped she didn't drool all over him.

CHAPTER SIXTEEN

The lyrics to *I Don't Want To Miss A Thing* by Aerosmith formed readily in his mind while Dec stared out his bedroom windows, trying to blame the terrifying emotions on the full moon. He was more than accustomed to not sleeping, but his own coping mechanism mocked him. The quiet of the night strengthened the calling's voice. He'd learned to use music to drown out the incessant craving for something to ease the burn.

This time the truth refused to be dammed. Just as Aerosmith suggested, he would indeed stay awake forever just to hold her and know she was sleeping soundly in his arms. He had never felt this way about anyone, never Evie, certainly never Victoria, and the dozens of nameless, faceless women he'd had in between the two. Holly was everything to their nothingness, and he had never been more frightened.

She deserved better. She deserved more. She had no idea what he did for a living. He had no idea how his cowgirl existed in the middle of a city, and what if she didn't want to stay in the city? What then? What now?

Tomorrow, he reminded himself, but it did nothing to soothe his nerves.

He had no real idea how to be in a relationship. He espoused to know how every fucking day to his patients, but it was all a textbook ruse. He was nothing more than a fraud. He could quote and play lyrics about love, but he'd never actually experienced it. Was this love? He knew it had to be. Was it supposed to be this terrifying?

She managed to twist him up in knots he had no idea how to unbind. He'd seen the longing in her eyes. The desperation to experience submission. That had been his goal. He'd lost that entirely somewhere in her pleading gasps and sinful moans. He didn't know what the hell he'd been doing. All he knew was that when he had her in his arms, that constant, exhausting call of the substances, that at one time had been his master, was silenced. She dammed his demons. How was that even possible?

It wasn't. Addicts were forced to live with their demons their whole lives. They were inescapable, but somehow she'd made them seem so far away they could never hurt him or anyone else ever again. She silenced their incessant howl.

He tucked her closer, needing to feel her sweet breath whisper across his chest. Needing to have her wrapped in his physical strength and in his emotional weakness.

He'd have sold his soul for her to wake up and want to talk right then, but she slept peacefully in his arms, with an occasional sigh of contentment. He decided those sighs were better than talking just then. They could talk in the morning.

By what had to have been the sixteenth ring, Dec understood two things. The damn thing wasn't going to shut up, and Holly wasn't going to awaken to answer it. His sweet baby slept on in his arms despite the glimmer of sunlight dancing on the dresser mirror and the shrill call of her cell phone.

Easing away from her, he carefully tucked her back in the covers, pulled on a pair of boxers, and headed down the stairs. A sense of unease twisted in his gut. Someone wanted to talk to her badly. He had no right to go through her purse or answer her phone. Intent on simply turning it off, he located it quickly without having to rifle through her personal belongings too much.

When he saw the name on the screen he dropped the phone like he'd just inadvertently grasped a hot skillet. *Dad.* Nope. Nope. Nope. He was not talking to 'Dad.' Not now. He was beyond certain that *Dad* had not yet heard about *Dec,* and until Holly decided to change that, he wasn't going to fuck it up.

Besides, no father in his right mind wanted confirmation, via a male voice answering his daughter's phone early in the morning, that his little girl was keeping the owner of the male voice's bed warm. On top of all of that, he was not the kind of guy you took back to the ranch to meet Mom and Pops. Not that Holly had indicated that she wanted to make introductions, but Dec knew what his past mistakes had cost him.

The damn thing started ringing again. *Shit.* Clearly, Dad needed to talk to Holly. He couldn't send it to voicemail lest her father suspect she was up and refusing his calls. All he wanted in the world was to shut the damn thing up and return to bed with her. There were at least a hundred far sexier ways to awaken his sleeping beauty than to hand her a phone with her father on the other end.

A full minute passed between rings. Maybe he'd assumed she was still asleep and had decided to call back later. Dec reached to turn off the ringer, something he would have thought of earlier if he'd been more awake, when it started ringing again.

This time the screen read Luke. Who the fuck was Luke? An unhealthy level of possessive ire ticked in Dec's blood. Were the calls somehow related? Did Luke know her father? Was Luke some guy back home she'd dated in the past? Some guy waiting on her to move back to wherever the ranch was? Shaking himself, he drew a steadying breath. Holly was not Victoria. She wasn't the kind to cheat. He had to get it together.

Succumbing to his morning fate, he carried the phone up to the bedroom. There she was, clutching his pillow instead of his chest now. He noted the hesitant glints of auburn in her long brunette hair as the rising sunlight played amongst its long strands.

Settling back beside her, carrying the now silenced but still ringing phone, he brushed a kiss on her cheek. "Did my sexy cowgirl sleep well?"

She gave a few audible huffs and buried her face further in his pillow. Chuckling, he continued to kiss what portions of her cheek and shoulder he could access. "I agree. But your phone has been ringing non-stop."

She roused. Rubbing her face, she managed to sit upright. When her fingers scrubbed down over her cheeks and lips, she cringed. "Oh God, I drooled on you, didn't I?"

That did it. Dec laughed at her outright. "You did, and I found it completely adorable. Pretty sure that means I'm falling harder than I thought."

"I'm so sorry. I do that. I don't mean to, but I always have. I'm a drooly sleeper."

"Sweetheart, I had all kinds of you all over me last night, and it was easily the best night of my entire life. I really do think it's cute. Why don't you talk to whoever *Luke* is, and then we can go back to sleep and you can soak me down again." He tried to keep the disdain from his voice but hadn't quite managed it.

A mischievous smirk joined the sheet marks and rosy glow painted on her face. He longed to kiss her until he'd replaced the smirk with a genuine smile. "Jealous?"

"Should I be?"

"Definitely not," she giggled. "He's my big brother."

Feeling like a complete imbecile, he huffed, "I warned you I was possessive. You encouraged it. There's some American statement about sleeping in the bed you made or some other such thing."

"I like you possessive, but I should probably talk to him." She pointed to the vibrating phone still clutched in Dec's hands.

"Your father called as well. Unless you call someone besides me Daddy."

"I did not call you Daddy." She was still giggling. That intoxicating sound filled the hollow, empty places she'd filled the evening before with her delectable moans of his name.

"I'm still hoping." He winked at her and relinquished the phone.

. . .

"Is there some particular reason you're calling me at. . ." she held the phone out in front of her until it displayed the time,". . .nine o'clock on Saturday morning?" Holly didn't mean to be quite so irritated with Luke, but dammit, this was not at all how this particular morning was supposed to go.

"There some particular reason you're still asleep at nine o'clock in the morning?" Luke challenged.

"I was out late last night." Holly hoped her blush blended in with the afterglow of sex or sleep that was surely painted on her cheeks.

"Uh-huh. You were *up* late. Only time you ever sleep late is when there's some new asshole involved."

How did her brother even know that? She hadn't dated anyone in well over a year. That was the problem with having four older siblings that felt certain they should have some say in your life. She rolled her eyes. It made her feel better, even if Luke couldn't see her. "How's Indie?" Changing the subject seemed the best possible choice.

"Beautiful. Full of my babies, and also bitching at me on the reg'lar since she can't get under the cars to work on them anymore."

Holly grinned at that. Her sister-in-law was currently pregnant with twins due in a few months' time. "Well, it is totally your fault she can't wrench for a while."

"Never said it wasn't, and nobody loves that belly full of my little girls more than me, so she's welcome to fuss about it all she wants. But listen to me, Dad's been calling you all morning. He handed you off to me because he didn't want to think about why you weren't answering. We think you may want to come home."

Hesitation and concern perforated Luke's low drawl. Holly's heart sank. "Why? What's wrong?" Panic immediately set in. What if something was wrong with her mama, or one of her brothers, or Natalie?

"It's Aurora Belle, Holl."

Tears sprang to Holly's eyes. She tried to swallow around the rock-like enclosure that sealed her throat at those words. Dammit, she couldn't deal with this much emotion without coffee.

Dec's face fell. He'd been studying her while she talked. He scooped her up into his lap and silently brushed a kiss in her hair. His hands settled her. His steady strength held her tightly, and she hadn't even told him what was wrong yet.

Aurora Belle was one of the Camden horses. She happened to have always been Holly's favorite. She'd helped Holly fly whenever she wasn't sure she had the strength to do whatever had to be done. Aurora Belle had been her best friend since birth.

A few months ago, Luke, who was also the town vet along with helping run the ranch, had come to find Holly out in one of the barns, wrapped her up in his arms, and tried as delicately as he could to explain that Aurora Belle had Lymphosarcoma cancer, and that there was nothing he could do.

"Is she. . . ?" Holly managed, blinking back tears that Dec was tenderly wiping away.

"Not yet. She won't stand up anymore, and I can't get her heart rate down. I've tried everything I can think of. I'm sorry, Holl, I just don't think it'll be much longer. If she starts showing signs of pain, I might need to. . . . I just thought you might want to be here."

"I do. I'm leaving right now. I'll be there quick, just don't do it until I get there unless you really need to, please."

"I won't. Love you, Sis, and I'm really sorry."

"Love you, too."

Holly ended the call. Her heart, which had been managing a few erratic beats, shattered, and she collapsed on Dec's shoulders, sobbing.

"Hey, shh, I've got you, love. I'm right here, and I'm not going anywhere. Want to tell me what that was all about?"

Holly deeply appreciated the fact that he hadn't promised it would be okay or that he could fix it. He'd just promised to be there. He should consider becoming a psychologist.

"I'm sorry. I can't believe I'm crying like this. I hate it when I cry. What is wrong with me?" She tried futilely to erase her own emotions.

"You're crying because of news from your brother, sweetheart, and tears are a perfectly natural byproduct of emotion. Most of the time, people cry because they've simply been too strong for too long. Nothing wrong with tears."

She nodded against him and attempted several deep breaths. "It's my favorite horse. Her name is Aurora Belle. She's the horse I learned to ride on. She's been sick for a while, and Luke says she isn't gonna be. . .here. . .much longer." Another racked gasp of tears stole any further words from her lips.

"You don't have to explain it, baby. How about I take you to see Aurora Belle?"

"No." Holly knew she could absolutely not deal with Dec on the ranch. Not right now. Her brothers were likely to make his life a living hell as soon as they understood how much Dec meant to her. They'd never been able to stand any guy she'd ever brought home, and all of the ones before hadn't been heavily-tattooed, pierced musicians who they would instantly hate for not being a cowboy. She hadn't even managed to verbalize to him how much he meant to her. There would be no exposing him to the ranch for a long, long time.

Right now, she had to process Aurora Belle not being there to greet her when she went out to the paddock anymore. She had to try to understand that one of her beloved horses wasn't going to be there ever again. "It's okay. I just need to get there quickly. Can you take me back to my apartment for my truck?"

"Of course. Want some tea first?"

For some unfathomable reason this made Holly smile. "Because you Brits think a cup of tea makes everything better?"

"We don't think it, love, we know it, and I happen to make a perfect cuppa."

"I was always disappointed when no one in the Harry Potter movies offered someone a cuppa," she admitted. "But I'd much rather have a huge cup of American coffee before I head out."

Chuckling at her, he nodded. "Damn movie houses try to Americanize everything so tickets will sell out here. That's all that matters. I don't actually have a coffeemaker. I'll get one. How about we stop off somewhere and I get you coffee?"

"You don't have a coffee maker?"

"Sorry, sweetheart. I solemnly swear I will rectify this terrible lapse before you return from home."

Dec looked panicked, like she might decide to call this whole thing off because he couldn't provide her coffee.

"Stopping off somewhere would be great, and you don't have to get a coffee maker just for me."

"I was hoping you might like to be here often. I'm not above luring you in with coffee, sort of Hansel and Gretel style."

"And do you promise to eat me like the big bad wolf when I get here?"

"Believe you're mixing your fairy tales, cowgirl. Little Red Riding Hood was chased by a wolf. Other than that, you get the cape, I'll be more than happy to play the wolf."

"Can we go now?"

"Absolutely."

CHAPTER SEVENTEEN

"We were supposed to talk today." Holly slumped in the seat of Dec's SUV. The constant slam of emotions coming from every side made her feel like the mole portion of a whac-a-mole game. This wasn't at all how this weekend was supposed to go.

"Let's save all the big confessions for when you get back." His jaw tensed, and he cast a quick glance her way. Debate furrowed his brow. "Any idea when that will be?"

"I'm gonna miss you, too," she assured him. He wasn't the only one who could read body language. "I have to be back Monday for. . .the thing we're not talking about until then. I don't know how long every-thing will take. I just want to be there with her. . .you know. . .for the end or whatever. If I can, I'll be back Sunday night. If not, I won't leave until Monday morning."

Dec had laced their fingers together before he'd even cranked the car. He gave her hand a consolatory squeeze. "Mind indulging me in just a little bit about my past? I promise not to get too deep until you get back."

"I don't mind at all. I hate we're not making our confessions now like we planned to. You're not seeing someone else, are you? 'Cause I'm having a shitty morning, but I could still take a bitch down."

Dec's laughter filled the vehicle. Somehow that sexy baritone chuckle of his wrapped itself around her heart and reassured her that everything was going to be okay. Different, but okay. "I'm supremely flattered you'd take down a bitch on my account, sweetheart, and I'm relieved I'm not the only one with a tendency for being possessive. But this is about my past, and I told you last night I haven't been with anyone since my divorce, and that was over a year ago. I'm only seeing you, and I will only see you until you realize what an absolute piece of shit I really am and leave me. My ex cheated on me repeatedly. I could never and would never do that to you. I may be seriously fucked up in other departments, but not there."

Wow. Holly wasn't accustomed to him being so forthcoming. Maybe he'd been preparing to tell her everything. She hated this entire thing all the more for preventing their conversation.

"You are *not* a piece of shit, Dec, and if you say that again I'll remind you how good I am with a rope."

Giving her a sly grin, he shook his head. "Never say I didn't warn you."

"Thought you were going to tell me about your past."

"I grew up on a sheep farm in the Southeast. Tiny town called Bexinglee no one's ever heard of, in Chiltern Hills, or the Chilterns if you should ever find yourself in London and needing to get there. Anyway, I grew up riding horses as well. I had a grey Thoroughbred named Kingston. My dad gave all the horses ridiculously proper names. He fancied himself more than a lowly sheep farmer, which was really all we were. I'd been called a sheep-shagger from the time I learned to walk.

"Anyway, I loved that horse. Kingston got me. He understood that I couldn't wait to get off that fucking farm. He understood how fast I wanted to fly. When I was seventeen, I got caught nicking smokes from one of our neighbors. My dad was furious. He never liked me much anyway. He sold Kingston to buy. . . well, he sold him as a kind of punishment. I still regret that to this day. Kingston was the first thing that meant something to me that my own foolish decisions affected. I'll never forgive myself for him being sold off. I do understand how much Aurora-Belle means to you."

It took Holly several moments to remember how to make her lower jaw connect with her upper. "Wait, are you telling me you were a cowboy? Or a sheep-boy? What do you call them there?"

That smirk that made her heart and her stomach feel like they were exchanging locations formed on his features. "We call them farmers, and you sound more horrified by this than the fact that I'm an addict."

"I am. I mean, I'm not. I just wasn't expecting that. I'm sorry about Kingston, though."

"I'm sorry I disappointed you, darling. I kind of thought that confession might play well for me, seeing as you're heading back to cattle country." Genuine confusion darkened his grey eyes.

Holly lambasted herself for having no control over her own thoughts or tongue. She wasn't usually like this. The night before, being in his arms, it had all stripped away her guards. He'd crashed through every barrier, and she hadn't had time to process any of it. Now, everything that came to her mind sprinted out of her mouth.

"I'm sorry. I'm a disaster this morning. I'm not disappointed, just surprised. I love that you know how to ride. We could ride together sometime." There, that was an appropriate response, even though her mind was a spinning storm of questions and confusion. She wasn't supposed to fall in love with a cowboy. She'd sworn she never would.

"I haven't been on horseback in a few years, but I'd love to ride with you if that's something you'd like to do. I do have a question. Who named Aurora Belle?"

"My parents. They rescued her when she was a pony from a ranch that wasn't taking care of her. She's older than me."

"So, you know what her name means then?"

"Yes. It means a beautiful second chance, doesn't it?"

"It does, and it sounds like your family gave her that. I'm not sure anyone, neither man nor beast, could ever ask for more than a beautiful second chance."

Holly stared at him as he guided the car into her apartment parking lot. There was more weight in that statement than in any of his others. Is that what he saw her as? A beautiful second chance? She hoped so, because she definitely wanted a chance at a real relationship with him. "I want to give this a chance, Dec. I'm really sorry I can't stay and talk today. I wish I could."

"I know you do. I can tell. Don't be sorry. Just maybe call me if you need to talk while you're gone. Even if you want me just to listen or to sing you to sleep. Nothing would make me happier."

"I will definitely take you up on that."

He threw the SUV in park and lifted her chin. The calluses on his fingertips made her long for more of his craving caresses. Feeling like she was being rent in two, she leaned across the console, and Dec blistered her mouth with another one of those kisses that sent warm ripples of pleasure throughout her body.

When she was a little girl and her mother would try to kiss her skinned knees and elbows, she always wiped the kisses off on her dirty blue jeans, but Dec's kisses did in fact hold some kind of magical healing power. If he'd just keep kissing her, the rest of the world would disappear and nothing else would even matter.

She didn't want to leave. Every fiber of her being desperately wanted to remain in his presence. He thought being with her was some kind of drug. He had no idea the things he stirred within her. The intoxication of things she wasn't even aware of before he'd arrived on her scene, things she desperately needed to explore and understand. All of the conversations they needed to have amplified in the mating of their mouths.

She'd planned to spend the morning running her hands and her tongue over every one of his tattoos, and then up and down every chiseled muscle on his body. She wanted to count each and every tight bulging plane of his abs. Then she wanted to take her time with his cock in her mouth. She wanted to taste him again, wanted his salty flavors mixed with the metallic tang of his piercing on her tongue.

She had to leave. She would never let Aurora Belle go without saying goodbye.

He turned his head, cradled her face in his right hand, and stroked the hollow of her cheek as he extended the kiss.

"Dec," she managed in a breathless whisper.

"Shh, darling, I'm not near finished. I have to make this last until tomorrow night. My cock is fairly certain it's being sent back to prison."

Holly added the phrase *back to prison* to the lengthy list of things she wanted further explanation on.

With one last wave, Dec watched Holly's massive truck back out of her assigned parking space and head out. Rubbing his temples, he tried to decide what to do next. Tea. He'd never had any that morning. He'd procured her coffee from a burger joint that prepared perfectly symmetrical eggs. He always found that odd. He'd inquired about tea, but when asked what kind, he'd given up all hope. Fruit teas. Americans and their ideas.

Right now, he desperately needed to think, and that was either going to require a drag of something he had no business seeking to soothe his frayed nerves, or an outstanding cuppa. As always, he chose the latter.

Heading downtown to Trace's, he reviewed the evening before in his mind. When that only exacerbated the heavy loss of her leaving, he moved on to their morning. He'd stupidly offered to take her to see the dying horse, forgetting that her family would be there. Of course, she didn't want him on her ranch. Nothing surprising about that, but had he pushed his own family so far outside of his realm of reality, he'd mentally orphaned himself and her by proxy? Was there any possible way he could ever be a man that she'd want to introduce to her family?

Probably not, but that didn't mean he wouldn't try.

He'd walked her inside her apartment when she'd finally halted their kissing, insisting that she had to leave. His jaw tightened as he recalled her flinging out two highly captivating baby doll nighties she must've intended to wear for him. She'd quickly replaced them with another pair of Wranglers and two button down shirts.

The universe never failed to punish him. It wasn't like he didn't deserve to be punished. He just never wanted Holly punished for his mistakes.

"You look like your favorite cat just died," Trace sized him up as soon as he made his way to the counter, after his customary inhale of the soothing coffee and graphite-infused air.

"Don't have a favorite cat. Don't even have *a* cat. Could use a large cuppa, though."

"You got it. Thought you were spending the weekend with Holly. You want me to make her a coffee to go? You two are still. . .okay right? Things are the way they're supposed to be?"

The phrase 'supposed to be' resonated with his soul. Dec tried to remember that Trace was one of his favorite people before he called him on being intrusive. This little tea shop had made his transition to America something he could manage. Trace was friendly with all of his customers. That was part of his appeal. "Holly and I are still dating. Yes. Hoping that doesn't change anytime soon."

One of his many devious brain cells contemplated asking Trace about Holly's profession or what he knew about her, but he would never betray her. Never. He'd wait patiently on her to return and then they could hash out their lives, every gory detail.

"You told her you're the love doctor yet?"

Cringing at that particular title, Dec kept his eyes trained on the boiling water Trace was pouring. "How did you know I hadn't told her I'm a therapist?"

"She was in yesterday afternoon, and I asked if she knew where you worked. I might've pretended not to know. I was being nosy. Watching you two dance around each other while falling in love has me hooked. They took my soap off the air. You're as good as I've got."

Ignoring most of the explanation, Dec honed in on 'falling in love.' "I wasn't aware we were falling in love." It was when the words scalded his throat that he knew what he'd just stated was an outright lie.

Trace's kind, blue eyes locked on Dec's. "I was married for three dozen years before the cancer took her from me. That's the thing about love, you never realize you're falling in it 'til you're half drowned with no hopes of making it back to shore. And you'll do something about it 'bout the time you realize you never wanted to get back to shore in the first place. I hope you never experience this, but when it leaves you, you spend most of your time wishing you'd just gone on and drowned. But if you just keep treading water, after a time, it does get a little easier, I 'spose."

"I'm terribly sorry for your loss. I didn't know your wife had passed."

Trace's throat seemed to visibly expand as he began wiping down the counter to avoid looking Dec in the eye. "Not something I talk about too often, but I do recognize love when I see it. You and Holly are frantically treading water, but you're 'bout to give out and let the tides come on in. Don't fight it too hard. Woman like her don't come around too often."

"Yeah, perhaps you're right." Dec lifted the tea cup in his hand in salute to some outstanding advice.

So this *was* love. This horrible, wonderful feeling that felt entirely too much like being high was love, of all ridiculous things. Being high only had one problem: it was always followed by an inevitable crash that would irrevocably shatter him and make him desperate for another fix. The constant need and attraction to Holly was terrifying. There couldn't possibly be any kind of rehab where one could learn to deal with this level of addiction.

I am not a drug. You are not getting high with me. Holly's decree from the night before stamped itself in his skull. He swore for a moment she was saying the words out loud to him even though she had to have been miles from Lincoln by now.

If she wasn't a drug, if love wasn't an addiction, she was going to have to prove that to him because they felt so acutely alike. *Probably because you're such a fuck-up, and it's not her job to fix you.* Hating himself doubly for even having that thought, he settled into a vacant booth near the back window and gave himself several long moments, battling incoming obsessive thoughts.

She's gone for a while. She'd never know if you bought something. You're near campus, bet there's a dealer close by. Obsession. Inability to deal with the stress of her leaving without wanting something chemical to get him through. Depression. Insecurity in their relationship. Addiction was an asshole.

He simultaneously loathed it and accepted it. Feeling sorry for himself wasn't going to help him deal. Drawing a long sip of the tea, he closed his eyes and let it soothe him. He could do this. For Christ's sake, he was a psychologist. He may not have ever lived love, but he'd sure as hell knew what would be seen as healthy. He'd just have to keep his less-than-appropriate thoughts to himself. Maybe he could fake it long enough to actually make it.

Keeping things from people who are here to help. Not a good sign either, St. James. Dammit all to hell. He couldn't escape demons dammed in his own soul. His only choice was to carry them. They occupied his every breath, every beat of his heart, his every thought. Inescapable. Fishing his phone out of his pocket, he touched Kade's name on his favorite's list.

A sleepy grunt preceded, "Uh, hey man, you okay?" It was followed by a deep yawn.

"Sorry I woke you." Dec massaged his temples. It wasn't Kade's job to fix him either.

"No problem. What's up?"

Before he could apologize again, Dec heard the distinctive noise of another man sighing and then coughing. *Shit.* Clearly Kade and Wyatt's night had extended into the morning. "Nothing's wrong. I'm fine . . .just thought I'd see if you wanted to come over and work through a few songs this afternoon."

"Doubting that's why you really called. There's a meeting tonight. I'm needing to go. We could go together."

"I'm okay for now. You enjoy your morning." Dec ended the call. The despair began to construct its chokehold when his cell rang. Holly's name appeared, and he answered it instantly.

"Hey, love. You okay?"

"Kind of." Her tone was tender and raw with emotion.

"Sweetheart, I know you'll probably never want me to meet your family, but I could get a hotel room near your ranch. Stay away, but be there if you need me."

"God, I'm such a baby. You are not doing that, plus the closest hotel to the ranch is probably in Lincoln. And what makes you think I don't want you to come to the ranch?"

"I don't know." That caught him off guard. If he'd been in her physical presence, he would have been able to tell if she was lying. She sounded quite sincere.

"We live out in the middle of nowhere, and my family can be a lot to deal with. I didn't want to expose you and make you never want to see me again. Don't worry, I'll be fine. I'm a cowgirl. We're always fine, and if we're not fine somebody better run because when we get back up, they're gonna get the shit beat out of them. I just missed you already. How pathetic is that? I swear I will not be one of those girlfriends that wants to celebrate weekly anniversaries or freaks out when you don't answer your phone or whatever."

"You are absolutely not pathetic, Ms. Camden, nor could you or your family ever do anything that might make me not want to see you again. You are complete perfection. I like how the closer you get to home the more your cowgirl side slips into your verbiage, by the way. Very hot. And I'm sitting here in Trace's, feeling tremendously sorry for myself and missing you so much I ache, so if anyone is a sad sap, it is I."

"We both thought we were gonna have the whole weekend. Maybe neither of us is pathetic, just disappointed."

"That sounds far better."

"I really do miss you, Dec, a lot."

"I can still taste you on my tongue." He lowered his rumbled tone until he was certain no one but Holly could hear him. "I swear, my hands burn to touch your skin again. I long for you. This is stronger than missing you, love. Little worried I'm addicted." He was far more than a little worried, but perhaps talking to the object of his addiction was the healthiest way to deal with this. He had no idea. Cocaine was a terrible conversationalist.

"This isn't addiction, Dec."

He listened intently for a sigh of impatience or even a note of it in her tone, since she'd already voiced this several times. He came up empty.

"I feel all of those very same things, and I don't struggle with addiction. I can still taste your piercing and your cock in my mouth. All I can think about is kissing you again so I don't lose your flavors. I keep checking the marks on my neck in the rearview while I drive. I want to see them. It makes you feel more real. Like I said, this isn't addiction. Might be something else. Not sure yet. Besides all of that, the beginning of a new relationship is supposed to feel all-consuming, isn't it?"

"Trace would like to confirm the potential diagnosis you're referring to." The tight clench of Dec's chest eased. She felt it, too. Maybe he wasn't as screwed up as he thought.

"Oh yeah?" Holly chuckled. "Well, Trace is pretty darned smart, and, you know, psychologists believe that falling in love only takes a fifth of a second. They've studied this, and the study also said that your brain reacts the same way to love as it does from a small hit of cocaine."

Dec had to laugh. He was well versed in Dr. Ortigue's research. What he couldn't comprehend was how Holly had read that particular finding. It was somewhat obscure. "Psychologists say that, do they?"

"Yes, they do. One doctor at Syracuse University did an entire study of brain electrodynamics when someone falls in love. I used it when I was writing my. . . . Uh, never mind. It was fascinating."

"Very interesting, indeed." Dec shook his head and a grin expanded across the width of his face. His sexy little cowgirl was a psych student, a doctoral candidate to be exact. Had to be. That explained the late night lamentation about the advisor, and Trace's slip about hiring her every semester.

Quickly recalling the American university process to get a PhD, he grinned. So, she'd used Dr. Stephanie Ortigue's work on her master's thesis. There was no doubt. Explanation of his profession formed on the tip of his tongue, but he bit it back. He'd tell her when she returned. He didn't want to bring on a conversation she clearly didn't want to have. If she'd gone on with the word *thesis*, he'd tell her all about his work, but she hadn't, so he'd leave it be. Maybe he could help her with her with her studies. At least that was something he could give her. He could probably even pull a few strings and get her an internship at Lifespan.

"You told me last night love wasn't a drug," he teased. A lightness pervaded his soul. She was right. Ortigue's work had been spot on. Love *was* like being high.

"Well, may-be I was wrong. . .a little bit. . .but not much." She giggled.

"That's right, you don't like to be wrong. Perhaps my sexual minis-trations last night simply caused you to forget whatever it was you were reading about love being like cocaine."

"You made me forget most everything in the best possible ways. I'm looking forward to being fucked mindless again when I get back."

"Done. I'm very anxious for another hit of you."

"I'm going to allow that, and not insist that I am not a drug, given the nature of this conversation."

She'd gone right back to psych-student mode. He rather missed her cowgirl drawl. "I assumed you would." So, those were the two sides represented in her latest ink work. Now, he understood.

"Oh, no. Dec, that's Luke calling me. I need to take this."

"Go ahead, darling, and I was serious, if you need me to meet you somewhere or come out there don't hesitate to call."

"I won't, and Dec, I can't wait for another hit of you either."

"Promise?"

"Promise."

He was quite certain no woman in her right mind, not even one as perfect as Holly, would count that exchange as a vow of love, but to him, it meant the entire world.

They had far more in common than he would ever have hoped. Curiosity about her age played in the periphery of his mind, but that could be discovered later. It truly didn't matter. Not to him. If you'd lived as much life as any recovering user was forced to live, you began to understand how age meant absolutely nothing and willpower meant everything. Nothing improved with age. Experience level never guar-anteed success.

With the last sip of his tea, he allowed himself to feel the obsession as it sluiced through his veins. Constantly reassuring himself that this was okay, he headed out into the warm Lincoln sunshine. It held nothing on Holly's warmth and acceptance. Her love, he supposed. The word still seemed to tangle his mind.

He had some shopping to do. No reason he couldn't spoil his cowgirl psych student. Spending the day thinking of things she might like eased a little of the craving need that burned low in his gut. It didn't work nearly as well as being in her presence, but maybe it would be enough to get him through this weekend.

CHAPTER EIGHTEEN

The truck rumbled and bounced Holly as she made her way over the long dirt road that led her home. As soon as she opened the first cattle guard and drove her truck through it, she felt it. Her shoulders relaxed. A smile formed on her features despite the nature of her return. The scent of manure and tall grass whispered on the winds. It readily filled her lungs and eased her soul. She was home.

She stopped the truck for one quick moment when she reached the highest point along the road and could see out over the expansive flatland. Her parent's home was another mile in, but the nearby cottage was in view and cattle were spread out over the nearest fields. She tried to envision Dec there, but she couldn't quite manage it. She still didn't know how to make her two sides fit inside one body, one body that she desperately wanted to belong to him.

Driving onward, she performed the mental routine she went through every time she came home. Trying desperately to memorize the exact rust color of the old train cars turned barns that her great-great-granddaddy had secured when the train tracks had been built through the center of town. The low bellowed murmur of the cows. The bracing creaks of the metal sheds when the winds assaulted them. The snorts of the bulls and steers, and most importantly, the slap of the screen door on the home that had raised her when her mama, her sister, and both of her sisters-in-law spilled through it to greet her.

"There's my baby girl." Her mother, Jessie, all but hoisted her out of her truck and into her arms. Her sisters then buried her in a four-woman hug.

"Let her breathe, Jess, and let me see my little girl," her father's low soothing intonation rang from the front porch.

The hug broke apart, and Holly raced into her daddy's arms. "I've only been gone a week and a half, you know."

"I know, but it feels longer to me. I don't like it when my girls are gone." He pulled Natalie in for a hug as well. A twinge of despair twisted in Holly's gut. Her daddy knew as soon as she graduated, she'd get a job in the city if all went according to plan. The ranch wouldn't be her home after that, not really, and she hated to disappoint her father more than anything in the world. She was daddy's girl through and through. He'd love nothing more than for her to quit school, move back to the ranch, and start running cattle as soon as possible. Part of her longed to do just that.

"Yeah, he don't ever give a damn if we go anywhere though," Austin teased as he pulled off his deerskin gloves and joined the crowd.

"You and your brothers caused me more trouble. That's why I love the girls more." Everyone laughed at the absurdity of that. He adored all five of his children and everyone knew it.

"If it ain't Sister Holly come home to help me out with chores." Grant joined the crowd, carrying Austin's oldest son J.J. on his shoulders.

"Aunt Holl-yee," rang from her nephew. Holly extended her arms and J.J. leapt off of Grant's shoulders and into her embrace.

"You make me sound like a nun, and I ain't doing your chores for you, Grant Camden," she informed him just before kissing J.J.'s sweet face.

"Didn't Dad try and sign you and Nat up for a convent one time?"

"Probably." Holly shot a sly grin at her daddy.

"You can't blame a daddy for tryin'," Ev vowed.

J.J. started wiggling so Holly set him down, letting him race off across the wide open field towards Luke's Beagles, Bailey and Bella, who were flanking Luke on his way in from the barn.

"Thank God." Luke's wife, Indie, sighed, rubbing one hand on her lower back and the other over her massive belly. "My back's killing me. He owes me a massage."

"I'm coming," Luke called. "Knew you'd be fussing." He winked at her and Holly hid her grin. Some things were meant to be. Luke and Indie were one of them. *So are you and Dec.* The thought took permanent hold of her mind, her heart, and her soul simultaneously. Now, to convince everyone else of that.

"Well, it is your fault she's hurting, son," Jessie decried.

"The two of you never let me forget that. You don't have to take up her flag, Mama."

"Yes, she does." Indie laughed. "She loves me more than you."

"Probably true," Jessie winked to her son.

"Don't I know that, too." Luke managed to get his arms all the way around his very pregnant wife and began massaging her back.

"How's Aurora Belle?" Holly hated that Indie was miserable, but that wasn't why she'd come home.

"Not much has changed. Still won't eat and won't stand up. Maybe she'll get up for you. I've got her on her blankets out in the horse barn. Still got a high fever. I've tried everything I can think of. I can get Doc Halverson out here if you want."

Luke never seemed to mind that he hadn't finished his doctorate. He was perfectly happy being a full-time cowboy and a part-time vet. It struck Holly how much she would hate to quit now. Not when she was only a few years away from being able to practice on her own.

"If you say nothing can be done, I know that's the case, Luke. Besides, Doc Halverson's an idiot."

"Can't say I disagree, but it kills me to watch her suffer."

"I'll go sit with her." Holly turned and headed towards the barn, but Grant looped his finger through the back belt loop of her jeans, halting her progress while everyone else headed back into her parent's home.

"Don't think you would'a made a real good nun, sis," he huffed quietly enough that her parents couldn't hear him. He pointed to the hickeys just under the collar of her shirt. "Some shit-licker needin' my boot up their ass?"

"Grant, please stop with the typical Camden-men, caveman, cowboy routine. I really can't take it today, okay? I am a grown woman, and no one did anything to me I didn't want. And do not get Luke and Austin all riled up about this either, or I will call up Cheyenne and invite her over for the entire weekend." Holly felt bad for using her best friend, but that was the quickest way to get Grant to can it. He genuinely did not like Cheyenne, though Holly had no real idea why, and she simply couldn't break Cheyenne's heart by telling her.

Grant scowled. "She already follows me all the fuck over town every time I go in for supplies. I'm telling you, Holl, there's some'um about your friend I can't stand. My gut's never wrong."

"Well, I have always thought something was wrong with her. I mean, she has a crush on *you*." Holly laughed.

Rolling his eyes, Grant drew a deep breath. "I wish she'd get over it. Ain't happenin'. Ever. Like I said, my gut's never wrong. And as long as whoever left those marks is treating you right, I got no issues, but don't blame your brothers for trying to look after you. It's our job."

"I am perfectly capable of taking care of myself." Holly gave her standard answer. The same answer she'd given anyone trying to tell her what to do since the ripe old age of four.

Grant blocked the sun from his eyes as they made their way towards the paddock outside the horse barn and chuckled. "Oh yeah? That mean you don't want me to come with you to see Aurora Belle so our boy Matt can moon all over you like a heifer in heat?"

"Oh no." Holly narrowed her eyes, and sure enough, Matt Cartwright was pacing in front of the barn. Grant and Holly's cousin Brock had hired Matt as a ranch hand. Ev and Matt's daddy, Sal were the best of friends.

Matt had an ongoing crush on Holly for years and seemed to feel that if given enough time and enough of his awkward attention Holly would suddenly fall madly in love with him, want to marry him, and live out their lives on Camden ranch together. The fact that he drove her completely crazy with all of his cowboy-ness and ideas about the world, not to mention the six-year age difference, didn't seem to matter.

"Okay, scratch that. I can take care of myself, but since Dad and Brock would like to keep the little shitlet employed, stay with me so I don't scalp him."

"Aww, Junior ain't that bad," Grant goaded.

"Grant, before I left for school, he informed me that I didn't need to get an education, that he'd take good care of me, and I quote, because he's a real man.' According to little Matthew, I'm a real woman that don't need nothin' but a cowboy who'll look after her."

Grant choked back hysterical laughter. "He wants to look after you? I wish the poor sap luck," he harassed as they swung opened the gate.

"Uh, hey there, Holly. I figured you'd be coming back home. I tried to tell you, ya don't need to keep leavin'. I got everything you need right here." Matt edged closer, cautiously. Holly resisted the urge to deck him.

"Ease up, Matt. If you ain't noticed, Holly does what she wants when she wants. Let her see her horse," Grant commanded.

"She just needs. . . ."

"You to leave." Holly wished she'd taken Dec up on his offer to come with her. She'd pay good money to see the look on Matt's face when he got a glimpse of Declan.

Stubborn as a penned bull, Matt followed Holly and Grant into the barn. A heavy weight slipped from Holly's throat and took up residence in her chest as she settled beside her beloved horse in the hay.

Aurora Belle gave a soft neigh and lifted her head to lay in Holly's lap. Tears pricked Holly's eyes, and Grant settled beside her. "She loves you, Holl. You know that. She's lived a good long life."

"That doesn't make it any easier."

"I know." Grant put his arm around her shoulders and handed her a handkerchief from his pocket.

"I've been telling Luke I think he oughta go on and put a bullet through her skull," Matt said.

"Oh my God," Holly gasped.

"Dude, what the actual fuck?" Grant bellowed. "Get 'fore I get after *you* with a pistol. My God, you really ain't the brightest bulb on the Christmas tree, are ya?"

"She ought to know what's gonna have to happen," Matt huffed.

"It ain't gonna have to happen. This ain't gonna go on much longer. Go on home, Matt. Try to get your brain outta your lower head 'fore you come back."

Just then Brock, Holly's cousin, entered the barn. "What'd you say to her this time?" he sighed.

"I was just saying. . . ."

"Do not under any circumstances say those words in my presence again, you got that? I ain't in a good mood, and you do not want to flip my cowgirl switch right now." Holly sneered furiously while keeping her hand gently soothing Aurora Belle's mane and side.

"I've seen that switch flipped several times in my life, man. You need to get on. It ain't pretty." Brock shoved Matt out of the barn.

When they heard Matt's ancient Dodge rev, they all relaxed.

"Kid's a good hand. Gets everything I need him to done, but I swear he couldn't find his ass with two hands and a mirror."

Grant and Holly's laughter pierced the shadowed barn. It brought a little light into the situation, which Holly wasn't entirely certain she wanted. It felt wrong.

"Hope saw you pull up. She's putting Nathan down for his nap. I'll go up and sit with him so she can come love up on you," Brock explained.

"Good. I miss her. I need to squeeze baby Nate too, though."

"If you can catch him, you can squeeze him all you want. Kid's on the move constantly. Figured out how to climb out of his crib last night. Woke me up at three this morning by taking a'holt of my foot. I near about shed my own skin." He studied Holly for a minute. "You pissed about Aurora Belle, Matt, or at the asswipe that left those?" Brock pointed to the hickeys.

Holly ground her teeth. "As usual – cowboys. Cowboys are inherently annoying."

"So we've been told," Grant sighed. "I take it said asswipe ain't a cowboy, which is why you won't say nothing about him. You think we're prejudiced against non-rancher types."

"You are prejudiced, and I'm not talking about him because I don't need to. I'm here for Aurora Belle. You can meet him later."

"Do we even get a name?" Brock inquired.

"Nope."

"Must not be too important then," Grant concluded.

"He is extremely important." Holly clenched her teeth to keep from saying more. Dammit, why did they have to do this? Why did she let them goad her in to saying too much?"

"Who's extremely important?" Luke asked as he entered the barn followed by Austin.

Great. All the brothers and the cousin. Maybe the whole damn town could show up in the Camden barn and offer her advice on her love life. Not like they all hadn't tried in the past. Holly kept her gaze fixed on her horse and ignored Luke's question.

"Shit-licker that left those all over Holl's neck," Grant explained.

"Yeah, I seen those. Just figured I'd let you love up on Aurora Belle 'fore I figured out whose ass to whup," Austin vowed.

"Oh, for crying out loud." Holly rolled her eyes.

"All right, all of ya, get. Leave Holly be. Brock, Hope's looking for you. The rest of you go find your wives or some work to do." Jessie entered the barn and laid down her decree. Holly had never been so pleased to see her mama.

"I ain't got a wife," Grant argued just for the sake of arguing.

"Well, then maybe you should go out and look for one, Grant Camden. Lord knows I ought not to have to be the only woman in this world that has to put up with you."

Holly's mother unfurled another blanket to cover Aurora Belle and settled on the other side of the horse. "No sense in trying to keep the fever down now. Can't stand for any of my babies to be miserable."

Another round of liquid emotion singed Holly's eyes. "When Luke told me what she had, I didn't want to believe it. I should have prepared myself."

"Oh, honey, you can't prepare yourself for this. Like getting thrown. You feel it 'fore it actually happens. You know what's gonna happen. Still takes your breath away when you hit the ground. Eating dirt still tastes just as bad."

"Yeah. I guess so." Holly didn't care for her mother's wisdom. Surely, if she'd taken time to process how sick Aurora Belle was this wouldn't hurt so badly.

"Can I ask you something, sweetheart?"

"Sure, Mama."

"You ever plan on telling me and your daddy that you're actually specializing in sexual psychology or have you really convinced yourself we'd be appalled?"

Another weight stacked itself in Holly's leaden gut. "Should'a known you already knew. You always do."

"That don't answer my question."

"It's just. . .it's a hard thing to say to Daddy. He wanted me to be a nun, remember?"

Jessie shook her head. "You plan on getting a job talking with people about their sex lives, but you can't look your daddy in the eye and say the words sex therapist to him? That sound as strange to you as it does to me?"

"Do I really have to have this lecture right now? I'm kind of in the middle of freaking out about a lot of things, my horse for one."

"Holly Suzanne, you have been on the receiving end of enough of my lectures to know that this ain't one of 'em. I was just calling you on what I saw. You've tried so hard to keep your life here away from your life in Lincoln, sweetheart. Living two lives, that ain't an easy thing. You ever thought about melding them and just being you?"

Her mother's words pricked the blasting cap of emotion Holly was trying desperately to keep locked away. "I've been trying for the past six years, Mama. I don't want to lose being a cowgirl. I don't want to leave the ranch. It kills me to even think about it. But I want to be a psychologist. It fascinates me. When I help someone, counsel them or whatever, when I learn something new that might help people that need to be helped, it makes me feel like I'm flying. I feel like that's what I was put here to do. Same way I feel when I used to ride Aurora Belle out to check the calves or to pull bulls. How can there be two things I was put here to do? How do I make that work out?"

"We were all put here to do a great many things, sweetheart. What I'm trying to help you realize is that your daddy and I don't expect you to be everything to this ranch any more than we want you to give up your goals and aspirations to be a doctor. All of the pressure you put on yourself comes from inside of you. It ain't us. We love you just the way you are. The doctor side. The cowgirl side. You're our little girl, no matter which role you're playing. And you know what else?"

"What?" Holly sighed. Her parents loving both sides didn't make them any easier to balance.

"We also love the girl that's fallen head over heels in love with someone quite unexpectedly. Some man that she won't tell her brothers about, and we're all gonna figure out how to love him, too, because we're a family, Holly. You've been trying to get away from us since you were three years old and your daddy finally let you ride by yourself. But, baby, we've always been here waiting to catch you if you fall. We're always here for anything you need help with. We want to be there for every single side of our girl."

"How did you. . . ?"

"A mama always knows."

Holly gnawed the inside of her lip as she debated. It wasn't like her mama hadn't already figured everything out. Might as well go on with it. "Can I ask you something?"

"I was hoping you would."

Guilt iced the brick of confusion weighting Holly's soul. "I'm never trying to cut you out, Mama. I just. . .I like to figure things out on my own."

"Mm-hmm, I know that, too. Sometimes other people can help you along the way of your figuring. Might help you get where you're going a whole lot quicker. 'Specially if the person you're asking for help has already been where you're heading."

"What if I don't know exactly where I'm heading?"

"Then I'd dare say my little girl's all grown up. By the time you figure out that life's a lot like trying to drive a truck uphill in the fog, and that you don't have any idea what you're doing, you can actually crank the engine and get on the road, but that ain't what you wanted to ask me."

"Maybe you should get a psych degree," Holly sighed.

Her mother's knowing smirk somehow soothed her. "Honey, I have birthed five children, raised six, been married to a cowboy for most of my life, seen more cattle born and shipped on the ranch than I ever hope to count, have looked after all kinds of ailments, broken bones, skinned knees, snakebites, and more than a few broken hearts. Have buried horses, dogs, bullfrogs, and cats. I even took care of my littlest girl when at barely four years old she up and decided she knew just how to brand the calves all by herself and grabbed the wrong end of the iron. I don't need a degree. I'm a mama."

Holly instinctively turned her right hand over to see the white scar that ran the length of her palm the approximate shape of a branding iron rod. "Can I ask my question now?"

"You're the one that keeps hemming and hawing. I'm right here, and I'm listening."

"Yeah, I know, and I know you've always been there, Mama. I'm sorry I'm so stubborn sometimes."

"Well, I kinda 'spect you get that from me so I can't really complain too much."

"You know how Daddy always talks about how when he saw you in your broken down car on the side of the road that he knew he was gonna marry you? He knew you were the one."

"I do believe I've heard that story more than a few times." Her mother's smile said she valued each and every retelling.

"And you know how Austin swears when he first saw Summer out in Wyoming he knew she was the one. And Luke, too, when he saw Indie the first day of high school or whatever."

"And your Granddaddy Camden, and your Great Granddaddy Camden, and your great-great Granddaddy Camden, and Brock and Hope. I've heard them all, sweetcheeks. What's this got to do with my girl, though?"

"Did you know when you saw Daddy get out of his truck to help you? Did you know you were gonna marry him? Does it work like that for the Camden girls, too?"

Her mother's warm smile eased the tense set of Holly's shoulders. She studied Holly intently for a long moment and then closed her eyes. "Mama?"

"Must be dust in my eyes or something."

"Why are you crying?"

With a few rapid blinks, her mother ridded her hunter green eyes, duplicates of Holly's, of emotion. "I'm not. It's just that's quite a question from my youngest baby." Holly and her mother were momentarily distracted when Aurora Belle shifted oddly and groaned.

"Oh God, I can't stand for her to hurt, Mama." She bit back the demand for her mother to make everything okay. To make the pain stop, both hers and the horses. That's what her mother had always done when she was a little girl. If realizing your mama can't always make everything better was what it required, Holly wasn't certain she was really ready to grow up.

"There. She's all right for now." Jessie tenderly eased her hand down the horse's side until she settled once again. "Now, let's see about this question. Before I answer that, I think you might want to figure why you asked."

"I asked because I want to know if you knew, too."

"That ain't why you asked me, Holly. You asked because you want me to tell you that I knew as soon as I saw him that he was the one, and you want me to tell you that because you desperately want there to be a reason for why you're feeling the way you're feeling about this gentleman that's got my girl on a runaway horse without any reins. You want me to tell you that I knew I was gonna end up being Mrs. Everett Camden, owner of the legendary Camden Ranch in Pleasant Glen, Nebraska. You want me to tell you that this is all gonna work out just the way you want it to, but I can't do that, sweetheart.

"Life doesn't give us any kind of assurances that things will work out the way we want them to. I guess what I'm trying to say is that the reason you asked the question is far more important than the question itself. If you want it to work out a certain way, baby, you got to *work* for it just as much as you *hope* for it.

"I will tell you this, though. When your daddy hopped down outta that old Ford truck, I knew he was different. I knew he was worth something, and you know I never gave one hoot or a holler about his money. I knew he was worth getting to know. He was worth loving. Knew if it ever came down to it he was worth saving. Worth so much more than any of the boys I'd chased back in Denver. His worth somehow made me understand my own. I did take one look in those eyes, and I knew I wanted to know him. And that night when he brought me out here to this very barn we're sitting in and kissed me, I felt something I'd never felt before. It wasn't about me knowing he was the one for me forever. It was figuring out that I was willing to work to make *us* be forever. That's when I knew. So, let me ask you, sweet girl, is he worth something? Is he worth your forever?"

"I think he might be, Mama." Holly damned back her own stubbornness and told her mother the truth. "I've never felt like this before. I've only known him a week. How can I feel this way?" Her mother scooted closer and opened her arms. Holly fell into her mother's embrace. "I'm scared."

You are a completely pathetic fuck-trumpet. Dec stared down at the four coffee makers in his cart at the housewares store. He was still in awe of the size of the store. In London, stores were stacked four deep and one could not possibly push a cart large enough to even hold the coffee makers he'd chosen.

Buying her all four probably crossed into some kind of deranged stalker territory, but the offered bells and whistles made no sense to him. He needed guidance. He also desperately wanted a hit and shopping for her provided a decent distraction from the constant need clawing under his skin.

"Can I help you, sir?" The saleswoman hoisted her cleavage outward, licked her lips, and adjusted her brown apron. Dec made no effort to hide his eye roll. *Those don't interest me, dear. I held the holy grail of tits in my hands last evening and those are the only ones I want to stare at.* Dear God, what was happening to him? He paused for a second to recall the heady sensation of Holly's perfectly imperfect nipples pulsing against his tongue. His cock heralded its immediate approval. Okay, nothing was wrong, just love proving itself once again to be completely terrifying.

"Perhaps. My girlfriend has a deep and abiding affection for American coffee. I've recently decided that I live to make her smile. I'm sure you understand this. Which of these makes the best coffee?"

Sales-chick redacted her proffered cleavage. "Girlfriend, huh?" She scowled.

"Was I unclear? Perhaps it's my accent."

"You from Australia or something?"

Dec reflected her scowl. "I sound Australian?" He panicked. This simply could not be. His accent could not be slipping. He might never want to return to London, but he had his dignity.

"I don't know. You sound kinda like that guy that played the sparkly vampire in those movies with the talking dogs."

Fighting not to gag, Dec shuddered at the thought. "I'm from London," he managed.

"Oh, yeah, my grandma went there with a church group a few years ago. Her name's Olive. You might'a seen her."

"That is highly doubtful as over eight million people live in London and three times that many tourists visit every year. The coffeemakers?"

"I thought you all drank tea?"

"You've been terribly helpful. I'll just go."

"Okay. It was my pleasure. I'm supposed to say that we pride ourselves on customer service here at Sheets and Shit."

Dec halted his escape. "The name of this store is Sheets and Shit?"

"Oh no." Blood flooded the girl's cheeks. "Well, I mean that's what we call it, but it's Lincoln's Linens. It sucks to work here, though."

"I see."

After deciding to just buy all four makers, Dec loaded them in the back of his SUV and tried to think of some productive way to spend the rest of this endless day.

CHAPTER NINETEEN

By two, the burn that Holly had managed to keep at bay through the night crawled constantly over Dec's skin. *Can't be that hard to find something to make the time pass faster. She'd never know.*

He shook himself, trying to violently dislodge the cravings. He'd run out of things to purchase for her. He didn't want to take her time away from her horse or her family by calling. He needed something to do. Something that might douse the burn, ease the chokehold of the call.

Pacing in the basement of his home, he headed towards his sound-proofed music room but stopped before he'd switched on the light. Music wasn't going to cut it. The demons were playing particularly dirty this afternoon, and his sweet demon-tamer was a hundred miles away by the sounds of it.

He stripped down to his boxers, threw on a pair of workout shorts, and leapt on the treadmill. Nothing as metaphoric as attempting to outrun the hellish beasts of addiction on a fucking treadmill. You could never escape. You could only keep moving. He knew this. Currently, his knowledge wasn't helping.

When he'd run until his muscles wept sweat out every pore, he kept his heartrate up by hopping off the treadmill and mopping off his forehead and hands. Working quickly, still damming the monsters he wrapped his wrists, pulled on his gloves, and beat the shit out of his heavy bag like it was his addiction.

It never appeared battered or bruised, just continued to swing with every blow of his fist.

Two hours later, he slid down the tile wall of his shower, buried his face in his hands, and let the water cascade over his back.

The psychical exertion had at the very least weakened the summons to ease the ache of Holly not being nearby. That was the one problem with working behind a desk. Physical release was the only thing he'd found to ease the desire for a substance when music didn't work. It was the reason he ran every day at lunch.

Standing, he lathered his hands in shampoo and worked them through his hair. Keeping his eyes shut tightly, he replaced the craving for a line with his craving for Holly. *'Now, please. Take everything you want. Then take more.'* The memories of her pleading filled him momentarily.

His audible grunt echoed against the rhythmic drum of the water as he ran his slicked hands down his chest, leaned his head back, and let the water rid his body of the workout. He began the fantasy from her begging him to take more. His hand wrapped tightly around his cock. His piercing throbbed as he began to tug.

She was naked and blindfolded, bound to his bed, since this was his fantasy. He dragged his cock between her lush tits, drawn into stiff peaks from arousal and curiosity as to what he might do next. Pre-cum leaked down her belly and pooled in that adorable bellybutton he longed to drink expensive whiskey out of.

His hand worked faster, pumping out his need. 'Lick your lips and ask me for a taste,' he commanded.

She complied readily this time. Trembling as he indulged her body in several nibbles and sucks, keeping her guessing as to where his hands or his mouth might touch next.

He attempted to dip his cock between her lips. 'Suck me like a good girl.'

She shook her head. A sexy pout on her lips. 'I don't want to be a good girl. I want to be naughty.'

His body tensed as he envisioned his hand smacking her firm little ass, turning it deliciously pink.

'Yes,' she cried out for more.

'Need more? Want me to make you count them, or are you gonna suck me like a good girl?'

'More.'

Another strike before he massaged away the sting. Then another.

The fantasy shifted rapidly as his sac drew to his body and his hand pumped faster and harder, bringing on the relief he required. The reality of the evening before, better than anything he could ever have conjured, took over. He pounded inside of her slick walls cinching around him tighter and tighter with every thrust.

He released the blindfold, needing to see the hunger in her eyes. The lust. The love. He knew now. Another pump. His weary muscles trembled. His hand slicked up his wet cock, twisted at his head, and down, up, twist, down and he unloaded inside of her.

When the hot jets of cum mixed in with the wet rush of water on his abdomen he tried to enjoy the release and not feel the disappointment that he'd once again come alone thinking of her. God, he needed her to come back to Lincoln. Now.

If only the monsters resided in his cum or in his sweat, he would have been rid of both, but later that afternoon he was anxious again. The burning sensation licked at his spine. He'd texted Holly but hadn't gotten an answer.

What if something happened to her? Then what are you going to do? You'd never be able to get through that without a little help. Why not take it now?

Dec lifted his favorite Stratocaster and settled in a seat in his music room. He closed his eyes and strummed out the first few chords of *The Sound of Silence*. Silencing the devil in his head, he began to sing the lyrics over and over.

The noise of applause ripped him from the reprieve the sound offered. His eyes jerked open. Kade offered him a sheepish grin and continued his one-man applause. Dec wondered if there was any sadder sound in the world.

"Knocked on the front door several times. Got a little worried after your phone call this morning. Used my key to get in down here. Man, if we could write lyrics like that we could blow this popsicle stand and make your dreams of playing Wembley come true."

"I can write lyrics like that. I just have to be high to do it," Dec huffed. No point in lying, and Kade would generally put up with him when he was being an asshole. For a little while, anyway.

"Then it ain't worth it, and you know that, but I'm not gonna lecture you."

Kade. Solid as they came.

"Thanks. I'm sorry. Rough day."

"I gathered. Surprised you gave Holly the vampire treatment. I had a good feeling about you two."

"The vampire treatment?" Dec's brow furrowed.

"Yeah, you know, they're welcome to come over in the night but gotta be out by the morning light."

"I didn't do that. I didn't want her to leave. She had to go back home. Her horse is apparently dying."

"That sucks. Poor kid. Maybe you should've gone with her."

"I offered, but you and I both know I'm not the kind of man you take home to meet Dad."

"I don't know that at all. Wyatt says her family's all right. He knows her brother or something."

"Luke?"

"Nah, I think he said his name was Austin. Something about a PBR champ."

"I haven't heard about him yet. There's a lot that remains to be said between us, honestly."

"Not gonna lie to you, Dec. You don't look like you're handling life all that well right now. I'm enacting the privilege you extended me after you joined the band. There's a meeting at First Baptist tonight. Kind of think we should go. We'll grab dinner before."

"Thank you for having the guts to call me on it. I thought I could handle this. Had the weekend all planned. Dammit, I should be able to handle a change of plans. It's been eleven years since Evie died. Eleven years since my last hit."

"You've handled the last eleven years taking them day by day and moment by moment and attending meetings often. You haven't been in a few weeks. This day and a few of these moments got to you. You and I both know it happens. Let's get."

"You have to give me more than sleeping with Dec is life-altering," Cheyenne whined. She'd invited herself over for dinner as soon as she'd heard that Holly was back home. Grant was irked. He'd inhaled dinner and headed back out to sit with Aurora Belle.

For some reason, Holly had no desire to talk about Dec with anyone. She supposed she did owe Cheyenne for calling her so late the other night, though.

"It wasn't just sex, Chey. It's everything. Everything about him is different. Everything about us. I'm not sure I'm ready to talk about it."

"What about the piercing?" Typical Cheyenne — only heard what she wanted to hear.

"I'll just say this — you should get over Grant and find a guy with an apadravya piercing for yourself. So, so worth it."

"Maybe I could get Grant to get one."

That cracked Holly up. "Grant would no more let someone pierce his cock than he would set himself on fire."

"Well, I don't really know anyone who would. Why on earth did Dec do that?"

"Not sure yet. I was going to find out this weekend, but I had to come home."

"Hey, Holl," Luke leaned his head in Holly's childhood bedroom. "You might want to come out here. Breathing's getting awfully shallow."

"Oh gosh, I shouldn't have left her."

"Call me if you want to get breakfast in the morning." Cheyenne headed out of the house.

Holly sprinted back to the barn. She saw the headlights on Cheyenne's truck fading away as she drove down the dirt road off the ranch.

At one o'clock, Holly fell into her bed with fresh tears tracking down her face. It was too dark to bury Aurora Belle that night, and Holly just didn't have the emotional fortitude to help dig a grave. Her entire family had promised to help in the morning. They'd stood in a solid mass in the barn watching her slip away. Luke and Austin had damned the non-existent dust in their eyes. So had her daddy. Indie sobbed uncontrollably and blamed her hormones. Even the boys seemed to have realized the magnitude of the situation as they'd laid quietly on their mama's and daddy's shoulders.

The light on the screen of Holly's phone split the darkness. Leaning up in bed, she scrubbed her hands over her face and saw four texts from Dec. They eased her weary soul.

Just wanted to say goodnight, my love. I miss you. I need you.

She called him back immediately.

"This is the best possible answer to a text." His voice was soft, soothing.

"I miss you, too. I didn't have my phone with me in the barn." Her voice hung as the pain of loss took another blow at her heart.

"It's all right, sweetheart. I'm so sorry. Wanna talk about her?"

"Not right now. That'll just make me cry. Tell me about your day."

"Started out okay, then got less so."

"What happened?"

"I'm an addict. That's almost always what happens."

"You didn't use?" Holly knew he hadn't. She also knew abrupt changes of plans that might've left an addict bored with nothing to do could be difficult to navigate. She should have woman-ed up and brought him with her. She'd left him to deal with all of this on his own. Some girlfriend.

"No. Did all the things I do when I'm fighting. Most days are a little easier than this one. But every now and then things just really suck. I went to a meeting tonight."

He was testing her. She could hear it. Did he think knowing he attended a Narcotics Anon meeting would make her run? No, but if she had to guess, she'd say some part of him, the parts of himself that he believed unworthy and unlovable, hoped she would. They wanted to prove themselves right once again. Well, she'd let them win over her dead body.

"Good. That's precisely what you should have done. Did you go to the one at First Baptist?"

"Yeah. How did you know about those?"

"Worked there a lot last year. Also work the meetings we have here at our little tiny Methodist church in the summers. It's the closest one in five towns, and they only have a leader there once a month. I always worry about that. What if it's too far for some people?"

"You are absolutely incredible, did you know that?"

"I think the very same thing about you."

"Holly, could I . . . ?"

She knew what he needed, and hated herself for being two hours away from him right now. "Why don't you tell me your story? I'd really like to hear it."

"I shouldn't do this on the phone. I need to see you when I tell you this. I'll wait. Your horse just died."

"No. You won't. No more waiting. Life isn't for waiting. Turn the camera on your phone on. That way you can see me. I'm not going to sleep tonight anyway. Talk to me. All night long."

"Holly, sweetheart, not now. I need to be stronger than this for you. You're hurting."

"I need you to be *you* for me. Here, would it help if I said I'm actually a PhD student at UN. I'm getting my degree in Psychology, so I have some experience with this. That's part of why I didn't tell you about being a student, actually. I was scared you'd think I was only dating you because I wanted to study you. Please, know that isn't it at all. I really care about you, Dec. More than I've ever cared about anyone.

"I also grew up with an uncle who was an alcoholic. I saw the pain he inflicted not only on his son and wife but on all of us because he refused to go to meetings, to deal with his addictions. I know what kind of strength it takes to talk about this, to know when you need help dealing. I want to help you if I can, if you want me to."

"Thank you. If you really don't mind helping to hold me accountable, I'd never turn you down. I figured out you were a Psych student this morning when you were talking about Dr. Ortigue's work. I never suspected that's why you were dating me. If you really don't mind doing this over the phone, I could work through the story and explain how it is that I own this house without a record label. I didn't want to tell you what I do because I didn't want my job to intimidate you."

"I won't be intimidated. I'm a cowgirl, remember?" Holly found herself laughing softly in the peaceful serenity of her bedroom. Maybe the phone wasn't at all a bad way to have this conversation. She needed to spend the night with Dec. If it couldn't be in his arms, the next best thing was to listen intently to his voice.

"That's right. My stubborn, sexy, cheeky, and extremely brainy cowgirl who I find myself falling more and more in love with every passing moment."

"Glad we're finally saying that. Not sure how sexy being brainy is though."

"Whoever told you brains weren't sexy as hell is a bastard without enough brains to get in out of the London rain."

"Dec, tell me your story."

"I need to see you."

Holly switched on the camera on her phone. Dec did the same. She studied him. He looked rough. Raw from fighting with his own demons most of the day if she had to guess. Her heart lurched. Why hadn't she brought him with her?

He cleared his throat and looked anywhere but in her eyes. "I don't know where to start."

"Start at the beginning."

"Jesus, baby, there have been so many beginnings."

"Well, start at the first beginning then."

"You're sure about this? Now? You want to hear all of this tonight?"

"If I have to walk out of my parent's house and drive back to Lincoln I'm going to hear all of this tonight. One way or the other. Your choice."

He gave a single nod. His eyes were ravaged with fear and rejection that wasn't coming. They were swollen and red-rimmed. He hadn't shaven that day. His stubble was a little longer than she'd seen it before. He was physically beautiful and emotionally wrecked. In that moment, Holly knew he was worth it. He was worth her forever.

"My mother died when I was born. I'm not blaming my addictions on my past. I'm just trying to start at the beginning."

"I'm so sorry, and everything in our past shapes our future, Dec. You're not blaming anything on anyone. I understand."

"Thank you. Uh, my father naturally blamed me for my mother's death. He hated me, not that he said that outright. He never said anything outright. We never seemed to be able to hear one another. I felt deaf, and for most of my childhood, I swore he was mute. I'm the youngest of three boys. He barely spoke twenty words to each of us a day. My mother's absence was more than he could deal with without a bottle in his hands. You have to understand, the drinking culture in London is so prevalent.

"It's a nightly event to go out and completely smashed until you pass out or vomit or pass out in your own vomit. No one thinks anything of it. I never wanted to be like my father so alcohol never appealed to me. It wasn't strong enough to dull the pain I was trying to kill. I refused to let it be because that would make me just like him, and I made myself hate him because he hated me for killing my mother. Took me until I was twenty-one to see that I was just like him, just chose a different route to my own funeral."

Holly absorbed all of this. She wanted to ask if his father was still alive, or if he ever saw him, or spoke to him, but she needed to show him that she would never be a source of judgment in his life.

"That makes sense, Dec. You sought out something different to ease the pain. That's okay."

"It's not okay, but it is the truth."

"You didn't kill your mother. You do know that, don't you?"

"Maybe."

Holly shook her head. She couldn't imagine him living an entire life believing he'd had anything to do with his mother's death. "What do you think made you decide to try it the first time?" She hoped she didn't sound too much like a therapist. She wasn't a therapist right now. She was his girlfriend, his friend, and someone he loved.

"Same thing that makes any sixteen-year-old male do anything he does."

"There was a girl."

"I'm not actually certain she was a girl. She was more a hurricane with female attributes."

Holly chuckled. "And how did this hurricane get you caught up in her storm?"

"She listened to me."

CHAPTER TWENTY

If Dec had stabbed her brutally with a knife, Holly didn't think it could have possibly wounded her like his last statement had.

She listened to me would forever weight her heart. My God. She blinked away tears. He was so strong to confess this. She couldn't be weak. Not now. "I'll always listen to you, Dec. I want to always be there to listen."

"You've only known me a week, love. Don't make promises like that."

"I'm making a promise I know I'm going to keep. One-fifth of a second, remember?"

That got a half-smile. "Her name was Evie. She was nineteen when I met her, and I was young and stupid, and she listened, and God, I was so weak, but that was all I desperately wanted someone to do. She listened to my music, and never asked me to play Wonderwall, which was all anyone ever wanted to hear. Listened to me talk and told me I was smart. See, in the beginning, *she* was the drug. She was my addiction. First time she pulled out a baggie of weed and told me it would make my music better, I never even questioned her. Didn't take me long to figure out that I was never satisfied with pot or cigarettes. No. Evie could get harder stuff, and that was what I needed."

"Dec," Holly's voice sounded distant and tunneled. She'd listened intently about Evie, but one sentence had struck above all others. "Why did you say her name *was* Evie?" She knew the answer, obviously, but suspected the hurricane's death had a great deal to do with Dec's getting himself cleaned up.

"Caught that, did you?"

"I'm a really good listener. Figure it will help me in my career choice."

"It will, and in just a second I'll tell you how I know that."

"Whenever you're ready."

"Let's see here, I stayed high most of the time. Went from hash to cocaine. Even dealt a little, which isn't easy to do when you're an addict yourself. I was rail thin, looked like walking death. My father never cared enough to call me on anything. My brothers tried, but I'm an asshole when I'm high, a complete terror. I don't blame them for throwing me out and not seeing me again.

"Evie was always there, and I'm sure you know precisely what she sold to keep us supplied. I would usually make it a few months in one lame ass job or another and the band I was in got decent gigs that made good money. Occasionally we bought food. Mostly we bought things far less sustaining. We were so certain you couldn't have sex without Ecstasy and you couldn't deal with life without a line. I told myself I had to have the tragedy to make music worth listening to, but that was total shit.

"I refused heroin. I'm still scared of needles. Never let anyone tell you that your fears can't save your life because they can. Evie got into it. Only she never told me about it. I came home one night and had sold off all of my vinyl collection, which a few year's prior had been my prized possession besides my guitars. I'd gotten what I'd thought would make for a fan-fucking-tastic night. I honestly don't remember what all I brought home.

"She was coming down off a heroin hit. I saw the needles, but I didn't want to think about them so just like my father I ignored everything I didn't want to see and started making snowcaps. Do you know what those are?" He stopped abruptly.

"Uh, yeah," Holly had forgotten to breathe for the majority of the story. With a few breaths she managed coherent thought. "Cocaine sprinkled over marijuana right?"

"Yeah. I had a hash mix, but same basic thing, only the hash I'd purchased was bad."

"And she'd had heroin," Holly gasped out the inevitable conclusion. "Oh God, Dec."

He only nodded. He didn't speak.

"Is that when you got arrested?"

"I called the cops. I couldn't wake her up. I turned myself in trying desperately to save her, but she was gone before I ever came to."

Holly's hand covered her mouth. She couldn't make herself take her hand away from her face. He thought he'd killed her, too. It was painted on every chiseled feature of his face, in the weight of his eyelids, in the length of every eyelash blinking away tears.

"Dec, it wasn't your fault," she finally managed.

"It was, love. It definitely was."

"No, it wasn't," Holly insisted. "You have to know there are two kinds of suicide. Some people do it all at once, and other people do it one day at a time. She was lost long before the heroin or the hash or whatever."

He went on without any acknowledgment of what she'd said, but she knew he'd heard her. "The rest was a haze. I was arrested. Evie was gone, so I didn't particularly care. Some great uncle I never even knew on my mother's side was an attorney. I remember staring at him through a metal divider in prison. I couldn't understand the words he was saying. Between the horrific withdrawal and the weight of the loss, all I ever heard were murmurs of death. Most of my prison life was spent in the infirmary, sweating profusely, convinced the nurse was trying to kill me.

"The days bled into the nights until one morning I was standing in front of a judge. All I remembered was that my father wasn't there and something about rehab. When I arrived at Betel, I was shaking so badly I couldn't walk. It wasn't until then, when other men had to fucking help me walk, that I finally found the will to fight the addiction."

"Dec, you are incredibly strong. How do you not see this?"

"Because I was so incredibly weak, darling. And the shame was enough for the first week to make me determined. All I could think about was how I hadn't even known Evie's parents. I was with her for years and knew next to nothing about her outside of the malignant world we lived in. I needed to apologize to them, but I didn't even know who they were. How fucked up that was.

"Then something happened to me in rehab. Again, people listened to me. They cared about me. I was safe there. I couldn't access drugs and people listened to me when I wasn't high. I never wanted to leave. They let me stay on for another session. I worked as a janitor just to be there and not have to leave. By the end of the second session, I had a plan. I owed it to Evie and to the world to be a person that would listen. I talked to my counselors and told them that I knew the only way I would ever stay clean is if other people were depending on me and I knew I was helping them.

"I'd blown off university after high school, of course. But you can go to school very inexpensively in London, so one of the counselors saw me through the entry process to Middlesex University. They had a program for students starting late. I got my degree in Behavioral Psychology. I'm a sex therapist, Holly. I treated sexual addiction in London. I would never be allowed to treat drug addicts, but addiction is addiction, no matter what form. And as long as we're digging out all of my baggage, I married the daughter of the head of a major psychological institution in London. His daughter was a wild child that he wanted looked after in exchange for giving a former addict a job."

"That's why you said you never loved her. You married her because you knew you wouldn't get addicted to her. You just wanted to help people, and she kept cheating on you. Oh my God, Dec, I am so sorry."

"Don't be sorry about that. It truly never bothered me until she up and filed for divorce so she could marry her French pilot boyfriend. Her father refused to keep me employed unless I was married to her. Said I couldn't work in a counseling center if I was divorced, but that was bullshit. I hadn't kept her in line and that was the only reason I'd ever had a job. That's how I got here. I didn't want to tell you I was a sex therapist because I was afraid you'd be intimidated. That sounds ridiculously pompous, saying it here in the dead of night after telling you I'm a drug addict and a murderer. I don't treat addicts anymore, which is what I really want to do, but I do work for Lifespan Counseling."

"You are not a murderer, Dec, and as long as we're all about confessions, I plan to specialize in sex therapy. Working at Lifespan is kind of my dream job. I would definitely not mind sleeping with my tutor."

Dec couldn't stop staring at her sweet, sleepy smile on the screen. She'd just listened to all of his shitty mistakes and was teasing him about their relationship, a relationship she still wanted. No one could be this good. He would never deserve her.

"I will do anything in my power to help you get your degree, sweetheart, and a job at Lifespan after you graduate. It would be another way I could give back, and that is the only thing that keeps me clean. I need to be needed. It's a weakness."

"Or it's an incredible strength. Depends on who you're asking, I guess."

Unbelievable. Absolutely unbelievable. He wondered if he was being given a dose of heaven for all the hell he'd been through in the last thirty years. That didn't seem likely, but he had no hopes of turning it down.

"Why did you choose sex therapy? People choose pediatric psychology, or clinical counseling, or something like that, unless there is something else driving them to want to learn about the human mind," he asked.

"Don't guess I get to get out of that question, do I?"

"You don't have to tell me anything, but I'd really like to know everything about you, sweetheart. That whole one-fifth of a second thing, after all."

"Yeah, that," she sighed. Whatever had driven her to pursue a specialty in sex therapy, she didn't want to verbalize it. Dec wondered if she'd ever said it out loud to anyone or if she was only keeping it from him.

"No one's ever asked me that before. Not a lot of psychoanalyzing out here in ranch land, I guess."

"I'm asking and I want to listen to whatever it is."

"It fascinates me. The way women are wired to need sex yet we're constantly told that if we want it we're bad. And then when women go through seasons of not wanting to have sex for whatever reason, that's our fault, too. I want to shatter those stereotypes, preferably with a great deal of dynamite or something equally as explosive."

Dec chuckled. "Very admirable use of explosives in my book. I'd love to help you with your quest, but I know there's more, sweetheart." He forced himself to wait patiently. She'd heard his entire sordid tale. He would wait forever to hear anything she had to say.

"Yeah, don't guess we could ever really keep anything from each other given that we're both trained to read body language."

"If I hadn't had such an exhausting day and your horse hadn't just died, I would make some ridiculous innuendo about loving the way your body speaks to me."

"Aurora Belle would want you to flirt with me. She would want both of us to be happy."

"I desperately want you to be happy, sweetheart. I just don't trust that I'm the guy to make you happy."

"I do trust that, Dec. I know it's only been a week, but you're worth this. We're worth us, if that makes any sense at all. I was talking to my mom and. . . ."

"It makes sense. Maybe more than anything else has ever made sense to me, but you still haven't answered my question."

"I know. Like I said, I've never told anyone this. I never want to make light of it or make it out to be worse than it was. I don't know how to talk about it, which probably means I'm going to be a really shitty therapist."

Declan's heart, which he finally was willing to admit must still exist as he was handing it over to her, ached. "Hey, that isn't true, and you know it. Whatever you're about to tell me obviously affected you. Stop trying to qualify it as not bad enough to discuss or so bad it shouldn't be talked about, just tell me from your perspective what happened."

"You're the lead sex-therapist at Lifespan, aren't you?"

"Yes, but what does that have to do with anything?"

"You're really good at this."

"Come on, baby. Talk."

"Remember me telling you my uncle was an alcoholic?"

With the sheer force of his jaw, Dec locked away the threats set to spew forth. If her uncle had touched her, he'd upgrade his own personal judgments on himself from two counts of manslaughter to murder in the first. He managed a half grunt, which she must've taken as a yes.

"Well, he got worse and worse while we were growing up. I'm the youngest of five kids. My sister is several years older than me, and my brothers are all older than her. Mama lost a baby between me and Natalie."

Extraneous details were a normal part of a confession like this. Dec knew that but his mind kept trying to fill in the information she wasn't supplying. Each scenario was worse than the one before.

"Anyway, my cousin Brock was my aunt and uncle's only kid, but my parents really kind of raised him right along with the rest of us. They had no idea when they kicked my uncle off of the family ranch that they would take Brock with them. They were sure they'd leave him here and they would become his guardians. They never meant. . . ."

"Holly, deep breath for me, okay?" He heard her audible breath. "Good girl. Now, it doesn't sound like your parents did anything wrong, sweetheart, but tell me what caused them to make the decision to remove your uncle and his direct family from the ranch."

"He'd always been an angry drunk. Got his hands on Brock several times. Dad wanted to petition for full custody. He didn't because everyone felt so sorry for my aunt, but it got worse. The more he drank the more demanding and angry it made him. He made a few passes at my mom when he was drunk. Dad was furious. It came to blows, but we didn't know what he was doing to Natalie then. I caught them in the barn one afternoon He didn't know I was in there. I was really little. I screamed because he wouldn't let her go, and I didn't know what he was trying to do to her. Dad and Luke came running. They'd heard me screaming. It had been going on for a long time. We didn't know. It could've been even worse, I guess. It's such a weird thing to quantify though. Why do we do that? Why do we take bad things and rank them according to how much worse it could have been?"

"Because it momentarily restores our need to believe that everything will be okay. Just never discount what happened when you're talking with your sister."

"I never have. I just meant... he never raped her. But of course it affected her. Mom and Dad spent three years driving Nat back and forth to Lincoln for counseling. It helped, and it didn't."

"Let me guess, she was a child when it happened and the therapist was able to help her regain confidence and security because your parents did everything right for a child. The problem returns when the adult tries to re-process the memories from their perspective and knowledge base, as a sexual being. That's why you want to do this. You want to help your sister."

"Well, that's not the only reason, but yeah, she struggles with dating and getting close to guys. When Brock and his wife first moved back to the ranch a couple of years ago, she was a total bitch to both of them."

"Sins of the father must be paid by the son."

"Exactly, but Brock is absolutely nothing like my uncle. He would never do anything like that. I've never even seen him drink. He also doesn't know what his father did. We've all kept it from him. It's this big family secret. None of us want him to feel any more guilt over my uncle, but he really doesn't understand why Natalie challenges him on everything. I just wish I could learn something that would help Natalie rediscover her sexuality in a healthy way."

"It's not your lack of knowledge, sweetheart. Natalie has to learn that, and she will in her own time and space. I'm guessing an understanding partner that would be willing to guide her might go a long way as well."

"Yeah, I know, but I don't like the idea that I can't help her."

"That is probably the very hardest part of the job you're after."

"Hey, Dec, would it be weird to ask you not to talk about our relationship at work until I graduate? I don't want people thinking you got me a job there."

"Plan on sticking with me through graduation, huh?" Abject delight pushed the demons he'd been running from all day further away.

His sexy cowgirl wanted to earn everything she got all on her own merit. Didn't want a hand up. That was something he understood, but it wasn't the way the world worked very often.

"I do plan on that, if you like the idea."

"I would like that more than you could ever know, sweetheart, and I won't say one word about my girlfriend at work. But after work, you have to promise to be all mine all the time."

"Your wish is my command."

"Be careful, darling. That phrase could get you into all kinds of trouble."

"I'm hoping."

CHAPTER TWENTY-ONE

Holly's hair whipped out behind her as she flew out of the paddock on Lightning, one of the Camden's horses that got cycled in and out of work but hadn't been claimed as primary horse by any of her brothers or sisters. Holly rather liked him. He was jet black with a white snip on his forehead.

Best thing about Lightning — he would fly when that's what you wanted, but didn't mind slowing down so you could think. He rarely fussed and loved to be ridden. Her kind of horse. Maybe she should claim him. No one would mind, especially after Aurora Belle. She'd already helped Luke and Grant dig the grave. The ache in her arms paid homage to the work. She'd said her goodbyes, but a part of her still felt like it was missing. Every breath she took aggravated the hollow in her chest.

The conversations she and Dec had in the dark of night replayed in her head as the ranch extended its open arms embracing her ride. The rapid rhythmic hoof-falls of the horse soothed her soul. She pressed her boots against his side gently. He readily picked up speed. Yep, definitely her kind of horse.

She should probably head back to Lincoln, but something kept her riding west. She missed Dec desperately, but didn't want to leave just yet. All of the words they'd shared via a phone screen, spoken and unspoken, spun in her mind.

He was a sex therapist. They were falling in love. She could ask him to show her the things she so wanted to know. He would understand. *What guy in their right mind wouldn't agree to playing out my fantasies with me, sex therapist or not? If you want him to enact them, you have to spell them out.* The two halves of her brain continued their opposition. They coupled with her mother's blunt question about being able to talk with other people about their sex lives when she couldn't even manage to say the words 'sex therapist' to her own father.

Dec would never make fun of you or think your fantasies are weird. He's probably heard of several you don't even know about. That was the thing about fantasies. No one wanted to confess their own for fear of rejection or ridicule, which left women embarrassed about perfectly natural desires. Yes, she could quote shit like that all day on research papers and even her thesis, but that didn't make it easy to discuss them in reality.

Trying to play out the conversation she longed to have with her new boyfriend wasn't any easier to imagine. *'Dec, would you mind being my sexual tutor and helping me explore my desire to be dominated, spanked, and a few other things we don't have to discuss now? I'm also open to suggestions. I mean, you already alluded to a few of those things and I've never been more turned on in my entire life. Maybe I could awkwardly write down some ideas for you or something.' Dear God, Holly, you won't even think the words, how are you going to say them?*

Lightning slowed when she slumped on his back, always attuned to his rider. She patted his side. "I can't even talk about any of this with a guy I'm pretty sure I'd like to marry. How the hell am I going to talk about it with patients, boy?"

Lightning gave her a less than helpful snort.

Dec answered his phone before the completion of the first ring. "Hey, sweetheart."

"Hey." Anxiety played in her tone.

"You okay?"

"Yeah, I just keep thinking last night was some kind of dream. We both said we wanted to do this, right? And by this I mean. . . ."

"A committed, monogamous, long-term, healthy relationship."

"Exactly."

"What are you listening to?"

"Why did you ask me that?"

"One surefire way to tell what's on your mind."

"Rhianna."

"Mm, glad I asked. Would you like to have *Sex With Me?*"

"I would, but I'm listening to *Good Girl Gone Bad.*"

Dec shifted on his sofa, trying to loosen the chokehold his jeans had on his cock. "Somebody done you wrong, love, or is it the idea of the title that intrigues you?"

"Definitely the title."

"Gonna have to take another shower."

Holly's sweet giggle slipped from his ear to his heart and then headed directly south in a flood of heated blood surging to his member. "Am I to take it that my innocent cowgirl might like to be a bad girl for me?"

"I'm not all that innocent. . .but yeah. . .maybe."

His mind conjured a thousand images readily. Her slight defensiveness said he'd hit the nail squarely on the head, but she didn't really want to admit that out loud.

"Maybe taking your innocence is one of my fantasies, you ever think of that?" Debating momentarily, he decided that was in fact the truth, and he would never mind covering her wishes with his own if she was afraid of expressing them.

"Really? You fantasize about that?" The irritation in her voice turned quickly to hope.

"My fantasies of you come by the greedy dozen, darling."

"Are you feeling better today? Little more steady?"

Well, that was an abrupt change of pace. He was going to have to work on her expressing her needs and desires. Making love was going to have to lose a little of its stigma if she was going to become a sex therapist. "Much better. Sometimes I have to remind myself how much better I am now than when I first got clean. The rough days still come, but they're not as bad or as often as they used to be. That has to be good, right?"

"Definitely."

"Not going to lie though, I missed you terribly. The cravings for you are stronger than the cravings for something to take away the pain of you not being in my arms. I went back and re-read Dr. Ortigue's study. Still trying to convince myself what I'm feeling is normal. It's easier to believe when I can see you and touch you. Where are you?"

"I'm an hour outside of Lincoln. I'll be there soon."

"Promise?"

"Promise."

Dec made it to the door of her truck before she even had the engine turned off. She fell into his arms.

"Damn, I really missed kissing you."

"What are you waiting for then?" she sassed.

With that, he plastered her mouth to his own. Tasting her. Capturing her gasp of breath. Feeling her body as she melted into him. Her warmth penetrated his skin, easing his restlessness, soothing his soul.

Her fingers knotted his t-shirt and pulled him closer. Her hips bumped readily into his in a slow grind. She might not want to discuss what she wanted, but her sweet little body knew precisely how to ask for what it needed.

"You're already wet for me, aren't you?" He dipped his hand down the back of her Wranglers in the darkened parking lot of her apartment complex and kneaded the ass he'd been fantasizing about paddling most of the day.

"God, yes," she whimpered in his mouth.

"Naughty girl."

The volume of her moan slammed his heart into overdrive. Dear God, she was going to be his undoing. When she finally pulled away to chase her elusive breath, he forced himself to slow down and relish.

Studying her, he called himself every unsavory name he could come up with. Her eyes were red-rimmed and swollen. Her body weak with desire certainly but also with exhaustion. *Stop being an asshole for once. Stop taking more and give.*

"Come here to me." Sweeping her off of her booted feet, he cradled her close.

"Dec, I can walk. You don't have to carry me." She looped her hands over his neck and cuddled into him. Her body disagreed with her statement.

"I want to carry you. You look exhausted, sweetheart. Let me take care of you."

"We stayed up talking until four in the morning. You're tired, too."

"Hush." He took her keys from her fingers and balanced her in the strength of his arms while he let them inside. He settled her on her feet and attempted to kiss her again, but he was denied.

"Did you just tell me to hush, Dr. St. James? Finally occurred to me this morning on my ride why you always grinned when I called you *Mr.* St. James. You could've corrected me, you know."

"Doctor, mister, I don't give a damn. I'm still pulling for Daddy or sex god, and you're still talking, which is delaying my ability to take care of you."

"Just so you know, I would never shut up for anyone but you." With a mischievous grin, she sealed her lips with the turn of a pretend key in the lock then grabbed the waistband of his jeans and dropped the invisible key in his boxers.

Dec's rumbled growl vibrated the thin walls of her entry way. "Very, very naughty, Ms. Camden." He grasped her hand and pressed it to his burgeoning erection, forcing her to paw him, to bring him some sort of relief. She bit her lips together, refusing to give away any reaction.

In challenge, Dec wrapped his hand over hers fully and proceeded to show her how to jack him off through the thick denim. Her eyes dilated and a rush of heat blistered her cheeks, but she kept up her end of the game, saying nothing and pretending to be unaffected.

"Fine. Retrieve the key. I missed your voice. I just didn't want you arguing with me about what I'm going to do." He popped the snap on his jeans. Without further provocation, she snaked her hand down his boxers and wrapped it tightly around his fevered cock.

Hot air hissed between his teeth. This. This was what he'd needed for what felt like a lifetime. He thrust into her hand. She spun her fingertips up over his head then pulled her hand away, making him burn.

With another turn of a pretend key she unlocked her lips, giggled, and then tasted the pre-cum his body had provided. "And what are you about to do?" she asked after she sucked the last of him from her fingers.

"Jesus Christ, you taunting me, sweetheart? That isn't nice."

"I know. I'm being naughty, remember?"

"Oh, I remember. To answer your question, I'm about to give you a bath."

"I was hoping you were about to fuck me."

"Anticipation, my love. Anticipation is everything. I need to take care of you in every possible way. Wash you with my hands. Feel you inside and out. Sate you. Then take you to bed and hold you all night long. I've decided I can't sleep without you drooling on my chest."

Holly found herself swept back up in the cage of muscles that constructed his arms and chest. The whirlwind of Dec always managed to blow her off-course. She'd been trying so hard to communicate even a fraction of the fantasies she had about him, the things she wanted to explore. He'd been on board, she could tell, but he constantly held himself back.

A bath sounded amazing, but she was thinking something far dirtier. Being clean was not on her agenda, and he was fighting with himself again. Anytime they were naked it seemed he raged against himself. She could watch it in his eyes. The light and the dark in constant conflict producing the most beautiful stormy grey she'd ever seen. Constantly at war with taking when he thought she needed him to give. She debated.

"Dec, wait." They were already inside her bedroom. She eased away from him and settled on the bed. He joined her. "I would love for you to give me a bath, but I'd also love to hop in the shower with you, have wild, hot, wet, kinky sex and then go to bed. I don't want you to fight with yourself. It feels like you think you *should* give me a bath instead of taking what you want. I don't want to be a concession."

"Holly, baby, no." He eased a few strands of her hair behind her right ear. "You are never ever a concession. My God, you are perfect, and you care about someone as completely worthless as me. Everything we talked about last night. . .I don't know. . .I just. . .don't think I explained it well. I have to do this right.

"Addiction isn't a lack of willpower or about making incredibly shitty decisions. It's putting my wants above the needs of everyone else. It's letting that part of me rule. I need to take care of you. I thought I was in love with Evie. I wasn't. I was addicted to her. I need to prove to myself that this is different. I'm sorry if this isn't what you want to hear. I'm sorry if I'm screwing this up. I probably am, but I don't know any other way to do this. I have to always know that I'm not fucking up your life the way I did hers. So, yes, I fight with myself every single time we're together, but you are never a concession. I have to protect you. . .from the way I can be if I lose myself. I need to love you the right ways. Not let my addictions rule and ultimately ruin this relationship. You're the best thing that has ever happened to me. I won't ruin this."

"Hey." She leaned in and brushed a tender kiss across his lips to make him stop talking. "Just promise you'll try to remember that you're not taking something if I want it, too. You're giving me what I desperately want to experience, but I know we both had a rough weekend, so give me a bath." A relationship with an addict wasn't going to be easy. That much was obvious, and that was fine with her. Every cowgirl knew nothing worth having ever came easy.

Two hours later, Holly traced her fingertip along the lyrics of Metallica's *Master of Puppets* inked in heavy black lettering from Dec's left shoulder over his breastplate to the bottom of his ribcage. The lyrics butted into what appeared to be smoky demons curling up out of his boxers to cover his side and parts of his back. His body was chiseled perfection. Every ripped muscle carved with a steel blade.

"I'm probably going to drool on your tattoos again," she warned.

His chuckle jostled her body and steadied her heart. "I'm hoping."

His arm was covered in more lyrics, demons, and a cross made of numbers, dates, she assumed. Perhaps his mother's birth and death dates and then Evie's. She didn't want to ask about the dates. There was something else she found far more intriguing. His left side was entirely covered in ink. His right untouched.

He sighed contentedly as she continued to touch and explore him.

"Can I ask you something?" she spoke softly, not wanting to disturb the air surrounding their afterglow. She was warm, naked by his side, and freshly bathed, inside and out just like he'd promised.

"Anything."

"Why did you only ink your left side?"

"You're the psych student. You tell me."

"It's either because you feel like you're constantly at odds with yourself or you're constantly at odds with addiction."

"So bloody smart with a killer ass. How did I get so damn lucky?" He brushed a kiss in her hair. "But being at odds with my addictive nature is being at odds with myself, sweetheart. No matter how hard I try I can't separate myself from my demons."

Holly nodded against him. She hated that he always had to fight so hard. She wanted nothing more than to wage the war on his behalf, but she had no idea how to do that.

"Shit!"

Holly groaned as she heard Dec's curse and felt the mattress quake the next morning. "What's wrong?" She blinked rapidly as she sat up and watched him throw on his t-shirt and jeans.

"It's ten 'til eight, love. Get up. Or maybe you don't have to get up yet. I don't know. But I'm supposed to be on the other side of town in ten minutes. I sleep when you're in my arms. Haven't slept in years." He planted a quick kiss on her open mouth. "Stay with me tonight."

"Promise," she managed. Her first class wasn't until 11:00 so she was trying to process all of this. Her only coherent thought as she heard her front door slam shut was that she needed coffee, or maybe a few more hours of sleep. Yeah, sleep. She collapsed back in the bed.

CHAPTER TWENTY-TWO

Dec sprinted through the doors of Lifespan un-showered and wearing the suit he'd worn Friday. The term *fuck it* replaced the lyrics that usually resided in his head on constant repeat. He planned to go home and shower at lunch instead of running. Being with Holly last night made him sure he could get through the day without the physical exertion.

Nearly colliding with Sherry from accounting, he leapt over a file box to avoid a pile-up.

"Oh, goodness, Dr. St. James, there you are. Dr. Gibbons and a few members of the board are waiting in your office."

"What?!" Panic rose like a tidal wave in his gut. His vision swam. *No. No. NO. No. No. This could not be happening. Not now.* "I'm only twenty minutes late. My first appointment isn't until 9:00."

Sherry's brow knitted. "Well, you're not being fired, Dr. St. James. I believe you're just being reassigned."

"What?" Reassigned. What the bloody hell did that mean? Was there some kind of satellite office he was unaware of? Oh God, what if it was out of state? *Holly.* No. Just no. He wasn't moving out of Lincoln.

"I've working on reassigning all of your patients."

Dec bit back a long string of expletives, not wanting to horrify

Sherry. Instead he turned and marched to his doom. Choices weren't something afforded ex-pats with addiction records. Without this job, he couldn't stay in the country. Unless he could talk his way out of this ridiculous re-assignment he was on the first flight back to London, back to the past that had nearly eaten him alive, back to face his father with another failure tucked firmly under his belt, back to that damned graveyard, back to every mistake he'd ever made, and a culture that wanted him to drink them all away.

Fury and defeat ricocheted through his body. Why did the universe hate him? Why couldn't he just have one good thing without it being taken away from him?

"You're late, Dr. St. James," Dr. Chad Corrington, resident asshole and Dr. Gibbons' favorite golfing buddy, sighed as Dec managed his way to his desk.

"Sorry," and, "Traffic," were the only two words Dec could force from his lips as he studied the four men standing uninvited in his office.

"It's fine." Dr. Gibbons shot him a glare that said it wasn't fine but that he wasn't going to call him out in front of half of the board. It was such an oddly humane gesture, the tension in Dec's gut intensified with every passing second. "Got a call late last night from Rich Newsome from UN-L. This all works out well, really, even under the unfortunate circumstances."

"What circumstances? What are you talking about?" Dec demanded.

A contract landed on top of his desk, and his stomach landed somewhere near the vicinity of his feet.

Holly grinned as she answered her cell phone while stirring cream in her second mug of coffee. "Hey, Beth. You want to grab breakfast before class?"

"Sure, I'll meet you at *Bread and Cup,* but did you hear?"

"I'm going to go with no since I have no idea what you're talking about. I went back home this weekend."

"Dr. Benders *died* yesterday."

"What?" Holly almost dropped her mug. "Are you serious? Oh my gosh, okay, I should not be excited about him dying, but this is so, so good for the department."

"I agree. We will only be internally excited because he was four-hundred and ninety-seven years old and still did not believe in the existence of the clitoris, but we will be outwardly saddened even though he died in bed with his wife's sister beside an open bottle of little blue pills."

"Oh my God."

"Yeah."

"Wow."

"Yeah."

"Wait." A horrifying thought dampened the news. "He was teaching our Foundations of Human Sexuality research class. They don't offer it again until next Fall. That delays us graduating an entire year."

"No. Already checked. Class hasn't been cancelled. They got someone to cover it, I guess."

"What about all of his undergrad classes?"

"No idea, but we might actually learn something this year. I'm so excited."

"Inwardly."

"Right. Now, get to campus so we can drop by Dr. Newsome's office and remind him of how awesome we are before class. Word is he's announcing who he's going to supervise before Christmas."

Twenty minutes later, Holly and Beth settled in their favorite booth at Bread and Cup. It had decent breakfasts and good coffee and they could both afford it on their stipends, which made it the perfect before-class eating locale.

Beth studied Holly closely as she downed a long sip of coffee. "Why, Miss Camden, I do believe you have been fucked recently." She giggled while she pointed to the fading marks on Holly's neck.

"They're not that noticeable." Holly fixed the scarf she was wearing tighter around her neck.

"No, they're not, but I noticed them, so tell me who the lucky guy is."

"He's amazing."

"Amazing like he wears a cape or amazing in bed?"

"Haven't seen him in a cape, but trust me, he could rock most anything. He's a psychologist at Lifespan, but I'm not advertising that we're getting pretty damn serious since I really want to intern there next year."

"If you get the internship, I vow to forever tell everyone that you slept your way to the top."

"I feel certain you will." Holly and Beth both dissolved in a fit of laughter. "No, but seriously, I don't want Treavor 'the asswipe' Singleton to have anything to say about my degree or how I got it."

"Agreed. You know I'd never tell anyone. I'm excited for you. I know it sounds silly, but you look in love."

"It's not silly. I *am* in love. It's complicated though."

"Aren't all good things? We need a girl's night so I can hear more about your out-of-cape superhero."

"Beth, he's unlike any other guy I have ever been around. Dec is serious and smart and so damn sexy. Perfect mix of bad boy with a heart of gold. He makes idiots like Singleton look like a toddler."

Beth's eyes goggled, and she shook her head frantically.

"What?" Holly spun in the booth to see Dr. Singleton Sr. taking one of the tables nearby. *Crap.* She was going to have to learn to keep her mouth shut.

CHAPTER TWENTY-THREE

"No. I'm sorry, sir, I simply cannot accept a position at the University. My patients need me," Dec continued to insist, though it was getting him nowhere.

"Need we remind you, Dr. St. James, that your work visa is tied to this practice? Teaching hours count towards your supervised professional experience hours required to be fully licensed to practice here in the States. This is the perfect opportunity. You were a guest scholar at several of the fancier universities in London. This shouldn't be difficult. We'll be paying your salary still, and Dr. Newsome from UN-L has added in a very nice bonus for you serving as a visiting professor for the year." Gibbons wasn't backing down.

Summoning herculean restraint, Dec refused the words he so desperately wanted to pierce Gibbons' sweaty visage. *You're doing this because you don't want me here, and you don't want me here because I make you look like the piece of shit you really are.*

"What about my ongoing patients?"

"That is a legitimate concern, Gibbons." Corrigan seemed to have located some fragment of his soul in the last half-hour. "How about this, as long as you can work it around the class schedule they've assigned you can see any patients you have time to see."

"At the University. Not here," Gibbons decreed.

Mother fucking jizz-trumpet.

Every argument he'd tried had been denied. This wasn't going away. Dec flipped through the standard visiting scholar contract on his desk until his eyes landed on the words *Ethics Codes and Violations Agreement.* His breath seized in his lungs. Bile lodged in his throat. He somehow wished he was surprised, but he wasn't. Nothing good ever remained in his life. He never deserved for it to. He was nothing more than an addict with a record and two deaths that would forever damn his soul.

He read the line: Visiting Professors and Scholars shall not fraternize, keep company with, or have any romantic involvement with an enrolled student *while student is in their class.* Hope sprang anew from the depths of his despair. There was a chance, a slim chance, but a chance none the less that Holly wouldn't be one of his students. Maybe he wouldn't even see her on campus. He knew he didn't deserve the prayer he silently offered. *Just please, let me have her. I'll never ask for anything else. I never really have.* He'd never even asked for help with his addictions, but he knew he had no hope of existing without her. His conquering angel. His saving grace. All he'd ever needed when every other quest had been nothing more than a want, no matter how badly he'd fucked that up.

He read the rest of the clause. 'If any inappropriate relationship develops with a current student and is reported, the University of Nebraska has the right to expulse professor, file a formal complaint within the American University System and the visiting professor's home institution, and seek arrest if any laws in the state of Nebraska have been broken. They also hold the right to withdraw student, deny stipend payments, scholarships, or any other financial aid, and withhold all funding to either professor or student.'

Deep breaths. The lyrics to Holly's song played in his head. *I want to dance in your light*

Affect the chemistry of my longest night Vanquish the darkness in the heat of your sun

Let your touch give me sight.

As long as she wasn't in any of his classes, he could survive. He could do this. He'd taught before. He hadn't even sucked at it. It was only a year, and it guaranteed his visa for longer than that. Who knew what he and Holly would look like in a year? Taunting images of her in a white gown stabbed through him.

Ridiculous. She deserves someone so much better. You'll always be a user, and when this blows up in your face too, you'll go right back to the lines.

No. Not this time. He refused the craving for the tenth time that morning alone. He had to remember he could never exist in years. He only survived moment to moment, and as he'd discovered recently, he only survived if those moments contained her.

He accepted the Cross pen Corrigan thrust in his face. As he signed the contract, he swore the weight of the pen was heavier than the weight of Evie's gravestone. God, he hated pens. Their permanence. Their heartless cruelty. Their inability to be undone.

He would not ruin Holly's life. He'd rather end it all right now than do anything that might keep her from everything she deserved. With the strike of the ruthless instrument, he made one more prayer that he wouldn't even see her on campus. Somehow, he knew he would never be that lucky.

"Did you hear about the visiting professor?" Beth slid into the desk beside Holly in the lecture hall where their two o'clock *Modern Foundations of Human Sexuality* was being held. They sat fourth row, center just like every other class.

"Beth, how the hell do you hear everything?"

Beth's cheeks pinked as she shrugged. "I have really good hearing, and I grew up in the middle of nowhere where absolutely nothing ever happened. I got very adept at listening to my grandma and mom talk on the phone. I'm an expert eavesdropper, basically, but I swear I only use my powers for good."

Holly shook her head. "I promise not to hold it against you."

"Thanks. There's a reason you're my friend. Anyway, the new professor is apparently ripped, tattooed, and completely freaking gorgeous. Also, he's British."

A sinking feeling weighted Holly to the ancient cushioned seat though she couldn't fathom why. "That does not at all sound like the kind of professors UN generally hires."

"I know. That's why this is so exciting. I ate lunch over at Union and the two girls sitting behind me were calling him Professor Sex."

"I can honestly say I don't care. I have my own Professor Sex, and I don't want anything else."

"Well, we can't all be that fortunate. Be happy for me. At least we have something good to look at during the two hour lectures."

"Fine, I'm happy for you. Now, do you want to partner up for Standson's Psycho Anal Fun project?"

Beth giggled hysterically. "I seriously cannot believe the University abbreviates Psychology Analysis and Functions to that on our schedules, but I do appreciate the laugh, and of course."

"Get this, Single-ass texted me and asked me to team up with him," Holly rolled her eyes.

"Not surprised. He knows you'll get the top grade and I still say he has crush on you, or maybe he wants to try out psycho anal fun with you."

Holly gagged. "Never say that out loud again. He has a crush on not doing any work and still getting an A. He's a douchebag and he's never getting anywhere near my anal fun."

"A whale-sized douchebag."

A half-second later the whale douchebag himself entered the lecture hall and took the seat directly behind Holly and Beth.

"Holly," he sneered. "I just talked to my father and he said you'd declared your specialty as Sexual Psychology. That has got to be a joke, right? I'm pretty sure cows don't need you to talk them through mating season. What are you going to do with a specialty in sex?"

Holly spun in her seat, wishing the fire surging through her veins could shoot out of her eyes. "Oh, I don't know, Singleton, deconstruct your entire social reality. Here, let me begin with — cattle do not have a mating season, dumbass. How are you even a doctoral student? Oh, right, Daddy's head is stuck all the way up Dr. Newsome's ass."

A wave of hush silenced the chatter in the lecture hall. When Holly spun around, she almost fell out of her seat. What. The. Actual. Fuck?

Her mouth hung open stupidly as she watched Dec set a laptop case down on the desk at the front of the hall. He glanced her way, pale like he'd just encountered a ghost. Holly's heart stalled. This just couldn't be.

He took entirely too long settling into the classroom. A hiss of intrigue rose from few of the women in the class seated nearby. Holly couldn't breathe. She could barely even see.

"Holly? Are you okay?" Beth whispered frantically. She pressed her hand to Holly's arm, either checking for fever or pulse. Neither of which currently felt present. Her traitorous eyes refused to look anywhere but at him. This had to be some kind of dream. Trying to pinch herself, she twisted Beth's skin instead. Beth jerked her hand away and stared at Holly like she'd lost her mind.

"Good afternoon, I'm Dr. Declan St. James, visiting professor from Lifespan Counseling. This is *Modern Foundations of Human Sexuality.* Your syllabi are available online, but I'm passing back a paper copy. For the purposes of this class all notes, papers, and tests will be turned in written in pencil."

Holly slunk down in her seat. No amount of squeezing her eyes shut seemed to be working. She willed Dr. Benders resurrection.

Singleton's hand shot upwards.

"You already have a question?" Dec's voice was harrowed and distant. It carried a note of death in its tone. Fear crawled up Holly's spine. What did this mean? What was he thinking? When had this happened? Obviously, he'd been assigned Bender's classes but. . . ? No. Just no. She'd left for the weekend, and he'd come unglued. He wasn't equipped for this. It was cruel. Suddenly, Holly understood for the first time in her life that there was something she wanted more than this degree, and he was standing at the front of her classroom.

"Look, I don't know how they do it in jolly Ol'England or wherever the hell you're from, but here in the U.S. we have these handy dandy things called computers. No one uses pencils anymore."

"Singleton, right?"

"Isn't it obvious?" Trevor postured for Dec. Holly would have laughed at Dec's responding glare, but her entire world was crashing around her currently.

"Pencils make it far more difficult for students like yourself to purchase your papers online, and it is my personal belief that you should be able to make mistakes."

His eyes landed on hers with that declaration. No. No, no, no. She was not a mistake. *They* were not a mistake. This was not over. The devastation that weighted his entire body cut through her like a frozen dagger.

"Holly, what is wrong?" Beth was more audible this time. Dec pretended not to notice. He moved back to the front. Whatever he was saying, Holly had no hope of making out the words. They drowned in the nauseous pit that had once been her stomach. Discreetly fishing her phone out of her purse, it took her less than five minutes to locate the University policies page on the college website.

The words, "If any inappropriate relationship develops with a current student and is reported, the University retains the right to withdraw the student, deny stipend payments, scholarships, and any other financial aid, and withhold all funding to either professor or student. . . ," levied another blow to her soul. Her parents could more than afford to send her to school without her stipend, but she was an adult and would never ask them for that. Besides, they already helped her out with books and groceries. Being expelled from a university meant she would likely never be able to attend another college.

Making no attempts at being discreet, Beth leaned over the arm of her own desk to see the screen of Holly's phone. It took her less than two full seconds to realize what was going on.

"He's. . . ?" Her eyes were the size of dinner plates.

Holly managed a nod.

"Oh my God."

Another nod.

At some point class ended. Holly couldn't decide if it had lasted five minutes or five hours. Nothing made sense to her. Time was oddly variable. Had Dec talked the entire time? Beth elbowed her when half of the lecture hall had emptied. "What are you going to do?"

Unable to formulate coherent sentences, Holly stood and forced her feet to move towards him. He was packing up his laptop and doing a damn good job of ignoring her completely.

"Dec. . . ." she choked.

He lifted his head. His eyes were almost black in their pleading desperation. She noted a slight shake of his head.

"It's Dr. St. James. If you have any questions about the class that can't be found in the syllabus, see one of the department assistants." With that, he grabbed his bag and left her rooted to the carpeted flooring.

"Damn." Beth reached to steady Holly, who hadn't yet figured out why the world was shaking. "Guess you know where he stands on breaking University ethics codes."

Doubling down on her refusal to cry, Holly shook her head. "No. This isn't over." With that, she marched out of the room. She'd think of something. There had to be a way to make this work.

CHAPTER TWENTY-FOUR

The agony in Holly's beautiful eyes would remain forever burned in Dec's mind. He'd dismissed her. He'd sent away what was probably the love of his life. One never recovered from that. His heart that she'd so recently begun to stitch back together shattered into a million irreparable pieces.

He sat at his newly minted desk in a third-floor office in the Psychological Sciences building and pulled up her student information. Invasion of privacy, hell yeah, but she was all he could think about, and he didn't have another class to teach for fifteen more minutes. He needed something to do lest he drive in loops around campus seeking the dealers that inevitably lurked nearby.

Two of his students smelled distinctly of pot. There had to be something stronger somewhere.

Her student ID photo appeared on his screen. *Dear God, she's only twenty-three.* His brilliant cowgirl had completed her Masters in under two years. He was ten years older than her. What the hell had he been thinking? How had he not known that?

A sleek, black truck with no tag circled the student parking lot again, driving entirely too slow. Tell-tale sign of a dealer if ever there was one. The weight of all he'd lost magnified the intensity of his cravings ten-fold with every breath he managed.

He had his wallet in his hand a half second later. *Dammit.* He had no cash. Of course, this was the very reason he never carried any cash. When he'd started making more money than he knew what to do with after he'd graduated, he'd carefully fixed it so he bought everything on a credit card and paid the bill at the end of the month. Dealers did not accept credit that didn't come in the form of sex.

His hands shook badly enough to remind him of his walk into rehab.

You know you're fighting a losing battle. Be easier to give in now. That truck's nice. Bet he's got good stuff.

No. Whatever was going to happen, he had to fight harder. Matt was coming for a session at five. Matt needed him to be clean. He had to do something. His cell phone dropped from his hands to his desk. Steadying his grip, he picked it up and touched Kade's name.

"Hey, man, was just about to call you. Got a potential gig tomorrow night. Some bar in Omaha. Be a drive, but it's good money."

"No."

Kade's tone changed instantly. "Dec? What's wrong?"

"Can you come to the campus and pick me up at 6:00? I'm. . .I don't need to be in charge of where I drive."

"You high?"

"No. But that's a distinct possibility."

"Ah, hell, Dec you know better. Never campus. Campuses are not a good idea."

"Yeah, I fucking know that, but I had no choice. Long fucked up story of my fucking life."

"Got it. How 'bout I head that way now?"

"I have to teach a fucking class."

"What?"

"I'll explain later."

"Look there. That was one sentence without an f-bomb. You can do this, whatever it is. I'll be there soon. Where am I coming exactly?"

"Psychology Sciences building. I have no fucking clue where it is exactly. I could barely see when I drove in."

"I'll find you. No parking lots, okay?"

"Yeah. I know."

Four hours later, Kade was pacing in Dec's living room. Dec's head was in his hands, and he hated life hard. "I cannot even put into words how much I already love her. Love her like she makes the cravings weaker than they've ever been. Love her like I would gladly lay down my life to keep her safe. I sleep, Kade. I bloody fucking sleep when she's in my arms. You of all people have to understand what that means."

"I do, Dec. You bought her four coffee makers." He gestured to the boxes lining the kitchen counters. "You not only love her, but you love her to excess, and I still see no reason why you two can't see each other on the sly. Who the hell would find out? Who even cares? She may be young, but she's legal. It ain't anyone's business but the two of you. You didn't even want this job. Fuck Gibbons. This entire thing is ridiculous. You said she has a 4.0. She probably doesn't even need your class. It's rules like this that were made to be broken."

"I will not ruin her life. She deserves better anyway. Just don't let me do anything stupid."

"I'm not going anywhere. You want me to find another meeting?"

"No, I can't be around anymore people. Not now. Maybe not ever. How fucking long do I have to be punished for Evie? I'm just damned forever, I suppose."

"You're not damned, and for the thousandth time, what happened to Evie wasn't your fault. Was it shitty? Hell yeah. But she did that all on her own. It wasn't the bad hash that did her in. It was the 500mg of Smack she shot up before you ever got there."

"Have you ever been crazy in love with someone you were just forbidden to see?" Dec didn't care for rationalizations. He wanted to feel sorry for himself. The most dangerous way for an addict to feel.

"Okay, I know this is rough, man, but are you seriously asking *me* that? I got kicked out of my house when I was fifteen just for the *idea* of loving someone forbidden."

"Sorry." Yeah, he was an asshole of epic proportions.

The front door shook under the force of a knock. Kade's eyes goggled. "Tell me you do not have anything in this house, and if you do, tell me where it is so I can flush it."

Dec rolled his eyes. "There's nothing here. That's why you're here, so nothing gets here. It's not the cops. Just send whoever it is away."

Holly pounded on Dec's front door with enough vigor to break the damn thing down. She'd peeked in the garages. His SUV and bike were here. There was an old Camaro that she didn't recognize in the driveway, too. He had to be inside and they were going to talk.

She raised her fist to pound again when the door swung open.

"Kade, what are you doing here?"

"Holly, thank God. Maybe you can talk some sense into him."

Dec appeared. If she'd thought he looked haggard and raw the night he finally told her his story, it was nothing compared to the anguish that marred his face that night. "Holly, baby, you can't be here. Please tell me no one saw you drive up."

Narrowing her eyes, she stepped inside, pushing Kade out of her way. "I'll take it from here, Kade."

"I'm all about you stepping in and talking some sense into him, sweet thang, but have you ever dealt with him when he's itching bad for a fix?"

"No, I haven't, but I'll learn to deal. Have you ever slept with him?"

Kade's laughter further bolstered her courage. "All I'm saying, man, is she's worth breaking a few stupid rules for."

"We, *we* are worth breaking a few ridiculous rules for," Holly corrected.

"Holly, I will not do anything that will ruin your life or your plans for your life. I won't. You could lose your stipend. You could get expelled."

Mustering every bit of resolve she'd ever hoped to have, she leaned in, gripped the reins, and took the leap. "*You* are my plans for my life, Dec. You and only you. There I said it. I'm in love with you, and I will not let some decree that was written in 1869 decide that I cannot be with the man I love. I won't."

Kade, at least, looked very pleased.

"I'm not sure you've seen me in full-on cowgirl mode, so stand back." She marched into the living room, followed by Dec and Kade. Spinning around she met a quick glance shared between the two men. Dec was trying not to grin, so they were getting somewhere.

With a deep breath, she went on with what she'd come to say. "I spent all afternoon in the library. There have been four instances since the founding of the school, where a professor and a student were dating and it was reported. In two of the cases both were either fired or kicked out." Dec opened his mouth to speak, but she held up her finger to stop him.

"Both cases took place before 1967. The other one, which took place in the nineties, neither the student nor the teacher were kicked out, but the visiting professor did return to his original job early. Two years ago an acquaintance of mine, Emma Barrett, threw herself at Dr. Singleton because he has an affair with one of his students every single semester. She wanted him caught and kicked out. She actually uploaded their sex tape to the internet, but things didn't go according to plan. She got kicked out. He was never named because his wife also sits on the board. Therefore, there is no recent precedence to suggest that even if we were caught, which we will not be, that it would be detrimental to either of our goals at the school."

"You know, I think she's got this. I'm gonna go. If either of you need me, call me." Kade grabbed Holly's cell phone out of the front pocket of her purse and entered his contact information before he made his way back to the door.

"Holly, honey, believe me, if there was any way we could ensure that we wouldn't get caught I would be all over it, but there's a lot more at stake here than you realize."

With her frustration rising like a thermometer in a pot of boiling water, Holly ground her teeth. "What don't I understand then?"

"If we continue to see each other and were to get caught, I would not only lose the professorship, which I don't even want nor did I ask for, I would also lose my job at Lifespan. My boss despises me. He's been looking for a reason to sack me since I was hired. The job at Life-span is what my work visa is tied to. If I lose my job, sweetheart, I have to go back to the UK and never return."

"What?"

"On top of all of that, I will not let you be reckless with your life."

"I like reckless."

He shook his head. "Does it bother you at all that I am thirty-three and you are twenty-three."

"No. Well, I mean I didn't know that, but it doesn't bother me. Am I going to get lectured about being too young, too?"

Dec's eyes closed in what Holly sincerely hoped was defeat. "I would never blame you for your lack of age or experience, sweetheart. What kind of asshole would I be if I held indefensible things against you? You have your entire life ahead of you. Just forget about me. I'm not worth any of this."

"No." Defiance lit through her. "No, I will not forget about this or you ever. We won't get caught. How would we? We're not stupid. No flirting on or near campus. No going out together. It's only for one semester."

"You don't know that. I have no idea what I'll be teaching next semester, and do you really want to be in a relationship where I can't even be seen with you?"

"I'm standing here looking at you right now."

"Yes, but you shouldn't be."

"You don't believe that."

"No, I don't, but this seems to be how I'm destined to live my life. With everything that makes it worth living out of my reach."

"I'm not out of reach," her voice strangled over everything that had happened, everything she felt slipping through her fingers. "I'm not a mistake, Dec." She just wasn't strong enough. Tears burned brutal paths down her cheeks.

"Sweetheart, no. Please don't cry." As soon as his arms were around her, the incoming doubts fled again. She knew this was worth fighting for. She knew he was her future. "You are never a mistake. I am the mistake. I will always be the mistake. That's what I meant when I said that."

"But you're not. We're not a mistake. Just please don't push me away. I need you."

He planted a kiss on top of her head, and she forced herself to lift her head from his chest. She knew he wasn't convinced. He was placating to keep her from crying.

"I need you to be my future, Dec. I don't care if it's only been a week. I've never felt like this with anyone else and I never will. Never. I need you more than you even know. More than I've told you. It's more than just being in love with you.

"I can't even look my own father in the eye and tell him I'm going to be a sex therapist. I don't have any idea how to do what it is I've thrown myself into doing. I have so many questions. There are so many things I don't understand. Things about myself. Things about the way you make me feel. Fantasies I want you to fulfill. The things I long for you to do to me and with me. Please, please don't let some stupid rule keep us apart. It isn't fair. I need you. You may not believe this now, but someday I'll show you, *you* are my future. I know it. And you know what else, if we do get caught and everything blows up around us, I'll go back to London with you. That is how much I believe in us."

CHAPTER TWENTY-FIVE

Dec could have told her she wasn't thinking straight or that she was being overly emotional. Hell, he could have told her that she just wasn't old enough to have the cynicism required to understand why this was a terrible idea, why *he* was a terrible idea. But he couldn't access any of those words. He couldn't lie to her, and somewhere deep in the recesses of his soul, he knew she was right. It had taken every ounce of strength housed in his ample musculature to rebuke her earlier in the day. He couldn't do it again. He just didn't have the strength. His heart, which he'd noted seemed to have returned to its cage as soon as she was back in his arms, wouldn't allow it.

Her tears pierced his skin like jagged blades, yet suddenly he could breathe. Every tremble of her body shook his soul, yet he felt whole for the first time since early that morning. And the burning craving that slithered constantly beneath his skin, resided in defeat. The demons recognized their warden. He would never allow her to go to London with him for any reason. There were far too many crypts in London where he might fall. Together, they would make this work.

"When I was in rehab, one of my counselors used to say that life is just like walking a tightrope. You can run across it or you can take it slowly, calculating each step. The only thing you can't do is stand still.

We don't have to stand still, but I need you to understand that I cannot go back to London for so many reasons, but the number one reason is that I cannot be that far away from you. No flirting in class just because it would be fun. We take no chances. None at all. I cannot lose you, Holly." She shuddered against him, and he held her tighter. "By the way, I love you, too."

"Promise?" she managed in a timid squeak.

Smiling was such an odd feeling given his day, but a broad grin spread the width of his face. "Promise. And I really like your cowgirl side. I'd like to see a lot more of that."

"That can definitely be arranged."

"I was hoping. We have to have some rules, if you're sure you want to do this."

"I doubt everything in my life, Dec. I always have. I second guess things. Should I give up on getting my doctorate and go back to the ranch because so much of me is in that land? Should I sell my portion of the ranch to my family and move here permanently? Once I graduate and get a job, I won't be able to work the ranch anymore, and that kills me. I never want to leave the ranch, but I want to be a therapist. I have no idea what I want to do moment to moment, but I swear to you I have not one single doubt about you and me."

Every word washed over him in a healing tide, mending his battered soul, suturing his heart, curing him. The moment two orderlies who'd been almost a foot shorter than him had to help him walk into that rehab facility sizzled up his spine. A mix of spite and grit surged through his veins. He would fight. He would be everything she needed him to be. He wouldn't let the world take her from him. No more. He owed it to her. He owed it to himself to be happy. He had to stop existing in Evie's tomb. Whether he'd put her there or not, he was still here, alive, and she wasn't. It was time to stop merely existing and really live, and his redemption was staring up at him with tear-stained eyes, holding out her hand, ready to carry him back to the land of the living. All he had to do was reach out for her.

"Let me have your keys," he instructed as he tried to ensure that this decision wouldn't cast both of their lives on the pyre.

"Why?" She supplied her truck keys.

"I'm going to pull it in my garage. Your truck is very recognizable. No one can see you over here, and I certainly cannot come to your apartment. You're too close to campus, too many students must live there."

"Okay, I could borrow another truck from the ranch. We have several spares."

"If you're seen driving it ever, it shouldn't be seen at my house. I hate the idea of this, but we probably shouldn't see each other except on the weekends. Your truck needs to be in your parking lot every night. You need to keep going out and doing things college students do. Suspicion is an extremely dangerous thing."

"Fine, but I'm a doctoral student. We do nothing but study. Ever."

Dec had to grin at that. "Then go wherever other people go and study." The words singed his throat. He never wanted her out of arm's length, but he would learn to deal with it. He had to.

"But I. . . ."

He placed his finger over her mouth. "My stubborn little cowgirl, I do love you, but we have to play by the rules."

"Fine," she sighed. "But I'm already here. Can I please stay tonight? I need to stay. I'll leave early, drive all over town, go back home so when I go to campus I'll be coming from my apartment. No one will know."

"I don't know any of my neighbors, sweetheart. The Dean could be living in this neighborhood. I have no idea."

"The chancellor lives much closer to campus in the historic district. Three of the other deans live out there, too. I've attended events at their homes. The rest of them could see me driving out of here and would have no idea who I am. I only know the Psychology department."

"You could take the Pilot. I drove the bike today so no one at the University has seen it. You can just have it."

"I don't want to take your car, Dec. I'm not actually sure how long you've lived here, but very, very soon it's going to be colder than a witch's tit with four feet of snow on the ground minimum. Your bike is going to be useless until Spring, and everyone knows my truck. It would be far more weird for me to show up in a different car. Besides, I only drive trucks. I will only ever drive trucks."

"It is unfortunate when your stubbornness makes sense."

Holly's laugh filled him once again. "Why is that?"

"Because how will I ever talk you into anything?"

With one single step forward, she wrapped her arms around him again, and he knew he was home. "You'll have to be very persuasive and use all of your God-given talents and gifts."

The gift she was referencing was rather pleased with this arrangement. It swelled its approval.

"When I get back from moving your truck, we're going to talk about those talents and gifts, and you're going to tell me all of these things you're afraid of and the fantasies I'm going to fulfill."

Dammit. She had said that out loud, hadn't she? Holly watched Dec stride purposefully through his kitchen to the garage. Now she was in for it. He wouldn't let her get away with backing out. *You made it this far. Don't chicken out now.*

He returned, sporting that smirk that sizzled across her skin, and took up residence between her thighs. "Pretty sure you were going to win weren't you, darling?" He held up the duffle bag she'd haphazardly packed and her laptop bag with her books.

"I don't like to lose, and also I was freaking out during your entire class so I have no idea what you told us to do. Might need my boyfriend to go over that again."

His dark chuckle returned, and her heart sprinted towards her throat. "I will be happy to help you with your school work, love, but I can't just give you A's on everything. That would look particularly bad. As for today, I have abso-bloody-lutely no clue what I said either. All I could think about was how fucked up my life was. I spent most of class trying not to remember the lyrics to *Under the Bridge,* and wishing I could kiss the heartbroken look off of your face, pick you up in my arms, and run away."

"Channeling Kiedis were you?"

"Trying my damnedest not to."

"He did get clean though."

"Eventually, but that song is sort of how much harder life is when you're clean."

"I know."

"I'm almost certain I didn't assign anything today, which now that I think about it was an incredibly stupid thing to do given that this is a doctorate level class. I didn't know if you needed this tonight for one of your other classes." He lifted the laptop bag before setting it on his sofa.

"I'm taking three classes this semester because yours is my first research class. I haven't been to Statistics yet. I do have a project for Anal Fun that I'm doing with Beth, though."

"Please tell me that you are not actually taking a class called anal fun, and if you are, tell me how I can become the professor for said class."

All of the tension and despair that had been pent up inside of her, escaped in her hysterical laughter. Her emotions were on a death-defying rollercoaster that evening. Another round of tears, this time from joy, cascaded down her face. Dec hadn't stopped smiling since they'd made their decision. It was risky and reckless. She could never deny that, but she also didn't care. Making him smile like that was worth it.

When she regained a little control, she wiped her eyes and nodded. "It's actually Psychology Analysis and Functions, but on our schedules they abbreviate it to Psycho Anal Fun."

"I should probably point that out to Newsome, but that is simply too good to spoil."

"We get so little. Don't take away what we have."

"Never. Now, tell me, did you pack anything more comfortable to wear since you knew I was a weak bastard that would never turn you down?"

"I packed my sluttiest lingerie. I was prepared to pull out all of the stops if I had to."

"Damn, I should've held out longer. Come here to me." Dec lifted her into his arms as if she were weightless. Currently, she felt like she might be. He carried her upstairs to his room and peeled away the layers of clothing concealing her.

His eyes held darkened need and white hot fire as he stared at her naked. She fought the urge to cover herself.

"So, damned gorgeous." His hands raced over her flesh like he couldn't decide where to touch her first. "We're going to talk, but I spent this entire endless day convinced I would never be able to touch you again. Just let me get a fix of you. You're irresistible."

She shuddered as he slipped behind her to cup her breasts, letting them spill through his fingers. His left hand glided downward to her bare mound.

"All mine. All for me. You're sure that's what you want? I'm a greedy bastard, Holly. I will always be an addict. I will always take what I want when we're together."

"Yes. I told you, that's what I need. I want that more than anything." She swayed against him. The rough denim of his jeans taunted her ass. She felt empty, a need only he could fill.

"Needy, baby? Say the word, and I'll make it feel better." He knew she was. The wet heat slicked the lips of her vulva, swelling them. He could feel her need.

"Please."

"Please what?"

"Touch me."

The calluses on his fingertips abraded her tender skin. Her arousal perfumed the air. She wanted to be embarrassed at her own desperation, but his deep inhalation of breath was coupled with a growl of approval.

"I am touching you, love." He circled her mound. "Tell me *where* to touch you."

"Dec, please. Touch me everywhere. Touch me in places no one else has ever touched. Make me feel things no one else will ever make me feel."

She stared in the mirror and knew she'd made her point. His eyes darkened with every slip of his control. Suddenly, she was back in his arms being laid on his bed. The cool, rumpled sheets against her fevered body carried his musk to her lungs. "Spread your legs for me. Keep them open. Do as I say, and I'll make it feel better."

"Yes," quaked through her as she complied.

He traced up and down her inner thighs. Liquid desire seeped from her slit. She could feel herself weep for him.

"Fuck it, I was just going to get you off, but you're too damned tempting. I need a taste." His tongue lapped up her juices. She ground against his face until he pulled away.

"Be still and let me give you this. Then, we are going to talk."

With that he ran his left hand over his mouth, ridding himself of her flavors, and dipped two fingers deep in her channel.

"Jesus, you're so tight. Drives me wild."

Holly trembled against his force as he pounded his fingers in and out, giving her what she needed to come.

When his other hand caressed her ass, she cried out for him, hoping he'd understand her desire for more without her having to say it.

"Like that, don't you, baby? So many things to discuss." He plied her flesh and then teased the puckered opening of her backside.

Pleasure pervaded every cell of her body as he drained the tension and the terror from her with the masterful strokes of his hands. Her pussy began its frantic rhythmic flexes.

"You're so close aren't you? I can feel it coming. Tell me what you need, sweetheart."

"You. Please. Harder," she whimpered.

"You beg so sweet. Makes me crazy." He pumped into her harder and faster, driving her closer to the edge with every pass.

"Please, please." She would do most anything to make him understand the power he held over her. She met his every forceful stroke, undulating against him.

"Who do you belong to?"

"You."

"And who's going to let you come?"

"Oh God, you."

"Good girl. When I bring you, I want to hear how good it feels."

Constant pressure coiled behind her mound until pure pleasure and relief unfurled as she cinched tightly around his fingers, quaking and writhing in his bed. She called out for him, and he eased his strokes as she came hard and fast.

When she finally stilled, she stared up at him. He leaned and cleaned her once again with his mouth like he simply couldn't get enough of her.

She sat up, intent on returning the favor, but he caught her hand as she stroked over the steel-hard bulge in his jeans. "Not until we talk. Every dark fantasy. Every question you have. Every thought you're scared to own. They all belong to me now. I want to hear them. I'm going to own them. Then, when we're finished talking, I'll show you a few of mine. The first being taking you so hard you feel me with every single step you take tomorrow and remember who you belong to."

CHAPTER TWENTY-SIX

Dec shed his shirt and jeans and crawled into bed beside her. He still couldn't believe she was there, that she was his. As long as they were careful, never taking any risks, there was no reason he couldn't have her and keep his job. If only the little devils that occasionally darkened her angelic eyes didn't like to play with matches, he might've really believed that.

He pushed his worry away. There were far more important things to focus on. Things she was feigning exhaustion trying to get out of. Propping up the half dozen pillows he owned, he seated her between his outstretched legs with her back against his chest and covered them loosely in the sheets and blankets.

"So, we're just going to talk naked?"

"There could not possibly be a better way to have most any conversation with you, but most certainly one of this nature. I'm a sex therapist, love. Trust me, you're not going to tell me anything I haven't heard."

"Yeah, but I'm assuming you've never slept with your patients as that is absolutely unethical, so this is very different."

"Unethical like sleeping with my student?"

"That isn't unethical. We're in love, and when we started sleeping together you were not my professor."

"Pretty sure that reasoning would not stand up in court."

"We're not going to trial."

"You are aware that sexual fantasy is something you're going to hear a great deal about in the profession you are currently obtaining a degree for, right?"

"Yeah, but I keep hoping I'll handle other people's fantasies better than I handle my own."

"Holly, baby, you're making me feel like a predator forcing this from you. Come on. I do understand that this is far more intimate than sex, but intimacy like this is what was meant to be shared between partners. You've done the very thing you said you want to fight against. You've let society dictate to you what is and is not okay to want."

"I know. I told you, half the time I want to drop out and go back to being a cowgirl full time. I'm obviously not cut out for this."

"Hey, that is not at all what I meant." He kept his hands gently tending her. She calmed as long as he soothed her. "Let me help you."

"I could listen to you tell me what you want us to do and be wildly turned on. I can listen to my friends talk about kinky things they want to try, and it doesn't bother me at all. It's just when it comes to myself, I panic."

"You panic because you feel like you'll be judged, and because this country has done such a fantastic job of making women believe that sex should look like it came directly out of a movie script or should be nothing more than a grind session with someone you'll never see again relegating it to a meaningless task no one actually enjoys.

"Making love is meant to exist on a different plane. Somewhere between the harshness of reality and the softness of our best dreams. But women feel guilty for having pleasure. Sex is supposed to be a place to explore and to trust the person you're sharing it with, deepening the relationship. What all of that means is I need to create a safer space for us to explore the private recesses of your mind. What can I do, honey? What can I do to prove to you that I would never betray you or your desires? To show you that you have absolutely nothing to be ashamed of? I do love you. You know that?"

She turned her head to stare up at him. "I do. I feel so safe with you. Just let me get my thoughts straight, and I'll tell you."

"Whenever you're ready."

"I feel like it might all come out in a bizarre jumble of words."

Dec tucked a few hairs behind her ear. The heat of her climax still clung to her cheeks and her body was soft against him. He'd been intent on hearing the words come out of her mouth, but the need to protect her at all cost was far too consuming.

"How about we start at the top?"

"What does that even mean?"

"This is where it's handy to date a sex therapist." He winked at her simply to watch the grin that always made her eyes dance when he did that.

"Handy or hand-sy?"

"Touche, Ms. Camden." He stroked her thighs. "Shall we begin your love map?"

"I don't know what we're doing, but I do know about Money's love map concept." A little of her confidence had been restored and the sparks of curiosity had returned to her eyes.

"Money did good work. Now, from the top, eighty-five percent of women fantasize about having sex in a romantic place."

Holly rolled her eyes. "That seems fairly obvious. Mine is more like sex in a cozy, romantic place, where you sort of baby me. I just kind of lay there and you know what to do, and. . .you tell me that you'll take care of me, but it's also like I'm there to be the object of all of your attention. Also occasionally blends into my virgin fantasy."

"Now, we're getting somewhere." Dec memorized every detail. Once he got her started, she'd jumped right in. Maybe he hadn't done such a shitty job of creating a safe sanctuary for her.

He fought the erection currently pressing against her tail bone, but it was useless, and they'd only just begun. "The virgin fantasy where you have the perfect first sexual encounter with a far more experienced partner, in the romantic locale with me playing the knight in shining armor?"

"Not exactly."

"Please elaborate."

"I'm far more interested in the bad boy showing me all that I've missed out on than I've ever been in a knight in shining armor."

"Oh, honey, believe me, I don't have to *play* the bad boy. I'm the real deal."

"Why the hell do you think I fell so hard for you so fast?"

"You're killing me."

"I could take care of that for you." She reached her hand back between them to stroke his engorged cock.

"I'm gonna let you take care of me. Have no doubt. But right now I have several more fantasies to get through. Tell me, do they get dirtier, baby?"

"Much, much dirtier."

"Good. You seem to like going down on me. I'm adding that to the map."

"With instruction," she added quickly.

A low, hungry growl crawled up his throat and sounded in her ear. Perfection. She was absolutely perfection. "Speaking of that, nearly seventy percent of women fantasize about being dominated. Do you fit into the majority, sweetheart?" He already knew the answer, but he needed to hear her say it.

"Pretty sure you already knew that, but yes. I fantasize about that a lot."

"So, you wouldn't mind hearing *my bed, my rules* then?"

The tender tremble of her fevered body spoke volumes. "I'd really like that."

"Done. How about the other way around? Want to tie me up and have your way with me or make me beg and then deny me?"

"Maybe. Would you let me if I wanted to?"

"Most definitely. You know wanting to be dominated is a completely normal, healthy desire, right?"

"Yeah, I know, just feels odd asking for it."

"Bondage?"

"Yes."

"Psycho Anal Fun?"

With that she dissolved in another fit of giggles. "Maybe without the psycho part."

"Excellent amendment, my love, and I have noticed that you seem to enjoy my hands being on your delectable ass." He squeezed both of her cheeks, making her wiggle against him. "I highly suspect you might like to be spanked."

"I noticed you stopped giving me the percentages of women who share these fantasies. I take it I'm now in the minority."

"You dodge like a pro, but it doesn't matter. *Your* fantasies are my only concern. There are no fantasies that are wrong to have. Their individuality is what needs to be explored personally."

"All right, fine, yes, I've definitely dreamed about you spanking me. Since the first time we slept together when you said something about it beforehand I've wanted you to do that."

"My hands or some kind of instrumentation?"

"When I think about you doing it, you just use your hands. I kind of think if you hit me with anything I'd remove your spleen via your throat."

"Ah, there's my cowgirl. Glad I asked. I'm pretty sure I'm using my spleen."

"I get to ask questions, too."

"Of course."

"What do you fantasize about doing with me?"

"I told you, they come by the dozens. Got off in the shower while you were back home thinking about you tied to my bed with a blindfold on, while I took everything I wanted."

"Wow."

"But that can all remain in my head, or heads as the case may be, if you don't care for that."

"I do. I mean, the blindfold, everything. I want to try it all. I'm tired of understanding the concepts but having no actual experience with them."

Holly had no idea how she was verbalizing any of this. He'd once again shattered all of her barriers. She felt safe. Shocked at herself, but safe.

"I shouldn't ask, but I have to. How about role playing? Perhaps professor and student?"

Laughing at the very odd predicament they'd managed to land in, she nodded. "Yeah, definitely have that one. Guess I'm living my fantasy. How about you?" She smirked. "Actually, let me guess. Nurse fantasy, or maybe a band groupie?"

Dec all but gagged. "Been in too many treatment facilities to have a nurse fantasy, and I've slept with groupies. Trust me, it isn't something I relish recalling."

"Okay, so what is your role playing fantasy then, Dr. St. James?"

"It's horrendously clichéd."

"Tell me or I'll tickle you."

"You are completely adorable."

"Tell me."

"I'd rather see you try to tickle me."

"Declan."

"Fine, I have a very detailed fantasy about a naughty librarian."

"Pretty sure I can pull that off."

"Oh, darling, I have no doubt."

"There's something else I wanted to ask, but I don't want to kill the mood we've got going on?"

"Ask me."

"Did Evie want you to get your piercing? Is she why you had it done?"

"She is not, actually. I had it done when I got out of my second round of rehab. Back then, before I knew what my specific weaknesses were, I was hyper-aware of cross addictions. I wouldn't drink. I wouldn't even go to bars which basically meant I did nothing but stay in my shitty apartment and study. I refused to even go back to the farm because I knew there might be painkillers there. Piercings interested me. I had a tongue ring for a little while, and I got my brow done before I was legal, but the apa piercing takes months and months to heal. That kept me from using sex to distract me from my junkie habits, and somewhere in the clusterfuck that is my head, I hoped my future wife might enjoy it."

"I do." She couldn't help herself. She wanted him to have some idea what she was thinking about their future.

"Cheeky girl, the things you say and do to me. Someday, you're going to figure out how much better off you would be without me."

"Not gonna happen."

"Promise?"

"Promise."

CHAPTER TWENTY-SEVEN

Every rectified loss the day had levied, every blow he'd endured, they all eased their vice-like grip as she brushed a kiss on his neck. His devious side conjured a dozen ways to help her discover and explore herself as a sexual being, and a dozen additional ways to figure out just what she might like, given that she was now quite literally his student. His other side, the side that so desperately sought redemption, was desperate to prove to her that he would be worth the love she held for him. He would make himself better for her. He would not only meet her needs; he would prove himself to her *for* her.

"I bought you four coffeemakers," spilled out of his mouth before he could bite the words back.

He swore her hysterical giggle should be written into music and sung by some kind of angel choir. "Uh, why exactly?"

"Mostly because I have no clue how to do right by you, but showing you that I love you is all that matters to me. If I like something, I do everything to excess. If I like a song, I'll play it over and over again until I know the lyrics backwards and forwards and can play it as well as the producing band. I'm telling you this because I want you to know me, the real me. Being in a relationship with me can't be an easy thing. Also, because the entire store was bloody confusing and the sales chick kept talking about sparkling vampires and tea. It was horrid. Also, I need to hold your tits." He cupped her tender cleavage in his hands and felt her nipples pebble beneath his caress. She was laughing again. His cock throbbed against her back. "There, now I feel better."

"Can't say I really have any problem with being spoiled to excess or being felt up, but why don't we look at them tomorrow morning and maybe return three of them to the store?" The stars outside his window on the darkened night were nothing compared to the shimmer of delight in her beautiful eyes.

"Can you promise me something else, since we've decided to go on and throw the entire box of matches in the forest fire?"

"Anything."

"If I do something you don't like, if I screw up in this whole boyfriend department, which I admittedly do not fully understand, please tell me. I can learn. It's just sometimes I don't know healthy ways to express love."

"Dec, so far, you've been perfect." One of her sweet kisses landed on the corner of his mouth. He instantly wanted more. Needed more. Couldn't exist without more. "What girl doesn't want gallons of coffee at her disposal?"

"I'm about to do something you don't like." He quirked a smile and hoped she knew he was teasing her. Her respondent grin, said she knew him better than he'd guessed.

"Oh yeah? What's that?"

"I'm about to tell you to hush, so I can do this." With that, he scooped his hands under her thighs, eased up on his knees, and then laid her back so he could levy his body against hers. Desperate for her, he slid his cock against the slick, fevered folds of her pussy. Her lips were still swollen and tender from the force of his fingers a half-hour before. Their soft heat blanketed him. He shuddered from the heavenly sensation. Her entire body was soft against his solid strength.

"Baby doll, you're so wet you could take me just like this." He moaned before capturing her lips with his own, taking them hostage as he drew her tongue into his mouth and sucked. He nipped her bottom lip as she spread her legs further, an invitation he could never deny.

"Take me," she gasped. The scent of her arousal, ripe with abandon, filled him. A heady fog of lust wrapped around them from the heat of their breath. A concealment against the world that longed to tear them apart.

"Is that what you want? Want me to open you wide? Make you all mine. Make you ache with it."

"Yes," she thrust against him. "You promised. You promised you'd fuck me so hard I'd feel it tomorrow. Every time I walk, every time I move I want to know who I belong to."

Fucking hell, she was too much. He'd spent half his life turning down things he craved, but he would never possess the strength to deny himself this pleasure.

She blew his restraint straight to hell. She always did. Promising himself that soon he would take his time with her, he would fuck her so often he'd eventually be able to summon patience enough to fulfill every fantasy she'd described and those yet to be disclosed. But tonight, tonight they needed this without pretense, without complication. They needed to exist as one before they had to weave the web of lies that he prayed wouldn't ultimately be their undoing.

Rocking his hips forward he penetrated her gently, filling her full in one long fluid thrust.

The hitch in her breath and gasp from the tender pierce drew a low groan from his lungs. "So tight. So perfect," he grunted out his pleasure. He made two shallow strokes, reveling in every silky ripple of her pussy. With another full thrust he drowned himself in her, making her tremble beneath him as he filled her to overflowing.

When his piercing hit her g-spot she bucked against him. "More, please."

"Shh, baby, let me enjoy this. I'm gonna get you there. Just relax for me."

Her delectable little body cinched around him as he pressed harder, staking his claim. On his next thrust he stared down at her. Eyes closed in ecstasy, body rolling against him, so hungry for more.

"Look at me, darling." Another slow thrust before he picked up pace, giving her what she wanted. Her eyes blinked open, emerald fires of need on his withdrawals and warm pools of contentment when he permeated her fully. "So damn beautiful."

Her hands pressed against his biceps and traveled to his shoulders, clinging to him, making him her ballast in the storm, the only role he'd ever desperately needed to fill. He continued to rock, making certain she felt his piercing slide against her as he pervaded her body. She would feel it in the morning. Feel what belonged to him now. Feel his occupation and long for more.

Lifting up on one arm, he reached his hand between them and gathered the slick essence of the two of them before he hesitantly caressed at her clit.

"Oh God," she seized as he gently rotated his fingers, bringing her closer with every pass. She came in a wild cry of carnal noise. It ripped him apart. He gave two more frantic thrusts, forcing her orgasm to continue, as he gained his own. This time he unloaded fully inside of her, bathing her walls in everything he was, owning her thoroughly.

Holly's eyes blinked open before the sun made its appearance over the lake. She felt Dec slip from the bed. Why was he leaving? It couldn't possibly already be time for work. She'd willed the night to extend, wished for it, even tried demanding it from the universe. Once they were out of bed, she'd have to leave and pretend that she was once again alone.

"What's wrong, baby?" His sleepy voice calling her baby reminded her yet again why every sacrifice they had to make was worth it.

But damn he was good. She couldn't get anything by him even in the dark. "Where are you going?"

He slid back in bed and positioned her on his chest once again. When his fingers worked through her hair, just the way he'd soothed her to sleep the night before, she gave him a sleepy sigh.

"I usually work out before I leave for work and then run at lunch. I don't know where to run on campus that would be safe. The workouts ease the strain of my addictions and give me the equilibrium I'll need to get through a day trying to pretend you aren't the most important thing in my world."

Holly wondered why he thought campus was somehow unsafe, but was enjoying his admission that she was just as important to him as he was to her. "There are bike trails on campus. There's even a whole bike group or whatever. I'm sure you could run there."

"That might not be the best idea."

Forcing herself to sit up and study him, her brow furrowed. "Why?"

"You're so damned gorgeous, did you know that? I could definitely get used to waking up beside you looking thoroughly sexed."

"Dec." Was he dodging her again all of a sudden?

"Dealers aren't hard to come by on college campuses, sweetheart. This is difficult for me. As weak as it makes me to struggle with this, I had my routine figured out and it worked for me. The way to fight addiction is to create a life and a routine that makes it difficult to buy and use. Now, I have a completely different job, in a new place where dealers are ever present, and I'm with a woman I desperately need to protect. I need to not screw up this relationship. I'm also breaking the number one ethics code, and if I get fired I quite possibly will never see you again. The stakes are higher than I'd like. I have to take every precaution I can. Slipping is far too appealing when I'm not with you. Bike trails, parking lots, being outdoors on campus removes a barrier between me and the dealers."

Guilt ransacked Holly's stomach. She'd been pouting about him getting up before her and he was trying desperately to not only save their relationship, but to save his very life. "You aren't weak, Dec. You're the strongest person I've ever met. Can I do anything to make this easier?"

His half smile was somehow broken. "Thank you. Just don't be afraid to hold me accountable, but this is my battle to fight, my war to win."

"But. . .couldn't I be one of your soldiers? I'll do anything I can to help."

"Just give me a little time to work through all of this. I eventually learned to be in bars for gigs without it bothering me. I got through a divorce and being fired. I'll figure this out, too." He brushed a kiss in her hair.

"Okay. Go workout. I'll. . .make breakfast." There. That was something she could do.

"Make yourself at home. If you get lonely, I'll be in the basement."

Holly showered quickly and then wandered around Dec's house, feeling somewhat nervous, like an invited intruder. The odd sensation kept her from exploring much. She made her way to the kitchen and laughed when she saw the four coffee makers lined up on the countertop. *Declan St. James, I love you, and we're going to figure all of this out.* She shook her head and investigated each of the makers. Several of them had to have cost a small fortune. She'd grown up drinking coffee strong enough to take the paint off a barn, or strong enough to get cowboys up and out of bed to work cattle long before sunrise. She wasn't picky.

Scanning the bells and whistles, she selected a mid-range maker and set the others in the entryway to be returned. When she'd run enough water through it to make coffee that wouldn't taste like new plastic, she searched for breakfast food.

As it turned out, Dec's kitchen was stocked. He must've liked to cook. There was still so much she didn't know about him. It occurred to her that they'd never really been on a date. He'd come over to her apartment a few times before the night his band had played at Duffy's. She was supposed to spend the weekend with him but hadn't. The oddities and complications of the relationship weighted her again. Maybe that was best. Not having gone out meant fewer people would ever have seen them together. Still, it felt like they'd skipped several of the normal relationship steps. What if those mattered? What if they were trying to build a skyscraper without a foundation?

'You want me to tell you that all this is gonna work out just the way you want it to, but I can't do that, sweetheart.' Her mother's words welled in her chest. He was worth it. They were worth fighting for, and that was their foundation.

With a determined nod to the empty stovetop staring back at her, she took a dozen eggs from the refrigerator and found some bread to make toast. Holding an egg in her hands, she pressed with her index finger and thumb, applying equal pressure, and watching nothing at all happen. The delicate strength of the shell. When she slammed it against the side of the bowl, it split and spilled its contents. They just had to keep it together for a semester or two, never applying too much pressure from either side. That was it.

CHAPTER TWENTY-EIGHT

"You really are entirely too good to me." Dec tried not to be uncomfortable as Holly sat a plate full of eggs and toast in front of him. She'd even made him tea. He wasn't accustomed to being taken care of, and this all harkened decidedly too close to some kind of fifties sitcom.

"I know, it feels weird. We'll figure it out." Holly slunk into the chair beside him.

"I've never even eaten at this table."

"I've never spent the night at someone's house and then made breakfast the next morning before they went to work."

She was lost and seeking something he couldn't quite discern. This wasn't them. The entire thing felt rehearsed. It pricked at his skin. His gut churned. It was like trying to sweep concrete with a rake. It would eventually accomplish the task, but the cost was more than he could stand.

Shaking his head, he lifted his mug of tea and his plate. Then he balanced her coffee and her plate delicately. "Come here, my sexy little cowgirl."

He sat the plates on his coffee table, handed her the coffee mug, and settled in the corner of his large couch. Patting his lap, he watched her tense disposition melt as she cuddled into him and sipped her coffee. "This is so much better," she sighed.

"Let's never force anything, okay? We're good together, Holly. Really good. I know it sucks we can't see each other this week, but there's no reason we can't talk on the phone. We're good on the phone."

"Yeah. We are good on the phone. I just wish I didn't have to leave. Going back to campus scares me. I feel like I'm too easy to read. You seem to have no trouble knowing what I'm thinking."

"Not I nor anyone else can read your thoughts, love. That's why communication is so important. And people pay drastically little attention to anything that is not themselves. We're both nervous enough right now we'll be on constant guard. It will be in a few months when we've figured out how to interact in class without suspicion that will be the most dangerous, but I am about to ask you to do something that I abhor having to ask you to do."

"What? Anything."

"I saw the moment your friend realized who I was to you. I've never wanted to have the ability to erase a person's mind more than I did right then. I need you to tell her we decided not to pursue a relationship once we figured out that I'm your professor. We just can't take any chances."

"Beth is my friend. She'd never say anything."

Oh, to be twenty-three with that much innocence and faith in humanity. Dec hated himself all the more for being the one that was going to force her to give up those last few fleeting markers of youth. He wondered if he'd ever believed in anything as much as she believed in her friend. *Her. Them.* His mind readily supplied two things he believed in that much, but it was a very short list.

"God, I hate myself for making you lie." He tried to delicately disagree and leave no question as to what had to be done.

"I'm a terrible liar."

"We don't have to do this. I'll wait for you forever, but I have to teach for an entire year. That will get me enough hours to take the Nebraska Licensing Exam. After that, things get easier."

"We are not standing still, remember? I'll tell her. It's fine. Next year we'll come clean."

"If you aren't in my classes next semester, we can come clean then."

"She'll understand whenever we're able to tell her."

Dec sincerely hoped that was true. He cradled Holly closer, rather enjoying the scent of his body wash on her skin coupled with her coffee. Invisible notes of his possession she would carry with her throughout the day.

"Would it sound terribly clichéd to say that I'm jealous of that mug getting to touch your lips this morning?"

"Have you ever tried coffee, Dr.?"

"Got me through the psych program at a very advanced pace. I much prefer tea."

"Oh really?" She leaned in and mated their mouths. When she opened for him, he swept his tongue through her mouth, memorizing the flavors of her coffee-laced kiss.

"When you put it that way, nothing could ever taste better."

Apparently satisfied with his answer, she nuzzled her head against his neck. "Could I just sit in your lap and drink coffee for a little while and pretend we never have to leave?"

His first class wasn't until 9:30, and there was nothing he wanted more than to hold her just a little longer. "Nothing would make me happier, but we should eat the delectable meal you prepared."

"It's just eggs. Nothing special."

"You made them for me. Therefore, they are very, very special."

An hour later, Holly drove her truck down Dec's long driveway and nervously glanced up and down the street, terrified someone would see her leaving. Successfully escaping his neighborhood would be followed by trying to convince Beth that they'd broken up. *Whoever thought forbidden love was exciting and romantic was an idiot. It's simultaneously the most magical and the most terrifying parts of your entire life.*

She quickly made her way out of the subdivision and eased a little as she blended into Lincoln traffic. Thoughts of Dec being deported made the cold eggs she'd finally eaten turn to concrete in her stomach. She would not allow that to happen. This would be fine.

Taking her time, she swung by the drugstore and browsed for nothing in particular. She picked up toothpaste, tampons, and a few romance novels since her nights would not be spent with Dec, and she didn't feel up to going out with friends. After that, she headed to her apartment for the purposes of leaving from there to go to campus.

When she slid into a chair at the library beside Beth she attempted to look heartbroken. Beth studied her oddly. "What's wrong with you? I tried to call you last night but you never answered."

"Yeah, I sort of spent the night in tears." That wasn't entirely a lie. She had cried the night before.

Beth took another inventory of Holly. "You are aware I'm getting a degree in behavioral psychology, and therefore, I'm aware when you lie. You're one of my best friends, Holl. You look like you're trying to look upset."

"Dammit, I am upset. I'm not trying to look upset. Who even does that?"

"A person who's hiding something."

"I'm not hiding anything." This was never going to work. Holly was the worst liar ever.

"Holly Camden, you go set your riding pants on fire. You are a liar, liar. Now, what is it you're lying about?" She leaned closer and Holly jerked backwards.

"Mm-hmm, you smell like sexy expensive dude. You were at Professor Sex's house."

"Shhh,hhh,hhh!" Holly all but strangled her friend.

"Oh my God, this is so exciting."

"Beth, no. You can't tell anyone. At all. Ever. Please. It could ruin his life."

"Holl, I would never. I'm just a hopeless romantic. I want this to work out. You look so happy. Kind of settled, but in a really good way. Like content maybe. Can't I be excited for you?"

"It would really be better if you just pretended you didn't know."

"Okay, can I act excited if it's just the two of us?"

"Not on campus."

"Deal. I'm so excited."

"Beth," Holly pled. "Right now we have to focus on anal fun."

"Oh, I'll bet Professor Sex can help you out with some. . . ."

Holly clamped her hand over Beth's mouth. "You will not say what you were just about to say." Beth managed a nod. "Until you leave this campus after our classes, you will not even think about the two of us, and if you do think about it, you understand I will be forced to throw you on the ground and tie you up calf-roping style." Another nod. "And you know that I know how to do that with only one hand while blindfolded." And another. "Good girl." Holly released her.

"Speaking of blindfolds. . . ."

"Beth, I swear on my best saddle, I will hurt you."

"Kidding. I'm kidding."

Beth managed to keep her mouth shut through their statistics class, which was slammed full of doctoral students in their first semester. Holly dutifully took notes on bell curves and outliers, though she'd been over this review in the four stats classes she'd taken in the last three years.

She'd only seen Dec once so far and hated that she was almost glad of that. He'd been crossing the quad from the psychological sciences building to the research center. He'd rushed across the parking lot, fleeing his demons, she assumed.

Seeing him made her weak-kneed and panicked. It confused her soul. Her heart wanted to rush to him to kiss the tense frown off of his face. She wanted to ask how his day was going. She wanted to follow him into his office, lock the door, and do something extremely naughty that would plant a permanent smile on his face for the rest of the day. Her brain knew those things were absolutely the stupidest ideas she could possibly even consider. She spent the last half of Statistics drowning out Dr. Simpson's laborious drone with her own internal lecture about having thoughts like that on campus. The term *deportation* took on the gut punch words like failure, rejection, and disappointment used to carry.

.   .   .

Dec sat in his office attempting to work on his lesson plans, keenly aware that Holly was still on campus somewhere. He sensed her presence the same way he could sense a user or a dealer. *Nice analogy, St. James. You're an asshole, by the way.* His brain mocked him, but he couldn't help himself. She was the only thing in the world whose love roared even louder than his demons. How did he have any hope of ignoring her siren call?

It took every ounce of fortitude he possessed to stay in his posh leather seat. He could text her to meet him somewhere discreet. Hell, he could instruct her to meet him at his house and never to leave, and she would have obeyed. Tossing down his pencil, he reached for his Gibson Les Paul he'd brought just for this purpose. He didn't need an amp to play. He wasn't looking to piss off his colleagues. Besides, his entire life had been muted by this stupid job, so why not mute his music, too?

He strummed through the first few chords of *Lay It Down* by Aerosmith. The lyrics slipped quietly from his lips, half sung, half spoken. The knock on his office door and the text on his phone sounded at the same moment, severing the music, severing his life.

'I'm alone. I'm in my car. I just miss you and I love you and I needed to say that.' He read the text, cringed, hated himself even more for cringing, shoved his phone in his pocket, and ordered whomever was standing at his door inside.

"Sorry to interrupt your little practice session, Dr. St. James. Kind of assumed you'd be working," Dr. Treavor Singleton Sr. entered Dec's office. He extended his hand and Dec reminded himself to scrub thoroughly before touching his precious cowgirl, lest she contract the jizz-trumpet's slime. When Singleton attempted to out-grip Dec in the handshake, Dec chuckled, flexed his forearm, and felt Singleton's hand begin to throb.

"I was working." Dec offered nothing more. He simply dropped Singleton's now limp hand and stood the guitar on his nearby stand.

"We didn't get to chat much yesterday. I was kind of surprised you'd been hired. Normally all hirings within the department are approved by me."

Dear God, the man clearly had a half-inch dick he was having trouble locating. "Did you need something, Dr. Singleton?"

"Man of few words. I like that."

Dec refused yet another comment.

"Listen, my son, Trevor Jr., is in one of your foundations research classes. Just thought I'd see how you thought he was gonna do."

"I've only had one session with each of my classes. I have no idea how your son will perform."

Frustration tensed the plastered appearance of Singleton's face. One too many face-lifts, if Dec had to guess. "Well, you know what I mean. Doctor to doctor."

"I have no idea what you mean. Their first paper will be due next Monday. I might could tell you more after I've read Jr.'s work."

"Newsome's being disagreeable about whom he's offering his preferential treatment to this year. Everyone's jumped on this absurd politically correct bandwagon. In my day, a man's name meant something. Rich is just being stubborn. Says Trev didn't put forth any effort on his thesis work. Has his eye on some ridiculous cowgirl no one in Lincoln's ever even heard of. Women's lib and all that. Either that or he'd like to get her out of her boots. I'm trying to talk him into taking the girl and doing whatever he wants with her, but also giving Trevor a spot. He'll come around once he's graduated. Just sowing his wild oats like his old man. Rich keeps insisting that Trev's grades improve before he considers being his supervisor."

The pencil Dec had picked up off of his desk snapped in his hand. Possessive fury rocketed up his spine. *Do not react. Pretend she means nothing to you.* He vibrated in his seat. Bile lodged in his throat. He tried to reason through Singleton's mindless drivel. Newsome not wanting to become Trevor's supervisor had nothing to do with Holly. He didn't seem the kind of man to abuse his power. Of course, until last night, Dec would have sworn he wasn't the kind of man who would ever be caught in the predicament of dating one of his students.

He managed a half breath and tried to steady his heart, hellbent on escaping his ribcage to pummel Singleton on Holly's behalf. "Sounds to me like Trevor needs to improve his grades if he wants the coveted position of being Newsome's protégé."

"That's why I'm in here, St. James. I see no reason why you can't help Trev do just that."

"What exactly are you suggesting, Singleton?" Dec discreetly reached into his pocket and withdrew his phone.

"I'm just saying that if Trev should need any kind of *help* it would behoove you to give him that help. I did my research. I already know your visa has been funneled through Lifespan and then through the University. Set all of the dominoes up in your own favor, St. James. Don't be stupid. It only takes one screw up to send you packing, and I am keenly aware of that."

With a desperate prayer that Holly wouldn't text him again for a split second, Dec held up the phone. "I'll be more than happy to give Trevor as much *help* as he needs, seeing as he is one of my students. In fact, I'm sure you'll be more than happy to know that I took the liberty of recording everything you've asked for just so I can remind myself of your expectations for me in the department."

Singleton's eyes flashed with hatred, but he recovered with the skill of the well-trained sociopath he was. "You can't scare me, St. James. There's a reason my family's name is all over this campus. My wife and I are both deeply ingrained in the department and the board. Not to mention the depths of our well-lined pockets."

"Noted." Dec was quite certain he'd never hated anyone more than the man currently seated before his desk.

"Glad you understand."

Another knock sounded on the office door before Dec could order Singleton from the premises. Dr. Richard Newsome himself poked his head in.

"So sorry to interrupt, gentlemen. Everything okay in here?"

"Just fine, Rich," Singleton lied quite naturally of course.

"Dr. St. James, everything okay?" Dr. Newsome seemed to have Singleton's number. Dec felt a little of his sanity return.

"We were just discussing Trevor, Jr., Rich," Singleton continued to answer on Dec's behalf.

"Oh, I feel certain you were. Listen, Dr. St. James, I know Gibbons and myself threw you under the bus with this position. To tell you the truth, I've been so impressed with your background and your work I'd been trying to figure out how to hire you on for the past several months. Lifespan's loss is most certainly our gain. If I can do anything at all to make this transition easier for you, do not hesitate to ask."

You could give me a pass to date the woman I'm quite certain I'd love to marry that got caught in the crosshairs of this ridiculous situation. Dec ground his teeth to keep that particular request trapped in his throat. "Thank you, sir," he managed a full minute later. "I'll do my best. Been several years since I taught."

"It's like riding a bike. You'll be great. I have every confidence, and listen, I have several things I'd like to discuss with you, off-campus perhaps. How about dinner Saturday evening at Rodizio with my wife and me? Feel free to bring a date."

"I'm not seeing anyone." Fucking hell. He'd answered far too quickly. Now, he'd given up one of the only nights he could see Holly and had left himself without any viable excuses to get out of it. Newsome studied him for far too long. An odd smile formed on his features. Dec felt like he'd been locked in a pressure cooker. "Saturday night would be lovely. Thank you. I'll see you then."

"Perfect. Singleton, let's let Dr. St. James get back to his work. I feel quite certain he doesn't need any instruction on his methods of teaching or on playing the guitar." Newsome gestured to the Les Paul. "I've heard he's rather gifted at both."

"Thank you, sir." Dec watched the men leave his office while he held several debates in his mind. What the hell had Newsome meant when he'd said he was impressed with Dec's background? Drug addiction wasn't an admirable thing and that was the only real background Dec was aware he had. Surely, Newsome hadn't meant he was impressed with Dec's ability to work a sheep farm. And how badly had he just fucked up, showing Singleton his hand too quickly? It was a grievous tactical error. He could have held onto the recording if anything should go wrong in the future. Singleton fucked his last nerve repeatedly, but that was no excuse. He had to play the hand he'd been dealt, not continue to lament his cards.

Taking his phone out of his pocket, he texted Holly back. Told her he loved her and he missed her, too. Refrained from scolding her for texting him during school hours or telling her that his phone had been laying on his desk and Singleton had been standing outside his office door. None of that was her problem. It was his. *He* needed to be more careful. And merciful Jesus, he needed to see her. He needed to touch her and kiss her. He desperately needed her to lie to him again and tell him that everything would work out just fine.

CHAPTER TWENTY-NINE

"Can I ask you something rather loathsome, darling?" Dec asked as soon as she answered the phone. He stepped inside his home and willed it not to feel so empty without her there.

"Hi, babe. How was your day? I missed you, and this is a lot harder than I originally thought it was going to be, but I still know what we're doing is the right thing. I know we're worth this. Now then, yes, you can ask me whatever you want."

"I'm very sorry I left out the pleasantries. I told you I'm no good at this, and don't think I didn't hear you say this was harder than you thought it was going to be. We'll talk about that in just a minute. I just need to ask this."

"Dec, it's fine. I was teasing. Ask me anything."

"What can you tell me about either Trevor Singleton Jr. or his father?"

"Pardon me while I go vomit, then I might be able to talk about those no-good shitlickers, both junior and senior."

Every single thing he'd endured that day washed away in the sound of her voice when she let that cowgirl drawl slip in. He grabbed a can of soda from his fridge and settled on his sofa. "Is there any way at all I could convince you to revert back to your cowgirl way of speaking permanently?"

"Like my drawl, do you?"

"It's brilliant. I'm adding it to the unending list of things I adore about you."

"You think my speaking's bad, you should hear my brothers or my daddy. You'd get a kick out of them."

"Well, maybe I'll eventually survive long enough to meet your family, sweetheart."

"I certainly hope so. Now, what did you want to know about the Trevor dickhead-triad?"

"Triad? Please tell me there's not three of them?"

"Yup. Grandpa's still a major donor. Used to be on the board. Technically, he's not a Trevor. I think his name is Bankston or something, but trust me, the Singleton blood runs thick with shit."

"I figured that. What I need to know is if you were aware that Singleton Sr. asks Jr.'s professors to give him good grades and threatens them if they don't."

"Oh, yeah, everyone knows. It's standard behavior from that family. What I don't know is why Dr. Newsome continues to allow it."

"And what do you know of Newsome?"

"He's always been very nice, outstanding professor, genuinely interested in the students, available to help. Why?"

"Singleton dropped by my office right about the time you texted me."

"Oh geez, Dec, I'm so sorry. I wasn't thinking."

"Probably be best if we had no communication until I leave campus."

"Yeah, I know. This entire thing is just so stupid. I'd drop your class but they aren't offering it again until next year, and I can't take any other research classes until I've completed yours."

"It's fine, love. Listen, Singleton alluded to the fact that Newsome is interested in naming you his protégé for your dissertation research."

"Really?" The lilt of excitement in her tone had Dec regretting even asking about this.

"Yes. But. . .uh. . .Singleton is trying to secure the spot for Trevor."

"Wait, does that mean Dr. Newsome isn't planning on choosing two students this year? Because he's never done that before, but Trevor kept telling me he was."

"I have no idea, honey."

"You know, that's who I was at Duffy's to meet the night we met. He told me his father had overheard that Newsome was choosing two students this year for his dissertation program and that if I'd meet him there he'd tell me how we could both be chosen. It was a trick. He stood me up. That's why I was so pissed that night. . .well, until you sat down at my table."

"I don't like to owe men like the Singletons anything, but in this case it seems I'm indebted to Trevor Jr. with my very life."

"What aren't you saying?" The woman was far too good. Dec couldn't help but grin.

"Dr. Singleton wanted me to believe that Newsome would like to work with you for less than ethical reasons."

"Of course he does. I mean obviously, that's the only possible reason he would choose me over Trevor. Asswipe. Dr. Newsome isn't like that. If I get that spot, I'll have earned it without what's in my pants."

"I have no doubt. I just don't know how to proceed. How much should I know about you when I'm talking to them? I'm trying to prepare myself so I'm not caught off guard again."

"Well, you're a new professor so nothing more than you would have been able to discern either from my work in your class or our interactions in your class."

"And you're okay with that?"

"Why wouldn't I be okay with that?"

"I want to help you any way I can. It's just a very fine line between helping you and outing us."

"Dec, I don't need you to help me like that. Same way I wouldn't have wanted you to help me get the internship at Lifespan. I want to do this on my own. Well, everything except the sexual exploration part. That I want to do with you, but I'm pretty sure it won't come up in my dissertation or on a test of some kind."

"You mean I don't get to test you on our exploration of your fantasies?"

"You know it's not only *my* fantasies I want to explore, right, Dr. St. James? I'm currently online searching for a pair of glasses and a conservative skirt befitting a librarian who needs someone to loose her bounds."

Dec's breath seized in his lungs. The fantasy began without his permission. He could see her dressed the part all for him. A low, hungry moan wrenched loose from his lungs. "You're killing me, love."

"I wish I could be there with you."

"Me too. More than you'll ever know, and I have more dreadful news to tell you."

"Oh, no. What now?"

God, he hated disappointing her. It stung his already battered soul. "Dr. Newsome would like to take me out to discuss some things involving the department. . .on Saturday night."

"But. . . ."

"I know. I swear I'll figure out some way to make this up to you."

"We were going to have naked weekend."

Dec sat the soda on his coffee table lest he drop it the entire can in his lap. "What happens on naked weekend?"

"We stay naked all weekend. That's as far as my planning had gotten."

"Oh, I could definitely help you flesh out that plan, my little minx. I tell you what, I have no choice but to assign a paper Friday in class. What I assign tomorrow will dictate what I assign Friday. If it didn't, I'd go ahead and give you the topic. Anyway, come over Friday night after the sun goes down. We'll spend every moment together until I have to go to this ridiculous dinner Saturday evening. You stay here and work on the paper while I'm gone. It surely won't take you long. When I get back, we'll get naked and return to our naked weekend festivities."

"That sounds almost perfect, but Dec you can't give me assignments early. That isn't fair to everyone else."

"Sorry, love. I guess I felt like we were both being screwed so royally in all of this we should take any advantage we can manage."

"Let's not. Let's just pretend you're not my professor as much as we can."

"Whatever you want."

Dec's phone beeped in his ear. He quickly checked the screen. "That's Kade, sweetheart. He hasn't heard from me all day. If I don't answer he'll be on his way over here, worried I've done something stupid."

"Go talk to Kade. Cheyenne's been calling me all day, too. I need to make sure she's okay."

"What the fuck, man?" Kade bellowed as soon as Dec answered.

"I'm fine. Well. . .I'm handling life."

"And how are you handling it?"

"Without the use of any illegal substances."

"Good." An audible breath escaped Kade's lungs. Another round of guilt levied in Dec's gut. "You don't sound suicidal. I'm guessing you two figured out a way to keep dating despite the professor thing."

"Let's not announce that to anyone else."

"Good. I'm really happy for you. She's good for you. I can feel it."

"I would never argue with that, but listen, I can only see her on the weekends. I need to move practice to some other day besides Sundays."

"Good luck with that. Andy'll shit four bricks and a backhoe."

"That is quite an image."

"It's the truth, is what it is."

"Speaking of Andy, it is imperative that he think Holly and I are over. We both know how much he would love for me to be deported and him to get his place in the band back."

"Even if that did happen, which it won't, he wouldn't get to be lead again. He fucked everything up too badly, but yeah, I get it. We'll keep you and your cowgirl on the DL."

"Do people still say that?"

"No idea. Don't really care. Listen, you better figure out when we're supposed to practice. Everyone's gonna show up at your place on Sunday afternoon. We're supposed to play that hole-in-the-wall out past Haymarket that night. We need to practice a little before we go."

"Fucksake, I *need* to see Holly. I get precious little time with her the way this colossal shitfest is going already. I've never even taken her on a proper date, and now we're stuck inside my house like prisoners."

"I'm sorry, Dec, but you two just decided all of this last night. I'm just hearing about it. Give a guy time to figure out how to help you get with your luvvah."

"That may be the queerest thing you have ever said to me."

Kade laughed hysterically. "Fuck off, man. You know you want a piece of this."

"We would make a brilliant couple, there's no doubt."

"Naturally."

Dec appreciated the laughter more than anything else. Trying to envision telling Holly that their naked weekend was going to be relegated to a few measly naked hours was highly unappealing. "I've never thought about running away as often as I have today."

"Don't run away. No one else can play *Hot for Teacher,* which, now that I think about it, is hysterical given your current situation."

"I'm hanging up now."

"Eeeek, guess what!?" Cheyenne squealed when she finally answered her phone.

"What?" Holly grinned at her friend's enthusiasm.

"Grant volunteered to help out with this year's Cattle Baron Festival."

"Yeah, I know. One of the Camdens has to pony up every year since we're the biggest ranch in town. It's really Luke's turn, but Indie's due date is before Christmas and since it's twins they don't think she'll carry to term. He didn't want to be tied up with anything around Thanksgiving."

"Holl, I don't care *why* Grant is in charge this year, only that he is. This is supremely exciting as I have decided that I will co-chair the event with him."

Holly cringed. Grant would probably donate his profits on every head he'd just sold to get out of working with Cheyenne on the festival. "It's just a livestock show and a fancy dinner, Chey. Trust me, Grant is not the kind of guy that relishes getting dressed up and showing off our heifers for what he calls, and I quote, 'useless citys-lickers with balls slung so low they couldn't climb up in one of his trucks if they wanted to.'"

Truthfully, Holly loved every single thing about the festival. It was her favorite time of year. She always showed for Camden Ranch and then spent the evening relishing every moment of the ball. To her, the entire day was better than Christmas. She could be a cowgirl and a princess at the same time.

"It's a livestock show and a fancy dinner where he'll need to bring a date and then a dance where he will also need someone to dance with."

"Chey, just please don't get your feelings hurt if he. . .isn't as excited about the festival as you are." Holly hoped against hope that Cheyenne would eventually get one of the million clues she readily offered that said for some reason Grant was not interested in her.

"I won't. I'm just excited to get to be around him more since you're never here, so I don't have a good excuse to go hang out at the ranch more. Are you coming home next weekend?"

Holly had been stuck inside the situation with Dec all day. It hadn't occurred to her until that moment that in years past she'd gone home almost every weekend to help out on the ranch, to see her friends, and ride her horses. Now, the weekends were the only time she could see Dec.

"Uh, no. I can't. I have several big projects coming up." She crossed her fingers, hoping that she lied better over the phone than she did in person.

"The next weekend?" Cheyenne sounded desperate.

"Maybe. I'll have to see."

"You know what we need to really make the party awesome this year?"

"People other than cowboys and ranchers to attend?"

"No. We need good music. Didn't you tell me Harry Potter is in a band?"

"Could we not call Dec Harry Potter, please?"

"You basically said he has a magic wand."

"Cheyenne."

"Fine, I won't call him that. Do you think you could get him to come out here and play? Offer him a blow job or something."

"I can't. I mean, I can give him a blow job, but I can't ask him to play. It's complicated." Technically, Cattle Baron's would be after final exams so hopefully he wouldn't still be her professor, but they couldn't announce they were dating until well into next semester at the earliest.

"You could. For me. Please."

"Really, Cheyenne I can't. A bunch of stuff you don't know happened."

"Did you break up?"

"No, not exactly."

CHAPTER THIRTY

Blissful abandon whispered in the breeze coming through Holly's open bedroom windows. The hazy pockets of sunshine warmed the earth providing the perfect mix of lazy summer and cozy fall spiked with just the right amount of mischief. Potential pulsed through her veins.

It was going to be a good day. The kind of day where absolutely nothing could go wrong, because the universe itself was happy. She could feel it. Shimmying into the short sundress she'd chosen for the unseasonably warm day, she turned to study her backside in the dresser mirror. Convinced that no one could really tell she'd decided to go commando, she ran her brush through her hair once more before throwing it in her duffle bag.

Their weekend had been cut short. She couldn't really complain since she was going all the way back to the ranch early Sunday morning to help with the fall-calving. Turning down her daddy's request for a little help wasn't an option in her book, but she intended to make the most of the nights she and Dec did have together.

Trying to hone her play-acting skills, she slung an empty saddle and tack bag in her truck along with her duffle bag, the only one that was actually packed. She had plenty of saddles and tack back on the ranch, but this way it looked like she planned to head home that night instead of Sunday morning. No one was watching, of course, but *no chances* had become her mantra.

On her return trip to the truck carrying her makeup kit, she spied a bright yellow Scion leaving the parking lot. Remnants of the mud she'd sprayed it down with still resided in his ridiculous custom wheels. What the fuck was Trevor doing there? He still lived in his parents' mansion across town.

A woman was standing outside her door at the building across the parking lot from Holly's. She was dressed in skimpy flannel shorts and a NU t-shirt, smoking a cigarette. Great. Trevor must've been leaving her apartment. She did not need Singleton that nearby ever. Reminding herself that Singleton had slept with the majority of the female student population at least once made her feel better. Poor girl probably fell for his idiotic pick-up lines and his money. As long as this chick never heard from Single-ass again, they would both be better off.

Dec arrived in the lecture hall several minutes before any of his students. He told himself it was to prepare his lecture. He knew it was solely to watch Holly walk to her desk. Longest fucking week of his life. His tongue thirsted for the confection of her lips, both sets. His hands ached to touch her soft skin. His fingers were stiff with need to race through her hair. They weren't the only parts of his body stiff with need, either.

After this class was over, the countdown until he had her in his house, and more importantly, in his arms, would only be a few hours. Watching the rhythmic sway of her hips while she passed his desk would have to tide him over until then.

He scanned the papers in his hands, feigning interest in them all. There was only one he cared about. He'd read over his other students, of course, but the lovemap Holly had created he studied until he'd memorized every curve of every handwritten letter. She'd called him on using the assignment to suss out the rest of her fantasies. He'd readily admitted to abuse of power. She was more than welcome to punish him however she saw fit. He hadn't asked to be her professor, but he intended to take every advantage it offered.

When she entered the room, his eyes tracked from the tips of her scuffed boots, up her long legs, and zeroed in on the swish of the dress she was wearing. A floral number that showed off more of her thighs than it covered. His mouth went drier than the Sahara while his palms began to sweat enough to fill the lake behind his home. The dress was the perfect representation of her, deliciously sweet and seductively sinful.

She dutifully ignored him while he couldn't order his traitorous eyes to look anywhere but at the very slight bounce of her breasts as she climbed the stairs up to her seat. His cock throbbed anxiously against his boxers, raw with hunger. Naughty, naughty girl was clearly not wearing a bra.

If she had any idea how hard up he was, she wouldn't play so unfairly. It wasn't until she spun to take the seat beside Beth, four rows up and in his direct line of sight, that he discerned she'd also forgotten her panties.

For one quick moment, their eyes locked on one another. A jolt of heat shot through Dec. He was a bloody inferno. He licked his lips and gave her a slight headshake. Her mischievous grin said she knew precisely what she was doing to him.

Forcing his gaze back to her handwritten map of her own desires, he was fairly certain he understood her signals. He was going to have to bloody teach sitting at his desk lest the entire class know precisely what was on his mind.

Closing his eyes for just a minute, he ran the lyrics to Wonderwall through his head. God he hated that song. Every idiot who'd ever rubbed up against a guitar at a party could play Wonderwall but would rather Dec play it for them. In short order, his cock eased its choke-hold. His little guitarist hated the song, too.

When every seat save Trevor Jr's. was occupied, he went on with class. If the kid wasn't even going to show up, there wasn't much he could do, and the sooner he got this over with the sooner he could show his little minx what would happen if she kept playing with fire.

"Wednesday in class we discussed sex researcher John Money's concept of the love map and then John Gottman's slight adaptation on the concept of creating a sex map. Each of our love maps began developing from birth and takes shape throughout early life. Expectations of relationships are often influenced by the examples around us in childhood. As you age, your love maps evolve based on your sense of self within the relationships you seek or you're involved in."

Holly tried her damnedest to listen. She really did. The sticky wetness between her thighs was distracting. Her pulse sluiced through her veins, tapping out a frantic rhythm in her mound. Her own emptiness felt raw. Her breasts ached. Her mind had no trouble conjuring the recollections of his pierced cock filling her fully, sating her soul.

The way he'd watched her walk to her seat, the way he'd licked his lips, always the perfect mix of soft hunger and brutal possession, made her desperate.

Her love map paper had been on the top of his stack. *Playing fast and loose, Dr. St. James.* She wanted to scold him, but not nearly as much as she wanted him to discover that she was naked under this dress and to punish her for being naughty.

She shifted in her seat, futilely trying to bring herself some relief. Another round of wet heat coated her lips. If this class didn't end soon, she was going to look like she'd wet the damn dress, which was admittedly too short for her to have forgone panties.

His eyes flashed discreetly to hers when she repositioned in her seat yet again. A wicked grin formed on his chiseled features. She tried to communicate telepathically. *Aware I'm craving your wicked ways, professor? Good. End the damn class and take me home.* His pompous smirk said there was a decent chance he'd actually understood some of that.

"As you know, or you should, given that you're sitting in this class, the love map largely covers goals in relationships. Gottman guided it further into a kind of sex map, a part of every healthy relationship, and all of this leads us to the exploration of sexual fantasy and the part it plays in our adult lives, relationships, psychological development, and careers in psychology."

Blah, blah, blah. Gottman and Money and whatever. Sex. Relationships. I want both with you. Now. Get on with it. Holly shot Dec an impatient glare. He almost laughed out loud. Biting his lips together he returned to his desk to regain his composure and pick up a stack of computer paper.

"I had you quickly chart out, as best as you could, both the influences of your love map and what your map might look like and give brief explanations of how your map might've been developed and how it could help you navigate future relationships as that is the entire point of the exercise. In therapy sessions, a love map is often the first thing you'll have patients complete. Then you were instructed to expand on the idea of the map and to detail out a kind of sex map for either yourselves or an imaginary patient you were in charge of counseling. A few of you made me concerned this was the first psychology class you'd ever taken." He clicked a remote in his hands and further reading on John Gottman's works displayed on the wall.

Holly fidgeted with the pencil in her hand and tried to think of anything but Dec. His sultry, graveled voice and that damned seductive accent filled her head with far too many ideas, however. She uncrossed and re-crossed her legs. The stale air in the room taunted her damp skin. Dec's eyes locked between her legs for a split second. It occurred to Holly that given the height of her desk in the room, he could see up her dress from his vantage point on the floor. Heat pricked her cheeks, but this was her only class in a lecture hall. No one else would've been able to view everything God gave her. Everyone's eyes were locked on the screen where Dec's class notes were displayed from his computer. Per orders given, everyone dutifully copied the information in pencil.

Taking advantage of the opportunity provided, she slowly uncrossed her legs again. Edged the fabric of her dress up ever so slightly. Licked her lips. Watched every muscle in his body tense. And then re-crossed her legs, swinging her booted foot like she had no cares in the world.

His pierced brow lifted in challenge, then he set the remote on his desk for the purposes of rubbing his hands together. Her nipples were hardened pearls beneath her dress. They ached. Every caress of the fabric sent a fresh jolt of fresh lust through her. Her mouth flooded with saliva. Heat surged outward from her pussy to her limbs until she was concerned she might spontaneously combust in the middle of the lecture hall.

Dec cleared his throat. His voice was slightly strained but he managed, "It is important to remember that our love maps do not necessarily lead to any other destination than the one of self-discovery. Also keep in mind that like all of us, it evolves over time. Marriage should never be viewed as the endpoint of either the traditional love map nor our expanded sex map. Different people may leave their mark upon your maps, but it is our job as therapists to guide our patients to the understanding that they and only they should ever be the compass of their own relationship desires."

The word *desires* whipped and whirled through Holly's imagination. *Dammit, Dec. End class.*

"I'm going to hand back your map work. We're going to expand the concepts beyond Money and Gottman's research. Attached to it is one of the many fantasies often discussed on maps. It will not be a fantasy on your own map if you included any, however. Monday in class you'll hand back a short essay on where the fantasy is believed to have originated, you will dismantle its stigma, and give examples of how the fantasy could be explored safely. If you believe the fantasy given is deviant, tell me that, but here's a clue, none of them are markers of deviance. Don't come in here with half a paragraph about how anyone with your given fantasy should seek counseling with an attached future business card. I will fail you. It won't even tax me to do so."

CHAPTER THIRTY-ONE

Seated on his sofa wearing nothing but a loose pair of workout shorts, Dec watched the sun sink low behind the cottonwood trees bordering the lake. She was on her way over. His pulse doubled the mark of the passing seconds. He sincerely hoped she was ready to start exploring a few of her fantasies because that was his plan for the entire evening.

His version of British curry bubbled slowly on the stove. The methodical preparations had barely distracted him through the late afternoon hours. He'd cook the rice after he had his say about her lack of undergarments and her flashing him in class.

The memory of her impish grin and the wildfire in her eyes branded itself in his brain once again. He had plenty to say about her behavior, all the things she'd used her wiles to ask for. Being possessive wasn't something he had to work at. With her, it came far too easily. Damn, but she was woman perfected. For the first time in his life he considered not resenting his entire existence. If it had all gotten him where he currently sat, maybe some of it was worth it.

The clock on the mantle chewed through the passing seconds too fucking slowly. He reviewed the psychology behind her relatively well-concealed requests. Desire was the ultimate female orgasm. Anyone with a dick and half a brain who was paying attention should know that. Being the single focused object of his desires was not a problem. She just needed to see and feel him react. Proving his rampant desire was his only goal.

He'd left the garage door open. The chug of her truck motor announced her arrival. Her quick rap on the kitchen door surged another flood of heated blood to his cock. "It's open, baby."

Her appearance affected every cell in his body. In one fluid motion, he was off the couch relieving her of her bags. She eyed him hopefully, but there was more than a note of nervousness tensing her pretty mouth. He said nothing, just set the bags at the bottom of the steps to be retrieved later.

Returning to the kitchen, he took her hand and jerked her forward. As she collided with the solid wall of his chest, he wrapped her up in his arms and growled in her ear. "You are in so much trouble, young lady."

The tender tremble of her body vibrated his soul.

"For what?" Her feigned innocence was perforated with reckless desperation and a small helping of fear. *Slow it down, St. James. Don't get ahead of yourself.*

She was so damned intoxicating he longed to forget the whole thing, but she wanted to explore. She'd made that more than clear. All he wanted was to take care of her. She wanted something a touch more erotic.

Whisking her up into his arms, he ignored her quick gasp of breath. Her body was far too tense for his liking. He settled her in his lap, cradling her face against his shoulder. "Quite sure you know why you're in trouble. Taunting me. Tempting me. Showing off what belongs to me and only me to any man fortunate enough to be walking behind you. Your gorgeous ass is mine, sweetheart. All for me. And I have plenty to say about you showing it off."

It took less than half a second for his hand to lift the flimsy dress, baring her to his voracious eyes. His right hand landed on her ass. He cupped a handful of her flesh making his cock throb against her. "All mine."

Her breaths came in quick bursts. "Yes." She ground against him now, abandoning the case of nerves she'd been unnecessarily carrying.

"It hurt, didn't it, baby? Hurt to sit there imagining all the things you needed me to do to you. Made you wet for me, didn't it?"

"God, yes."

"Good, because I had to stand up there in front of the whole fucking class so hard for you I burned. Thought you'd taunt me flashing your pretty little snatch all for me. Showing me what I already know is mine."

Her low, breathy mewl of need cinched like a vice around his cock.

"You really think you'd get away with it, honey? Did you really believe I wouldn't remind you that I'm the only one who gets to see you like that, and that I'll look my fill whenever and wherever I want?" She rocked her hips back and forth against his erection, desperate now. Just how he wanted her. "Answer me."

"I wanted you to know how bad I need you. How bad I want you."

"I think what you want is to be bad *for* me. You want me to make you be bad don't you, love?"

Her response came through loud and clear. She threaded her fingers through his hair. Her lips crashed down on his, full and ripe. She opened for him readily. Their tongues tangled, each anxious for the upper hand. That beautiful mouth of hers; he had several plans for it as well.

Catching her bottom lip between his teeth he sucked until he could feel the wet heat spilling from her vagina through the thin shorts he was wearing. The flavors of her succulent mouth took up residence in his groin. Sweet as candy and spicier than sin. Perfection. He'd been on knife's edge of arousal since long before he'd gotten a sneak peek of what he planned to thoroughly enjoy that weekend. She consumed his every thought. Longing had sharpened his desires and dominated his every waking thought. In the dark of night when he couldn't sleep without her in his arms, it was the sweet addiction of her that sang for him.

He jerked his head away, and gently cradled her chin in his hand. "You're all mine, all for me and no one else. Only I get to see you uncovered. Only I get to see you undone. You understand that?"

Challenge lit the pools of emerald flames in her eyes. Her long lashes blinked once in contemplation. "Might need a reminder."

If there'd been any doubt as to what exactly she wanted, she'd erased it all in one quick phrase. Shifting his hips, he turned her and laid her face down across his lap.

"Oh God, yes," she begged. Arching her back, she presented her ass all for him. Oh, hell yeah.

Flipping the dress upwards, he cupped his hand. He had no intention of actually hurting her. This was about freeing the constraints, taking what she didn't want to admit she needed to give. The round feminine globe of her right cheek jiggled and pinked slightly on his first strike. He made another then massaged away the sting. "All for me and no one else, ever."

Tracing his fingers up her slit, he groaned out his approval. She was drenched.

"More." Any inhibition or nervousness she'd had disappeared completely, precisely the way it was supposed to.

Two more strikes and he rubbed with more vigor, absorbing the shock. His cock stabbed hard against her abdomen. He didn't know how much longer he could go without getting off. That gorgeous ass, plump and pink, drove him mad. She was wetter than he'd ever felt her, saturated with arousal. He made another strike. This time he felt the sting in his own hand. "You need more, baby, or can you be a good girl for me?"

"More," she demanded.

He continued.

"Oh God." In one quick move she'd slipped from his knees to the floor. "I can be good." She played her part too fucking well. The pout of her lips, the feral look in her eyes, her body painted in a dozen shades of pink nothing as fevered as her ass and her pussy.

She jerked the elastic of his shorts down. That was all he was wearing. She purred her approval.

"There's a good girl. You're gonna suck me off. Swallow all of me down for making me hurt with wanting you." Gathering her hair in his right hand, he edged forward on the couch, certain he wouldn't last more than two sucks. She'd wanted instruction. He didn't know how long he'd be able to survive this. She was the walking, talking embodiment of his every fantasy, and she was on her knees before him.

"Lick my head and run your tongue around the ridge and my piercing."

She complied instantly. Her wet mouth mocking his staying power. Two swipes of her tongue and one quick, suckled kiss on his head and he writhed, crushing her hair tighter in his fist, releasing the soft feminine scents of her shampoo. It coupled with her musk, driving him closer to the edge.

"Now suck more. Wrap your right hand around my shaft and take as much as you can."

A carnal cry of wanton urgency vibrated through him as she obeyed. Dec gripped the arm of the couch, ordering himself not to thrust into her mouth lest he choke her, but sweet Jesus she was good, too bloody good. He gave a shallow thrust, unable to help himself. She relaxed her throat like a pro and took all he gave.

"So fucking good," he managed to grunt. His jaw clenched. The strokes of her tongue fried every nerve ending in his body. He tensed. Unable to give anymore verbal instruction he grabbed her left hand and showed her how to cup his sac. "Gentle, baby. Just like that," he managed in a breathless choke. Sweat sheened his brow.

Another sweet moan reverberated from her mouth through him. "I'm coming. Swallow it all," preceded his body seizing. He came with a savage cry of her name and three quick thrusts up into her mouth.

The room spun. His vision clouded and white pops of ecstasy flared against his eyelids. She stayed with him as he flooded her mouth, swallowing and licking him clean until he had to stop her.

Trying desperately to remember that he'd more than just pushed her boundaries with the spanking, he forced his muscles to work, though he would've paid a king's ransom for her to crawl up on his chest and take a nap with him.

Instead, he lifted her up into his lap and let her hide. She nuzzled her face against his neck and curled herself into a tight ball. Grinning at that, he wrapped her up in his strength. "That all okay, sweetheart?"

"That was so freaking hot. I've never been so turned on. I think that's what scares me."

"You know I would never actually hurt you."

"I know. It's more that it made me feel so out of control, and I liked it even more than I thought I would."

"Being safely out of control is supposed to feel good. I love you, Holly. I love that you let me own your fantasies and live out my own. I've screwed up so much in this life, but I swear I will do anything to keep this good."

"I know you will. I told you we're worth all of the having to hide and other crap that comes with you teaching at UN. And," she brushed a kiss on his collarbone, inhaling the musky flavors of Dcc aroused mixed in with his cologne, "I love you, too."

"Promise?"

"Promise."

Despite all that she did know, she hadn't expected being turned over his knee or being on her knees before him to add new dimensions to their love making, to their entire relationship. He'd managed to run his fingers through her soul. He'd revealed a deeper being, one she hadn't ever experienced before. He unfolded the complicated truths she kept locked tightly away and more than that he loved her still. On top of all of that, she hadn't even climaxed yet she felt fulfilled in every possible way.

Cuddling against his shoulder, she loved the grin she felt against her head. If he'd held her like that for another few minutes, she would have drifted off to sleep.

"Are you hungry, baby? I cooked. Just need to make the rice."

"You cooked?"

"Did you think I was going to keep you holed up here all weekend and not feed you?" Humor played in his drowsy tone. Must've been a good orgasm. Pleased with that she spun her tongue just under his ear, indulging herself in his every flavor.

"Mmm, honey, you do very wicked things with that tongue of yours. Don't worry, after I feed you I plan to see what other wicked things you might be up for."

"I can't wait, and now that I can focus, whatever you fixed smells yummy."

"It's British curry. Ever had curry?"

Holly shook her head. "No, but I like trying new things. We pretty much eat beef all the time, so something different sounds amazing."

"Then you sit right here and let me go make you dinner, Ms. Camden."

"We always call it supper." Holly had no idea why that was important. She suddenly wanted Dec to know every intricate detail of her life. "Can I help?"

"You can come with me and keep me company, but let me take care of you." Holly followed him into his massive kitchen and grinned when he lifted her up to sit on his countertop. The cool granite dissolved the remaining sting of the spanking she'd just received. She suspected that had been his plan all along. "Only fancy Brits call it supper. I've only just broken myself of calling it tea."

"You're not a fancy Brit?"

"Sheep-shagger, remember?"

"Yeah, but after you got your degree you weren't a sheep *farmer* anymore."

"True, but one does not move between social classes easily. Once a sheep-shagger, always a sheep-shagger. My ex's father never failed to mention what I'd done coming up to anyone with any influence in proper London society."

"Sounds like a shitlicker that needs to get his ass whupped. I have shit-kickin' boots just for occasions like that."

She loved Dec's laugh. Love the way it eased the tensed lines of his face and the way the light played in the grey of his eyes when she said something he found funny.

"I swear, I fall more and more in love with you with every passing moment. I suppose he would be Sir Shitlicker as he was knighted for exemplary service in Psychology. Your boots won't be necessary. I'm just thrilled to be done with the lot of them."

"Knighted like with the sword and the Queen and everything?"

"The Queen and everything. I attended the ceremony. His daughter, my wife at the time," he shuddered and Holly couldn't help but grin, "was in Paris with her lover, and was therefore indisposed and could not attend."

"I'm sorry about everything bad that happened to you, Dec. I'm sorry you had to be around people like that."

He turned on the eye under the pot of rice he'd measured out before he came to stand between her legs. "Most of it was of my own making. I'm sorry for what it cost my family and Evie. Mostly, I'm sorry you have to deal with my shitty mistakes."

"So you made some mistakes. We all make mistakes. I'm in love with you. We're worth everything we have to do to make this work." She wrapped her arms around his neck and pulled him close.

"I couldn't agree more. I just hope it doesn't end up like every other thing in my life seems to."

"It won't." Holly sat back when he went to stir the rice.

His brow furrowed when she ran her right hand through her hair. "What happened here, love?" He took her hand and planted a kiss in the center of her palm along the long white scarred skin.

"Grabbed the wrong end of the branding iron when I was four. See, documented proof that we all screw up."

"You were four. Pretty sure that does not qualify as anything more than being a curious child."

"My poor daddy. He'll never forgive himself for it. He'd laid the iron down while we were working cattle. I got to it before he realized. I feel bad he still feels so guilty about it."

"Speaking of your father, may I ask you something?"

"Sure." Holly wondered what he wanted to know about her daddy.

"Occasionally, being a sex therapist gets the better of me, and I can't quite leave all of my work at work. Feel free to tell me to blow off. I just wondered if your father ever spanked you."

A flood of heat scalded Holly's cheeks and her first reaction to that question was to laugh hysterically.

"Something funny?" Dec was chuckling too.

Holly scrubbed her hands over her face, hoping to rid herself of the rash of redness discussing being spanked brought on. She didn't fully understand why she found the thought of Everett Camden spanking either her or her sister so funny, but she couldn't seem to regain her composure.

"I'm truly lost, Holl."

Finally able to draw breath, she grinned, no longer caring that she probably looked like an overly ripe tomato. "You called me Holl. I love that."

"I heard Beth call you that in class Wednesday, and Trace calls you that. I liked how intimate it sounds. I wanted to try it out."

"Everyone who loves me calls me that, so you should keep calling me that. To answer your question, my daddy would never in this lifetime or ten others have ever laid a hand on me or Natalie. He barely ever even spanked my brothers, and trust me, occasionally they deserved it. It's just not his style. Plus, I'm the baby and I am a spoiled brat, just ask my brothers."

Still chuckling, Dec brushed a kiss on top of her head. "I completely understand your father wanting to spoil you, but you are far from a brat. I was ever so briefly married to a brat, so I would know. Now, tell me this — if this all goes as planned, what will your father and brothers think of me being the guy who wants to make you his forever? Former drug user, dealer with a record, sex therapist, the whole deal."

"You forgot heavily tattooed and pierced rock star. Have to paint the whole bad boy picture." Holly rolled her eyes.

"Okay, all of that."

"To borrow one of my mama's favorite expressions, I don't give a half a hoot or a holler what anyone thinks of us, baby. You're mine. You're the greatest thing that's ever happened to me. I can honestly say I didn't even know what love was until I met you. My brothers will get over it. All my daddy wants is for me to be happy. You make me very happy. Now, feed me, I'm hungry."

"Just fed you, didn't I?" Dec winked at her.

"Very funny."

"Oh, you mean something besides my cock."

"For now."

CHAPTER THIRTY-TWO

With her stomach full of warm, spicy curry and rice and her body limp from the first orgasm of many over the course of their weekend, Holly lolled naked on Dec's couch, tucked up on his chest.

"Absolutely incredible," he sighed.

"Me leaning over the couch with my ass in the air, or are you applauding your own prowess, Dr. St. James?"

"My own skill, obviously."

Giggling, she ran her hand up his chest and twisted his nipple.

"Don't make me spank you again," he teased.

"But that was my entire plan."

"I do love how incredibly naughty you are, darling, and this is the problem with dating an old guy. I'm beat."

"You're not old. I just wore you out. I could make coffee."

"Drugging oneself to stay awake is not really the best idea."

"We can go to bed if you want."

"Nah, just give me a minute. It's still early and after tomorrow night, I have to go yet another week without you. I don't want to sleep at all. I want to spend every moment I have with you."

"We do have to sleep some. Besides, I love sleeping in your arms. I never want to sleep any other way."

"You in my arms is the only way I sleep. Believe me, I want the same thing."

Glancing around his living room, Holly noted the three guitars mounted on display over the mantle. She wondered where the ones he actually played were located. "Hey, Dec?"

"Hmm?"

"Would you play for me?"

"Sit up." He patted her backside and then guided her up off of the couch. "Come with me."

"Where are we going?"

"My music room is down in the basement. I had it finished out when I moved in. The acoustics down there are brilliant, and it's soundproofed. I can play anything you want as loud as you'd like without making my neighbors despise me."

"I doubt they could hear much. They're so far away."

"Yet another thing I love about this house. Come on." Dec grabbed the t-shirt he'd pulled on for dinner and tugged it over her body. She inhaled deeply, loving the way it felt against her skin.

When he'd slipped back into his workout shorts, he took her hand and led her down a long stairwell.

Grabbing one of his favorite Stratocasters, Dec settled in his chair and grinned as Holly extended herself on the black leather sofa he'd procured for the music room.

She was framed between his wall of mounted vinyls. The Gibson signed by Dave Grohl and the Fender Telecaster signed by Eddie Vedder hung on the wall over the couch, two massive amps, his pick-guard signed by none other than Van Halen, and his massive Radio 1 tower sign took up all of the wall opposite the room. Had he not been certain the most stunningly beautiful thing he'd ever seen was her climaxing hard and fast on his cock, he would have assumed that this was beauty personified.

"Dec, this room is amazing. Did you meet all of these people?"

"A few. Opened for Pearl Jam once before I crashed and burned."

"Oh my gosh, I had no idea. I mean, not that you aren't a fantastic musician, I just didn't know how famous you were."

He tried not to let the word *were* sting, but it did. All part of what he'd lost when he'd chosen cocaine over music.

"What would the lady like to hear?" He made a few tuning adjustments while he let the regret wash over him yet again. Feeling that regret, the reminder, made it easier not to make the same mistakes again.

"Will you play my song?" She bit her lip like she wasn't certain that was an allowable request.

With that tender timid question, the regret was washed away. He couldn't access his mistakes. He was staring at his future smiling at him sweetly. As he began her song, the past slipped through his strumming fingers.

He hadn't expected the tears she was blinking away when he finished. "I can't believe you wrote that for me."

"I can't believe you love me."

"Well, I do."

"I know."

"Can I ask you something?" Holly shifted on the couch to study him.

"Anything, baby."

"You never told me why you hate The Beatles, but I get the feeling there's a really good reason."

"My father loved them. I spent the better part of my teens learning to play American rock because I knew deep down it pissed him off. I refused to ever play The Beatles, and that was all he ever listened to. I'm sure what I wanted was for him to finally blow up and shout at me, do anything but drink and refuse to communicate. It never worked, but I still can't listen to them without wanting to vomit."

"I knew there was a good reason. I'm sorry, Dec."

"Don't be." He shook his head. "Not worth being sorry over now. Hit me with another request?"

Her smile returned though it bore the weight of being forced. "Your Van Halen riffs are pretty amazing, but I also love old school Pearl Jam. Oh, and lately I've been all about Arctic Monkeys."

"You are without a doubt the most perfect woman there has ever been."

"That's right. I am, just never forget that," she teased.

"Never, baby."

CHAPTER THIRTY-THREE

There was another small puddle of drool on his chest when Dec awoke the next morning and grinned rather stupidly, he was certain. He loved that she slept deeply enough to allow herself that.

She'd also fucked him so thoroughly the night before that there was no real need for him to work out that morning. His cravings were at an all-time low. Sex, it was good for so many things.

He noted the slight change in her breathing and wondered if she'd awoken or if she was dreaming. In that brief moment existing between slumber and consciousness, he allowed himself to imagine a real life with her.

In a few months' time, if they were incredibly lucky, they could ease into letting his colleagues at the University know that they were dating. Sure, people would be suspicious that it might've started earlier, but there would be no proof and she would no longer be his student.

A year from now, he'd leave the University, go back to counseling full time, and resume the life he'd come here to live with permanent residence. They could work together. He could help her with her research and getting her degree. She didn't need Newsome. He could be her advisor. He'd help her do anything in the world she wanted to do.

Newsome. His dinner that evening weighted his future planning. Having Holly in his home felt so right. The house itself was happier when she was there. She fit. A missing piece to his puzzle that slipped right in quickly, like it had known where it belonged all along. He had no interest in going to dinner with his new boss. It robbed him of precious time with her. If they were going to develop a healthy relationship concealed from the world, they needed to be together as much as possible.

But the world was a cold cruel place. He of all people knew that.

"What are you thinking about?" Her sleepy tone eased his mind and his soul.

"How did you know I was up thinking?"

"You were sound asleep. Your heartbeat was steady. Then you moved a little and got tense."

"I'm sorry, love, I was lamenting my dinner with Newsome. I don't want to leave you to spend time kissing his ass when I could be here licking yours."

Leaning up on her arm, she grinned down at him with her hair in a wild mane that he found sexy as hell. "Newsome isn't the kind of guy that wants his ass kissed, I swear, and it's only for a few hours. My human sexuality professor assigned me a paper I have to work on anyway."

"What a tosser, giving you homework when he knows you only get to be naked with him on the weekends."

"I know. He's a real hard ass." That infectious giggle was going to be his undoing.

"He should be punished."

"Mmm, and how would he like me to do that?"

"Well, actually, he was thinking that you've been terribly remiss when it comes to our love making, Ms. Camden."

"Oh really? And what exactly is it I haven't done."

Dec ran his hands down her soft curves, naked against him. Shifting to his back, he guided her up over his waist, straddling her tender pussy against his morning wood. "You, my sexy little cowgirl, have failed to show me just how well you ride."

She slid back and forth against him making him lengthen and throb. His cock knew precisely how to get where it desperately wanted to be. A delectable shiver shook through her when his piercing found her clit. "Well, Dr. St. James, it seems I'm all mounted up, so allow me to show you. Fair warning, I like to ride rough and dirty."

"I like rough and dirty."

"I know."

"Ride me, cowgirl."

Holly refused to be one of those girls that pouted. That was so not her. Cowgirls got up dusted themselves off, and either got back on the horse or got revenge on whatever had knocked them down, but Dec looked way too sexy dressed in a suit and combing his hair to be going out without her. Not that she resented being stuck in his house working on a paper while he went to dinner at Rodizio, but she was disappointed. This time there was no one to even be mad at. There was no horse to get back on. He had to go. She had to stay. Neither of them liked it.

"If you keep frowning like that, I'm going to call him and cancel. Don't give, as you like to say, a half a holler and a hoot what he thinks about it."

Grinning at her mother's saying in Dec's accent, Holly handed him his chosen tie. "It's a half hoot and a holler. Get it right, St. James."

"Dreadfully sorry, love. I'm still trying to get the intricacies of American English down. I'll add cowgirl dialect to my studies next."

"You can't cancel on Newsome. Plus, maybe you can put in a few good words for me."

"Obviously, discussing you will be my only goal for the evening. We can go over how intoxicating I find your laughter, how bloody brilliant you are, how exquisite your taste in music is, or how addicted I am to your stunningly gorgeous body, and how I intend to know every square inch of your silky skin long before this semester is over. The way your tits rob me of breath, the perfection of your ass and how pink I can turn it when I smack your bottom, or perhaps that exquisite little sound you make for me when my apa hits just the right spots. Or, I know, I could tell him how adorable I find it that you drool in your sleep."

Holly narrowed her eyes, caught between laughter and shoving him across the large master bathroom for pointing out those things to her. "I feel you really should remember how skilled I am with a rope, Dr. St. James."

"Does that mean if I keep teasing you, you'll show me your rope skills, honey? Dr. Newsome, sir, terribly sorry to miss our planned evening, I'm all tied up, quite literally." He waggled his eyebrows.

Rolling her eyes, Holly pinched his overly firm asscheek through his trousers.

"I'll be home in a few hours, and we can get to more of that."

"Would you behave?"

"Probably not. Especially since I'm about to have to go sit through dinner pretending that I haven't just had the best twenty-four hours of my entire life and trying not to lament that you're leaving to go work cattle early in the morning, meaning I get to return to my miserable existence without you."

"Believe me, I'd much rather be here than preg-testing mama cows, but a girl's gotta do what a girl's gotta do."

Dec cringed. "I suddenly feel a great deal of empathy for both you and the cows."

With a squirt of the cologne Holly adored, he declared himself ready. Since Holly had spent the day lounging in one of his vintage Radiohead t-shirts, she took the liberty of adding a fresh squeeze of the cologne. At least she'd could smell him while he was gone.

"You're killing me, love." Standing in his bathroom, he drew her into his arms and held her close, both of them willing time to freeze in that moment.

Holly tried to shake off the feelings of abandonment lest she inadvertently become one of those clingy girls that she found despicable. "I'll be fine. I'm gonna work on my paper and watch the game."

"What game?"

"We're playing Fresno tonight."

"Who is we?"

"UN."

"Ah, that's what all of the insanity was about on campus yesterday."

"Don't Brits watch soccer all the time?"

"No, we watch football. Real football. I have no idea why you call football soccer or why you play football at all. Has it never occurred to anyone else that only one player's foot ever even touches the ball?"

"Definitely do not say that to my brothers when you meet them."

"Noted, now come with me."

He led her back down the stairs to a small room off of the entryway she hadn't yet seen. Opening two sliding pocket doors he revealed an elaborate office. The walls were lined with bookshelves and a massive desk sat front and center.

"Most every book I used to get my doctorate, along with a few dozen others on all things sex therapy and development, are right here. Computer, much better than the shitty one you have, for looking up source information." He opened his personal laptop and set it on the desk. "And of course, pencils." He lifted two mugs full of Tombow pencils, one from the desk and one on a shelf in front of a line of books. "Now, I love you. I will try to keep this short, and when you finish your paper I will reward your efforts mightily."

Beaming at him, Holly laughed. "Definitely looking forward to that."

"Good." He gave her backside a light swat before he shrugged into his jacket.

After an extended goodbye kiss, Holly settled into his desk chair. The office was a tad intimidating. She much preferred the creative flow of the music room downstairs. Dec's office somehow felt like a removable segment of himself, aside from the rest, like a coat he donned when it was far too warm to wear one. Being downstairs felt like being wrapped up in his soothing presence. She couldn't argue that the resources available in the office were better than the sciences library at the University though, so she settled in to write the paper.

"It's not going to be too short of an essay if I have to quote five different sources, Dec." Still feeling a little sorry for herself that he was out to dinner and she was there working, she scanned the copy of her lovemap until she landed on the fantasy she was to write her paper about. Her mouth dropped open. Panic sizzled up her spine and her thighs locked tightly together. He wanted her to write an essay on *this*. This, the most untouchable of all female fantasies. The most intimidating. Also one of the most common, she guessed she had to give him that. She was supposed to dismantle the stigmas surrounding this fantasy. What happened to giving her the easy topics?

CHAPTER THIRTY-FOUR

Thoroughly confused, Dec swung his leg off of his bike and stared at The Rodizio Grill. The place was packed, noise assaulted the exhaust-filled wind in the parking lot, and this didn't seem like the kind of place Richard Newsome would pick for dinner.

Reviewing his self-imposed rules for this meal, mainly that he would scrub his mind of any knowledge of Holly and behave like a man forced to work for the University despite his own wishes, he entered the restaurant and was immediately swarmed by servers dressed as gauchos wielding swords of meat, and by greeters whisking by patrons awaiting tables surrounding the largest salad bar Dec had ever seen. The live band on the back deck was horrendously off-key and garbling whatever song they were supposed to be singing.

"Bollocks," he seethed under his breath. He'd left Holly at home in the peaceful quiet of his house with money for ordered pizza when he could have prepared most any meal she might've liked and then spent the evening listening to her talk, and sigh, and laugh, and moan.

A greeter descended upon him. "Welcome to the Rodizio Grill. Table for one?"

"No. Uh, I'm meeting a colleague here. Dr. Richard Newsome."

"Yes, Dr. Newsome. He's a regular. This way."

Dec dutifully followed the woman to a more private area on the opposite side of the restaurant. Thanking the Lord for small favors, he noted the music wasn't quite as incursive here.

Ten feet from the table, Dec froze. Bile flooded his throat. Abject panic seared through his veins. *Shit.* This could not be happening. He rocked forward on his feet desperate to run away. There, in a private corner in the back of the ridiculous slaughter house, sat Newsome, a woman who appeared to be his wife as she was approximately his age and he was buttering a roll for her, and yet another far younger woman dressed for what appeared to have been a date. She sat alone opposite the Newsomes, and Dec fought not to vomit. This was a setup.

What the fuck was he supposed to say? He would never jeopardize what he had with Holly, even if it was to save his job. However, not saving his job meant losing Holly as maintaining a lifelong relationship some four thousand miles apart was not really a viable option.

"Ma'am." He halted the greeter on her path to the table. "You said the Newsomes were regulars. Do you know whom the woman seated with them might be?"

"Yes, sir, that's their daughter, Olivia."

———

Trevor tapped the steering wheel while he waited in his darkened car hidden across the street from his professor's house. He'd been there the whole damn day, and had finally caught a break in the form of a pizza delivery guy, an undergrad at UN. Lucky for him he had one resource pizza-boy did not, money. And his money was working for him.

Dr. St. James was a bastard, and Holly Camden wasn't going to stand in his way anymore. Starry-eyed cowgirl needed to go back to the ranch before she ruined everything. She'd taken one too many wrong steps this time, and he was about to own her *and* St. James. Idiots. Both of them. Holly needed to learn that you couldn't always do just what you wanted to do. If he didn't have that freedom, neither did she.

Besides, did they really think they wouldn't get caught? Holly always thought she could get away with murder and use her smarts to get her out of it. Well, not this time. Try talking your way out of an ethics code violation, bitch.

Finally. The pizza guy, Mike or Mark or whatever his name was, backed his late-model Taurus down the long driveway. Trevor flashed his lights. When Mike parked his car beside Trevor's, he got out.

"Dude, this feels really stalkerish. If she ends up on the news, I'm coming clean. I don't care how much you pay me," he stammered.

Rolling his eyes, Trevor pulled another bill out of his wallet. "I'm not gonna kill her, you jack-weasel. I just needed confirmation that she's there. I'm getting her kicked out of school, and that's it. Did you get the picture of them together?"

"No, she's the only one there. I texted you what I got, but it's uh. . .mostly my thumb. You can kind of see her, though."

"Did she act suspicious?"

"Nah, seemed kind of distracted."

"Just keep taking pics of her anywhere you see her. Here's a few extra Benjamins for your efforts."

Mike all but drooled when Trevor thrust the wad of bills into his grubby fists. "If you need anything else let me know," he volunteered eagerly.

Yeah, now he was willing to work. "You just keep your mouth shut. If you get called back out here, try to get something with both of them in it."

"No problem."

You're being paranoid. Holly grabbed a paper towel while she paced around Dec's home eating another piece of greasy pizza. *The pizza guy was not acting weird, and you've never seen him before.* She'd been telling herself this through the last two pieces. The blank paper still mocked her. She had no idea where to even begin. She had managed to locate a few sources on her assigned topic, but they hadn't been easy to come by.

Then there was Dec's frantic text, apparently from the restaurant restroom, that said not to text him back but that he needed her to know how much he loved her and that he had no idea until he'd walked into the steakhouse that Newsome was trying to set him up.

Holly tried to imagine Dr. Newsome setting Dec up to fail at anything. That just wasn't the Dr. Newsome she'd learned from for the last several years. She knew the head of the Psych department was a decent, hard-working man who wanted everyone to succeed. She could read people — that's why she wanted to be a psychologist for heaven's sake. What on earth had Dec meant? She didn't know and wasn't allowed to ask.

Yeah, you can read people, so you know the pizza dude was creepy as fuck. Listen to your gut, Holly. She checked the locks on the front and back door again. She wanted Dec to come home almost as much as she wanted to take Dec to her home. Not her apartment on the other side of town; no, she wanted the quiet rolling flatlands, the low bellow of the cattle, her big brothers, her daddy, the half-dozen cattleguards preventing anything from getting too close, and her horses. She was being a big baby, and she wanted to go home.

The roar of the flat screen TV in the living room said at least the Huskers were having a great night. That was something.

CHAPTER THIRTY-FIVE

Dec withered in the chair he'd tried to discreetly angle away from Olivia. This was a shitfest wrapped up in a clusterfuck, and after this, he got to go home and tell the woman he'd fallen madly in love with in one-fifth of a second that he'd been on a date. Being on the receiving end of her cowgirl rage was not something he wanted to experience, but he was doomed. If he managed to talk his way out of this, someone should give him an award. Hell, *he* should be knighted for exemplary damage control and conflict management.

Why, did the universe hate him?

"Olivia's a market analyst at Buckley Air Force base in Denver," Mrs. Newsome offered hopefully.

Dec feigned a semi-interested nod while wondering what on earth the Air Force needed with a market analyst. What was their market? As far as he understood it, they flew planes, dropped bombs, and did something with drones, maybe. Victoria had run off with a French pilot, not that Dec had particularly cared until it had cost him his job. He still wasn't a fan of pilots, though.

A gaucho-clad waiter slammed yet another sword full of non-descript meat down on the table. Certain he was going to vomit, Dec knew he was in hell, but going home to his heavenly angel would only bring on their first argument faster.

"We've just managed to add Dr. St. James to the psychology department recently. He was a lead therapist at Lifespan. Worked at London's top counseling center prior, and is also a rather gifted guitarist," Dr. Newsome continued to sing Dec's praises.

"Lead *sex* therapist. I'm also a recovering addict." *There. Take that, Dad.* He prayed Olivia didn't have a thing for bad boys.

Newsome looked more surprised than offended. "And always candid. I appreciate that."

Olivia, thankfully, looked rather put off. She picked at the chicken on her plate. "Uh, guitarist. That's interesting. What brought you to Lincoln?"

"Lifespan graciously hired me. I'm rather anxious to get back to counseling."

"Ah, don't give up on the University yet. Students are already singing your praises," Newsome urged.

Dec highly doubted that was true. He adjusted his collar yet again. Damned thing was choking him. And why was it so bloody hot in there? The meat-laced humidity wrapped around him like a straightjacket.

"So, what kind of guitar do you play?" Olivia seemed pleased she'd come up with a question that involved the words *guitar* and *play*.

"I own twenty-seven different guitars. I occasionally play all of them." What the hell was she even asking him?

"I meant what kind of music do you play?"

"I can play most anything. Classic rock is by far my favorite. Play a fair amount of metal as well. My gir. . . . Uh, I'm learning more country, currently. Don't have a lot of it in Britain, but I rather enjoy the lyrics." *Christ's sake, St. James, what is wrong with you? Go ahead and tell them all about how your girlfriend loves country and you're learning for her, you imbecilic wanker.*

"I really prefer jazz or classical. I also love opera. Rock is prosaic in my opinion, and the shouting in metal is highly unnecessary. I don't mind that song Wonderwall, though. I believe it's by Oceans or something like that. Do you ever play it?"

"No, and it's Oasis."

"See, I know nothing about that genre of overly-branded shouting." She laughed at her own joke. Dec shuddered in his seat. "I did manage seats at the Ellie for Lucia di Lammermoor. Fantastic production. Have you ever seen it?"

"I have no idea what it even is." Dec was more than over trying to keep Newsome happy. This ambush of a dinner was more than he could take.

"It's a fantastic opera about a woman who's forced to marry for money, loses her mind, and murders her bridegroom. Stunningly beautiful story." That remark was shot directly to Olivia's father.

So that was it. Daddy was trying to fix her up with Dec because of his money. Clean breath filled Dec's lungs. This he could deal with. She had no more interest in him than he did in her, but she'd come to keep her parents happy.

Newsome's white flag was all but visible. With that comment, he gave up the task of playing matchmaker for his daughter. Thank God.

"I did want to ask you to keep your eyes on a few students for me in your foundations research class, Dr. St. James, if you wouldn't mind," Newsome and his wife shared a discreet glance, acknowledging their loss.

"Certainly, sir."

"Have you had any interactions with Holly Camden? She's in the class I mentioned. Generally wears cowgirl boots." Newsome chuckled.

Oh, I've had so many interactions with my cowgirl, sir. Interactions that have changed my entire life. "I've not spoken with her outside of class, but her work on Money's love map reflected a brilliant mastery of the concepts of sexual psychology. I assigned a paper over the weekend." *That she's at my house working on.* "I'll know more when I see more of her writing."

"She's an outstanding student. Brilliant young lady. Turned down a generous offer from Stanford so she could continue to help her family run their ranch out in Pleasant Glen. Tiny town out in cattle country. I'd truly like to give her a hand up if we can. It takes quite a bit to pull yourself up from cowgirl to doctor, I expect."

In Dec's opinion, Holly didn't need to try to be one or the other. She needed to be who she was. Her profession did not and should never define her. "I agree, sir."

"And how is Dr. Singleton's son doing?" Newsome's entire demeanor fell with that question. Interesting.

"He puts forth little to no effort in class. Didn't even come to class yesterday. His work on the love map was something out of a dirty movie, pardon me for saying so," Dec offered the women seated at the table.

Olivia looked relieved that her father had dropped the fix-up charade and offered him a sincere chuckle. "I work on an Air Force base. You can't shock me."

Newsome sighed. "I'm between a rock and a hard place with Trevor. Not certain what to do. If you wouldn't mind offering him any hand you can. For my conscience, I need to know we did everything we could to help him succeed."

"I'm happy to help any way I can, but I cannot pass him if he doesn't come to class and do the work."

"I would never ask you to. I just need to know that the entire department has reached out to him. There's a bit more to the story than we can discuss here."

"I understand, sir."

Eventually, the Newsomes were meat-stuffed and thanking Dec profusely for meeting them for dinner.

He thanked them for the invite awkwardly and had almost made a full escape to his bike when Olivia appeared.

Another round of panic slammed in Dec's steak-lined gut. He backed up as she advanced. "I'm not going to attack you, Dr. St. James. I wanted to apologize. I've accepted a position with the Air Force that moves me to the Pentagon in two-months. Daddy cannot give up the idea that if I fell in love with someone here in Lincoln, I would move back and be close to them. I'm sorry you got yourself thrown under the bus. If it makes you feel better, I had no idea you were coming until you arrived."

"Thank you for your explanation. I had no idea your father thought of me as a potential mate for you. I honestly didn't even know he had a daughter."

"Mama's sister set my parents up on a blind date they didn't know they were going on. If it worked for them. . . ." she shrugged.

"I see."

"Forgive me for being forward, Dr., but I wanted to make you an offer. Whomever your girlfriend is, I'd be glad to tell her that neither of us had any idea we were being set up, and that you were a perfect gentleman."

Dec sank his teeth into his tongue. Treading on extremely dangerous ground. To acknowledge Holly or lie outright when his opponent seemed just as adept at reading people as any psychologist. Her father's daughter through and through.

Olivia chuckled. "I'm not really that appalling to spend a few hours with, but you looked absolutely horrified when they brought you to the table, and, uh, there's a smudge of something light pink on your collar. I'm guessing Chapstick."

Instinctively, Dec thumbed the collar of his shirt. "I. . .uh. . . I am completely, madly, irrevocably in love with her. I don't like to mix my personal life with my business life. I lied to your father. I told him I wasn't seeing anyone."

Olivia gave him a genuine grin. "I'm about to go back to Mom and Dad's to pretend that I'm not shacking up with a stunt pilot. They really prefer for me to date the stodgy type who'll keep me settled firmly on the ground. I like to fly. Little weary of them playing matchmaker."

"Yes, I figured that out when you brought up the murder of the bridegroom in the opera."

Olivia's harsh laughter irritated the cool night air. God, he missed Holly.

"Sometimes Daddy needs it spelled out for him."

"Understood. I'm going to head out."

"It was nice to meet you, Dr. St. James. I'll keep your relationship secret as long as you do the same for me."

"Not a problem." The rev of his Harley split the night. Whatever was going to happen when he explained this to Holly, he wanted to get on with it. If he ended up sleeping on his own sofa, so be it. He just needed to be in her presence. This fucked up night was more than he could endure any longer.

Scanning the moonlit lake for the tenth time in as many minutes, Holly told herself yet again that she hadn't seen some kind of recognizable human form in Dec's backyard. She was just imagining things.

Every light in the house was on. Cementing herself as a big baby in her own mind, she'd gone as far as to call Luke just to hear him tell her that her imagination had run away with her, but that had only led to a lecture from her big brother for staying over at some guy's house and questions as to why he wasn't there with her.

The garage door raised and every hair on her body stood on end. She flew to the door and collapsed into Dec's chest before he'd pulled off his helmet.

His warm chuckle eased her restless mind. "One second." When the helmet and leathers were off, he drew her back into his arms and kissed the top of her head. "You okay, baby?"

"Yes. No. I don't know. Just come inside and lock the door."

She half dragged him to the couch in the living room and tried to wait patiently while he jerked off his tie and button-down shirt, then she curled up in a ball in his lap.

"I'm loving this, sweetheart, but your heart is racing and you look like you saw a ghost. What happened?"

"You're going to think I'm a big huge baby that's entirely too immature to be your girlfriend."

"I would never think that. I'm right here. I will hold you like this forever if you'd like. You talk whenever you're ready."

"Now you're psychologist-ing me."

"I'm not trying to, I swear. Can't always take the psychologist out of the man."

Summoning courage she hadn't been able to locate until he got home, she lifted her head. "I don't know what's wrong with me. I was okay until the pizza guy came. He acted weird, super weird. He kept messing with his phone even when I was trying to pay him, and he kept asking if I was here alone. Then I thought I saw a man in the backyard. I'm sure it's nothing. All my imagination. I've been calling myself an infant for the last two hours."

"Sweetheart, I am so sorry." He tucked her head back under his chin, rubbed his hands up and down her back, and brushed kisses in her hair.

"You don't have anything to be sorry for." Unable to help herself, she nuzzled against his neck and fisted his undershirt in her hand.

"I do. I am an idiot of epic proportion, and I am so very sorry."

Holly raised her head ready to argue now. "Dec, you are not. You didn't do anything wrong."

"Baby, I left you home alone in this ridiculously huge house, that you aren't used to, and instructed you to write a paper on rape. I am sick. I cannot believe it never occurred to me that you might be unnerved by that fantasy. I am so sorry."

She slumped back against him in relief. That's why she was so jumpy. Of course. Why hadn't she realized? She'd never equated the topic of the paper to her case of nerves. It all made sense as soon as he said it. "Why *did* you give me that topic?" Okay, so she was a little annoyed now.

"It seemed to line up with your dissertation goals. I swear. . .I just never considered that it would throw you. I didn't expect it to even take you an hour to dismantle. I was completely insensitive to the fact that you are a woman and that even the idea of it as a fantasy might frighten you, rightly so. Please forgive my incredible stupidity, and that is unfortunately not the end of my apologies for the evening. I told you I'm no good at this."

"No, Dec. That isn't it. I guess it all just kind of got to me. What do you mean it lined up with my dissertation goals?"

"That fantasy is quite common for several reasons, but the underlying purpose behind every reason given is that society has shamed women's sexuality so thoroughly and for so long, women feel ashamed for feeling physical pleasure or for allowing themselves to be the center of attention for any period of time. The idea that they didn't have a choice, that they were forced to have sex, allows them to enjoy it without risk of shame. That is why it is such a common fantasy. Obviously the fantasy is nothing like the actual event, which is never about sex and always about power. It is quite honestly the lowest of human lows. The fantasy represents nothing more than the harm we've done to ourselves as sexual beings."

"By not having to admit that they wanted the sex they have no responsibility to have regret enjoying it."

"Precisely."

"That makes sense and makes me angry for woman-kind."

"It should. Like I said, I thought the paper might give you a starting point for your dissertation work."

"And that is the same reason submissive fantasies are also so very common."

"Brilliant girl. Women bear the brutal load of responsibility for most everything now and are constantly told that nothing they do is good enough. Letting someone else take over for a while is highly pleasurable. I was trying to help you with blasting the constraints we've put on women's sexuality straight to hell, just like you said you wanted to. I was handing you the dynamite so to speak."

"Now, I really want to write the paper. Women can fantasize about anything they want to and shouldn't feel guilty."

"There's my cowgirl, but I do have another confession, though I swear I have no idea how I could have done anything differently in this case."

"What happened, and what did you mean Newsome was trying to set you up? I told you he's really not like that. He's a good guy. You just have to get to know him better."

Dec's eyes closed and he rubbed his temples. "Not set me up like trying to catch me doing something wrong. He tried to set me up with his daughter."

"What?!"

"She was at the restaurant when I arrived. Holly, baby, you know I had no idea, and if I had I never would have agreed to go. I was incredibly rude. She cornered me in the parking lot and explained that this isn't the only time her parents have done something like this. Newsome asked me about bringing a date to the dinner. Naturally, I told him I wasn't seeing anyone. Lying to cover things up will always blow up in your face. Take it from me, an addict and therefore a liar by proxy."

"But Dr. Newsome and his wife were there the entire time? You were never alone with her?"

"I was alone with her very briefly in the parking lot, and I made certain we were never closer than ten feet apart. She is moving across the country to be with the man she is currently living with. She is wildly in love with him, and far more importantly, I am wildly in love with you and would never ever do anything to jeopardize what we have."

"I know." She did know. She could feel it. The entire insanity of everything that had happened was the cause of all of this. If he'd never gotten hired on at the University, none of this would ever have happened. She knew her part. She'd pushed him to go on with their relationship. She had to take responsibility for any complications that arose while keeping them a secret.

"You do?"

"Of course. I mean, I'm not crazy about the fact that you were set up on a date, but it isn't your fault."

"You are the most understanding woman in the world. You have every right to be upset. Please don't hide things from me. If you're mad, say so. I don't want anything between us."

"I'm mad at this night. It wasn't a good night, and I hate that we're in the mess we're in, but I'm not mad at you at all. Just part of the deal, right?"

"I'm going to keep apologizing for my part of royally fucking up your night in."

"I know you are, but you don't have to. I'm just glad you're home." Holly debated but couldn't keep the question pulsing in her mind at bay. "Was she pretty?"

"I quite honestly have no idea. I'm blinded to all other women. I'm holding my own personal sun in my lap. I can't see anything but your light."

"It's getting deep in here, St. James. I need a shovel."

"I'm quite serious. I couldn't describe her to you if you begged me. You are my everything. I will tell you that the only rock song she knew was Wonderwall and she called the band Oceans instead of Oasis."

"Okay, I feel better now, but if she's living with some other guy why did her parents try to set her up?"

"Sounded to me like she's living a bit of our predicament. Doesn't want the Newsomes to know about her relationship, so she placates to keep them happy."

"Sucks not being able to be with who you love and tell the world."

"Epically."

CHAPTER THIRTY-SIX

"Jay-sus, don't give them gloves to Holl. She apologizes to every heifer before she shoves her hand up 'em. We'll be here all day," Austin harassed as Holly prepared to preg-test cattle the next afternoon at the sorting pens on Austin and Summer's land. They'd already worked through Natalie and Luke's herds.

Summer promptly smacked her husband in the back of the head. "You ever been pregnant and had someone shove their hand up you, Austin Camden? No, you have not. You leave Holly alone. It's feminine solidarity."

Holly high-fived her sister-in-law before she went on with the business at hand.

At the end of the long day, Holly was covered in manure, dirt, and sweat and desperately wanted a long hot shower and a huge mug of coffee. She also wanted to curl up in Dec's arms and let him massage away her sore muscles.

She briefly tried to envision telling her parents or siblings that she was dating her human sexuality professor, that she wanted to bring him to the ranch, and also needed them to keep quiet about it, but visions of her brothers driving to Lincoln to let Dec know what they thought of their arrangement made her cringe.

"Mighty quiet today, baby girl. Some'em you wanna tell your daddy about?"

Holly grinned as she helped her father brush the horses and hang up bits. "I'm all right, Daddy, just tired."

"Nah, you ain't just tired. Your mind's a million miles away, or maybe only a couple hundred miles away, but it ain't here on my ranch."

"Mama told you about Dec, I take it."

"She didn't have to tell me. I saw it the last time you were home. Tell me about this young man that has my girl under his thumb."

"Daddy." Holly rolled her eyes. "He does not have me under his thumb. Don't say things like that. He means a lot to me. He's very good to me. Kind of the best guy ever."

"If he's from Lincoln, he ain't a cowboy and that means. . . ."

"He ain't good enough for me. Yeah, yeah, I know."

"No, now, don't get all huffy with me. You're my little girl. Hurts a daddy's heart when his baby goes and grows up and lets somebody else be her hero. I don't like it."

"Aww, Daddy, I'll always be your little girl, and you'll always be my hero, even when I'm eighty." She threw her arms around his broad chest and let her daddy's warm embrace ease the world, just the way it always had.

"You better be, and this boy better treat you right, and you can tell him I'll have plenty to say about it if he don't."

"He will." Holly had no idea how to explain to her father that Dec wasn't a boy. Another round of guilt weighted her exhausted frame. She didn't like all of the secrets and the lying, but there was no other way.

"He in school with you?"

"Uh, not. . .really."

"Where'd you meet him then?"

"Met him at Duffy's one night before classes started."

Her father scowled. Picking up a guy in a bar did not cast Dec in the best light, but at least that was the truth.

Dec was finally able to draw a full breath when Holly entered the lecture hall Monday afternoon. He'd talked to her for hours the night before, but hadn't spoken to her on her drive back from Pleasant Glen that morning. He'd missed her. His empty bed still held her scent and served only to make him ache, and it would be another long week before she would return to his arms.

Stifling a smile and a wink for his girl took practiced resolve. He studiously ignored her and she did the same. They repeated the awkward act as the class handed in their papers on fantasies. Their eyes locked as he passed her desk and took her paper, the paper he'd already read because he'd helped her write it. He lingered before her too long, desperate to say something, anything to her, to let her know how much he hated having to pretend that he barely even knew her name.

Beth Kinders cleared her throat and propelled him onward. So, clearly Holly hadn't managed to convince her friend they'd broken up. They'd gone from simply playing with fire to fanning the flames.

Climbing to the next row of desks, he glared at Singleton, who was rather pompously typing on his laptop. "This isn't kindergarten, Singleton, either turn in the paper or don't. Matters not to me. I'm not going to chase you down for assignments."

"Yeah, I was a little busy this weekend. I emailed you the paper since this is not 1986."

"I will not grade an emailed paper. In fact, I won't even read it. Good luck moving beyond this foundational class with a failing grade." Dec moved on.

"I don't have time to hand write papers, St. James. Some of us have lives."

Dec refused the bait. Trevor was a grown man. At some point he would learn there were consequences for his actions. Holly, however, looked ready to maim. Dec's heart swelled at her defensiveness of him.

"I can't even believe you got this job. My father says. . . ."

"Let me make something clear, Mr. Singleton, I could not care less what you or your father think. Lucky for you both, admiring me is not a course requirement. You will either follow the guidelines or you will fail. End of discussion. If you have anything else to say on the topic, you can wait until after class and direct your pathetic drivel to Dr. Newsome."

"Oh, I'll be talking to Newsome. Don't worry."

Tension muted the room. Dec sat the papers he'd collected on his desk, proceeded through his class notes, and assigned a lengthier paper on the current trends in sexual therapy due in two weeks.

When class was dismissed, Holly took entirely too long gathering her belongings. *Baby, don't do this.* He reached for his phone to text her to go on, but the rest of the class cleared out quickly, murmuring about Trevor. Before he could type the message, she was standing at his desk.

"Um, Dr. St. James," her voice shook. His heart fractured.

"Ms. Camden, excellent work on Money's love map last week. I look forward to reading your paper." *Go, sweetheart. Just go.*

"Thank you. I enjoyed the topic." She glanced nervously at the door. There were still a few students lingering in the corridor.

Dec discreetly shook his head.

"I know," she was barely audible. "It's just Trevor's family is really powerful. Be careful."

"I need to get to my next class, Ms. Camden. Was there anything you needed help with? I have office hours later this afternoon."

"No. Well, maybe. I wanted to discuss the paper that's due in two weeks."

"I'll be in my office at 4:00 or you can email me. There's a TA available in the research library as well." *What was she doing?*

"Great. Thanks." With that she spun on her boot-heel and fled the building.

'Baby, are you okay?' He immediately sent her a text.

'Yes. I'm sorry. I just got to thinking that Trevor could get you fired and I freaked out.'

'Let me take care of Trevor. You just go be brilliant.'

She sent a selfie of herself blowing him a kiss. He was certain she'd been careful and no one would've known whom she was texting, but a photo was worth a thousand words, and it was harder to cover up than ten thousand.

CHAPTER THIRTY-SEVEN

By Wednesday afternoon, the entire campus was talking about Professor Sex playing at Duffy's Friday night, and Holly was more than prepared to lodge her shit-kickin' boots up the next chick's ass that she heard refer to Dec as such.

"He is so freaking gorgeous. I swear, I'd lay down for more than one sex lesson from him," Amanda Higgins, a transfer in from Oklahoma State, drawled while Holly and Beth were sitting at a table with two other girls in the library working on their Statistics project.

Holly seethed, and if Beth didn't quit offering her sorrowful glances, they were going to figure out why Holly was being such a bitch.

"What are you wearing Friday to Duffy's?" Ella Carlson inquired.

"As little as possible, obviously," Amanda laughed.

"Agreed. Bet he's a rock star in bed and out. I'm lucky I'm not in his class. I plan to sneak backstage and see if Professor Sex might like to make me choke."

Holly's chair careened into the table behind her when she leapt up.

"Holly," Beth pleaded.

"I have to go," Holly slung her bag over her shoulder and marched towards the door.

"What's wrong with her? She's been a bitch all day." Amanda's drawl incited Holly's blood. She longed to show her just how bitchy Nebraska cowgirls could be when the need arose.

"Who cares? Where does she get off thinking she's better than everyone? Have you ever listened to her in class? Miss 'I'm a psychology major so I it know all.' She works with cows. It's gross," Ella huffed.

Holly spun past the racks out of sight to listen.

"Hey, she's my friend. You're being a bitch. You ever stop to think about the fact that without cowgirls you wouldn't be able to eat? You ever stop to think maybe she's sick of talking about some good looking professor when we have work to do. I seriously doubt Dr. St. James wants to have anything to do with either of you," Beth sneered. "I'm leaving. You two can figure out your own stats project. Holly and I will do ours on our own."

"But we're supposed to be a group of four," Amanda pouted.

"Yeah, we were, but you've done absolutely nothing so far."

"But you and Holly did all of the research. We don't have copies of it."

"Bingo, bitch."

Holly heard Beth's chair slam against the table before she escaped to the parking lot. Far too many emotions swirled in her gut. She hadn't eaten lunch. Her chest ached from the weight of the secrets that just kept building. Now she'd caused trouble for Beth.

"Holly?" Beth raced towards her.

"Hey, I heard all of that. I'm sorry about that. I'm so sick of hearing women talk about him like that, but I don't want to create more work for you."

"Don't be sorry. I can't stand them. Cowgirl pride, girl. Besides, I hate group work. I want credit for my own shit."

"Agreed."

"Wanna go get some supper?"

Holly should have gone with Beth, but the sheer number of times she'd overheard some other woman lusting after Dec, calling him Professor Sex, or making plans to see him sing at Duffy's roiled in her stomach like a building maelstrom. Her eyes landed on the Psychology

Office building. It was dark except for one lone light that pierced the night, like a beacon guiding her home. Her own North star was right there.

"I can't. I need to. . .do. . .something."

Beth followed Holly's gaze and grinned. "I see. Okay, well, call me later."

"I will." Scanning the relatively empty parking lot, Holly crossed the street and walked away from the streetlights. Her boots sank in the mulch, but at least her steps were silent.

There was really no reason she couldn't pretend she was going to talk to *Dr. St. James* during his office hours. No one would question that. She was his student. Avoiding the elevators lest she be seen unexpectedly by someone on another floor, she climbed the stairs, gaining speed the closer she got.

All of the offices on his floor were darkened, all except his. She listened by the door and could just make out the sound of a male voice that wasn't Dec's.

Panic jolted through her. Her heart threw itself against her ribcage.

"It can't be that bad, Dr. St. James. Just take it moment by moment, like you always tell me. I only get to see Megan once a week. Plus, I'm kind of getting used to coming up here for my appointments now. Your other office was kinda stuffy."

"You think?" Dec chuckled.

'Other office.' It was one of Dec's patients from Lifespan. Guilt stormed through Holly's stomach. She should never have come up here.

Suddenly, the lock popped and there he was. Scrambling for an explanation as to why she was there, she stammered out, "I had a question. . .about. . .something."

"It's fine, Ms. Camden. I'm working late this evening. This is my favorite patient, Matt. Matt, this is one of my favorite students, Holly Camden." Dec made formal introductions while Holly tried to decide how a normal student would behave in this situation.

"Holly? Didn't you say the girl you were dating was named. . . ?" Matt's eyes flipped back and forth from Holly to Dec like a perfectly paired tennis match.

"No," Dec insisted.

A knowing grin formed on Matt's features. He couldn't have been more than eighteen or nineteen. Holly told herself to breathe.

"Uh, okay, well, my mom's probably here, so I gotta go. See ya Friday, Doc."

When Matt disappeared onto the elevator, Dec offered her a stoic smile. "You okay if I close the door, Ms. Camden?" She hated the way he sounded like her professor. That wasn't who he was. He was her everything

"Yes." Why had he asked her that?

He not only closed the door, he restored the lock silently before turning to study her. "What's wrong with my girl?" His voice was barely audible, but that was how he was supposed to sound. The light in his eyes when he looked at her was how he was always supposed to look.

"I'm sorry." Her chin trembled and she clenched her jaw. She would not cry. She was not weak. "Just been a long day I guess." Her fingernails pricked her palms as she held back emotion with the force of her fists.

"I'm not sorry, honey. I can't think about anything but you. I was waiting on you to leave campus before I do just to be in your relative proximity, as lovesick as that makes me sound. I've thought of nothing but you since the last time I held you. Come here to me." He settled in his chair and guided her into his lap. "Dr. Newsome is still in his office upstairs, just be mindful of that. We need to let him leave before we do."

"But what about Matt?"

"Matt is delightfully involved in his first case of puppy love. He is so thoroughly consumed with Megan I feel certain he will have not only forgotten your name, but also that either of us were even here by the time he reaches his mother's minivan. He did offer me some good advice while he was here, though."

"What was that?"

"I tried to get a word or two in between his obsession with Megan. I mentioned I was struggling with working here and not getting to see my girlfriend as often as I'd like to. He used to respond to me rattling off struggles. I'd share a little, he'd share a lot kind of thing. This time, he quickly threw my own words back in my face so he could get back to Megan. Take everything moment by moment. It's something I need to hear often. I'm thrilled I get a few moments with you right now."

Holly nodded against him. "Me too, but I shouldn't have come here. I know that. Do you have any idea how freaking good looking you are and how annoying that is?"

Dec's chuckle eased her day. "I feel a little bit like I'm on trial for my appearance."

"Sorry. It's just you being Professor Sex is all I've heard about all damn day. You're mine, but I can't tell anyone that, so I just have to sit and listen to other women talk about you like you're a piece of prime rib. I want to throw them on the ground and tie them up calf-roping style."

"Professor Sex, huh?" Dec sighed.

"Do not sound happy about that."

"I'm not. I mean, it's ridiculously clichéd. That's the best thing they could come up with for a professor that teaches Sexual Psychology? Come on."

"Would you have preferred Dr. St. Jizz, or maybe Professor St. Clit, or how about Dr. Octopussy, something like that?"

"See, now those have merit. Far more creative than Professor Sex. However, you mixed your metaphors on Octopussy. You'd have to get rights from two franchises."

Holly rolled her eyes.

"Please tell me you know where my loyalties lie, sweetheart. Other women mean absolutely nothing to me."

"Everyone's going to go hear you sing at Duffy's Friday night. They all have plans for what they should do with you afterwards," she continued, trying to explain why she was feeling a little out of sorts. "Some chick in my stats class just informed me that she wanted you to make her choke."

Dec's scowl did more for Holly's self-worth than anything yet. "Well, I happen to have my own plans for after the gig at Duffy's Friday night. Would you like to hear them, Ms. Camden?"

"Maybe."

"I'd planned to go home as soon as we sing the final encore, race up to my bedroom where I'm praying you'll be laying naked in my bed, and then I plan on completely ruining you for any other man. Fast and hard, then slow and reverent, worship your beautiful body, up against the walls, on the stairwell, tied to my bed, in my shower, over every flat surface of my house, and I don't plan on stopping until Monday morning."

He captured her soft, needy moan with his lips, keeping her quiet, setting her on fire. He nipped and drank at her mouth.

"Dec," she managed as his hands roamed her body, never settling any one place until he landed on the top button of her blouse. He plundered her mouth at the sound of his name, taking possession of her tongue.

She gave herself over to him. To be owned was her only quest. This was why she'd come to his office. She should have known all along.

He worked through the buttons of her blouse with adept skill. His callused fingers explored until they'd popped the front clasp of her bra, and she arched into his seeking hands.

"I need you." His low grunt sent a flashfire of desire throughout her.

"Yes," she whimpered against the scruff of his five o'clock shadow.

Those perfect nipples, a flushed raspberry fire, stabbed against his palms, and Dec just didn't care anymore. He couldn't do this. He couldn't live without her. Moment by moment be damned. He was an addict. He would always be an addict, and she was the most addictive thing he'd ever encountered. Only this time there was no crash, there was nothing but her love, her body, her laughter, her needs. He required it all. He wanted to bury himself so deeply inside of her she had no hope of understanding where he stopped and she began. He needed her more than he needed to draw his next breath.

Desperate for her softness, he cupped her breasts and drew them together in his right hand. As she arched back in offering, he drew the turgid peeks into the heat of his mouth.

She rocked against his erection then maneuvered until she was straddling him, grinding against him while he nipped and sucked at her breasts.

He knew what she liked. He'd memorized every detail of her desires.

One hand wrapped around his neck and her other tunneled through his hair, her body begging for his. He scraped his teeth along the underswell of her right breast, and she whimpered out for more. The noise sated his soul and ignited his body.

Fixing his hand over her mouth, too far gone to stop himself, he lifted his head to stare her down. "Can you be quiet for me, baby? Be a good girl and let me have this. I need you."

A quick nod led the roll of her body against him. Her eyes closed in submission as he began to suckle softly. With every draw, he sucked harder until he found her rhythm. His cock made itself known against the denim of her jeans. Her fingernails bit at his shoulders now as she pressed harder against him.

The tang of sweat gathered between her breasts drove him mad with longing. He was going to fuck her. Nothing short of her telling him to stop was going to keep him from her. When she realized he was trying to stand, she made quick work of pressing palms against his desk and presenting herself. The few seconds it took to work through his belt was too damn long. Frustration to have her seared through him, drawing his muscles taught like a guitar strung so tightly it would snap on the first strum. He pulled her back to him, rocking his strain against her ass desperate for relief. There were far too many layers between them. Skin. He needed her skin. Now.

His fingers worked down to the button of her jeans and finally his hand landed on the soft flesh of her abdomen. She wanted to know whom she belonged to, he sure as hell would show her.

Like a runaway train on a downward track, his hand dove in her panties, naughty little number, white lace g-strings with a pink bow at the top of the crack of her ass that said *fuck me*. Her favorite kind to wear. His favorite kind to see her in.

His pulse thundered in his head. His cock damn near severed the zipper of his trousers itself.

"Dec, please," she begged.

"I said be quiet." He returned his hand to her mouth and used the position to thrust against her.

The knock on the door shattered through them. He jerked backwards. Panic barreled through his chest. His heart refused him the next beat. Her eyes goggled as she frantically buttoned her jeans, fixed her bra, and smoothed her hair.

Pushing away remembrances of rabidly flushing dime bags, eight balls, and papers down the toilet while the police beat on his door, he buckled his belt and tried to think of some plausible reason why his student was standing in his office, flushed with kiss-swollen lips and her nipples so hard and tight they had to ache.

She buttoned her blouse, grabbed a binder out of her bag, and took the seat opposite the desk. Flipping it open, she grabbed a pencil from the cup on his desk.

Dec took his seat and prayed this would work. The only problem was the majority of his brain simply didn't care. All he wanted was her.

"Come in," he called.

Dr. Newsome was smiling pleasantly when he entered. "Ms. Camden, I'm so sorry to interrupt, dear."

"It's fine, Dr. Newsome," her voice faltered. Newsome either didn't notice or pretended that he hadn't. "I just had a few questions about an upcoming paper. Dr. St. James was going over a few points I was unclear on. We were just finishing up."

Oh, naughty girl, we are not finished. Not 'til we're both spent.

The snap of her binder shutting reverberated through Dec's chest.

"I was just leaving."

You can leave, baby, but I'm coming after you. You can run, but you can't hide from me.

"If you're sure. I just need a few minutes of Dr. St. James time. I owe him an apology. I do hope to see you at the Behavioral Sciences symposium. I'd like to extend you a personal invitation to sit at my table."

The entire department had received an invitation via email that afternoon to a symposium on advances in Behavioral Psychology being held in none other than the Singleton Auditorium in a few weeks.

"Thank you, Dr. Newsome. I'd be honored. I'll see you there.

Thank you for your help, Dr. St. James. I'll check out those sites you suggested, and I'll review Dr. Rogers work. I haven't read it in a few years."

Well, look at his little cowgirl, flustered and fidgeting, but competent none the less, saving his sorry ass. *If she's still that capable of thought, you aren't taking care of her. Take more. She needs to be undone.* His mind was having none of this, and he was helpless against the calls for her that evening.

Searching his brain for anything but longing, he landed on, "Pay particular attention to Kramer's introduction. The bridge it offers between psychotherapy of the past and today is invaluable."

"Yes, sir. I will."

Oh, yes sir, you will, honey, and that won't be the only yes sir I hear tonight.

When Holly made her escape, Dec negotiated with the universe as a whole. Let him manage one fucking conversation with his boss without outing them and then he'd have her all night long.

"Lovely girl, isn't she?" Newsome gestured towards the door.

It took Dec two full breaths before any words other than *you should see her in nothing but a g-string and those boots* formed in his mind. "She works harder than any other student I teach." There. That kind of worked.

"Yes, like we discussed, she's very impressive."

Dec offered a nod and nothing more lest he begin gushing about her rosebud lips, her lush ass, her long silky hair, and her tits.

"Dr. St. James, I've been avoiding you all week," Dr. Newsome sighed.

Oh fuck, what was about to happen here? Dec tried to force more blood flow to the head on his shoulders.

"Avoiding what?" His heart couldn't locate a steady beat. *No one knows what you were doing in here. Get it together.*

"I owe you an apology. I'm terribly embarrassed. I admire you very much. The way you've taken bad situations and worked through them. The way you devoted your life to psychological studies. How hard you work. The way you used education to stay away from your addictions. I know how dreadfully difficult it must be, and I'd hoped my Olivia might see some of the same things in you I saw. To be truthful, I desperately want my little girl to move back home. I don't care for those reckless pilots she prefers. Saturday night, I stuck my nose in where it doesn't belong and I do beg your forgiveness."

"Not a problem, sir. Word of caution, if I might?"

"Please," Newsome took the seat Holly had occupied a minute before.

"Trying to keep the moth from the flame often times makes them more determined." Dec mentally called himself an asshole, offering up twisted reverse psychology to a man who'd been in the field three decades longer than he had.

Newsome laughed genuinely. "I know, but a father has to try. You'll understand when you settle down and have children."

Children? The foreign concept did nothing to quell the rampant desire still surging through his veins. Kids came after sex and all he wanted right then was the first part.

"I'm really not looking to get back in a relationship any time soon."

"Point taken. No more fix ups." Newsome offered him a kind smile, one he most certainly did not deserve. "We've been up here all day. Let me make up for my faux pas Saturday night, and buy you a meal."

"Thank you, sir, but I can't go out this evening. I have something that requires my full attention at home. Rain check perhaps?"

"Certainly, and thank you for your kindness. I'll see you in the morning Dr. St. James."

Dec shoved a few papers in his briefcase as Newsome saw himself out. When the door closed, he grabbed his phone to text Holly.

Go to my house. The garage key code is 1579. Let yourself in. When I get there, you should be in my bed and ready for me. Leave your panties on. Take everything else off. I plan to tear them off of you. Don't make me wait.

Her responding text made him vibrate with urgency. *Yes, sir.*

He flew out of his office, making it to his bike in record time. Using the bike lane, he cut around an obnoxiously yellow Scion that pulled out in front of him.

CHAPTER THIRTY-EIGHT

Since Holly was already half way to Dec's home, it was convenient he'd sent her the garage key code. Reckless abandon whipped through her. She didn't give a damn anymore. She needed him. Her pulse timed itself to the rapid thrum of her tires on the road.

Just a few more miles. She pressed the accelerator harder. Her entire body was a livewire, raw and desperate.

Breathless, she leapt out of the truck, keyed in the code, and pulled in. Shutting down the motor, all she could hear was the pounding of her heart in frantic rhythm. Racing through the house, she unbuttoned her blouse as she clambered up the stairs and toed off her boots. Her jeans made a soft swoosh as they landed on his carpet. The slight noise shocked her overexposed senses in the absence of any other sound.

Flinging her bra away, she climbed in his unmade bed and stretched out. The wet lace of her panties made her raw. Inhaling deeply, she let the scents of Declan fill her lungs as the soft sheets cooled her overly-sensitive skin.

The lurch of the single-bay garage door jolted through her. He must've flown. The slip of the opening door sent a shock through her nervous system. Suddenly, a speaker she'd never noticed in the bedroom clicked on.

She sat up, searching for Dec. The opening lyrics to *Chains* filled the room. A shiver worked up her spine. Her heart double-timed the backbeat. Where was he?

His entire body dominated the doorway, backlit by the moon from the picture window in the hall. Craving desire pulsed in the air between them. His eyes ate her up with a hunger that bordered possession. His hands landed on his belt. She watched as he slowly unbuckled the strap of leather, not certain what he was about to do. She'd never seen him quite like this. Savagery burned in his eyes. Every tensed muscle in his body was set to ravage.

Another tremor worked through her as the whip of leather slipped through the loops of his trousers. He picked up speed, unbuttoning his shirt. It hung open, revealing his intricate tat work and sculpted physique that would've made Adonis envious. Declan St. James in an open-suit — she'd never seen anything more tantalizing.

A moment later, he'd rid himself of any clothing at all.

He held out his hand to her, a sinful invitation she would never deny. Ordering her hands to stop shaking, she placed her fingers in his palm and stood off the bed. He jerked her forward and dipped her back in time to the music. Her body rolled towards his and his hand slid down the slight straps of her panties, kneading her ass while he worked her body in rhythm to the drumbeats.

Giving herself over to him, she ground against him, his erection burning like a hot brand against her abdomen. Her nipples pressed insistently against his chest as he rocked her to the music that she swore welled through their souls.

"I'm about to take everything I've wanted since the first time I had you. Say that's what you want," were the first words he spoke.

"It's what I want." Lost and seeking, confused and frantic, she clung to the only anchor she'd ever wanted. He danced them towards the wall by the door. The music changed. Something by Satan's Circus, she thought, but Holly couldn't breathe. She couldn't make out any lyrics. She could do nothing but give herself over to him.

He braced her against the wall and wrapped her legs around his waist. She clung to his shoulders. "When I tell you to do something, you say yes sir. Understand?"

An explosion of nerves careened through her. "Yes, sir."

"Pull your panties to the side."

"Yes, sir."

"I've got you. Let go of my neck and put your fingers in my mouth."

Again she complied. He sucked her index and middle finger until they wet enough for his purposes. "Touch yourself."

Scaling her hand between their bodies, she located her clit and hastily ran her fingers across it.

"Slow-ly," he growled.

"Yes, sir." Reaching lower, adding her own dew to his saliva, she slowed, this time watching him as she obeyed. Her body reacted to the caress, a back and forth mix of tension and relief.

A storm of fire resided deep in his darkened eyes. "Good girl. Get them nice and juicy then feed me."

"Oh my God."

"What do you say when I give you an order?"

"Yes, sir."

"That's right, honey, but when I'm finished with you, you won't be able to speak."

When her fingertips were wet with her own cream, she brought them back to his lips. His eyes closed as he licked and sucked. A low moan vibrated from deep in his chest. Managing her with one arm for just a moment, he grasped his cock and pressed inside of her. "Take it, baby. Take it all."

He pulled back and stabbed into her again. She gasped from the sensation of being so empty to being so full. Another pass and her body gave compliance. He rode her harder now, losing himself in her.

Frantic thrusts punctuated by rhythmic percussive beats she could barely make out through their gasps of breath. Her legs shook. He roared his approval.

"You don't come until I say. You understand me?"

A desperate moan preceded her responding, "Yes, sir."

His piercing taunted her resolve. She couldn't stop it. She cinched around him. His eyes flashed dangerously. "Not yet."

"Please," she whimpered as he continued to pound. Agonizing pleasure throbbed throughout her body. He gathered the slight lace of her panties and tore them from their delicate stitches. The rip of the tearing fabric and the pull of her skin stole the incoming climax. "I said not yet." On his next withdrawal, the panties slipped from between them to the floor.

Dear God. She'd never been more turned on. This was what she'd wanted from him for so long. Finally, he wasn't holding back with her. A wispy cry of need raced from her lips. His fingers dug into her hips as he pounded into her fast and furious.

Her head fell back and she gave herself over to the ride of her life. Faster. Harder.

"It's coming, isn't it, love? Coming so hard and fast I can feel it. Can't stop it, can you, baby? Now, say please, Dec."

"Please, Dec."

"Again."

"Please, please."

"Good girl. I love hearing you beg for it."

"Please," she whimpered.

"When you go take me with you."

Certain she was careening out of control, unable to recognize her own wanton screams, she felt the orgasm rip through her. Her legs cinched tightly around his waist. Her body shook violently. The ripples of her climax did indeed draw his release from deep within his body.

A thunderous roar tore from Dec as he arched his back and slammed inside of her once, twice, and then he somehow managed to cradle her limp body to his and carry her to the bed.

They remained connected as he held her, still wrapped around him with her head on his shoulder. "I'm not finished, sweetheart. I hope you're ready for more."

Nothing in his tone or demeanor said he was joking. Holly took inventory of her body. She felt weak with satisfaction and was still unable to move, utterly boneless. In fact, the only firm and unmovable thing currently in her body was his rapidly stiffening cock. Damn, he really was a stud. She made a soft sigh, but gave him no other response.

He chuckled. "Don't worry, baby doll, you don't have to do a thing. You just lay there and take it."

"That I can do."

"Good." He brushed kisses in her hair and on the tip of her nose when she finally lifted her head. "I'll never get enough, sweetheart, and there's so much more I want to take."

"Anything. Take it. Take me." Coming back to reality slowly as Dec gently laid her on her stomach in his bed Holly finally recognized *Closer* by Kings of Leon pumping through the speakers now.

Exhaustion tugged at her eyelids. She blinked a few times to clear her eyes while Dec went to get something from his closet. When he returned with three silk neckties, she was suddenly wide awake.

That wicked grin had returned to his gorgeous face. His eyes still held dark flames of craving want. Thoughts of him having his way with her sent her to another dimension entirely. She existed in a state of expectation and desire. "Have to make sure you don't move and let me take care of everything."

Something between a moan and a gasp lodged in the back of Holly's throat. Her pulse sped ten times faster than the song. Seeming to understand, Dec lifted her right hand and brushed a kiss at the pulse point on her wrist. "I want you bound for me, Holly. Vulnerable only to me. At my mercy. But if you don't want this just say the word, sweetheart, and I'll make it all go away."

"I do." The words took wing from the hive of nerves buzzing in her stomach. She did want this. She wanted all of this with him. "I want this, too."

The cool silk tie slipped along her wrist and with a few quick looped knots, her right hand was supported on a pillow and secured to his headboard. A minute later, her left hand was bound as well.

A spike of thrill zipped down her spine. She gave a slight tug and found herself without much leeway. Her thighs still quivered from their first session.

"Just relax, darling. I'm going to take good care of you."

Slipping into bed beside her, he lifted her chin and brushed a kiss on her lips. She could taste the reckless possession on his tongue. "Let me have this, baby. Let me free the desires in your soul. I know they're there. I know what you need to lose to control. Let me take you places you've only ever gone in your most forbidden fantasies. Let me show you, honey, let me take them from you. Let me make them come true."

She managed a single nod. Watching as he lifted the final tie. Holly closed her eyes as he gently fitted the silk tie over them. "A blindfold is never meant to be a barrier, baby. I'm not taking anything away from you. I'm right here, and the only things I will be taking are every orgasm I'm about to give you. My hands will be on you constantly. If you want me to stop, just say the word. The blindfold is a gateway to your other senses. You'll feel every touch, hear every breath, experience every sensation deeper."

"Yes," Holly's breathless gasp bolted through Dec as he secured the tie with a soft square knot. Gently he guided her hips up off of the mattress and eased two pillows beneath her stomach.

Keeping his hands on her fevered skin just as he'd promised, he allowed himself to take her all in. His cock throbbed, just as appreciative of the sight as his voracious eyes.

Her delectable, feminine ass, plump and perfect on display. Her head down, her arms bound, her body a feast of beauty and innocence. Innocence was the one other thing he knew he was taking from her, but he would protect that, protect her, until his dying day. She was his.

"Breathe for me, sweetheart. I'm right here." He ran his hands up her sides making her tense. His fingers tenderly parted her hair as he accessed the nape of her neck with his lips. Chill bumps charged across her shoulders. "Just relax. Let yourself enjoy this."

Kissing a trail of sweet fire from her tender neck down her spine, he worshiped her thoroughly. When he spun his tongue in the hollow at her tailbone, a needy moan joined the melody of the music. "Like that, baby? Sensitive isn't it. I want to know every square inch of your beautiful skin. I want to taste all of you." He dropped kisses lower on his path to her perineum and there he began his unrelenting devastation.

"Dec," she groaned.

"I'm right here. Spread your legs just a little more for me." She obeyed readily. Keeping one hand on her ass, he gripped the base of his cock to tamp down the rampant need to unload all over her. He'd just filled her full up against a wall, but he was just as desperate as he'd been before. She was his every need. The sweetest addiction. He would never be satisfied.

Her body quaked as he centered in on that tender patch of skin between her ass and pussy. She writhed as best as she was able. He continued his taunting until she was begging to be freed. Not yet. Continuing his path, he left hickeys on the sensitive skin where her thighs joined her ass. "All mine."

"Oh my God," she whimpered. "Please, please take me."

"No need to rush. I'm thoroughly enjoying myself."

She thrust frantically against the pillows, desperate for relief. "Keep doing that, baby, and I'll paddle that sexy little ass again. You come when I say. Be a good girl for me."

Her desperate cry surged a jolt of fresh lust from his cock to his limbs. If he was going to set her free, freer than she'd ever been, he had to remain in control. He continued his rash of kisses down her thighs and calves.

The slight whiskers of his five-o'clock shadow caressed the sensitive arch of her foot as he kissed her heels. Another shiver shook through her. Chuckling, he peppered another few kisses on her adorable feet. "Ticklish, sweetheart? Have to remember that. Also means you'll probably like this." Steadying her, he lifted her right foot and let her adjust to the new position before he suckled her two tiniest toes.

"Oh. Yes."

Pleasure darted constantly to his cock. He treaded a strained thread of tension. He had to have her.

"I'm about to show you what it's like to be fucked by a man on fire for you. I hope you're ready, honey."

"Yes. Please, Dec. I can't take any more."

"But you can, sweetheart. You can take it all for me." He tracked his mouth and hands back up her body. Positioning his groin at her face, he gripped his cock. "Lick," he commanded as he braced her cheek and guided her mouth to his strain.

She consumed readily, hungry for it. "Now suck."

"Yes." Her hot breath whispered over his sack as she drew him in. He was going to lose it all. Easing his cock out of her mouth, he gasped for breath. His mind scrambled, unable to think of anything but burying himself inside of her.

"Tell me where you want my next mark. I want everyone to know who you belong to." Just because they couldn't didn't mean that wasn't what he wanted. This wasn't about their reality. This was about their fantasies.

She writhed again. The bed creaked and shook under the force of her need tugging against the makeshift tie-ups.

"Tell me or I'll choose for you."

"My neck. God, it feels so good."

"It does feel good, doesn't it? Right here." He licked and sucked the back of her neck in that vulnerable spot where it met her shoulder and watched the tiny hairs stand in ovation. He punished with his teeth and then forgave with his tongue until he'd marked her thoroughly.

Unable to draw it out much longer, he raced his hands down her back and pressed his fingers through her soaking wet tissues, drawing a wanton scream from his cowgirl.

"That's it. Let me hear you scream. You're gonna scream on my cock after this."

Unintelligible moans were her only response as he primed her thoroughly. They spiked his blood. Too far gone to have ever managed gentle, he gave her the brutal pressure she required.

"Be a good girl and say please, baby. Say please, and I'll let you come on my fingers."

"Please," avulsed from her in a keening plea.

"Come." His every fantasy perfected, she shattered at his command. Rabid anticipation thundered in his blood.

Behind her in a second flat, he gave her no time to regain her breath. She gasped in a ragged shudder as he jerked her back over his cock, impaling her, taking every centimeter of the tight space and owning it. He rode the tide of her orgasm in waves of excruciating pleasure watching the sun and moon of her tattoo blend together with his every thrust.

The rhythm of the music he'd selected just for this worked through him. He thrust shallow, full, shallow, full to the steady beat of *Feel Like Makin' Love* by Bad Company, the perfect rhythm for her, he knew. If there had ever been any doubt as to whether or not she was put on this earth to be his, the song had been recorded at Wembley.

Reaching up her body, he gently loosed the blindfold and eased it off her face. It only took her a few seconds for her eyes to adjust to the room lit by the moonlight. "Look in the mirror and watch me, honey. Watch my cock fill up your greedy little snatch."

Again she obeyed, turning back to watch as her body shook. He pistoned his hips faster and harder. His own climax barreling through him. He fought. His jaw clenched tightly. Not yet.

"Dec, please, please let me come." Agony perforated her plea.

"That's a good girl. Asks me to let her come." He chased his breath. Every silky ripple of her pussy rendered him mindless.

"Please," she begged.

"You say my name when I let you have it. Scream it for me."

"Yes, sir," another whimpered moan, and he was done for.

"Come, baby. Come hard on my cock."

She shattered with the guttural cry of his name, and he caught himself on his hands, landing on either side of her shoulders as he lost it all deep inside the only thing he would ever need in this lifetime or the next.

Regaining his breath slowly, Dec managed to pull the slip knots on the ties loose. "Careful, love. Might be a little stiff for a few minutes." Massaging her wrists, he cradled her on his chest trying to ease any strain.

Her contented sigh completed the perfection of what they'd just shared. Chuckling, he painted her shoulders and cheeks with tender kisses. She was stunningly beautiful and so damn sweet. "You gonna talk to me or do I only get sighs?"

"That was amazing. I'm still processing it."

"I see. Well, I thought it was pretty fucking amazing myself. I love you so much, Holly. I'm sorry I lost control like that at the beginning."

"I love you, too, and do not apologize for anything. It was every-thing I've ever wanted from you." As if on cue, the opening chords of *Nothing Else Matters* by Metallica began playing.

"I have to ask. Did you make this playlist for us or. . .you know, have you *used* it before?"

"I spend hours and hours alone thinking about nothing but being with you, baby. I made it for us. Didn't think I'd get to use it before this weekend, but I'm sure as hell not complaining."

"Good answer."

"The truth usually is."

"Is it okay that I hate that this was so perfect and it happened because I was being stupid? I should never have come to your office. We almost got caught. I'm so sorry, Dec."

"Hey," he leaned and kissed away her contention, "none of that. This. . .this was everything. It was what we needed. I never want you to stay away from me if you need me. We'll figure it out. Listen to James Hetfield, *Nothing Else Matters* nothing but you."

"I like James. We should always listen to James." A deep yawn stole the end of her decree.

"I agree, but I think right now I should go turn off the music so I can put my baby to bed."

"No, don't leave. Just hold me."

Cradling her closer, he cossetted the covers around them. "There is nothing else I would rather do."

"Promise?"

"Promise."

CHAPTER THIRTY-NINE

"Well, everyone and their brother is going to Duffy's to hear you play so I don't guess anyone will see me driving to your house," Holly pouted on the phone Friday afternoon, sitting in her living room while Dec prepared for the show that night.

"Holl, come on. Not this again. You are welcome to come tonight, but that means we arrive alone and leave alone. You have to act like we broke up because Andy is a wanker of diminutive size. And if some slapper makes a comment about how I finger the strings or some other such nonsense you cannot show off your cowgirl temper."

"What's a slapper?"

"Uh, rough translation would be woman lacking great moral fiber."

"I thought you liked my cowgirl side."

"Oh honey, there are few things I adore more about you, but you can't show it off if someone throws a pair of panties on the stage."

Holly choked on her coffee. "Has anyone ever done that?"

"Few times."

"I am so coming tonight."

"Many, many, many times, but not 'til *after* the show."

"Funny."

"You are welcome to come, but you have to behave."

"I much prefer being naughty."

"Don't I know it. Don't I *love* it."

"Just feels a little like being the only girl without a prom date, and I would know exactly how that feels because my brothers threatened to kill any guy that asked me both my junior and senior years. I never got to go."

"I am both terrified and appreciative of your brothers."

"They're relatively civilized, just occasionally dumbasses."

"Sounds like they must have Y chromosomes. Listen, love, the guys just got here. I love you. I miss you. I will see you right after the show tonight. If you want to come, you are more than welcome, but remember the rules."

"Yeah, yeah. I love you, too."

"That's my sweet girl," Dec harassed.

"Go play, St. James. I'll see you later."

Still unable to shake the feeling that something weird had happened the last time she'd been alone in Dec's house, Holly saw no reason to go over early. He wouldn't be back until well after midnight.

But by eight-thirty, she'd finished most of her homework. The rest she needed Beth to complete, and Beth, like everyone else, was at Duffy's. Desperate for someone to talk to, she called Cheyenne. "Hey girly, how goes it?"

"It's so good. On my way to meet Grant and Wesley Kilroy to talk about the dance after the cattle show."

Squeezing her eyes shut, Holly wished on the starless night that maybe just maybe Grant would see that Chey was really a sweetheart and ask her out. "I am crossing my fingers that Grant does not act like an ornery bull."

"I think he's cute when he's stubborn."

"Chey, you thought he was cute when he got thrown a few years ago and was throwing up from his concussion."

"He should have let me take care of him, but like we just said, he *is* stubborn. So, what are you and the horny professor up to tonight?"

"Dec's playing at Duffy's so I'm stuck here until he's done."

"Why are you stuck there? Why didn't you go see him perform?"

"It's complicated. I can't act like I know him as it would effectively ruin both of our lives if anyone figured out we're together. It blows goats."

Cheyenne giggled. "I'm sorry, Holl. At least the guy you're hot and heavy for wants to get with you, too. Count yourself lucky. Maybe I should wear one of those mega-push up bras tonight."

"Your tits are already mega, Chey. You're gorgeous. My brother is a dumbass. We've already established this."

"Well, maybe you could call him for me and feel him out. Then call me back and tell me what I should say to get him to finally notice me tonight."

"Chey, that feels kinda desperate and very eighth-grade."

"You could be more helpful if you wanted to."

Holly heard computer keys clicking. "What are you doing?"

"Sometimes Duffy's livestreams videos of their performers. I want to see Declan."

"Really? I didn't know that."

"Yeah, here it is. They're just taking the stage."

"Is it on their site?"

"No. Check their Youtube channel. Damn, Holl, he's hot. How do you always end up with the hottest guys?"

"He's the only guy I've ever ended up with." Holly quickly found Duffy's channel. Someone had uploaded a short video of the intro and the first song. At the end of the video was some chick front and center right below Dec's mic. The video blurred but not before Holly saw the skank flash Dec.

"Oh my bulla shitta, did you see that?" Cheyenne gasped.

"Yes, yes, I did." Unmitigated rage blazed through Holly.

"Girl, if I were you I'd get myself down there and stake my claim."

"Already on my way." Holly stepped into her boots, grabbed her duffle bag, slammed the door, and sped to her truck. She arrived in time to see the woman from the video and two of her friends being escorted out of the club by two massive bouncers that looked like human concrete walls. "Think you've had way too many fishbowls, ladies. Go sober up and don't return."

"I can't. . .that doucheass. . .can't. . .kick us. . .out." The flasher stumbled forward. One of the bouncers caught her before she ate the pavement.

A twinge of compassion that Holly hated herself for feeling niggled in her chest. "You need to call them a cab."

"Bartender already did. Frontman of the band ordered them out. Scott okayed it. Good bands bring in customers. What they say goes."

The jealous girlfriend bit has to be highly unattractive, Holl. She scolded herself. She should've known Dec wouldn't put up with that. He loved her. "Are you going to stay with them until the cab arrives?"

"I don't get paid to babysit, honey. If you're friends of theirs, you can stay with them."

"I'm not, but I'll stay." The women began laughing hysterically at a rock, from what Holly could tell. Rolling her eyes, she willed the cabbie to speed it up. Thankfully, she arrived just a few minutes later. One of the women supplied an address, twice.

The cabbie rolled her eyes. "I've taken them home from here before."

With that, Holly slipped inside the bar. She wanted to hear Dec play, even if she had to act like he meant nothing to her.

"I was wondering when you'd show up, Camden." Trevor's spiteful drawl slammed into Holly as she made her way towards the tables.

Spinning on her boot heel, she narrowed her eyes. "What the hell is that supposed to mean, Singleton? You miss me or something."

"You think you're so smart, but you're so full of shit, Holly, and this time I'm gonna watch you drown in it."

Poking out her bottom lip in a mocking pout, Holly pretended to wipe her eyes. "Poor, Trevy, what's wrong? Is Daddy not gonna be able to get you everything you want this time? Gonna have to grow up and learn to be something besides a twenty-gallon sack of shit in a ten-gallon bag?"

Trevor was trying his damnedest to appear unaffected, but Holly had gotten to him, she could see it in his weasley little eyes. "I'll make you sorry you said that."

"Can't wait." Holly's eyes turned to the stage without her permission. Dec had spotted her as they prepared for their second set. Concern was tensed on his face. He lifted his eyebrows in question and discreetly gestured to Trevor. Before Holly could try to communicate that she was fine, Trevor stalked out of the bar.

"You came," Beth raced to her side. "There's no seats anywhere, but come over here with me."

She watched Dec, Garrick, and Kade lean in onstage. Dec gave instructions and got nods of agreement.

"I told him you'd show." Wyatt joined Beth and Holly as they staked out a spot near the back of the bar. "But I'm saying nothing. I've been given my orders."

"Thanks," Holly brushed a kiss on Wyatt's cheek.

"Wanna drink?" Wyatt pointed to the bar.

"Sure, but not a fishbowl," Holly wrinkled her nose.

"Knew you had good taste. Be right back."

"I have never seen so many people here," Beth shouted as the fierce thrum of Dec's Stratocaster shattered the smoky air.

"Me either."

A parade of emotions worked through Dec as he watched Wyatt carefully balance two glasses of wine for Beth and Holly. He was both nervous and thrilled she'd come, excited to play a few songs just for them, and furious at whatever Singleton had said to her that had her in full-on cowgirl mode for a few minutes. Once you recognized the sassy cock of her hip, slip of her jaw, and the fire in her eyes when someone tried to mess with her, you knew that someone was about to go down. . .hard.

Sure enough, Singleton had fled the premises. Having willingly agreed to play *Hot for Teacher* again that evening, Dec began the insanity. He saw Holly cover her mouth to keep from laughing and he had to close his eyes to play without messing the entire intro up.

Soon she was singing along, and he swore he fell even more in love with her. They followed it up with *Nothing Else Matters,* and he tried to stare anywhere but at her. Wednesday night was still potent and fresh in his mind. He could think of nothing else but her cuddled in his arms after their extended sessions.

He found himself hating their predicament more and more with each passing day.

CHAPTER FORTY

"I shouldn't be doing this, but I'm going to because I'm just that kind of guy," Dec sighed as he read emails on his laptop in Holly's lap as she was reclined against him, forcing him to watch American football two weeks later.

"What shouldn't you be doing?"

"Semi-grading Mr. Singleton's latest emailed paper."

"How do you semi-grade something, and why are you giving that asswipe special treatment?"

"I'm highlighting the entire paragraphs that he stole from either Reddit, Thought Catalog, or something called Love Shack Psych, and sending it back to him as the very reason I will not accept emailed papers."

"Those aren't even psychological studies. They're just random people spouting off their opinions."

"I am aware, darling. I'm doing this because Newsome asked me to."

"Asked you to grade his papers even though they aren't in pencil?"

"Asked me to help him in any way I possibly could."

"He asked you to give him special treatment?"

"No, just to really reach out to the kid. This is me reaching out."

"What was his topic?"

"Dismantling the stigmas behind calling a lover Daddy from both the male and female perspectives."

"You're big on dismantling stigmas, Dr. St. James."

"That is because stigmas can do a great deal of harm to humans as sexual beings."

"Okay, so why do men and women like the daddy thing?"

"Not all do, but generally it has nothing to do with either of their fathers. Nothing Freudian about it. It's a specific role he either longs to fulfill or she desperately wants him to fulfill. He wants to care for her every need, protect her, nourish her. He generally wants to be a solid, stable fixture in her life. The name has to be separated from her own father, however, and people struggle with that."

"I can honestly say I have never thought about my dad while we were fucking."

"Can't always control what pops into your head during sex. You already know that, seeing as you have the highest grade in my class, but as your boyfriend that makes me exceedingly happy."

"Does all of that mean you want me to call you Daddy?"

Dec growled in her ear. "I told you, either that or sexgod."

A blast of cool air whipped Holly's long hair out behind her. She cinched up her coat and quickstepped to her truck in the parking lot. She would've given anything to go back to the ranch to ride Lightning. This was perfect riding weather. The leaves on the campus ground were still crunchy, not quite waterlogged like they would be as soon as the first snowfall hit.

Just two more days and it would be the weekend and she could go back to Dec's. He'd looked particularly sexy that day, dressed in a button-down shirt and jacket. The top buttons of his shirt had been undone and he hadn't shaven that morning since they'd broken the rules again and Holly had stayed over the evening before. She'd given him something to do besides shave that morning.

Grinning at that, she ordered herself to stop breaking rules. They were well over halfway through the semester. In a few short weeks, they could come out, so to speak. And tonight was the psychology symposium. The very symposium where she had been asked to sit at Dr. Newsome's table along with Kyle Sapen, another contender for the supervisor spot who'd come out of graduate school in Oregon.

Climbing up in her truck, she immediately rolled her eyes. Dammit, couldn't the local pizza shops advertise some way other than shoving shit under her windshield wipers? Balancing carefully, she leaned out the door and yanked a large envelope off of her windshield.

When she tossed it in the passenger seat, a few pieces of computer paper slipped out of the top. Furrowing her brow, she retrieved the papers. Her heart leapt to her throat as she read the sloppy hand-written note on top.

'Hey, I don't know who you are, and you don't know me, but some guy's been paying me to take pics of you. It's getting weird. I thought you should know. These are all the photos I've taken. I swear, I won't do it anymore. Just be careful.' - M. A.

There were seven pictures. One was of some guy's thumb and what looked like it might've been the toe of one of Holly's boots. The concrete ground and brick border in the shot looked familiar, but she couldn't quite tell where it had been taken. There were four of her in full frame from the student parking lot where she normally parked her truck and two from the parking lot of her apartment building. Her hands trembled. Bile flooded her throat. The questions stabbed like icy shards through her. *Who* and *why* took several vicious blows.

She tried to breathe while searching every inch of the parking lot and Psychology annex. She saw no one out of place. Internet news-paper headlines scrolled through her mind. Stalkers. College girls. Harassment. Other horrific statistics racked readily behind the headlines.

Trembling, she jerked around in her seat but there was no one in her truck. *Think, Holly.* Dec was in a staff meeting about the sympo-sium that evening. She needed to tell campus security. For some reason, she believed whoever M.A. was. What would he have to gain from giving her those? It felt like a confession.

Telling herself that if this had anything to do with her and Dec, he would've also been in the pictures, she touched the first name of the last person she'd called.

"I never hear from you twice in one day. How's my girl?" Her mother's voice steadied her.

"Hey, Mama, I'm okay I think. Would you just stay on the phone with me while I walk back inside the building?"

"Holly, what on earth?"

"I'm going in to talk to campus security. Just, if I scream or anything call the police."

"Holly, what happened?"

"Just don't freak out. Someone's been taking pictures of me in the parking lot."

"Everett," her mother's shout nearly deafened Holly.

"No, don't tell. . . ."

"What's wrong, baby girl?"

"Nothing, Daddy. I'm okay. Look, I'm walking in the building. I'm fine. I'll call you and Mama later when I figure out what's going on."

She drew a deep breath as she entered the Psychology Sciences office building. Dec was standing with Dr. Newsome, Dr. Sinclair, and Professor Maven. He rushed towards her as soon as the door opened.

"What's wrong, ba. . . ." he caught himself just in time. "Everything all right, Ms. Camden?"

Putting on her game face, though her legs were the consistency of Jell-O, she handed him the envelope. "Dr. St. James, um, someone put this on my truck."

Dr. Newsome joined them. Dec's entire body was rigid as he flipped through the printed photographs. Fury darkened his eyes.

"Dear me." Newsome shook his head. "I'm so sorry, dear. Tell me this isn't your apartment parking lot?"

"It is, sir." Holly nodded.

"Is there anywhere else you could stay until we get this resolved?"

"Uh. . . ." *Do not look at Dec. Do not look at Dec.* "I guess I could go home and drive in every day. It's a long way, though."

"Well, that might be best."

"I know this may be a bit unorthodox, Dr. Newsome, but I have a very large home with a guest house. She'd be welcome to stay there. I'm not even home much," Dec immediately volunteered.

Guest house? He doesn't have a guest house. Holly shook herself. *Duh, Holly, no one has to know that.*

"I wouldn't want to be any imposition, Dr. St. James. I really don't want to go back to my apartment, though."

"No imposition at all. Any student's safety is always my top priority."

Dr. Newsome seemed torn but finally shrugged. "I certainly cannot tell a doctoral student where they may or may not stay. It's none of my never-mind. If you'd feel safer in Dr. St. James' guest house, it would certainly give me peace of mind. Not that I doubt your ability to take care of yourself, of course. It would let me sleep at night, though. I'd like to take these to the head of campus security. This has become a problem as of late. Several instances have been reported. We do have cameras in all of the parking lots. Surely, we'll catch our photographer soon. Would you mind walking with me there?"

"That's fine, sir. Thank you."

"Do you have any idea who might've wanted you photographed? Seems to me whomever M.A. is, he turned these in out of guilt?" Dec asked.

"I agree, Dr. St. James. The photographer risked his own neck clearly out of guilt. What on earth would he have had to gain from this?" Newsome studied the note again.

"Exactly." Dec's biceps flexed constantly. She watched his pulse hammer in his throat and his jaw tense. Everything about him looked severe. Intensity rolled off him in waves. Holly wanted him to hold her and to tell her that it would all go away. She wanted to promise him that she could take care of herself. She wished she felt that way.

"Let's go talk with the head of security, and I think we should also let the police department know. I will personally walk you to your truck when we're finished and follow you back to your apartment to get your things for this evening," Dr. Newsome vowed.

"Oh, no, sir, that's not necessary."

"It is absolutely necessary. I won't take no for an answer. If Dr. St. James is willing to share his home, the least I can do is walk you to your car." Dr. Newsome gestured towards the doors. Holly had no choice but to follow him to the security complex. "Dr. St. James, would it be all right with you if Ms. Camden followed you to your home after the symposium this evening?"

"Of course. No problem at all. I'll be here should anyone need anything." Dec's hardened gaze was laced with worry and vengeance. Holly had no idea how to reassure him that everything would be fine.

As she walked beside her second-favorite professor to the other end of campus, for the thousandth time that semester alone, she wished she could just go home.

Two and a half hours later, Holly and Dr. Newsome exited the security complex. She'd been interviewed by four security guards and a police officer who'd all managed to make her feel like it might've somehow been her fault she was being stalked. However, they'd also explained that ten other women in undergraduate and graduate programs all over campus had complained of either a man or two men photographing them or of pictures of them showing up online that they didn't know were being taken. All of them were from campus or nearby housing. Somehow, knowing she wasn't the only one made her feel a little better.

None of them had been given copies of their photographs, however. The police seemed to think it was nothing more than a peeping tom case. They agreed to review all security footage in the parking lots, but disagreed with Dec's assumption that the photographer was working for someone else. Apparently, it wasn't unusual for peeping toms to eventually turn over photographs to rid themselves of both evidence and guilt. The police had promised to patrol campus more often as well, but unless the photographer himself had been caught on camera and could be identified that was all they could really do.

Exhausted, uneasy, and embarrassed that Dr. Newsome was following her to her apartment, Holly tried to focus on the fact that she was going to get to move in with Dec at least for the near future. Only problem, Holly had never lived with any male other than her brothers.

This entire day was more than she could quite wrap her head

around. She pulled into her apartment parking lot with Dr. Newsome's Caddy on her tail.

"Of course," she sighed. "The cavalry's here." Standing in the parking lot, arms crossed, scowls etched on their chiseled faces, and shit-kickin' boots complete with spurs in place, were her three big brothers.

"Holly, dear, do you know these men?" Dr. Newsome's voice shook, though he bravely exited his car.

"Yes, sir. These are my brothers. You might remember Luke. He graduated from UN, and this is Grant and Austin."

"Tuck and Wes can be here in an hour if we need 'em," Luke informed her.

"Brock's already on his way," Grant explained.

"I do not need the Kilroy boys nor anyone else from the Glen to come fight my battles for me," Holly huffed. Truthfully, she was glad to see them. Caught in an odd moment where her childhood and her adult life danced far too closely, she let the relief wash over her as she raced into Luke's arms.

"I gotcha'."

"You know we ain't gonna let nobody do nothing to you," Grant vowed. "Luke brought his suit. He knows his way around campus. He'll take you to your fancy shin-dig tonight. Austin and I are going shitlicker huntin'."

Dr. Newsome gave them a placating chuckle. "I do appreciate you boys wanting to care for your sister, but we've let the police know and she's made arrangements to stay somewhere else for a while. I'm sure there's no need for violence."

"And who the hell are you?" Austin drawled.

"Austin." Holly smacked her brother's arm.

"I'm Dr. Richard Newsome, the head of psychological research at the University."

"Well, thank you for seeing Holl back here, Doc, but we got everything under control. We've got a fair amount of experience hazing tenderfoots."

"I will have no hazing on University property, Mr. Camden," Dr. Newsome decreed. Holly wanted to crawl inside her own boots.

"They won't do anything like that, Dr. Newsome. I promise they'll be on their best behavior, and hazing tenderfoots means teaching city-boys never to mess with cowboys. It's not hazing like you're thinking of, exactly."

"Yes, well, like I said, I do wish you'd leave this to the proper authorities."

"No offense, Doc, but she's our baby sister. We *are* the proper authorities," Grant vowed.

"Grant, would you shut up," Holly spoke through her clenched teeth. As glad as she'd been to see her brothers and get a reminder of home, she was going to Dec's after the symposium and nothing was going to stop her, not a stalker, not a peeping-tom, and not her big brothers.

Dec paced back and forth in the empty corridor outside the banquet room in Singleton Auditorium. He'd texted Holly seven times and then realized she must still be with Newsome and unable to text him back.

An hour before the symposium was to begin, his phone mercifully rang. He answered instantly. "Baby? Please say you're okay."

"I'm fine, just listen." Her whisper was so low he raised the volume on his phone as high as it would go just to be able to hear her. "My brothers are here. I freaked out in the parking lot and didn't want to walk all the way back in alone. I thought you were still in your meeting, so I called my mama. I should've known she'd send them out. I swear I will get rid of them after the symposium."

Dec didn't particularly care who was with her as long as she was safe. Just then he was elated her brothers were in town. He'd already alerted Kade, Wyatt, Garrick, and Brett to drive around campus and her apartment building looking for anyone suspicious. Her brothers could help them. "It's fine, sweetheart. Are they staying with you tonight?"

"No. I'll think of something. They need to get back to the ranch anyway. They just want to check everything out, I think."

"I'm just so glad you're all right. I went down to the security office myself when I hadn't heard from you. They told me about the other women."

"Definitely freaky." She was trying so hard to sound brave and unaffected, and she was failing miserably. His heart shattered all over again.

"I swear, I will keep you safe, honey." Dec still couldn't believe she was going to be able to live with him, at least until this thing was resolved.

"It's okay. We're leaving soon. I just want to be with you."

"I'll be right here."

It wasn't until Holly, bedecked in a low-cut satin blouse the precise shade of her eyes and a grey pencil skirt that showed off her delicate curves to perfection paired with a fancy pair of cowgirl boots, entered the auditorium on the arm of a man she favored, who was dressed in dark Wranglers, a suit-coat, a starched button-down complete with a bolo, rather nice cowboy boots, and a Stetson, that Dec managed to remember all that was at stake.

The hall was filling up with invited guests and speakers. He should've gone to find his seat but he stood there staring, speechless. She was so seductively sweet. She was supposed to be on his arm. *He* was supposed to keep her safe. She was his. Thoughts of what she was wearing under the dress had him dropping his clasped hands to shield his bulging zipper line.

"Dr. St. James, I'd like to introduce you to my oldest brother, Luke," she managed, though panic broadcast from every inch of her. The tiny freckles scattered across her visible cleavage darkened as she fought a blush.

"Very nice to meet you. Holly is a delightful student. One of UN's best." Dec offered Luke his hand. Everything about this was wrong. *I'm Declan. I'm madly in love with your sister and intend to make her mine in every possible way. I'll do anything in my power to take care of her and make certain she is happy for the rest of this life and the next.* That was how introductions with her family were supposed to have gone.

"Luke, this is Dr. St. James, one of my professors."

"Sir." Luke tipped his hat in what looked like a move he performed numerous times a day. "Been more'n a day or two since I was here. This building still kept by that sonuvabitch boot-lickin' family that thinks they own the moon?" His low baritone voice rumbled through the hall.

Dec had to laugh. Given time, he and Luke would get along just fine. "The Singletons, and yes. Also that is Dr. and Mrs. Singleton Sr. and their son right over there. Might want to keep it down."

"Luke got his veterinary degree here several years ago," Holly explained.

"I did, and they needed their horns clipped when I was here. Can't imagine what they're like now."

Before either Dec or Holly could respond, Trevor Jr. left his parent's side and descended upon them. "Ms. Camden, Dr. St. James, all the usual suspects. Who might you be?" He turned on Luke.

From the narrowing of Luke's eyes and the cock of his jaw, Dec wondered if Trevor was intelligent enough to see that Luke Camden was not a man he wanted to take on.

"Someone who ain't impressed with pompous city-slickers."

Holly's beaming grin said she was pleased her brother had sized Trevor up that quickly.

"What are you smiling at, Camden? Give me a little time. I'm gonna wipe that smile off of your smug face soon enough. In fact, Dad says Dr. Newsome's considering announcing his pick tonight."

Suddenly, Luke had Trevor by the knot of his tie. Trevor went up on his tiptoes trying to jerk away but only managing to dance in order to breathe. "Listen up, you half-wit corncracker, I hear about you gettin' anywhere near her face, I'll rearrange yours seven ways from Sunday. Won't even dirty up my coat. I take it by them ridiculous loafers you're wearin' that you ain't ever had a taste of work boots, but I'll bury mine so far up your skinny ass your first taste of leather will be covered in your own shit."

"Luke," Holly was trying not to laugh. "Let him go."

With the quick release of his hand, Trevor stumbled backwards. Dec ran his hand over his face to keep from laughing. This was too good. "Perhaps we should all go find our seats," he offered what he hoped sounded like a suggestion from a relatively uninvolved professor.

"We're sitting at the head table with Dr. Newsome," Holly explained for both Trevor and Luke's benefit.

"The Singleton family has their own table," Trevor huffed.

"Oh good, then you can sit in Daddy's lap and cry when I'm named Newsome's protégé."

Luke and Dec shared a sly grin. "Come on, Holl." Luke offered her his arm. It crushed Dec. She should've been walking in on his arm.

As it turned out, Dec had been placed at Newsome's table as well. Several top members of the staff had. Luke's name had been quickly added to a placecard and had been switched with Professor Dilentoie's, who'd graciously given up her seat after hearing about the photographs.

"All they have is sissy wine," Luke grumbled to his sister.

"This is a psychology symposium, Luke, not a night at Saddle-back's," Holly sighed.

"Much as it costs to go here, you'da thought they could at least get a cheap bottle of Crown." Luke flipped through the program at his place. "Merciful Jay-sus, Holl, there's like twelve speakers."

"You're the one who insisted on bringing me."

"Should'a made Grant come. Lordy knows he could use some learnin'."

"You used to say that about Austin."

"Yeah, but Summer beat some sense into him."

"So, maybe Grant needs a woman to teach him a few things."

"I ain't disagreein' with that a'tall. Please tell me they're at least feedin' us. I'm half-starved."

"They are." Holly shared a quick exasperated glance with Dec. He managed a discreet wink that no one else noticed.

CHAPTER FORTY-ONE

Okay, Luke was right. This is as boring as watching paint dry. Holly shifted in her seat as Dr. Singleton took his. He'd welcomed all of the speakers, thanked them for being there, and had then spent twenty minutes lauding his own credentials and enumerating his substantial donations to the University. He'd then given his own father some plaque for being a donor and had then gone on to exult his son for carrying on the family legacy.

"Crowbait horse thinks he's running Kentucky," Luke spat under his breath. Holly nodded her adamant agreement.

As dinner was served, Holly braced for Luke's inevitable analysis of the lobster and rice.

"Are they shittin' me? They're feeding us bait 'fore they jaw us to death?"

"Luke, please."

Dec, at least, found this comical and took a sip of his water to keep from cracking up.

"How do you even eat this?"

"Use the fork and the crackers." Holly pointed to the implements beside his plate.

"So, I'm makin' my own meal. You know, I left Indie home with a roast in the oven."

"You didn't have to come."

That brought Luke up short. "I didn't mean it like that, sugar. You know I'd do anything in the world for you."

"Yes, I know. Now shut up and stop complaining. You're embarrassing me."

"Fine. Fine. But can we go out somewhere after this?"

"You can."

Dec was still chuckling as the first speaker, Dr. Howard Gardner, began speaking on forms of intelligence. Even Luke seemed fascinated and settled in.

When Dr. Singleton returned to the podium, Holly eased away from the table. Luke and Dec both turned towards her. "Just have to use the restroom. I'll be right back."

Dec simply did not possess the strength it would have taken to keep from watching Holly's exquisite ass caught up in a fitted skirt sway as she exited the auditorium. Her long lush hair danced to the rhythm. He burned for her.

If he'd been her date, he would have escorted her himself. Her brother kept an eye on her until she was out of sight, but made no move to follow after her. Dec reasoned that brothers were likely never as overprotective as lovers, but it did nothing to soothe his agitated nerves.

However, when Trevor Singleton slipped out, Luke's eyes flared with irritation. They stood at the same moment intent on the same target. It was when he locked eyes with Luke Camden that Dec realized they were had.

Luke's jaw cocked to the side. His left eyebrow arched with suspicion. Ignoring the panic that roared in his ears, Dec headed out of the auditorium. Luke was hot on his heels when he found Trevor and Holly face to face.

"If you think playing teacher's pet for St. James' is gonna help you,

you're dumber than you look. I've got you by a string this time, Holly, and I plan to take full advantage."

"Ms. Camden, is everything all right, dear?" Fury throbbed in Dec's clenched fists. He longed to pound Singleton into the ground.

"Nothing I can't handle." Her fight was vicious, but a healthy dose of fear resided in those all-telling eyes.

"Boy, you ain't real bright now are ya?" Luke shoved Trevor away from Holly and stepped in front of her. "You get in her face or threaten her again, I'll take you outside and give you the whuppin' you clearly been needin' for a long while."

"Mr. Singleton, is there some reason you're standing in front of the lady's restroom?" Dec summoned his most professional tone.

"Yeah, I take issue with Holly thinking she can just get up and leave when my father speaks. Won't matter though. She gets away with everything."

"By my count, motherfucker, I've had to talk to you three times today. That's my shit-drivel limit. I'm all tapped outta patience for your family's self-serving gibberish, Singleton, and I had to pee," Holly lunged around Luke.

And there was his cowgirl. God, he loved her.

Luke's right arm shot out, keeping her back. "Boy, I've seen her fight. She don't take shit offa nobody. You don't wanna go there. Last chick that got into it with her lost half her hair to them claws."

Dec lowered his head. The image of Holly fighting both terrified and enlivened him. He called himself a bastard, ordered himself to act as a professor, and drew a deep breath.

"Trevor, return to your seat. Ms. Camden, calm down. Now." Oh, she didn't like that. For a split second, Dec was worried he was going to be the next target of her wrath. He offered her a pleading gaze. She returned an eye roll.

"Now, Mr. Singleton." Dec clapped his hand on Trevor's neck with more force than was warranted, not that he cared. Guiding the asshole out, Dec fought the bile swimming in his gut.

"You hang on a minute," he heard Luke instruct Holly, but he refused to look back and confirm her brother's suspicions.

CHAPTER FORTY-TWO

"What do you want, Luke? I'm supposed to be in there," Holly panicked. Her brother knew something. It was written all over his face.

"I may not be smart enough to be in there speakin', Holl, but I got enough brains to more'n get me by. I got a real good feelin' you and that Doc that just left are more'n teacher and student."

"That's insane."

"Too bad this school can't teach you to lie better than that. Spill it."

"There is nothing to spill." She prayed no one in the auditorium had super hearing or decided to make a trip to the bathroom.

"I'm waiting, Holl, and you know I am a patient man." He crossed his arms over his chest to prove his point. "He's the boyfriend you jumped all over us about when you were home for Aurora Belle, the one mama's so convinced you're gonna marry."

"We started dating and fell in love before he was assigned to teach here," Holly's whisper was so low, Luke leaned in to hear her. "Please, Luke. He means everything to me. I'm in love with him. I swear to you I'd walk away from everything for him, just like you and Indie."

Her brother's entire demeanor changed. His eyes softened and he dropped his arms. "There's gotta be some kinda rule about this, though." He sounded more concerned than agitated. Holly took that as a good sign.

"There is, but only because I'm in his class. After this semester, it won't matter. He's only teaching here for a year before he goes back to being a therapist."

"Holl, you're playing with fire. Seems to me you could get kicked outta here or lose your stipend at the very least, and he could get fired for messing around with you."

"Not if no one ever finds out. And. . .I don't care what happens to me anymore. I just need him not to get fired."

"I don't much believe that. You've wanted to be a therapist since your junior year of high school. You've worked your tail off."

"But I love him more than all of that."

"You sound like a love sick pup. He better be treating you right."

"He's the most amazing man in the world, Luke. And actually, since you know now, Dr. Newsome okayed me staying at his house until we figure out the picture thing."

"Wait, the head of the department knows about you two?"

"No. It just worked out."

"Sounds mighty suspicious to me, but okay. Next question, you ever think this deal with the pictures has anything to do with him? Somebody tryin' to get the two of you in trouble, maybe. Seems to me the little pipsqueak Mr. Amazing just dragged outta here is lookin' for something to keep you from getting whatever it is he's decided he wants."

A shot of terror stabbed through Holly. She'd been trying not to think that very thing all damn day. "I did think of that, but the pictures were only of me. What would that prove? Besides, there are lots of other women who've also had their picture taken without their permission."

"Just be careful. Don't get so hellfire determined to do things your way that you end up losing the guy his job and everything you've worked for."

"I won't."

Luke stared at her for the length of two heartbeats. "If you don't, it'd be the first time in your life you haven't."

The distinctive sound of an exterior door closing sliced through the moment.

"Shit," Holly raced towards the front of the building. Luke followed after her. She clutched her chest, trying to steady her racing heart. Mrs. Singleton was striding out of the building. She seemed to be leaving and didn't appear to have heard anything odd.

Idiot just wouldn't give it up. Dec followed after Trevor yet again when he returned to his parent's table, picked something up, and headed back out of the room. This time Trevor walked out the exit doors, however. Dec watched him hurry towards the adjacent building until he was out of sight.

Luke and Holly returned to the table several minutes later. The look on Holly's face said it all. Her brother knew, but he wasn't going to talk.

A rising tide of panic roiled in Dec's lobster-filled stomach for the rest of the symposium. Finally, Dr. Newsome took the stage. He droned on, thanking the speakers and the attendees.

If your caught, it's all over. Back to every failure with your name stamped on it. Back to that headstone. Back to the suffocating crowd where no one cares. Without her. Forever. You can't even handle the stress that someone else might know. You'll never make it through the night without a little help. Bet it wouldn't take much to find something nearby.

The cravings slammed through him, drowning him in a riptide of weakness. Wave after wave crashed over him. Dec could barely catch his breath.

"I know several students are hoping I'm going to announce my choice for whose dissertation I will be supervising this year. I have decided to wait until the end of the semester to make my announcement. Still too many students in contention for my help, though I have no idea why. They're all far more brilliant than I." Polite laughter followed Newsome's attempt at self-deprecation.

A cold sweat broke out across Dec's forehead. *Just shut up. I need her. I need a fix. Nice, St. James, do you love her or is she just your next addiction?* Brutal thoughts embattled his mind. He had no control over them.

Shaking himself, he grabbed a near empty glass of water and tossed it back, slapping his mouth with the half-melted ice. A constant buzz of contention took up residence in his ears.

Suddenly, applause broke out and the lights in the room were back on. Dec blinked rapidly. His eyes sought Holly. She was laughing at something her brother had said. Breath rushed into Dec's lungs.

She was right there, laughing and smiling. He was okay. She was all he needed.

Everyone made their way to the exit doors and Dec prepared to argue with Luke over letting Holly stay at his home. He doubted knowing what he now knew that her brother would be agreeable over this. Dec didn't particularly care.

When they spilled out into the cold night air, they were met by two other men wearing cowboy hats and boots that had to have been Holly's other two brothers. And they were dragging two other men by the scruff of their necks.

"What on earth?" Holly gasped.

"Found your photographers."

Dr. Newsome made his way to the front of the gathered crowd. "What is the meaning of this?"

"Larry and Moe here were snapping pictures willy-nilly outside the dining hall. We thought that was a little odd so we followed after 'em. Headed straight up two trees outside a dormitory. We yanked 'em down. Didn't put up much of a fight. Cityboys." He shook his head.

"That's Grant," Holly whispered to no one in general. That made the slightly shorter one with the massive belt buckle Austin, Dec recalled.

Newsome and Dec moved closer. "Do you attend the University, gentlemen?" Newsome demanded.

Neither responded until Austin shook the one in his hands. "Grown man asks you a question, you better answer lest I show you exactly what we do to peeping toms out in cattle country. I'll turn you out with the bulls, boy."

"No sir," vaulted out of the kid's mouth. He couldn't have been more than seventeen.

"We go to Lincoln High," the other volunteered without having to be prodded.

"Why are you here on this campus then?" Newsome sounded rather severe.

"We. . .uh. . .we're working on. . .uh. . .a project."

"Yeah, for school."

"Oh, so you were told to take pictures of women on UN's campus for school?" Holly stepped up. "I highly doubt that."

Dec watched the men closely. Neither seemed to recognize Holly at all. They shared a shameful glance.

"Give it up, gentlemen. What's the name of the site?" Dec couldn't possibly have been the only one to figure this out, yet somehow everyone around him seemed surprised.

"We don't have much up yet." One volunteered as the other elbowed him. "We're caught now. We weren't gonna put up nudie pics, I swear."

"My baby sister ends up on some kind of website nekkid, boy, the bulls'll be the least of your worries," Austin snarled. "I'll skin you alive."

"Who's your sister?"

"Dear Heavens, all right. If you don't mind holding them there for a moment. I'm calling campus security. We've got it taken care of folks. Head on home." Newsome pled.

The crowd begrudgingly slunk towards the surrounding parking lots. As they began to move, the one Grant was holding managed to jerk free and took off. Without thought, Dec summoned his past, every fight he'd ever been in either in a bar, or with a dealer, or user, or hell, with his own brothers coursed through his veins. In three quick strides, he dodged around Dr. Hennessy and his wife, caught the kid at his waist and had him on the ground. He planted his boot firmly in the idiot's chest.

"Damn," Grant admired. "You're quick. Not bad for a city-slicker."

"Came up on a sheep farm. I'm not a city-slicker." Shocked at his own decree, Dec jerked the kid off of the ground. Never before had he readily owned up to his upbringing.

Security pulled up followed by a police car. The fools were taken by a cop, not the security guard. Having been the guy shoved in the back of a police car himself, Dec cringed when they were pushed inside.

Grant and Austin began recounting getting them out of the trees to the security team and the remaining crowd, but Luke discreetly motioned for Dec to follow him to the side of the building. "Look, Holl told me what's going on."

Dec glanced around to make absolutely certain no one could hear them. He gave a quick nod.

"I got a wife at home and if you ever tell her I said this I'll scalp ya, but she's 'bout as big as the broad side of my barn with a belly full of my baby girls. Two of 'em. Most beautiful thing I've ever seen, but I can't stay out here. Austin or Grant could stay if they needed to, but that puts us short on the ranch and that's a lotta extra work. Seein' as you seem just as capable of taking care of Holly as we are, I'm holding you to that. Those idiots hadn't ever seen Holly before. They didn't take them pictures, and if they had, they sure as hell didn't return the copies to her. Something else is going on."

"I know that."

"Well, also know this, I got no issue with what you and Holl got going on long as you treat her right, and I'll keep my mouth shut about it 'lest this all gets fucked up bad enough to make a freight train take a dirt road. What all of that means is if something, if *anything*, happens to her, I'm coming after you."

"Understood. I'll keep her safe. I know this looks bad, but I swear to you, man to man, I love her more than life itself."

"Yeah, well you both sound like love sick pups. Just keep her safe."

Two hours later, Dec held Holly in his bed, content on his chest wearing another one of his Radiohead t-shirts.

"I can't believe I'm here," she sighed.

"I'm just so happy that you are. Not sure you're supposed to be now that your brothers caught the amateur photographers. Newsome never redacted the suggestion though."

"If anyone asks, I'll say that we figured out that they weren't the people who took pictures of me. Or that my brother asked if I could still stay here."

"Hopefully, no one will ask." Dec shifted so more of his skin was in contact with hers. Their current reality seemed far too close to a dream.

"We have less than three weeks until the end of the semester. Since you already met all of my brothers, do you want to come home with me for Thanksgiving? Please."

"I'd love to, baby, but don't you think the other members of your family might not like confirmation that you were sleeping with your professor?"

"Luke didn't care. He is probably the most civilized, but they all just want me to be happy."

"That's all I want as well."

"Then come with me. You make me happy."

"Promise?"

"Promise."

CHAPTER FORTY-THREE

Two days before finals began, Holly walked the circle in Dec's house from his kitchen to the living room to the entryway, past the office and bathroom and back again, reciting facts about the functions of the temporal lobes in monkeys for her Anal Fun exam. The playlist Dec had created just for her to study to blared through her earbuds silencing the incessant drone of the salt trucks. They'd barely gotten an inch of snow, but there was more to come.

Dec was once again playing Duffy's. This time she had no choice but to stay home and study. Other than letting Dec fuck her senseless each night, she'd done nothing the last week but go to class, go to the library, write papers, and study.

The music died in her ears when her phone rang. Cheyenne, again. She sent it to voice mail. Her mother, Luke, Grant, and Beth had all been relegated there that afternoon as well. Everyone wanted to wish her good luck on her exams. It was sweet, but she didn't have time to chat.

Keeping a close eye on the front windows, she glanced at the clock on the mantle then returned to the front of the house. The pizza would be there soon. A hint of nerves niggled in her empty stomach, but she'd repeatedly told herself that it was the topic of the paper that had weirded her out not the pizza guy. Besides, studying made her hungry, and before he'd left Dec had ordered her a deep dish supreme with extra onion, her favorite.

She laid her phone on the front table and went back to reciting facts. The buzz of the doorbell startled her. Holly peeked out the windows and summoned courage. It was the same damned pizza guy. Didn't anyone else work this neighborhood?

Opening the door, she mean-mugged the guy, but he refused to meet her gaze. His ball cap was pulled low over his eyes. "Uh. . .ma'am. . .uh. . .your pizza." Almost dropping the insulated bag the pizza was in, he finally managed to hand her the box.

"Thanks."

"And. . .your receipts." He dug in his pocket and produced the receipt for Holly to add the tip to and sign. She completed the tasks quickly and returned the paper. He handed her a copy, glanced back down the driveway nervously, and offered her a wave.

Carrying the pizza and the receipt back to the kitchen, Holly dropped them both on the granite. Damn thing was hot. The receipt fluttered to her feet. When she lifted it, something caught her eye. Driver's Name: Michael Ashbury was printed at the bottom of the receipt. M.A.

Her stomach turned inside out. She had no idea how she knew he was the M.A. who'd taken her picture, but she did. The last time she'd been at Dec's house alone. He'd been messing with his phone. He was trying to take her picture. That was the shot with his thumb in the way. The brick. She remembered. It was the brick border on Dec's front porch. *Shit. Shit. Shit.* He was taking her picture at Dec's house.

"I don't know who you are, and you don't know me, but some guy's been paying me to take pics of you. It's getting weird. I thought you should know."

The squeal of tires slipping on ice ripped through the twilight. "Oh my God," Holly stepped into her boots and raced out the front door. The brutal wind took her breath away. Her lungs burned as she sped through the trees towards the road, no longer afraid of M.A. but of the man she knew had to be behind his payments.

Freezing in place, she watched in horror as a yellow Scion chased an old Ford Taurus with Mario's Pizza Delivery on the top out of the neighborhood.

"Oh my God." Her words were whipped away in the wind. *Think, Holly, think.* She could call Luke. No, he wouldn't be able to help. Racing back in the house she tried to think of any possible way to figure out if Trevor had any usable evidence to convict either Dec or herself.

She couldn't possibly tell Dec. He would freak and, he'd told her that morning his cravings had been increasing. He'd planned to go to a meeting in Roca the next day with Kade. She could handle this on her own. She wouldn't worry him. She just needed someone to talk it through with her.

Beth's phone rang three times before she answered. "I haven't slept in eighteen hours. Why do we have to know all of this crap about monkeys?"

"I don't know, Beth. Listen to me." Holly quickly explained the hell raining down around her currently.

"Oh. My. God. Holl, what are you gonna do?"

"That's why I called you. I need to talk this through. I don't even know if he has enough evidence to get us in trouble."

"Okay, okay, let me think."

"Do you want to come over here? Dec will be out late."

"Uh, no, if Single-ass knows where his house is it would look particularly bad for your friends to be showing up over there. Let's not give him any real evidence."

'I've got you by a string this time, Holly, and I plan to take full advantage.' "He wasn't just threatening me at the symposium. He even called me Dr. St. James' pet."

"What?"

"He told me he had me by a string this time and that he was going to take advantage. I thought he was just being his typical douche-bag self. It never occurred to me he was serious."

"Okay, deep breath. Meet me at your old apartment. We'll figure something out."

"Okay, but I have to be back here before Dec gets home. He'll freak if he thinks something's wrong."

Holly threw on her coat, grabbed the pizza on her way out, and leapt in her truck.

"You got pizza for this?" Beth shivered when she entered the freezing cold apartment.

"Dec ordered it before he left for Duffy's. I didn't want to chance his coming home and finding it uneaten. I turned the heat up but, it'll take it a little while to warm up in here. The insulation sucks."

"It's fine. Can I have some pizza? It'll help me think."

"Of course. I can't eat. Pretty sure I'm going to be sick."

Beth offered her a sympathetic gaze. "We'll figure something out. We just need to think like psychologists. Understanding why people do what they do or don't do what they don't do is our job. We need to analyze Trevor."

"Okay, that's good. Let me think. Trevor never does anything the way he's supposed to. Dec let me see a few of his papers. He puts forth no effort at all. It was almost like he was trying to goad Dec into failing him or something. It was blatant."

"So, we could assume he puts forth no effort unless it's for his own gain." Beth took a bite of pizza and made notes on a notepad. "Do you think his plan is to threaten Dr. St. James with anything he's found out about the two of you so he wouldn't fail him?"

"Maybe. But he's the same way in his other classes, too. He went so far as to pay that Michael dude to follow me. That's kind of a lot of effort. And oh my God, Beth, Dec could get deported all because of me."

Beth studied her for a moment. "Not necessarily. I mean it probably wouldn't save you getting kicked out of school, but you could marry him. If you're married to an American citizen, you get to be a citizen too. My dad's from Germany. He got to move here as soon as he and Mom got hitched, well, not as soon as but a few months later."

"Really?"

"Yup."

"Have I ever told you how much I love you? If I wasn't going to marry Dec, I swear I'd marry you."

"We would make a kick-ass couple, but you lack all the right equipment for keeping my horny meter down."

Holly laughed. It was a strange sensation given what they were dealing with. Somehow knowing she could keep Dec in the country at the very least eased the terror in her gut. "That still requires getting Dec to marry me, which would probably freak him out right now. And I would still get kicked out of school, and he would lose his job. None of that is okay."

"Dr. Singleton didn't get fir. . .holy cheeseballs, Holly, that's it!"

"What's it?"

"Dr. Singleton had an affair two years ago with Emma Barrett, and he didn't get fired."

"So? He has an affair every semester and never gets fired."

"But I'm still good friends with Emma. She started going to school at Northeast. I help her out sometimes. Keep her in the loop with what's going on here. She owes me."

"Yeah, but she had an affair with him on purpose. She threw herself at Dr. Singleton for the drama and scandal. She wanted them to get caught. She was trying to get him kicked out. She freaking uploaded their sex tape online."

"Exactly. She was furious when she got kicked out but he didn't get fired. Furious enough to want to get back at the whole family." Beth retrieved her phone. A minute later, she was talking to none other than Emma Barrett.

Holly's phone buzzed on the coffee table. She sent another call from Grant to her voicemail. What the hell was going on in the Glen that night? Whatever it was she had more important things to worry about.

When another call from Cheyenne came in immediately, Holly's curiosity got the better of her. "What?" she demanded.

"Why are you yelling at me?" Cheyenne pouted.

"Not yelling at you. Just kind of having a major crisis here."

"Holl, Grant's dating Ashley Stender. I just saw them in town."

If Holly had rolled her eyes any harder, they would have lodged in her skull. "Cheyenne, Grant never dates anyone for any length of time. He just wants to sleep with her. Please, please, please get over my brother. He's just not into you, and he's the dumbass that doesn't see what a great girl you are. You deserve better."

"You could talk to him."

"No, I can't. I have to go," Holly insisted.

Beth gave Holly a thumbs up that brought a round of relief to her nerves.

"No, that would be amazing. You're the best." Beth nodded. "Get off the phone," she mouthed to Holly.

"I'll talk to you later Cheyenne. Beth needs me," Holly ended the call.

"Well, maybe, kind of, I'm picturing more of a blackmail scenario here, just email them to me." Beth reached in her bag and flipped open her laptop. "Yep, just came through. Thank you a million times over from me and Holly. I'll let you know what happens."

"Who are we blackmailing?" Holly demanded as soon as Beth ended the call.

"Trevor, obviously, although Emma really wants us to take down Dr. Singleton, too, but I'm not sure we can make anything stick to him. We just have to convince Trevor we can."

"How are we supposed to blackmail Trevor?"

"We tell him what we have, hope to the horses above that it's enough to get him to give up any info he has on you and to keep his mouth shut about you and Dr. St. James."

"But what do we have?"

"We have every single email, screenshots of texts, and even a few naughty pictures shared between Dr. Singleton and Emma. Apparently there's even a dick pic in here, but Emma advises us not to look at it. She says it's a sad old man dick. She just got him to send it in her quest to get him fired."

"Are you serious? She just sent all of this?" Holly yanked the laptop out of Beth's lap.

"I told you, she was furious she got kicked out, and he got another building named after him. It's her second chance to ruin him, even if it is vicariously through us."

Holly scanned down the file of dozens upon dozens of emails. "This is good stuff."

"You know it." Beth waggled her eyebrows.

"Seriously, I don't know what I would do without you. Thank you."

"Now that you have all of this, you won't have to find out. When do you want to show this to Trevor?"

"He was spying on the pizza guy or on Dec's house just a couple of hours ago. He must think he needs more on us before he goes to Newsome."

"If he has anything at all. We still don't know for sure."

"Yeah, but the best defense is a good offense in this case. I'll corner him at school tomorrow. I just need to calm down before I go back to Dec's. I have to act like nothing's wrong."

"That and we have to copy this onto something so we have more than one copy."

"You know way too much about how to do this, Beth."

"Please, girl, don't you watch Bachelor in Paradise? Do you have a spare thumb drive?"

"Yeah, hang on." Holly dug in her bag until she located a drive she'd used the year before. "All the rest of mine are at Dec's."

"Okay, copy them onto your laptop and make another copy when you get back there. It's going to be okay, Holl. Just promise I get to be your maid of honor."

"For this, I'll boot my sister out of the spot."

The quick knock on the door had both of the women gasping.

"Maybe it's Dec. He has to drive by here to go to his house. My truck's right out front." Holly panicked.

"It can't be Dec. It's barely 10:00. They're just warming up at Duffy's, don't you think?" Beth insisted even though she slammed the laptop shut. Holly shoved the thumb drive in her pocket, just in case.

Hating her super for never installing peepholes in the doors, Holly called, "Who is it?"

"It's Trevor."

"Holy shit!" Holly gasped.

"Open it. You have the upper hand. Just keep it together." Beth swung the door open when Holly continued to stand there motionless.

"What are you doing here?" Trevor huffed.

"I live here," Holly spat. Rage and vengeance jerked her out of her shocked stupor. Singleton was going down.

"Not you. Her." Trevor jabbed a finger at Beth.

"Why do you give a shit where I am, Trevor? You scared of girls in packs?"

"I'm not scared of anything, Kinders. I'm here to talk with Holly. I saw you run out in his front yard. I know you're living there. I know everything. You really stupid enough to think if you ran back over here I'd believe this is your house?"

"You know nothing, Singleton. Newsome told me I could stay there. Why do you even care where I live?"

"Right, Newsome said you could live with our professor. You hit your head when you went running out of his mansion or something?"

"What do you want, Trevor?" Holly channeled her own inner-bitch and tried to remember that she wanted him to show his cards first.

"What do *I* want? To make you drop off the face of this planet, but that brings up all kinds of police investigations, so I have something far less complicated."

"Oh yeah? What's that?"

"Well," Trevor dug in his pocket for his phone. "Dad told me St. James had the audacity to record a private conversation between the two of them at the beginning of the semester. Pissed me off at first, but then I saw the brilliance of it."

Holly narrowed her eyes as Trevor played a recording on his phone. She could just make out her own voice talking to Luke at the symposium. *'I'm in love with him. I swear to you I'd walk away from everything for him.'* Beth's eyes goggled. Holly chased her breath. *Think Holly. You still have the emails.*

"That still true, Holly? You still willing to walk away from everything for Professor Sex?" Trevor taunted.

"Maybe," Holly choked.

"Wrong answer. Correct answer is, yes, Trevor, I'll do anything to keep his ass from getting shipped back to wherever the hell he came from."

Holly ground her teeth.

"Here's what happens to whores who offer BJ's for A's."

Something inside Holly unhinged. She existed in pure reaction. Her backhand flew across Trevor's smug face.

His eyes flashed dangerously. "Bitch, you do not want to go there with me." He rubbed the glowing outline of her fingers on his cheek. "Here's what you're gonna do. You're gonna fail every single one of your final exams. I'm going to be named Newsome's protégé. My parents will chill, and you can repeat the entire semester. And if you don't, I'll let the entire department hear this recording I have."

Adrenaline scalded Holly's blood. It cleared her thoughts. "That's why you wanted my picture. That's why you hired Michael or whatever his name was to photograph me. I never say his name on the recording and you can't hear half of it. It's not enough proof. You need a picture that you don't have."

"Oh, I've got more. That's just the icing on the cake. I was there that night at Duffy's before school started when he was licking your spit, grabbing your skanky ass, and jumping off the stage to get to you. Made me sick to watch and that was before he was a professor. But I knew he was a therapist at Lifespan and I intended to keep you from getting an internship there. I have pictures from that night as well. I've been following you two all semester. I have a long list of indiscretions, including pictures of you packing your truck to go to his house. Do you recall the night you snuck up to his office and then went running out? Yeah, when he took off after you he almost ran me down with his bike. I got a pic of the plate, and shots of your truck in his garage. I've got you in my cage, Holly."

"Oh, Trevy, you don't." Holly yanked the thumbdrive out of her pocket. "Know what this is? I'll be nice and tell you. It's every single email, text, and photograph shared between your daddy and Emma Barrett. You remember her, right? I mean, she almost became your step-mommy. That would have been awkward, having a stepmom younger than you." Holly tsked. "What's the saying, you show them yours I'll show them mine? Bet Daddy would love that."

Trevor reached for the drive, but Holly was quicker. She had it back in her pocket before he could get his grimy hands near her. "My God, you really aren't the brightest bulb on the tree are ya, Trev? This ain't my only copy."

"Where did you get that?"

"From Emma herself," Beth sneered. "She was a little put out that she got kicked out of school while your father got away scot free, rightfully so."

"What's it going to be Trev? I'm up for a truce if you are," Holly baited.

"Do not show those to anyone, Camden, or you'll be sorry."

"Right back at'cha Singleton." She gestured to his phone.

With that he slithered back to his car, and Holly slammed the door.

"How creepy is it that he's been following you all semester?" Beth gagged.

"It's sad, really. If he'd put all of that effort into learning something, he wouldn't need to fuck with me."

"Did you see him, though? He was shaking in his boots. He'll keep his mouth shut. Mark my words."

"He sure as hell better." Holly pulled back the window shades and watched Trevor drive away.

"I think he was lying. If he really has all of the pictures he says he does, why did he get pizza-delivery boy to take more pictures? Why did he chase after him at Dec's tonight?" Beth asked.

"He needs one of Dec and me together. None of what he has will ride. It's all circumstantial. The pictures of us kissing were before Dec started working at UN. Pictures of me loading my truck. That's easy for me to get out of. Even my truck in his garage. Dr. Newsome told me I could stay there. Michael fucked it up and only got a picture of his own thumb and my toe. Betcha he'd been told to get a picture of me and Dec together in the house."

"Devious little ass-weasel. I wish we could broadcast the info Emma gave us all over campus anyway."

"NO. We keep our word and hold him to his."

CHAPTER FORTY-FOUR

Dec watched Holly glare hatefully at a rather defeated looking Trevor Singleton as they took their seats. He wanted to believe this was typical behavior for Trevor being such an ass, but it was unlike Holly, and she'd been acting a little off. Something was wrong. Whatever it was, he would deal with it in. . .he checked his phone. . .two hours and seventeen minutes. The exact moment he would be able to breathe again. The exact moment she would turn in her final exam and no longer be his student.

Impatience swirled through his musculature. The sooner they got this exam over with the sooner he could move her into his house permanently, put the massive ring he'd purchased on her delicate finger, let the entire world know she was taken, and actually live a life worth having.

He tapped the test booklets on his desk, hoping to prod time along. At 2:00 PM on the dot, their assigned exam time, he stood. Holly was performing some kind of deep breathing routine. As he began handing out the booklets, he tried to discern if tests always made her this nervous or if he should panic. She'd had her Analysis and Functions exam that morning. Maybe it was too much in one day.

When she gnawed on her thumbnail he assumed that was it. She was going to ace both tests. She had no reason to worry. He'd done his best that morning to reassure her, but apparently his assurances hadn't lasted long. Her nerves were getting to him. A low level of dread ran through him constantly. His cravings were amped by the bizarre feeling of impending doom. They needed to get this over with so they could both relax.

Promising himself that he'd spend the entire afternoon making her forget all about her exams, he returned to his desk and pulled out a piece of blank sheet music. Another song had been playing on repeat in his mind. Another song she'd inspired. He intended to put it on paper while she worked and play it for her later that day.

"You may begin." The test pamphlets opened in an orchestrated contagion around the room and everyone settled in.

A half hour into the exam, a knock sounded on the door, ripping everyone from their intent focus.

His heart careened downward when he opened the door. His blood ran oddly cold. Nausea turned his stomach. *Oh fuck* were the only words he could access. Dr. Newsome was front and center, flanked by Singleton and two women Dec had never seen before.

Stepping back as they advanced, he tried to breathe. "Dr. St. James, it is imperative that we see both you and Ms. Holly Camden in the Psychology Sciences office building immediately."

Terror rocked through Holly. Her entire body vibrated in dread. Barely managing to stand, she took a single breath that brought oxygen back to her brain. Turning to glare at Trevor, she stopped short of screeching at him.

He shook his head frantically. "I didn't. I swear."

Bile singed her throat as she fought tears. Dear God, what had she done? What was going to happen? A single moronic brain cell offered some ridiculous hope that this had nothing to do with her and Dec's relationship, but she'd been a disaster all morning. She'd felt this coming.

All of the blood housed in Dec's body appeared to have left his ashen face. Holly eased forward, concentrating on nothing more than putting one foot in front of the other.

The world tilted and roared. She drowned in a mass of hysteria and confusion.

"Let's go, Miss Camden. Now," Dr. Singleton sneered.

Somehow Holly made it to the corridor. She tried to see Dec's face, but couldn't make out much of anything in front of her. This was entirely her fault. She'd just lost him his job and quite possibly his citizenship. *You can marry him.* She tried to hear Beth's reassurances through the roar, but somehow knew it just wasn't going to be that simple.

"Holly," shouted from somewhere behind her. She spun back and stumbled. It was Dec who kept her from falling forward. His capable hands steadied her. The scent of his cologne cleared her head.

"Dad, wait." Suddenly Trevor was before her. "Listen to me, I didn't do this. I swear to you. I don't know who did, but it wasn't me. You have to believe me. You can't give them those emails. Please. Don't do this to my mom. Just please. She's sick, Holly. Don't put her through this."

Trevor continued to plead, and for some unfathomable reason Holly believed him. He hadn't done this, but who had?

"Trevor, return to your test." His father's vicious tone took another blow at her psyche. The next thing she understood was that she and Dec were being separated. He was being led into Dr. Newsome's office and she was escorted into Dr. Sinclair's along with two women she'd never seen before.

"Dec," her voice was distanced and tunneled. No real noise accompanied her plea.

"Shh, just blame me," was the last thing he said to her before Dr. Newsome's door shut.

"Ms. Camden, I'm Rebecca Forester, a counselor from the student health center. This is Dr. Anderson, the head of student mental health and abuse awareness here at the University."

Mental health? Abuse awareness? What the actual fuck was happening here? "I'm fine," Holly insisted. "Why am I in here?"

The women in the room shared a concerned glance.

"Answer me," she demanded.

"We received a phone call last evening explaining to us that you and Dr. St. James have been involved in a sexual relationship while he was your teacher. I'm certain you understand that this is a very serious accusation. The caller had a great deal of information about your relationship. It seems highly unlikely that she was lying. Our main concern is that you understand that if Dr. St. James pressured you to become involved with him, we need you to tell us that. Mental abuse can make everything feel very confusing," Dr. Anderson's placating tone made Holly want to vomit.

She measured her words carefully, tasting them before she spit them out. Confirm nothing. "Dr. St. James would never be abusive to anyone, and he certainly has never tried to pressure me to do anything at all."

"Are you confirming that you are involved with Dr. St. James?" Ms. Forester leaned closer. Holly scowled.

"I'm confirming nothing, and quite frankly, I don't really believe my personal life is any of your business. I'm a grown woman. I can take care of myself, and I can certainly make my own decisions." Wait. She? They said she. It seems highly unlikely *she* was lying. Holly's heart leapt to her throat then made a crash course towards her feet. Not Beth. No. She wouldn't. Would she? She was the only other person that knew. "I do, however, feel that I deserve to know who made such outrageous accusations about either me or Dr. St. James."

"We are not at liberty to give you their name. In fact, it was an anonymous call."

"Dr. St. James, I honestly don't know what to say. This is extremely damming evidence." Newsome did look rather sorrowful, not that Dec was capable of understanding any sympathy. *You've ruined her life, too. You're nothing but an asshole who can't say no. Might as well damn your soul now. There's nothing left worth living for and there's got to be something near by that can take this all away,* chanted constantly in one form or another in his head.

"Sleeping with a student in your class is highly unethical," Dr. Singleton had the audacity to berate.

"Way I hear it, Singleton, you would certainly know," Dec sneered. He needed to get the hell off of that campus, away from Holly before he did anything else that would ruin her life and find something to make this go away.

Pure hatred flared in Singleton's eyes. Dec couldn't possibly have cared less.

"I have to admit I suspected something like this was going on. At least tell me you were seeing her before you were hired on here," Newsome pled.

"I was."

"Why didn't you say something when you were presented with the contract?"

The incoming loss of his only reason for living unhinged Dec. "What was I supposed to say? I was never given a choice," he roared. "I never wanted this job. I fell in love with her, but being in love wasn't an option I was allowed."

"I suppose I understand that," Newsome sighed. "I do wish you'd confided in me. We could've found some way to keep you from being her professor. Now, I have a recorded report from an anonymous source that has to be handled. You gallantly volunteering to let her stay in your home makes me look like a fool. I don't appreciate that."

"Oh yeah? Well, I don't appreciate a lot of things. The first being that I was forced to work here and now I've managed to fuck up not only my life but hers as well. Look, I'm leaving. I'm sure I have no fucking choice, yet again. Just don't punish her for this."

"Dr. Gibbons has asked me to communicate to you that you have been terminated from Lifespan."

"Asshole couldn't even show up to fire me in person?"

Newsome's eyes closed in what Dec assumed was a plea for patience.

"I do understand that this affects your H-1B work visa, but please don't do anything rash, Dr. St. James. As for Ms. Camden, at the very least she will have to repeat the class you were teaching. I highly doubt either of you would vow that you gave her no preferential treatment. She has the highest grade in your class."

"She has the highest grade because she's brilliant. Not because of me."

"Either way, you are both liable for your actions. I simply cannot make this go away for either of you. In two weeks, both you and Ms. Camden will return to campus for a hearing about where we will go from here. Then we will decide whether or not either of you will be allowed to return for spring semester. She is being placed on academic suspension until the time of the hearing. Her grades for the entire semester are null and void." Newsome set several sheets of blank paper and a pen in front of Dec. "I need you to outline in detail the nature of your relationship with Holly Camden."

Dec stood and walked out of the room.

CHAPTER FORTY-FIVE

"Have you ever been in love?" Holly demanded of the vultures surrounding her. "Really, truly in love with someone? Has anyone ever told you that you weren't allowed to be in love with them?"

"We do not believe you are in love, Miss Camden. You're simply too young to understand such a thing," Dr. Anderson tsked.

"Thank you so very much for your insight into my life. I just met you. You know absolutely nothing about me, or my life, or what I understand. You want to suspend me, go right ahead. I don't really think I have any interest in obtaining a degree from a university whose psychological response team is this apathetic and devoid of any understanding of human emotion. Just please do not fire one of the only teachers in this department that does understand what you're so unwilling to. You're doing nothing but a disservice to the University and what it should stand for. I'll leave and never return, but don't fire Dr. St. James."

"He hasn't been fired. That decision remains with Dr. Newsome and the board. You'll both return here in two weeks to plead your case."

"I'm not pleading anything to anyone. I shouldn't have to. I'm leaving."

"Ms. Camden, you're not free to go."

Holly narrowed her eyes, "No, Mrs. Forrester, you're not free to hold me here. I've done nothing wrong." With that, she stormed out of the makeshift cell she'd been forced into.

Racing down the hall, she burst into Dr. Newsome's office.

"Holly?" Newsome somehow looked startled. Did he really think she'd leave Dec to deal with all of this?

"Where is Dec?"

"I think it would be best if you returned home, Ms. Camden. As your parents were responsible for what portion of your books and supplies that your stipend did not cover they have been alerted to the fact that you have been placed on academic suspension. I expect they'd like to hear the explanation from you."

"Dr. Newsome, I mean this with all of the respect I used to have for you, I do not give a half a hoot or a holler what my parents want right now. I do not care if I never get to return here to finish this degree. I do not care if either you or they are disappointed. In fact, I have no idea why I ever cared so much. I need to know where the man I intend to marry is, and that is *all* I care about."

"Dr. St. James left fifteen minutes ago. He was escorted off campus by security. I have no idea where he is now."

Sprinting towards the parking lot, she nearly toppled over Beth who was racing towards her. "Holly, what happened?"

"I can't believe you did this to him," Holly raged.

"Did what? I didn't. . .I mean. . .you don't think. . .I don't even know what happened."

"I'm pretty sure you do. I have to go."

Somehow she knew he wouldn't be there, but she had nowhere else to check. Her truck protested her speed. She floored the accelerator. Skidding past his driveway, she backed up and raced down the path to the house, praying for an impossibility.

"Dec, just don't do anything you'll regret," she pled to the ether as she leapt out of the truck and opened the garage. The Pilot wasn't there. "Dec!" she screamed as she flew through the house. Nothing.

Another idea sprang to her mind. Ten minutes later she crashed through the front door of Trace.

"Holly?" Trace came around the counter staring at her like she was a ticking time bomb. "You haven't been around for ages. You okay?"

"No. Has Dec been here?"

"No, sweetheart. I haven't seen him since I last saw you. Want me to call you if he comes by? Want a cup of tea or something? I don't know what happened, but if I can help, say the word."

"Thank you." The hysteria returned, stampeding through her this time. She knew Dec. She knew addicts. She knew he would blame himself for this entirely, even though it was all her fault. She knew he thought he was going to be deported. She knew he now believed he'd ruined her life the same way he believed he'd ruined Evie's. She knew what he thought he was returning to, and she knew where that would most likely lead him. "If he comes by or you see him anywhere call me. Here's my number." She grabbed a pencil in a nearby cup and scribbled her cell number on a yellow pad.

Back in her truck, she scrubbed her hands over her face. "Think Holly. Just fucking think." Panicked breaths gasped from her lungs as she pulled out of the parking lot and drove to the other side of town.

The streets narrowed and somehow the sunlight seemed unable to reach the ground here. She drove on, slowly scanning every house, every business, every human being she saw clearly for the first time in her entire life. People who were hurting, cold, hungry. People who thought they had no hope because the sunlight didn't reach the ground here. It was owned by someone else.

Calling herself a fool an hour later she recalled that drugs were not a plague of the poorer end of town. She drove back towards Dec's house. The homes here shot upward towards the sun, desperate to claim it, but only managed to manufacture it differently, to bend its rays and band its infinite colors into one blurred bar of perceived warmth that provided nothing at all.

As she drove down street after street of perfected facades, realization tore her apart. There was no way to find him because what he thought he couldn't survive without existed everywhere, hidden in plain sight. Tears finally seeped from her eyes and burned her cheeks. She had no idea where to go or what she was looking for. She had to find him.

One last thought managed its way through the impossible maze of her mind. She pulled over along the curb-and-gutter street and found her phone.

"Holly? Everything okay?" Kade's shocked tone bled quickly to concern.

"Where do I find a cocaine dealer?"

"Whoa. Back up. Where's Dec?"

"Kade, please, just tell me where he would go if he were going to buy a lot of it."

"Where are you, Holly?"

"I don't know where I am. Please help me help him. You have to help me."

"Okay, I am. I'm gonna help. Deep breath. Are you in your truck?"

"Yes."

"K, drive until you see a cross street and let me figure out where you are. Then tell me what happened."

Another hour passed. The sun sank low on the horizon and Holly was a disaster. Kade continued to drive slowly from 17th to 20th and up and down Euclid. She'd been right there hours before. Trace's was just a few streets over.

"Only hope we have is to spot the Pilot. Keep your eyes peeled," Kade instructed. His knuckles were white on the steering wheel, his entire body rigid as though an internal war waged on inside of him.

"Kade, I'm so sorry to make you do this. I know it has to be hard for you."

"I'm fine. Just need to find Dec."

Holly continued to scan every building and alleyway.

Dec crossed over the river having no idea where he was going or what he was looking for. He couldn't see anything in front of him. Holly and Kade had been lighting up his phone all fucking afternoon. Both of them deserved better. He'd shut his phone down.

What are you waiting for? You can't have her. You'll never have her. You never deserved her and you never will. London awaits. The headstones. The crowds. The farm. The faceless people. The muted silence. Your father. You'll never get another job. Not now.

Pressing the accelerator harder, he made a hard left on 9th. Human beings were incapable of unknowing what they knew, and he knew where to get the only thing that could take away this level of abhorrent pain. There was no reason to avoid the inevitability. It was all he would ever be. The persistent call drowned out any other options.

CHAPTER FORTY-SIX

"Kade." Holly grabbed his bicep. "There." She blinked, making certain she wasn't dreaming, but the scene before her looked far more like a nightmare. Dec's SUV was parked on the street near an old home. The single light on the porch faded against the darkening skies. A slush mix of snow and rain pricked Kade's truck. The entire world was grey.

"Fuck, this ain't good Holly." Kade parked his truck in front of Dec's Pilot so he couldn't escape. She understood.

"So. . .so is this a dealer's house or something?"

"Or something. Do you see him on the porch? Do you see anyone on the porch?"

"No, I don't see anything."

"Dammit, Declan. You're better than this." Kade slammed his hand on the steering wheel. "Look just stay here. Lock the doors when I get out. I'll get him."

"No, I'll get him."

"Holly, I cannot let you walk in on a deal. Things could get ugly really quick like."

"I don't care. Bring it on. Life is ugly sometimes. But we're going to live it." Holly flung open the door and raced through the bracing cold to the front door. It was open just a crack, too swollen to close. Her heartbeat flew. Her head throbbed. She had no idea what a drug deal even looked like or what might happen to her once the dealers saw her. What if he was already high? What did you do with a person that was high?

You clean him up and you take care of him. You show him that you accept every single part of him. You love him and you help him fight this.

Determination surged through her veins. She was in this with all of her heart, with all of her soul. She had to show him how much of her belonged to him.

Placing her hand on the knob, she pressed in as someone else jerked the door back. She stumbled forward almost toppling over, "Dec," she gasped. "Don't do this."

"Holly? What are you. . . ?"

Suddenly two very large men flanked Dec. "You don't get to walk away, man. You came in asking, you make the buy."

Dec grabbed her hand. "Run!" He motioned for Kade to go. "Hurry," his shout shook the trees.

Holly grabbed his keys from his hands. "Get in. I'm driving." The Pilot edged dangerously to the side as she skidded in a 180 degree turn in the middle of the street and took off.

He sat in silence. The life she was so accustomed to seeing in his eyes when she was in his presence was gone. They were grey just like everything else, a blurred line between the darkness and the light.

"You sit there and you listen to me and do not argue," she spat furiously. "This is entirely my fault. You said we should have broken up and waited until the semester was over. I wouldn't listen. I did what I always do. I got stubborn. I wanted *what* I wanted *when* I wanted it. I decided I could get away with it. I decided for you that *we* could get away with it and Dec, I am so, so sorry, but *we* are not over. *We* will never be over.

"I am taking you home. Not to your house, or to my apartment, to *our* home. And I know you've never even been there and that I never realized how lucky I am to have a place that will always catch me if I fall, but I do and now you do, too. I have no idea what's going to happen at that stupid hearing in two weeks, and I don't care. We're getting married. You are not going back to London. You are not going back to this life. Ever."

"Don't you see, baby?" His voice was eerily soft almost absent. "Don't you see how weak I am? You deserve better."

"No, no I don't. I don't want anything else. I don't want anything but you. My stubbornness got us into trouble, but dammit, I'm gonna use it for as long as I need to. You will not go down because of my stupid mistakes."

"I have no choice. I have to go back to London."

"Did you not hear me say that we're getting married?"

"It doesn't work that way. It takes time and proof and a lot of other things."

"We will do whatever it takes, even if that means I go to London with you. We are not going to function as two separate entities. Never. Kade said your visa has a few more months on it anyway. That gives us time to figure everything out."

"Holly." He shook his head.

"Don't. I take it by the fact that we were just chased out of that house that you didn't buy anything, but if you did, you tell me now."

"I couldn't. I just kept seeing your face, and I couldn't. Can I please hold your hand? I need to touch you. I need to feel you. Please."

"Always." She laced their fingers together. His eyes closed and his head fell back against the seat.

This was going to work. She wouldn't let it fail. "Get ready, Dr. St. James, we're going home. Hope you like cattle and wide open spaces."

"This isn't going to work. I'm not worth this. I don't get to have a home."

"You've had a home from the moment you sat down at my table in Duffy's bar all those months ago. You know it, and I know it. One-fifth of a second. Stronger than a hit. We were done for. This," she lifted their joined hands, "is our home. Wherever you are is where I'll be, forever. You're worth my future, and we're going to the one place on earth where life makes sense. Just stick with me."

"Holly?"

She turned to him, the terror in his eyes cutting her to the quick.

"Do you promise?"

"I promise, Dec."

CHAPTER FORTY-SEVEN

Holly begrudgingly released Dec's hand to answer Kade's call. The glow of her phone disappeared in the fog enveloping them.

"Well, that was invigorating," Kade quipped. "You all okay?"

"We're getting there."

"He agree to go home with you?"

"I didn't so much give him a choice."

"'Atta girl. All right, take him to Trace, I'll go by his place and pack him up. You said two weeks right?"

"For now. Ultimately it will be forever, but two-weeks worth of stuff will do."

"He's gonna insist he's fine to go home. He isn't. He needs to stay away from anything that reminds him of possibly losing you because of his work or the school. I'll meet you two up at Trace with his stuff as quick as I can."

"Hey, Kade, thanks for everything."

"No problem. You take care of my boy. Maybe Wyatt and I will come out and visit in a few days when he's feeling more himself."

"You better."

"I can pack my own stuff," Dec insisted when she ended the call.

"Yeah, I know." Holly tried to study him discreetly. "But tonight, what I say goes. I'm in full-on cowgirl mode."

"I love you, Holly. I love you as best as I understand how, but I'm not okay."

"All I will ever need is for you to love me as best as you understand how. *We* are going to be okay."

Something outside caught Dec's attention. His head turned away from her to face the lights of the Baptist Church as they warmed the cold night. They shattered the oppressive grey. "Do I get to make requests?"

"It's Wednesday night." Holly understood. "Let's go."

"You can wait in the car."

"Never. This is home, remember?" She laced their fingers together again and squeezed his hand.

A minute later, she followed Dec down several corridors to the basement of the church. More than thirty people were already seated. More chairs were added.

Holly kept Dec's hand locked in her own. She sat there steadfastly listening and smiled at him as he stood. "My name's Declan, and I'm an addict."

———

"We'll talk about all of that when you get here," Jessie Camden assured her youngest daughter. "Just come on home, baby. I'll save supper for ya."

"Thanks, Mama." The relief in Holly's tone broke her mother's heart. "We'll be there in a couple of hours."

"You go take care of Dec. I 'spect a lotta things are about to change around here."

"Yeah, but I'm ready for that."

"Nobody's ever ready for life, little one. You just take it as it comes and ride the heck out of it. We love you."

"Love you too."

Jessie ended the call and turned on the line of cowboys in her kitchen. Her husband, her three sons, and her nephew fidgeted anxiously. Never a good sign from cowboys. No one knew quite what to think. "You all listen up and you listen good. If you so much as lay one hand on this boy or make him feel less than welcomed on my ranch, you'll answer to me about it. You hear me?"

A round of begrudged yes ma'ams chorused from the boys, but Ev still looked ready to maim.

"That goes for you too, Everett Camden. Don't get to thinking you're too good to sleep in one of my barns. I'll put you right out with the horses."

"Sweet Jesus, Jessie Camden, this is our daughter that's been suspended from school 'cause a' some no good. . ."

"You stop it right there or so help me you'll be calling on sweet Jesus to save your sorry ass when I get through with ya. Your daughter is in love with him, and we're gonna love him, too. Maybe not exactly who we'da picked for her, but we don't get that say. I trust my girl enough to know if she picked him for her forever we owe her respect enough to honor that. This boy has some problems, but don't we all. He, just like every other being on God's green earth, needs some love and he needs some work to do and we're gonna give him that, no matter how this ends."

Austin still thought he could roll his eyes and she not catch him. God bless her daughter-in-law who saw it, too, and smacked him on his shoulder.

"You brought me here and I wasn't exactly in a great place either, Austin Camden. This ain't no different. And don't think I won't put you out in the barn with your daddy if you so much as give him the stink-eye. Them bulls you used to be so fond'a riding won't hold a candle to what I'll do to your sorry ass," Summer spat.

"No offense, Summer, but this ain't the same thing," Brock argued. Jessie had been expecting this. Might as well cut it off 'fore it went to root. "We've all lived with an addict. I ain't too thrilled for Hope and Nathan to be in the presence of another one. I played that game my whole damn life. There's a reason my good for nothin' daddy don't get to come up here."

Jessie tried not to glance at Natalie. Once again, her daughter's face went to stone as soon as anyone broached this topic.

Hope, Brock's wife, studied him carefully. "Brock, I know you're worried about Holly and about all of us, but you have to stop judging every man that walks on this ranch by holding him accountable for the mistakes your father made. Aunt Jessie says Holly loves him. Trust her judgment." Brock scowled. Hope narrowed her eyes. "And no offense, dear, but you've made your fair share of mistakes as well. We all have."

"I'm just gonna go ahead and say this 'fore you get all up in arms about your baby sister. Luke Camden, if you say or do anything that makes me have'ta get up outta this chair I'll back over you with your own truck. Be nice. Pretty sure our daughters are trying to kill me, and I ain't got patience for you to get pissy," Indie called from the living room where she was laid out in a recliner, trying desperately to ease the sciatica she had from carrying twins.

"I ain't said nothing, Indie Jane. I got no problem with the guy. I honestly like him. He's good for her and we all know Holly don't never take no for an answer. You're all crazy if you think she wasn't the one steering this ship headlong into the shore," Luke huffed.

Jessie couldn't have been more proud of her girls, but that left Grant. He said nothing and looked mighty guilty. Jessie hadn't quite figured out what part he'd played in all of this, but she was working on it.

Dec had no idea how Holly knew where she was driving. The last street light had been five miles back. Squinting into the darkness, he could just make out what appeared to be a tiny hamlet.

A minute later a honkytonk offered the neon glow of a Budweiser sign to the road ahead. Saddlebacks — he could just make out the name of the bar — was flanked by a feed and seed and a few other tiny store fronts.

This must've been Pleasant Glen.

They turned off the two-lane and drove further into the night. It was blacker outside than his soul. Yet somehow none of the bumps or brushing tree limbs unnerved her. She pressed onward.

He could make out the low murmured bellow of cattle, though he had no hopes of seeing the calling animals. Knowingly, Holly slowed his car, threw it in park, and leapt out to open a gate a foot in front of the car that he could just barely make out.

"I could've gotten that," Dec sighed. Feeling useful would've been nice.

"Don't worry, sweetheart, we'll put you to work bright and early tomorrow morning."

Dec weighed that possibility. Weakness pervaded his bones. The nightmarish day still felt surreal. The meeting had grounded him somewhat, but he still couldn't make sense of anything. He focused on nothing more than the moment he existed in, just like Matt had told him so many weeks before. In this moment, he was okay. The only way to deal with anything at all was to live life one split-second at a time.

Three more cattle guards and she pulled the Pilot up beside a picturesque home set on a slight hill that overlooked the expansive land surrounding them. All the lights in the house were on, welcoming them in. The look he received from her father when he followed her inside the large kitchen stole the room of most of its welcoming warmth, however.

"Dec, this is my daddy, Ev, my mama, Jessie, and you already know Luke, Grant and Austin. That's my sister Natalie. And this is my cousin Brock, his wife Hope, and Luke's wife Indie is in the chair in there, and this is Austin's wife Summer," Holly managed introductions. "Everybody, this is Declan."

"It's nice to meet ya, sweetpea. Come on in and take a seat. I'll get you two some supper. Been a helluva day, I 'spect." Holly's mother directed them to the kitchen table.

"Thank you." Dec momentarily wondered if part of this had been a bizarre dream. Maybe he *had* drawn a line. This entire thing was surreal and a little trippy. Holly squeezed his thigh reassuringly under the table.

A plate bursting with meatloaf, mashed potatoes, and okra landed in front of Dec. It smelled heavenly. Not exactly something he would normally have prepared for himself, but he'd never complain. These people, a few of them anyway, were offering him something he'd never experienced before — love and acceptance.

"Thank you very much," he offered again, not certain what else to say.

Holly's father seated himself across from Dec, and her mother shot him a warning glare. Dec braced for the incoming anger he'd more than earned, but it never came. Her father's voice was relatively calm. "I know it's been a long day, baby girl, but I need a little explanation. Kinda want to hear what in blazes you were thinking."

Dec begrudgingly swallowed down a delicious bite of perfectly prepared meatloaf with iced tea. Why did Americans insist on ruining tea? "Sir, this was all my. . . ."

"Stop it now," Holly commanded. "Dec and I met and fell in love before he ended up teaching at the University. He had no idea he was going to be a professor, but had to take the job in order to keep his job at Lifespan Counseling Center, which is who holds his work visa. He said we should break up when we discovered that he was my professor. He also said he would wait for me, remaining faithful to our relationship until I was no longer his student. I insisted that we go on seeing each other. I'm in love with him. Not sure what the school will decide, but I'm done with the likes of them, anyway."

This was the first Dec had heard of her walking away from her education. "Holly, baby, you can't quit because of me."

"I have'ta agree," Ev vowed.

"And I'll thank both of you to let me make my own decisions, thank you very much," Holly retorted before devouring her mother's mashed potatoes.

"Piece of advice, never try to tell her what to do," Grant offered Dec quietly. "'Bout the quickest way to get her to do whatever it is you don't want her to do."

"Yeah, I already figured that much out for myself. Just a little off tonight."

"Get Holl' to take ya ridin'. Nothing better for clearing your head."

Dec tried to understand why Holly's brother was being so kind. He'd expected accusations that he'd ruined her life and threats to skin him alive.

"We got a few more things to discuss 'fore you get him up on horseback," her father huffed.

"And we have plenty of time to discuss them later." Holly glared at her father. "Not tonight."

"They've been through quite enough, Ev," her mother warned. "Tomorrow's another day."

"I am well aware of what tomorrow is. What I want to know is what their plan from here on might be."

"We're getting married," Holly vowed.

Dec tried to process this. It wasn't at all how he'd planned it. He'd envisioned a Christmas Eve engagement at some romantic B&B somewhere. Everything about this was wrong. He'd crashed and very nearly burned again. He wasn't worth her future.

"Married?" Her father gasped. "You're just a little. . . ."

"I am not a little girl anymore, Daddy. I'm sorry. I know that's hard for you to hear, but I am a grown woman and this is what I want."

"You cannot fence time, Everett Camden. And you ain't gonna stop love."

"Merciful Heaven, Jessie, that's blasphemy. You just up and used sweet Sara Evans against me."

Suddenly feeling more himself, Dec downed another sip of the affront to tea everywhere to keep from laughing.

Holly shared a sly grin with him that brought another jolt of life to his weary body.

"And if you don't quit trying to turn our daughter back into a three-year-old with pigtails, a lisp, and a saddle four times her size, I'm gonna call up sweet Sara and have her come pick your sorry butt up. She can have ya. There will be more talkin' in the morning and the next few weeks. Tonight we're gonna be pleasant and try to help ever'body do a little healing. Dec, darlin' can I get you some more tea?"

"No. No, ma'am. I'm. . .good."

Holly laughed. "Sorry, I wasn't thinking. Mama, do we have any hot tea?"

"Sure, what kind?"

Dec fought not to shudder.

"I'll find some." Holly searched her mother's cupboards until she located a box of Earl Grey. She prepared it perfectly. He'd learned to fix her mugs of coffee just to her specifications, and she'd done the same with his tea.

"Have I mentioned how much I adore you, love?" Dec spoke without thinking as he accepted the mug. He longed to dive into the warm soothing liquid.

All of the women in the room looked quite pleased at their exchange.

A full minute later, Luke's wife, Indie, waddled into the kitchen. Dec felt terrible for her. Luke hadn't been lying. She did look like the broad side of a barn, and Luke looked desperate to help ease her strain.

"You ain't supposed to be up and around, sugar. Sit," he pled.

"Sittin' ain't helpin'. I'm miserable. It's shooting down my leg now." She turned to Dec. "You're a doctor, right?"

"Uh, a psychologist, yes."

"I don't care what kind. Ever done a c-section? Preferably one on a kitchen table."

"Indie," Luke sighed.

Dec's heart ached for her. "I haven't, but I might can help. Is it sciatica?"

She nodded.

"Recliner's not going to help. Let's try laying you on the side in the least amount of pain, place a pillow between your legs, and place cold compresses on the hip that hurts the most. Take a little aceta-minophen. It won't hurt the babies and will ease the strain."

"You sure it won't hurt them?" And with that question Dec knew once again that he'd never actually experienced a mother's love. She was willing to be in excruciating pain for her daughters for as long as it was required.

"I'm sure."

"My doctor said to put heat on it but that isn't helping."

"The nerve endings are already inflamed. You don't need more heat."

The entire family leapt into action, shocking Dec once again. Luke settled her on her right side on the couch. Austin provided compresses from one of Jessie's outdoor freezers. Holly grabbed a bed pillow for her legs and Jessie handed Dec a bottle of Tylenol to dispense.

A half-hour later, she was sound asleep.

"Thank you," Luke slumped back into his seat at the table, relieved. "She hasn't slept in a month."

"No problem. When's she due?"

"Got another three and a half weeks."

It wasn't until Holly went upstairs to shower that Dec understood they were going to be staying in her parent's home. The awkwardness of that added to the weight of the day.

Grant motioned for Dec to follow him out on his parent's porch. *And here it comes.* Dec wondered how well he'd even do in a fight just then. If pressed, he could probably defend himself, but quite honestly he felt he deserved to let her brothers take a few swings.

"Hey, listen, has Holly figured out who told on you yet?" Grant asked quietly, his deep voice barely audible over the freezing wind.

"What do you mean? I thought you were going to. . . ?"

"Chew you up and spit you out about Holl? Nah. I used to threaten any guy that looked her way, but I knew you were a good guy when I met ya. 'Sides, this is kinda my fault."

"What is your fault?"

"That you two got caught."

"How on earth is that your fault?"

"Guess she hadn't figured it out yet then."

"Given the detailed information the school had on us, me in particular, I assumed it was her friend Beth. She was just a few notches below Holly in the pecking order at school. I assumed she'd decided to take out the one on top."

"Doubt that's who did it. I don't know for sure, but maybe ask Holl what she told Beth. If you don't mind letting me know what she figures, I'd say I'm gonna have to eat crow for my baby sis."

"I'll ask her. We haven't really talked about much of anything yet."

"Sounded to me like you two were gettin' hitched and moving back home."

"It can't possibly be that easy," Dec sighed.

"Maybe it will be. Maybe it won't. Ain't nothing easy 'bout running a cattle ranch, but we can make a cowboy outta you yet. Just give me a month or two. You need any help, just ask."

"Thanks." Dec had no hope of making decisions about his future just then. All he wanted was to crawl in a hole, preferably with Holly tucked up beside him.

"Holly's room is right at the top of the stairs, sweetheart. 'Cross from the bathroom," Holly's mother informed him when he returned to the kitchen.

"Oh, uh, okay. Thank you."

"Things have a way of workin' themselves out. I know it's gotta feel like you been thrown and trampled right about now, but you'll see, everything'll figure itself out."

"Mrs. Camden, thank you very much for your hospitality and. . . ."

"For my little girl." She laughed. "Once you're on my ranch, you're family, Dec. We'll get you squared away. You just promise to take good care of my girl, and we'll take good care of you."

"I hope I can promise that. I still expect to be sent back to London, and she truly deserves someone better."

"Oceans can't stop love either, and none of us are saints. If you think she deserves someone better than the man you are right now, then become the man you know she deserves. You and only you can do that. Like I said, things'll work themselves out. Go get some sleep."

Climbing the stairs, Dec weighed Jessie Camden's words in his mind. He'd tried to become better for her, and he'd failed miserably. That didn't mean he couldn't keep trying, but what if he just kept failing?

Grant's odd half-confession plagued him. He didn't particularly want to bring up Beth that evening. He knew Holly already blamed herself for this. The fact that he'd instructed her to tell Beth they'd broken up was only going to levy another round of guilt.

Much to his dismay, Holly's father was coming out of the master bedroom as Dec crested the stairs. The door he'd been instructed to enter by her mother was currently blocked by her dad. The infuriated glare on Ev's face didn't make the situation any easier to handle.

"She's my baby girl." The threat was implicit.

"I am keenly aware of that, sir. I never meant to hurt her or her future."

"But you did hurt her and her future."

"I am also aware of that. If you want me to leave your ranch, say the word."

"Jess'd have my hide, and Holly'd never speak to me again. Do you really believe you deserve to marry her?"

"No, I don't, but have you ever tried to tell her no, sir?"

Ev put forth valiant effort but Dec got a half grin. "Yeah, I have. Wasn't pretty. Just give me a few days to wrap my head around this. Don't you dare leave. You hurt her again, you gon' have me to answer to."

"I have no intention of ever hurting her again, sir. That's precisely why I agreed to come here. Believe me, I could use a few days to get used to my entire life being different than it was less than twelve hours ago."

"'Spose you have had a helluva day. You ever ridden a horse before?"

"Yes, sir."

"You any good?"

"I can hold my own."

"Good. Be on horseback 'fore sun-up. We got cattle to feed and prep 'fore there's two feet of snow on the ground, and bulls that need to be moved to another field for spring calving."

"Yes, sir." Dec had absolutely no idea how to do any of that, but if her family was willing to take him in and help him be the kind of man Holly deserved, he'd do his best.

CHAPTER FORTY-EIGHT

"Quite certain your father despises me," Dec sighed as he closed Holly's bedroom door. She couldn't believe he was standing in her childhood bedroom. She honestly couldn't believe any of this. All she knew was this felt right. This was where they belonged.

"He'll be fine. He just wants me to be seven eternally." She patted the side of the bed he normally slept on at his house. Of course, she only had a queen and he had a California king, so this would be a little more snug.

"Feel like talking?" he asked as he shed his jeans and shirt and crawled into bed with her. She clambered onto his chest and let that feeling of being in his arms wash over her like a healing tide. There'd been far too many hours in this endless day where she'd been terrified she'd never be in his arms again.

"Definitely."

"You are not quitting school for me."

"Not about that."

"Okay, want to talk about what happened today?"

"That, we can do, and I have several confessions. Stuff I should have already told you."

"I knew something was bothering you. If we're really going to get married, we can't keep things from one another."

"We are really getting married, but not until you understand that not everything that goes wrong is your fault. Not this. Not Evie. Not your marriage."

"I'll give you my marriage, but not Evie and not this."

Holly sat up. "Did you or did you not tell me that we should've waited until the semester was over to start dating?"

"I did." His eye roll said he somehow didn't believe that counted.

"And did Evie or did Evie not consume a lethal amount of heroin before you ever even arrived at your flat?"

"You've been talking to Kade."

"Answer the question."

"She did."

"Then how is that your fault?"

"I could've stopped her if I'd just gotten there earlier, and I wasn't there because I was out buying."

"Using and buying was your fault, Dec. No one's denying you that. But her actions are not your responsibility. You can mourn for her. You can even miss her, but you cannot go back to drugs when things get too difficult to handle. That's what she taught you. It isn't you. That's what the drugs make you believe, but that isn't how you and I are going to work. I will be here each and every day to help you handle your addictions in a healthy way. I want that responsibility. You don't have to fight this alone."

"It has to be my responsibility, and I swear sometimes I'm just not strong enough to fight them."

"But you are. Baby, you were leaving a dealer's house, not because of me, or Kade, or anything but your own power. You stared down the face of temptation and walked away. Do you have any idea how strong you are?"

"I will always need help, Holly."

"And I will always be here to help you."

"I wish I didn't need your help. I want to be everything *for* you. I don't want to require anything from you."

"Well, Mr. Sex Therapist, that isn't how relationships work." She brushed a kiss on his bare chest and ran her fingertips along the tattooed lyrics once again.

"Can I ask you something, sweetheart? I don't want you think I blame you for any of this. It's just something Grant asked me."

"Of course."

"What exactly did the women who took you in that room ask you? I nearly broke down the damn door, by the way. I thought I was going to lose my mind. I didn't know what they might be doing to you in there."

"They just asked me stuff. Tried to insist that you'd pressured me into this. It was ridiculous. But listen, I figured out that the guy who'd taken those pictures of me was the pizza delivery man. The one who'd asked me if I was there alone that night a few months ago."

"The one who'd scared you when I had dinner with Newsome?"

"Yeah. Remember I said he kept messing with his phone and asking if I was there alone? Well, he was taking my picture. That was the one of his own thumb. And he was taking my picture because Trevor Singleton paid him to. He followed us all semester and then threatened to go to Newsome with what he had. I figured out what he was doing, and Beth and I got the woman his father had an affair with a few years ago to send us their texts and emails as blackmail to keep Trevor from talking. I should've told you. I was scared you'd freak out, but then Beth turned on me. I still can't believe she did that."

"And that's why Trevor ran out into the hall after you saying he hadn't done it."

"Exactly."

"How do you know it wasn't him?"

"The information they had on us wasn't what he had, plus they said the anonymous caller was a she. What all did they ask you?"

"I left when I was handed a piece of paper and a pen, of all things, and was asked to elaborate on our sexual relationship. I gave everything away when they asked about my piercing. I wasn't expecting that. Lost my poker face."

"What?!" Holly shot upwards in the bed again. A cold fist of realization gripped her.

"Darling, you're a bit like a jack-in-the-box. Come here. It's all over now. It's fine you told her."

"But. . .I didn't." Fury exploded throughout Holly, but it was quickly drowned by the hard blow of betrayal. Her cheeks burned, her chest ached, her stomach bottomed out somewhere near her thighs. This day was simply too much.

"Then how did she know?"

"She didn't. It wasn't Beth."

"Grant said something about it being his fault. Does that make sense to you?"

"I can't believe she did this. She was my best friend."

"I take it we're no longer talking about Beth."

Holly collapsed back on Dec's chest, and gave herself over to every terrifying, agonizing emotion the day had held. She sobbed and he kissed away tear after tear until she'd finally cried herself out. Then he cradled her in his arms, easing the sting of being betrayed by your best friend, until she finally fell asleep safely on his chest.

Dec managed to open one eye when some despicable person continued to ring some kind of bell.

Holly groaned and burrowed deeper under the covers and closer to him. Grinning at that, he wrapped her up in his arms and attempted to mentally banish the bloody bell to the depths of hell.

It didn't work. "What's that bell?"

"Time to get up. Gotta feed. Horses. Ride. Sleepy," she whimpered.

Clearly her father hadn't been joking when he'd told them to be up before sunrise.

An hour later, he saddled a gorgeous copper quarter horse, much to her father's shock, and mounted. His entire childhood settled firmly in the saddle, and this time he didn't push it away. With the click of his mouth, the horse moved. A minute later, he was flying across the prairie. The rhythmic hoof-falls soothed his soul. The cold wind cleansed his lungs and washed his weary soul.

The Camden's ranch surrounded him in every direction. It embraced him. All of his problems felt too far away to reach. Even if he'd wanted something, it certainly couldn't be accessed in this tiny town.

For the past few months, Holly had been his only sense of peace, his only redemption. He began to understand perhaps this place could be a sanctuary for both of them. He just had to work out how to stay here.

CHAPTER FORTY-NINE

"Well, the boy can sure as hell ride. You gotta give him that, Dad," Grant vowed.

Holly couldn't help but grin as she nuzzled Lightning, but Cheyenne's betrayal still rooted her to the ground. If she never left the ranch, she never had to see Cheyenne again.

Ev only grunted his allowance that Dec could most certainly ride.

"You're just being stubborn, Daddy," Holly smarted.

"You're my little girl. I don't care how old you are."

"Doesn't mean I'm not going to marry him."

"Doesn't mean I have'ta like it."

By the end of the day, Dec had been given lessons on winter feedings, busting up icy lakes, calving, preg-testing, pulling bulls, and had even cleared a little snow off the dirt roads through the ranch with the tractor-driven snow plow.

Holly didn't know how he felt about any of this, as they hadn't really had any time to talk, but he'd certainly thrown himself into the work. Even her father was complimentary by the time everyone sat down to her mother's beef stew supper.

"I have a surprise for you." Holly was excited to show Dec what she'd been working on while Grant was teaching him to drive the tractor.

"Does it involve a bed, because I swear I'm going to collapse." He brushed a tender kiss in her hair. She'd never love anything more, and as she studied his eyes, no longer clouded with tension and felt the ease of his breath, she knew he belonged here, too.

"It will involve a bed someday soon, but right now it doesn't. Just come on."

"You ain't gonna go out there in that sissy car you drove in on. Snowing too hard now. Take my truck. I'll meet you out there in one of the other." Grant tossed Holly the keys to his Sierra. "Where's your Silverado, anyway?"

"Back in Lincoln. I'll get in later."

"Want me to take you back out there to get it?"

"Not that you aren't always a good big brother, Grant Camden, but why are you being so nice to me?" Holly demanded. She knew he had to have something to do with Cheyenne's insanity.

"How 'bout you take Dec out to your surprise. I'll come out there in a few and we'll chat."

Dec climbed in the passenger side of Grant's surprisingly luxurious truck. "I take it my Pilot is not ranch worthy?"

Holly giggled. God, he'd missed that sound. In the middle of her sobs the night before, he'd wondered if he'd ever hear it again.

"Won't pull or haul much of anything and it's not heavy enough to cut through the snow as well as the trucks do. We have plenty of trucks here, though. You don't have to sell it if you don't want to."

"Holly, honey, if this is where you want to live, I'll do my best to figure that out, but we do have an entire life in Lincoln. There's no guarantee that they're going to kick you out of school. My band is there. And there is absolutely no assurance that even us getting married will keep me here in the States. I'm going to call my immigration attorney tomorrow, but I expect to hear that I'm going to have to go back at least for a little while."

"I'm doing it again, aren't I? I'm deciding what I want and being stubborn about it. I'm sorry, Dec. I kind of hoped you'd love it here." Devastation weighted her tone.

"I could definitely fall in love with this ranch, baby. It's just a lot to consider, and I'm still not okay with you not finishing your degree if that's what you want."

"I'll try not to be so stubborn."

"I don't ever want you to change for me. I just know we have to deal with our pasts or we can't have a future."

Just then, she slowed Grant's truck in front of a two-story clapboard home a little smaller than her parents'. The lights were on and there was smoke billowing out of two chimneys. "This side of the ranch is my land. I kind of thought maybe this could be our house, after we deal with Lincoln."

If she'd actually stabbed him, it couldn't possibly have hurt as much as his enumerating complications of their current situation and taking away from her surprise.

"I'm sorry. I had no idea where you were bringing me. I never meant to say that I didn't want to live here."

"I know. There's a lot on my mind. It's just so tempting to hide out here and never leave. I keep insisting that I'm a grown woman, but I'm not acting like one."

"I'm ten years older than you, baby, and I sure as hell don't have it all figured out. Not dealing with everything back in Lincoln sounds just as appealing to me. I just know we have to. Come, show me our home. I'll figure out some way to make this all work. I want to be the kind of man that provides everything you need. The only way I can allow myself to marry you is to vow every single day to be better for you." For the first time in a long time, thinking about the future wasn't so terrifying. There had to be some way to give her what she wanted.

"I don't want you to change for me either, Dec. I just want you to keep fighting your addictions and I want you to let me help you. Now come on, I've been working on this for hours."

She led him inside what was apparently going to be their home. The hardwoods were in need of some repairs but had been scrubbed recently. He doubted she'd want to keep the dated wallpaper, but the living room had built in bookshelves and a reading nook by the front windows.

"I found some old lamps and end tables. We can bring my bed here. Have to buy some furniture, but it's a great house. I used to play here when I was little with. . .never mind. Anyway, I used to imagine living here with my husband. Well, when I wasn't pretending to fly to Jupiter. I wanted to be an astronaut for a while. Just come see the kitchen." She took his hand and led him to the back of the house. There was an expansive kitchen that he could easily turn into a chef's paradise. "There are two bedrooms and a study upstairs. The master's over here."

There was a half bath on the main floor. The master wouldn't hold his California King. It did have another brick fireplace, however. The crackle of the second fire welcomed them into the room. The master bath had a clawfoot tub that delighted Holly. "Maybe we could get a King sized bed in here. Yours is a little small, and mine's going to be too big."

"I feel a little like Goldilocks suddenly," she laughed.

The study upstairs had more built-in bookshelves. Dec mentally planned out an office until he realized that if he moved to the ranch there would be no more treating patients. He'd worked so hard to help people. He just wasn't certain he wanted to give it all up for tractors and horses as much as he'd enjoyed the work that day.

"Basement?" He pointed to a door in the hallway once they were back on the main floor.

"Yes, but it's dark, and gross, and a little scary." Holly wrinkled her nose.

"I'll keep the monsters away, baby." He offered her his hand, knowing he couldn't outrun his own monsters, but he'd spend every day of his life keeping them from ever hurting her again.

"The acoustics down here are brilliant," he declared in the center of the massive room.

"Want to finish it out and make it a music room?"

"Naturally."

"Deal."

"I'm here and if I'm about to walk in on you banging my sister, dude, I'm not gonna be able to keep on being a nice guy," Grant bellowed.

Holly rolled her eyes and gave Dec a wicked grin. "Oh, Dec, oh, Dec, oh right there, yes, yes, yes," she cried.

"Ah, Jay-sus Christ," Grant gagged as she bounded up the stairs laughing hysterically.

"Gotcha."

Dec shook his head and offered her brother a sorrowful gaze.

"You oughta turn her over your knee," Grant informed him. Dec tried valiantly to look unaffected by that instruction. It was a very appealing idea.

"You. Talk." Holly ordered her brother.

"Fine. You got anywhere to sit down here yet?"

"The floor." Holly directed them to a few quilts she'd spread near the fire.

"I take it you figured out who told the school about the two of you."

"Cheyenne." A cold shiver worked through Holly. Dec wrapped his arm over her. This was the part of the story he hadn't gotten the night before.

"Who's Cheyenne, love?"

"She *was* my best friend, since I was a little girl."

"I tried to tell you," Grant started but shook his head and started over. "She wasn't ever your friend, Holl. Did you ever notice how she only wanted to be friends with you as long as you were there for her? You weren't ever really yourself around her because you adapted to whatever she wanted you to be. Whatever Chey wanted to do, you did. She wanted to talk, you listened. But if you needed something, she couldn't be bothered. Hell, Holl, your favorite horse was taking her last breaths a few months ago and she couldn't be bothered to hang around.

"She's been doing nothing but making my life miserable since she up and decided to co-chair Cattle Baron's just because I'm in charge this year. Drove me up four walls and over a hay bale. I'd kinda taken up with Ashley Stender. Things were going real good like. I'd asked her to the barn dance after the cattle show. Took her to Ogallala for dinner, then to the drive-in they were having out at the Kilroys. We ended up dancing at Saddlebacks and then might'a made our way back to my truck."

"You fucked her in the back of your truck. I got it," Holly scowled.

"Not in the back. Too damn cold for that, but we were heading all kinda good places in the front."

"Remind me to wash my hands in just a second. I just drove that truck."

"Cheyenne was at the drive-in and then at Saddlebacks, of course. I didn't think much of it since she follows me around all the damn time. She was downing tequila shots like there was no tomorrow. 'Bout five minutes into me and Ashley doing what we were doin', she threw open my truck door and informed Ashley that I was going to the barn dance with her. Said you'd told her I'd go with her. Told Ashley I was cheatin'. Ashley was furious. Crawled off'a me and left. I told Cheyenne off, and I wasn't kind. I'd had enough. I'm sorry. She makes me crazy. Way she takes advantage of everyone to get what she wants, and Ashley was in tears 'fore she ever got to her brother to take her home. That tipped me right over the edge. I said some things I regret. All of 'em were the truth, but I'm sorry for what it did for you all. She got her feelings hurt and decided to take it out on you."

"Grant, I'm so sorry," Holly's head fell in her hands. Dec felt helpless. Her best friend had betrayed her and was an outright liar. Not an easy thing to find out one day after being suspended from school.

"No, now, don't apologize to me. I just wanted to tell ya 'cause she ain't ever gonna change, Holl. She's a user through and through. It's always gonna be all about her all the time."

"Did Ashley believe you? Did you try to tell her that Cheyenne is a lying bitch?"

"I went over there to tell her, but Taylor Swenson was there and his tongue in her mouth would'a made it difficult to talk."

Defeat fell over the entire room.

"Grant, I'm so sorry." Holly tried yet again.

"I know, sug. Don't worry 'bout it. There's an ocean full 'a fish, right?"

With that, Dec knew whoever Ashley was she'd meant a great deal to Grant. He scooped Holly off of the quilt and into his lap. He couldn't fix Grant and Ashley, but he could take care of his baby.

"Yeah, I'm gonna leave you to that," Grant nodded to Holly. "Get some blinds 'fore you two christen your new home, or at least wait 'til I'm back on my side of the ranch."

"I have to call Beth. I have to apologize." Holly was on the phone before Dec's next breath. He could make out a little of the conversation.

"Beth, I'm so sorry I accused you. I know it wasn't you."

"Well, I guess I'm glad you figured that out." Beth didn't sound ready to forgive. "I can't believe you ever thought I would. I did everything I could to be a good friend to you. I tried to help you cover up everything."

Holly's eyes closed, and Dec wasn't certain how much more she was going to be able to withstand. She was so damn strong, but everyone had their breaking point. Suddenly, the weakness he'd carried with him since he'd given into the call the day before eased its grip. She needed him to be strong, and her need all but silenced the endless demon song that ruled his life. His every choice mattered because his choices affected her now. That's why he hadn't been able to make the buy the day before. He understood.

"I just wanted to tell you how sorry I am. I understand if you hate me."

"I don't hate you, but I don't want to see you for a while. I'm not sure I can be friends with someone who believed even for a moment that I would've done that." The call ended with that.

Dec strengthened his hold. He'd never let her down again. "Pretty shitty what humans do to each other, huh?"

"Cheyenne hurt Grant, and me, and you, and now I hurt Beth. I just don't know how everything got so fucked up. I'm going to go out to Ashley's farm tomorrow and apologize to her for Grant. Might not help, but I have to try."

"Permission to psychologist you for a minute?" Dec planted a kiss on the top of her head.

"Permission granted."

"Seems to me that you're willing to talk and make amends to

everyone that was hurt at your own expense, but you keep avoiding talking about and ultimately talking *to* the inflictor of the pain."

"I can't talk to her. I can't even look at her. I get sick to my stomach when I even think about it. I trusted her. I've trusted her most of my life, and I never saw that she was always using me. She used me for the last decade trying to get to Grant. See, this is why I shouldn't be a psychologist. I'd suck at it."

"Hush," Dec put his finger over her mouth. "Yeah, I know you hate it when I tell you that, but I will not allow the woman I love more than life itself to sit here and blame herself for being human. Psychologists are not above being taken advantage of. You are so incredibly sweet. You want so badly to see the best in people or to help people be their best. That's one of the things I love most about you. Your friend chose to use you for her own gains. You allowed it because you wanted the best for her even if it was at your own expense."

"Sometimes she was nice. Sometimes she listened to me."

"Believe me, honey, I know precisely how addictive it can be when someone you care about finally allows you a little light. The problem is their darkness is always the victor. They want to pull you into the darkness and when you resist or you don't feed their wants, they unleash it vengefully. I wouldn't have stuck with Evie as long as I did if I never got to be the center of her attention. She trained me to do whatever she wanted for a hit of her. Attention can be addictive all on its own."

"I didn't want to see what was right in front of my face."

"You didn't want to see it, sweetheart, because you loved your friend."

CHAPTER FIFTY

"You look so fucking good in those chaps, Dr. St. James." Holly wrapped her arms around his waist Saturday morning long before the sun was up. She loved having him here. She never wanted those two weeks to end. If they never went back to Lincoln, she never had to worry about Dec possibly going back to London and what she would do if their marriage didn't qualify him for immediate citizenship. She'd gone as far as getting a passport photo, and had read up on what all she needed to do to get a passport and a visa for an extended international stay.

"You're the one that told me you didn't want me to be a cowboy."

"Maybe I wouldn't mind it too much. You do look damn fine on horseback."

"Do you have any idea how much I'm enjoying the work here? I'm in shock, but between it and you I haven't had a craving in almost a week."

"Told you things made sense here, but I'm taking most of the credit for keeping your craving meter on low. I still wish we didn't have to go back to Lincoln." *Or London.* She refused to say that out loud.

"You have always been the key to the meter. We still have to deal with Lincoln though, baby, and I'm still not sure I can just walk away from being a therapist."

"One moment at a time, remember?"

"I remember."

"Dec really likes it here. His cravings haven't been bothering him. He even likes getting up early. I think it helps him that other people and animals are depending on him. I wish we never had to go back to Lincoln," Holly explained to her mother that afternoon while they had coffee. Dec had gone with Grant and Austin to help out with something for the Cattle Baron festival the next Saturday.

"Can't run away from life, baby girl. It's been good for both of you to be here, but you don't get to pick points on your timeline and ignore all of the things that helped move you from one place to the next. Dec must miss some things in Lincoln. You have to let him have those feelings and go back if that's what he wants."

"I know he misses Kade and the band."

"Would they be willing to come out here? They'd be more than welcome."

"They were waiting on Dec to get his bearings here, but I think he already has."

"If you'd be willin' I sure as heck wouldn't turn ya down," Grant vowed again.

"I'm more than willing to play for this thing. Have to see if the rest of the band wants to come all the way out here," Dec explained. "I'll call Kade tonight." As if on cue, his cell rang, but it wasn't Kade.

"Tell me something good," Dec ordered his immigration lawyer, Sarah Nicholls.

"I wish I could, Dec. Your H-1B is up in three months. Just to get to the interview phase for permanent citizenship for you and Holly will take four to six months. And they'll interview you both again in two years."

"That won't be a problem. It's the months between my current visa and the one for marriage I'm worried about."

"Well, there is also the fact that Holly has to show employment able to support you both. Since she was a student that's going to be another issue. Is there any way you could get another therapy center to take over your H-1B? If you could get another year on at a founding firm, you can marry Holly and eventually gain permanent citizenship."

"I doubt anyone would be willing to hire me after being fired from Lifespan and the University."

"You haven't been fired from the University yet. Let's keep our fingers crossed. Go ahead and plan a ceremony. I might can work a few months to let you be back here for your marriage. I'll see what I can do. Try to get a job, any job that requires your level of education."

"I'm out in the middle of cattle country, not a lot of need for a therapist out here."

"Then I'm going to work on getting Holly her passport. The UK will allow her to stay there without a job for six months. Maybe by then we can get you both back here."

"I don't want Holly to have to come there."

"I'm not a miracle worker, Dec. I'm doing everything I can. Without you having a job, my hands are tied. I'll try to think of something."

The gnawing anxiety of having to return to London ate at him constantly. If Holly went with him, which was the only way he would survive, she would have to put off school for far too long.

Grant was staring at him when he ended the call.

"That was my immigration attorney. Not looking very promising that I'm going to get to stay here. I don't know how to tell Holly."

"I thought if you two got hitched, you got to stay."

"There's quite a process to that. Interviews, things like that, and it's months and months before we could even get an interview. I don't have that kind of time left on my current visa."

"You thinkin' what I'm thinkin'?" Grant elbowed Austin.

"That Nebraskan cattle country needs a therapist. Lordy knows we gots loads a crazy right here in the Glen."

"Exactly."

Dec appreciated their candor, but this wasn't going to work. For a moment, he tried to remember the things he'd missed about London, the things he could show Holly if she did come with him. He knew what he'd tell her as soon as they stepped off the plane—to always look up. The buildings, the skyline, the history of it all. If he could just keep his head up, maybe they could survive. That is if she was really willing to come with him, and he just couldn't bring himself to ask her if she was sure she wanted to leave her home for him.

When they returned to the Camden's farmhouse, Holly and her mother were sitting at the table with a man Dec had never seen before. Holly was such a part of the ranch he decided then and there that she just couldn't leave it, not for him.

"Dec, this is Pastor Higgins. He came to pick up a few casseroles for meals on wheels." Holly raced out of her seat to welcome him home. God, how was he supposed to exist without this for six months?

"Nice to meet you, son. I hear you've swept Holly right off her feet. Must be a very special soul." Pastor Higgins' kind face reminded Dec a little of Father Christmas.

"Not sure about that, sir, but she definitely makes my life worth living."

"That's all that matters. I hope I might get a call to perform your nuptials soon."

"Yes, sir, we'd like that," Holly urged. Dec didn't have the heart to tell her right then that even with a marriage he wasn't going to be able to stay.

"May I impose just a minute more? I was hoping I might get to meet you, Dec."

"You can stay just as long as you like Pastor. I got plenty of supper. I'll set you a place."

"May I speak with you, son?"

"Of course," Dec wondered what on earth a religious man wanted with him. The only time he'd ever had a foot inside a church was to attend NA meetings.

"You'll find that word travels a bit like wildfire through Pleasant Glen. I heard a bit about your past and what happened at the University from a friend of a friend. Anyway, we do have a need in the community, and I know you've only just arrived here and might be returning to Lincoln soon, but I wondered if we could ask you to run our NA meetings at the church while you're here. We haven't had a proper leader here ever. I'd like to have them once a week, but we're on a rotation with a host of other churches in surrounding towns. The leader only gets out here once a month and you must know that simply isn't enough. I suppose I thought I'd ask for the moon and see if you might take them over while you're here."

"I've been to dozens of them, sir, but I don't have any kind of training to lead them."

"The only thing it requires is willingness to help, understanding of the steps and traditions, and we prefer that you have been clean for at least a year."

"I haven't used in eleven years, but I came very close to ending that."

"Then I suspect you're more than qualified. Not only have you remained clean, but you turned away a great temptation when you were tested."

"I'll help you organize them," Holly vowed hopefully.

"I'd be honored sir. When do they usually meet?"

"In about two hours."

CHAPTER FIFTY-ONE

It was Monday when Luke found Dec out at his and Holly's potential home that Dec realized Holly's family was trying to help him with the job hunt. So far, he'd talked to the feuding owners of the local honky-tonk, who were in a tiff about whether or not to have the waitresses wear shorter skirts in the summer. The wife had taken to smacking the husband with her bible. The sheriff asked if Dec would mind becoming an impromptu marriage counselor.

The day before, Austin had brought in two brothers worried about their mom. She'd been working sixty hour weeks at four different jobs, was exhausted, and still not able to fully provide. Her teenage sons had picked up on her depression.

Dec agreed to meet with her in a couple of days free of charge. He'd worked two NA meetings and had been asked if he would mind expanding to AA meetings.

Now Luke was standing before him with a man who looked like the world hadn't treated him fairly. The hollowness of his eyes bore more than any man should ever see. There was a hunger about him, not necessarily for food, but for nourishment.

"Hey, Dec you got a second?" Luke inquired.

"Sure, just trying to figure out how to get all of this wallpaper off of the walls."

"That mean you've decided to stay here?"

"Means I want Holly to have every option available to her. Still have to go back to Lincoln Monday. Still have to figure out if I'll even be allowed to stay in the country. I can't ask her to go to London. She needs to be here."

"I could hire you, or dad could, hell, Holly can claim all the cattle we're running this year and she could hire you as a hand or something."

"Has to be a job that requires my specific degree."

Luke, just like all of the Camdens, didn't take no for an answer. "I'll think of something. Listen, this is Aaron, good friend of mine. He was in the army for years. Special Forces."

"I'm honored to meet you," Dec offered Aaron his hand.

"I'm not anything special. I don't know why he introduces me that way."

"Luke must think you are, and I'd have to say I agree."

Aaron rolled his eyes.

"You mind if we tell him a little more?" Luke inquired.

"I've got nothing to hide."

"Aaron has to drive all the way into Ogallala twice a week for counseling for his PTSD. That's almost seven hours by the time he gets there, sees the doc, and drives back. That's fourteen hours a week he ain't getting paid. That means he can only work twenty-something hours a week, and they're nice and try to work around his sessions but he's barely making minimum wage. Be nice if he could go to counseling here, work more hours, take my sister out, things like that, don'tcha think?"

"Am I to take it you might like a session now?"

"If you've got some time."

"I've got time, but there's unfortunately not much I can do about there not being a counseling center nearby."

"I'll leave you to it." Luke waved.

"Alcoholic?" Dec asked.

"Oh, no sir, I'm a bartender."

"I was going to offer you a beer, but maybe after our session now that I think of it. How about a soda?"

"Sure." Aaron sat down at the card table Holly had placed in the relatively empty kitchen.

He studied Dec intently as he joined him. "If I was going to treat you officially, I'd need to see your release papers from the Army and your records from your other therapist. We can talk about anything you'd like, but you might have to give me a little back story."

"That's fine. Luke says you were sex therapist. I was our team's Intelligence Sergeant. Spent a lot of years learning how to read other people and anticipate everything heading our way. Kind of makes me nuts that I can't figure out what the hell is wrong with my head. Do you know much about PTSD?"

"Sex therapy was just my specialty. I have a full-fledged degree in cognitive behavioral psychology. I can attempt to treat it all."

"Could I ask you stuff about sex?"

"Certainly."

"Been out of the Army for three years. I was in an Army crazy-ward for eight months."

Dec frowned. "Let's maybe not refer to it as such. You were in a treatment facility."

"Whatever you say. Anyway, I been in the Glen for two years. Wandered around for the months in between. The meds help with the nightmares. Last time I freaked out was about a year ago when someone accidentally shot my dog. I think I'm getting better, but, uh. . . ."

"Three years is a long time to not have sex, and you think you might be ready for a relationship?" Dec supplied the inevitable conclusion.

"Yeah."

"Is your dog okay?"

Aaron looked relieved at that question. He needed Aaron to relax a little if he was going to be of any help. "She's good. Luke saved her."

"He's a good guy."

"He's the best. All of the Camdens are, really."

Take my sister out. Luke's laundry list of reasons there should be a therapist in Pleasant Glen became crystal clear. "Natalie."

"Yeah. Natalie's *really* great. Here's the thing, though, before I was discharged I had way more sex than I should have. It was a skillset I'd honed, I guess. Before Natalie, I never thought much about the lead ups to getting a girl in my bed. Kissing. Rounding the bases. All the other stuff. I... didn't always make the best choices. I even made out with Holly once, but honestly, I was trying to get her sister to notice. Holly seemed to think it would work."

"I'm going to need you never to mention that to me again."

"Sorry, I swear it meant nothing to either of us. She was drunk."

"Still talking about kissing the woman I'm about to marry."

"Why don't we go back to Natalie?"

"That would be good."

"I've taken her out twice. We're good friends. I just can't quite tell if she'd like to be more than friends. We talk for hours almost every day. When I talk, she listens to me like she cares what I say." He shrugged. "Kinda makes me forget all the stuff I have to go see the therapist about. Both times when I've tried to do more than talk, she..."

"Became uncomfortable?"

"Yeah."

"Any idea why?" Dec would never reveal what he knew of Natalie.

"Like I said, I was an Intelligence Sergeant. I can read people, maybe even better than you can, Doc. It's either because she knows I was kind of a man-whore back in the day, and she doesn't want to have anything to do with a guy like that. Or somebody did something to her that would make me want to kill them."

"Since she did agree to go out with you twice, I doubt she has any issue with your experience level before her. If you think someone might have been sexually abusive with Natalie, be very patient with her. I might also suggest asking for every step you'd like to take. Make sure you have consent for each and every thing, even holding her hand or rubbing her leg. That can actually be very sexy if you do it right. Or tell her what you'd like to share with her, but that you want her to make the first move whenever she's ready. Never ever pressure her."

"I would never pressure her to do anything, and I'd have plenty to say to anyone that tried that. You think telling her to make the first move would really work?"

"Won't know if you don't try."

"Have you gotten to really talk to Nat since you got here? She's amazing."

Dec grinned. "I haven't talked with her much, but her family clearly adores her as do you. Piece of personal advice that I would never have believed until I met and fell in love with Holly — the best things in life often take too damn long to come, but they are worth the wait whenever they arrive."

"Yeah, I figured you were gonna say something like that. Thanks. You really should open a center or something nearby. There are a lot of people that have no access to help anywhere. And the way I hear it, Pleasant Glen might do for you what it did for me."

"And what was that?"

"Made me remember life is worth living and that there are people outside of my team who will be there if I need them."

"What are you doing? I haven't seen you on your laptop since we got here," Holly snuggled up beside Dec in the bed as he researched.

"A brilliant young vet gave me an idea this afternoon, and I was researching the possibilities of it."

"Aaron?"

"Yeah, apparently you snogged him a year ago."

Holly cringed. "I was drunk. He looked sad, really, really sad. I felt bad for him. It was a very weird night. It never went anywhere. I used to have a thing for pierced, tattooed bad boys."

"Used to? I'm a little worried."

"Now, I just have a thing for you. Never anyone else."

Dec shut his laptop and set it on the bedside table. "Is that so?" He scooted down in her bed and drew her body to his.

"It is."

"Please tell me that after this ridiculous hearing Friday we can at least go by my house long enough to have wild, crazy, loud sex. Living with your parents is getting to me."

"We can definitely do that. We can also pack if you want."

"What if Newsome decides you can go back to school for Spring semester?"

"Then I'd have to really think about that. The other night when we did the NA meeting I loved feeling like I was actually helping people. More classes, more years of school, an entire year of research for my dissertation, all of the Supervised Professional Experience hours, it all feels a little useless when I'm here. It's very daunting. It's like I told you when we first met, I can't ever seem to fully blend my two selves."

"You don't have to decide tonight, sweetheart. I just don't want you to look back twenty years from now and regret anything."

CHAPTER FIFTY-TWO

———

"I hate you have to be here for Thanksgiving, Mama." Trevor Singleton took his post in the chair beside his mother's hospital bed. The nurses would be bringing around some version of turkey and stuffing. No one should have to be in a hospital during the holidays. There should be a law.

"You look pale, Trevy."

Trevor forced a smile for his mother's sake. "I'm fine. You're the one in bed. Want to watch TV?"

"How much did you give this morning? Surely, they shouldn't let you donate blood so often. There has to be a rule."

"I'm following the rules. I'm fine. You need the blood. Soon as this transfusion kicks in maybe we can get you home."

"Sweetheart, I don't know how many more of these I'm going to be able to endure."

"Don't say that." That damned knot that had taken up permanent residence in his throat expanded. He hated it when she talked this way. The weight this conversation pressed on him was too much to bear.

"Being here, watching you, I have so many regrets."

"Mama, come on, don't regret anything. Please."

"I'm allowed my regrets, son. No one gets to live a life without a few. Look at me, Trevor."

He did as she asked. He always did as she asked no matter what it cost him. No matter what he wanted. She was all that mattered. "Your father and I tried to choose a path for you that we thought would be best. My parents did the very same with me, and I'm laying here about to die, realizing I never lived. If there's something you want to do, if the path your father and I chose doesn't fit you, please baby, choose something else. Your father will understand."

"I'm not so sure about that."

"Well, even if he doesn't it's not his life to choose. It's yours. He's made his choices. A lot of them were terrible decisions as you and I both know. You get to make yours."

"I don't think you really want to hear my choices, Mama. Why don't you try to sleep? That always helps the transfusion work faster."

"I'm tired of sleeping. They've promised me a few more months with the transfusions. There are a few things I'd like to do and see. Want to go with me?"

"What about school?" Trevor couldn't believe what she was saying.

"Fuck school."

"Mama!"

"I always wanted to try out that word. It's fun. Say it."

"Mama, what kind of pain meds did they give you?"

"Now you sound like your father. I'll be up and around by tomorrow morning. We have to go to that blasted hearing your father's so thrilled about, but after that I'll have seven or eight days before I'll need another treatment. Take me somewhere you've always wanted to go."

"I don't know. What about Dad?"

"Fuck your father."

"Please stop saying that. You have never cussed before. You're wigging me out."

"It's a fantastic word. You can use it in so many ways. And look, I wasn't struck by lightning or scolded by anyone. Life has too many rules. Why do we do this to ourselves? I spent my whole life trying to follow arbitrary rules made up by someone else. I wish I'd broken more rules and let you break more rules."

"I know, Mama, just take it easy, okay?"

"Just promise me, after I'm gone that you'll choose your own path. Stop letting me and your father bleed you dry, literally." She gestured to the bandage on his arm.

"If we go on this trip, where do you want to go?"

"Somewhere we've never been before."

Trevor brushed a kiss on his mother's cheek. Somehow a little of the weight he always felt when he was with her eased. "You really want to know what I want to do with my life? All I've ever heard is I'm the only one who can carry on the Singleton legacy at the school. You'd really be okay with me getting the hell out and doing my own thing?"

"Only if you sit and tell me all about every detail of it. Don't keep living with the mistakes your father and I forced on you."

"Dad's making another mistake with this trial."

"I know he is, and I get the impression you'd like to do something to stop him."

"You know I hate him."

"I know that, but what I don't know is if you're going to stand up to him."

"I can't believe you're saying this to me."

"Death makes things very clear, sweetheart. Life is grey, some good, some bad, hopefully more good than bad, but death clears the grey. Degrees are great and wonderful if they get you where you want to go, but if they get you to a place you never wanted to be, what's the use in that?"

CHAPTER FIFTY-THREE

Thursday night, Dec unlocked the door to his home and guided Holly inside. Life as they'd once known it stood around them, but nothing about it fit now. Everything had changed in two weeks' time. They'd decided to come back tonight to re-center themselves, reconsider everything tomorrow's decision would hold, and to spend the night forgetting every single thing that had ever gone wrong.

He wanted to drown in the perfume of her arousal, get lost in her sighs, and fill her full of everything he would ever be.

Smiling as he drew her into his protective embrace, he brushed a kiss on top of her head. "Only takes one-fifth of a second. . . ."

"To fall in love." She nuzzled against his clean t-shirt, squeezing him tightly as if she was afraid he was going to disappear right along with the rest of their life.

"To fall in love or for everything to change."

"I'm glad we came back tonight. I know it feels like everything has changed, Dec, but we haven't and, we won't, ever."

"Incorrect, my sweet little cowgirl. We will change. We just have to make sure we change together, that we grow together from here on. I still don't think I'm going to be able to stay in Lincoln, baby. I need you to know that I'll wait for you forever, and I cannot ask you to come to London with me."

Leaning up on her tiptoes she brushed her lips across his. "I'd wait for you forever, too, but I don't want to talk about leaving tonight. You're not going to London without me, but right now, I want you to carry me up those stairs and make me yours. I can't exist without you, Dec, and I need to be full of you. I just. . .I need to. . .I need you. . . ."

Words had never been necessary for the two of them. He knew this. "Your wish is my command, Ms. Camden."

"Be careful, darling, those words could get you into all kinds of trouble." And there was his giggle.

"I'm hoping."

Reaching across his cold bed the next morning, Dec came up empty. Momentarily terrified that the last two weeks had been a cocaine-induced dream, he crawled out of bed. Holly's duffle bag was on the chair in his room. The panties he slipped down her legs the night before were on the floor.

His heartbeat steadied. Shrugging into a pair of boxers, he began his search. By the time he'd canvased the main floor and came up empty, he was on edge. The cravings had come back last night knowing the hearing was today. Nothing he couldn't handle, but being in Lincoln made everything far too close for comfort. He missed the soothing sounds of the ranch and the space to think and exist without intrusion.

A neighbor's car alarm blared through the sunlight's dance on the fresh snow that blanketed the grass. Out of places to look, Dec opened the basement door and continued. He found her sitting in his music room holding a mug of coffee and staring at his wall of signed memorabilia.

"Baby? You okay?"

"I don't know." She shrugged. "I just like this room. It feels like you in here. What if you don't like the ranch because this is you, and I'm trying to make you be me?"

"Come here to me." He scooted beside her and wrapped her up in his arms. "I think the reason you like this room is it's the only room in this massive house that I like. It's the only room I had any say in. I do love the entire ranch because I feel you there the way you feel me in here, but I also love other things about it. I love the community there. I love the work. I love that people depend on me, and I can't let them down. I miss it already. I'm anxious to get back."

"What if they don't fire you or they don't kick me out of school? What happens then?"

"That's up to you, sweetheart."

"That doesn't help. I never know what to do."

"When you're here in Lincoln. . . .?"

"I want to be there."

Dec wasn't surprised at that answer, but was a little shocked at the quick response.

"Then you just answered your own question."

"But I don't want to be there without you. The ranch isn't my home without you there. If they don't fire you, and they agree to take over your visa, you have to work here. It feels like too many choices, and there's only one thing I know for sure."

"What's that?"

"You're my home, and if that means we have to stay in Lincoln or we somehow figure out how to be at the ranch, or we have to go to London, I'm home when I'm with you."

"I love you so much. I'm going to do everything in my power to make Camden Ranch our home, just give me a little time."

"Is that really what you want, too?"

"It really is."

"Promise?"

"Promise."

While Holly showered, Dec called Sarah Nicholls. "What did we find out?"

"It still depends on what happens today. Even if they fire you, your hours in the classroom do count towards your required SPE hours, unless the University contests them. Between your hours working for Lifespan, and teaching, and seeing patients you have the required number. After that, all that stands in your way is the licensing exam. Just try to talk the University into not contesting your hours with the state."

"Not sure I have any favors to call in there, but I'll do my best."

"As long as you pass the exam, you can go through with your plan. You can carry your own H-1B until your citizenship is approved via marriage and open your own non-profit."

"My cowgirl needs to be on horseback on an open range. I'm going to get her there."

"I have no doubt. I am researching getting Holly a student visa for the UK should this all go south, though. I don't think it would be difficult, but if she is removed from UN-L that could complicate things. Maybe try to sweet talk them into allowing her to remain enrolled just until I can secure a student transfer to a school in London."

"We'll do our best. Thank you for all you've done."

"I better get an invite to the wedding."

"You got it."

Holly clung to Dec's hand as they entered a board room she'd never seen before. They had nothing to hide now.

Dr. Newsome was seated at the head of the table. Both Dr. and Mrs. Singleton, Dr. Anderson, Dr. Sinclair, and Dr. Simpson sat along one side of the table. The other side was empty. Dec pulled out a chair for Holly and took the seat beside her.

She'd pictured some kind of courtroom. Something like she'd seen on television. She'd been worried that being back on trial might get to Dec. He'd endured a brief stay in prison and several courtrooms according to him. Despite there being no bench or gavel and no one being dressed in black robes, the room was fraught with tension.

The stale air was difficult to breathe. The clouds outside the windows were bruised with another impending storm.

"Did you have a nice holiday, Dr. St. James?" Newsome asked. Holly wondered what he was playing at, exchanging pleasantries before placing someone's head on a chopping block.

"Holly's family welcomed me in very graciously. I helped prepare the family meal after feeding cattle, and then Holly and I spent the rest of the evening sharing the meal with a few members of my NA group that had no family to celebrate with. It was a lovely day. And yours, sir?"

"It was fine."

Holly wanted to scream. Why wouldn't they just start? Just say something, anything useful. She was a baited rat circling a trap.

"So, that's your plan. You're going to become some kind of twelve-step counselor?" Dr. Singleton sneered.

His wife looked bereaved. "Trevor, that's a lovely thing to do on Thanksgiving."

"I'm sorry, would there be some issue with that Singleton? Not prestigious enough for Singleton blood?" Dec apparently wasn't putting up with much of anything, and Holly had never heard Ms. Singleton disagree with her husband.

"I'm sorry, we're dragging this out," she explained to Holly. "Trevor's on his way."

"Why is Trevor coming?"

"Felt he needed to be here." *Of course he did. Wants to see me go down. Assweasel.*

A few minutes later, Trevor Jr. appeared. He was carrying a folder and looked ridiculously excited. Holly rolled her eyes.

"Let's begin. As both of you stormed out of our initial session I do still have a few questions," Newsome explained.

"I will not ever elaborate on anything shared between Holly and myself," Dec laid down the law.

"And I am sorry we asked you to that day. I suppose I was hoping if you provided enough information I could find a way to help you, Dr. St. James. What I would like an answer to is why you did not come to me when you realized Ms. Camden was your student?"

"Sir, I didn't know you. We'd never met. Lifespan informed me I was to teach that very day. I was never under the impression I had any other choice. Any time a human being falls in love, it begins with a lie. We lie to ourselves long enough to believe that we could somehow be good enough for the person we so desperately want.

"Unfortunately, our lies had to spill over to other people for circumstances we had no control over. And that is always the problem with a lie. At what exact moment would the truth have set us free?

When should I have come clean about my relationship with Holly? When was the exact moment in time that it wouldn't have brought on disaster for both of us, and how would I have ever known that moment even existed? My choices were to give up the woman I am madly in love with or to lose my job, meaning I'd move four thousand miles away from her. Surely, you understand how neither of those were viable options in my book."

"Sir," Holly leaned in. "It does seem to me that the ethics code that we broke was put into place to avoid either party manipulating the other. We do understand why it is there, but we fell in love before Dec was ever hired here. Nothing that we did was for ill-gotten gain. Neither one of us was in a position of power over the other. We're in love. I suppose I'm asking if you're going to stick to the letter of the law or the spirit of it. One seems far more logical in this case."

"I have to agree with that, Ms. Camden, but there must be consequences for your actions," Newsome vowed.

"Really, because there weren't any for my dad." Every head in the room turned to stare at Trevor in shock. "Don't sit there and pretend every single person at this table doesn't know what you did. You do it every semester. You've just only gotten caught once."

Holly couldn't seem to remember how to join her lower jaw to her upper.

Trevor continued. "Look, I followed them all freaking semester. My plan was to take them down, and the thing is I have no idea why I wanted that. Mad at the universe. Mad that I have to be here at this University. All of those reasons, but none of them have to do with Holly and Dr. St. James. I followed them around and tried to record what I could, because if I was doing that I didn't have to think about how shitty my life was going to be. I can tell you this — they were in love before he ever started working here. I saw them before school was even back in session together.

"Holly drove me nuts because she got things I'll never get. She gets to come here because that's what she wants for her life. If she decided she didn't want this anymore, she could leave, and I hated her for the freedom she has. But I'll tell you this, she's a kickass student, and she'll make a great psychologist. Dr. St. James is the best teacher this department has. He didn't let me get away with all of my usual shit. He actually taught me things, and I don't even want a psych degree.

"I thought my mom and dad desperately wanted me to be your chosen student, Dr. Newsome, so that's what I tried to do. Anything to make them happy. It used to be to keep them from fighting constantly. After that it was because Mom is sick and I wanted to do everything right. It was like I thought I could fight Leukemia by doing what she wanted for me. I could negotiate with God, or the stars, or whoever and buy her more time by doing what Dad wanted mc to do, but I can't, and I am so fucking sick of towing this line. I'm out."

"I told you it was a fun word to say," Ms. Singleton patted Trevor's arm as tears rolled down her face.

"My father has been buying or bullying my grades for the last seven years. He's also had dozens of affairs with students. I have proof of all of them right here." He lifted the folder. "By the way dad, your passwords on your laptops are lame. If you people want to fire someone, fire him. If you want to kick someone out of school, I'm your man. I'd say those are infractions worthy of being suspended. But falling in love? I don't think so."

Trevor's mother threw her arms around him, and Holly was certain she had to be dreaming. Dec looked equally as shocked.

Fury rolled off of Dr. Singleton in waves. No one spoke.

Each minute felt like an hour. Finally, Dr. Newsome, cleared his throat. "Well, that is all certainly something to consider, Trevor. Thank you. I would like to look at that folder you have there."

"I actually have a recording of Dr. Singleton threatening me if I didn't give Trevor a good grade." Dec laid his phone on the table.

Newsome shook his head. "I'll deal with Dr. Singleton later, but Dr. St. James, I have to echo what Trevor said about your teaching. We have your student reviews in. They all lauded your methods and up-to-date information. They felt your work in the field helped them more than any of their other classes."

"I'm glad they were pleased." Dec shrugged.

"And Miss Camden, your work here at the University has always been exemplary, but these things do not erase what the two of you did."

"We know that, sir," Holly assured him. She'd wanted him to make this easy. She'd wanted him to kick her out so she could go home, but she also wanted him to employ Dec and take over his visa for another year so they could be together. And in her wishes she found her truth. When the flipped quarter spun in the air, she knew what side she wanted it to land on.

"I haven't heard anything today that I feel would change my recommendation to the board on this ruling, which passed ten to one. Ms. Camden, you will be allowed to return to UN-L, however, you will have to re-take your foundations research class as the grade you received when Dr. St. James was your professor will be stricken from your transcript. The class will not be offered again until fall semester next year. Your research will be halted for a year. The lack of judgment you showed by continuing your relationship with your professor has also cost you your candidacy to work with me as your dissertation supervisor."

Holly nodded her understanding. Terror crawled over her skin. What if he'd saved her and Dec was the one going down? No. Please.

"Dr. St. James, up until this indiscretion was revealed we had been extremely pleased with your work here at the University. However, word has already gotten out and parents do not want you having access to their students."

Holly couldn't breathe. London held all of the things Dec was afraid to return to. Even if she went with him, he would be miserable there all over again.

Dec said nothing as if he'd expected this, as if he'd never had hope.

"However, I believe we have a workaround for this if you'd be interested."

The pent up air in Holly's lungs escaped audibly. Dec looked confused. "A workaround?"

"Yes, UN-L has an outstanding online graduate degree program in other fields of study, but Psychology is severely lacking. We'd like you to take a full load of classes online for spring semester. You would be in charge of developing the curriculum for the program as you see fit. We'd like to expand and add additional classes each semester. You would need to be on campus for the hiring of the online staff. If you agree to this, the University agrees to take on your H-1B visa for the next year."

"But I could work from anywhere?"

"You would need to be on campus occasionally, but the rest of the time, yes."

"And if I wanted to found my own non-profit psychological treatment center outside of Lincoln, would that be allowed under my new contract?"

"I see no reason why not as long as your work here never suffers."

"I'll do it."

"Is there anything you should tell me now? You do have choices and options, Dr. St. James, and I apologize that you were not given those luxuries when you were originally hired."

"Thank you, sir. I assure you there will be no more elicit, forbidden affairs. I'm hoping to be a married man very, very soon."

Holly beamed at him. He was going to get to stay, and even with the new options before her, her truth never faltered.

CHAPTER FIFTY-FOUR

"Does your chest hurt?" Holly asked as they eased out of the gravel lot onto the road.

"In a good way," Dec assured her.

"I can't believe you did that."

"You watched them do it, love. It was your artist."

"I know, but. . .can I see it again?"

He slowed the Pilot at a traffic light and gently edged his shirt away from the bandage covering his newest tattoo. Her cattle brand was the only marking on the right side of his body. Nothing could ever have meant more to her. They were fighting together now forever.

"I love it," she vowed knowing she could never verbalize what it meant to her.

"I love you."

"Promise?"

"Oh, baby, I promise."

"Do you have any idea how much it means to me that you want to open a counseling center in Pleasant Glen?"

Dec laced their fingers together as he continued to drive them further outside of Lincoln loaded down with the most essential items for their new home, mainly his guitars. They'd be back Sunday with a moving truck and her brothers and cousin to pack up his house and her apartment.

"Well, we have to find a place to put it. I'm not sure if you've noticed, sweetheart, but the Glen is barely a town. It's more a hamlet with a few horses and half a traffic light."

"And several dozen tractors. Don't forget the tractors."

"The tractors have been noted. There are people there and in the surrounding communities that need help, probably not enough people to be open full-time, but they need somewhere to go. I want to expand to AA meetings along with weekly NA meetings. And you're going to need somewhere to work to get your SPE hours after you finish your degree."

"You're going to have to help me if I'm going to attend online school from Northcentral."

"I think I've proven myself to be an excellent instructor for you, love." He winked at her. "You're certain you don't want to continue at UN-L?"

"It never even occurred to me that I could finish online. I've spent the last few years trying to live two lives in two totally different places. Then I met you and you gave me a way to make me whole again. You merged my two worlds because you're my home. Since my future husband is going to be teaching all of the online courses at UN, I think it would be better for me to attend a different university."

"I have no idea how I got lucky enough to be your home, baby, but there is nothing else, not teaching online classes, not opening my own therapy center, not even being a rock star that means more to me than being the place you fall when the world doesn't go our way. I've fucked up so much of my life, Holl, and I know I let you down, but I swear I will never let you down again. Every day I'm going to be a man worthy of you."

"You already are, Dec. You're worth everything. Our mistakes don't define us. We saved each other." She held up their clasped hands. "I'm going to be right there no matter what happens. We deal with everything together."

"You know, I'm going to need you to help me study for the licensing exam. Have to pass that before I can establish a new center."

"I could be your tutor. You should know I'm very strict."

"Mmm, I'm hoping you'll dress up like a naughty school marm for me."

"I thought you wanted a librarian."

"Can't I have both?"

"You can have whatever you want, Dr. St. James."

"Promise?"

"Promise."

"Could I speak with you, sir?" Dec should have worn one of those cowboy hats Grant had loaned him so he could actually have gone to Holly's father hat in hand.

"I 'spose," Ev sighed.

"Thanks," Dec climbed up the front porch steps. They'd gotten a reprieve on snow just in time for the Cattle Baron festival that day. "I wanted to thank you very much for letting me live here in your home and welcoming me in." Not that Holly's father had been overly hospitable, but Dec had expected nothing less. Former addicts with records who got your daughter kicked out of school didn't deserve hospitality. All he wanted was the chance to earn Holly's father's trust no matter how long it took.

"Sir, I'd like to propose to Holly at the dance tonight. I've had the ring for a while. I know I'm not going to get your blessing now, I just hoped you might give me a chance to be the man you'd be proud for your daughter to marry."

"Don't sound to me like you're asking for my permission. Sounds more like you're asking for my forgiveness. Less you and my baby girl got hitched at the Lincoln courthouse while you were there yesterday, try again."

"I didn't expect to get your permission."

"And even if you don't, you're going on with what you want, right?"

Dec's jaw tensed in frustration. He tried to let the cool air ease him, but the thin ribbons of icy air only served to agitate his lungs. "Look, I know I'm not the kind of man you would've pick out for Holly, sir. Okay, I get that. But I swear to you I love her. I didn't even know what love was until I met her, but I did know what it wasn't. That was all I'd ever known, until I sat down at a table across from her and she smiled at me.

"I will do everything in my power to make her happy, give her anything she might ever need, take care of her constantly, and be there for her. She needs to be on this ranch, sir. What she wants to do, the degree she's getting, it isn't easy. There are days you just can't leave the patients at work. You carry them with you. Their stories haunt your dreams. You never know if you've done enough to help them. I want to be there to pick her up at the end of a long day and reassure her that she did everything she could. I want to practice beside her. I want to help people. I want to help her help people."

"That was a little better," Ev allowed. "I've known all along my baby girl needed to be on this ranch. What I want to know is why you think you need to be here."

"I want to be with her, no matter where that might be."

"Declan, son, stop telling me about her. Tell me what this ranch can do for you and what you can do for it."

He called me son. Maybe we're getting somewhere. "I grew up working a sheep farm, but that was nothing more than an exercise in futility for my brothers and I and the sheep. My father couldn't be bothered to stop drinking long enough to teach us how to do what we were trying to do to survive. I've learned more here in the last two weeks than I learned in several years of college. Not only about how to run a cattle ranch, sir, but about how to live a life I could actually be proud of.

"To be perfectly honest, the work here, the hours, it makes my addictive cravings all but disappear. That's ultimately how you success-fully treat addiction. You create a new life where it's easier not to use. I've tried to do that twice now, and neither really worked. My addic-tions will always be with me. I know that. I'm an addict. Being here is a constant reminder that I don't have to let them be my master. This life is one that makes it so much easier not to use. Helping people is how I fought the addiction for the last several years. Being here, I could help people in this community and beyond, and you and your family and the animals, they depend on me, and you see, sir, that has always been the saving grace for me. If someone or something needs me, I try not to let them down. I swear, sir, I just want a chance to earn your respect. I know I don't deserve it, but I will never stop trying to earn that."

Ev took another long sip of his coffee. "My little girl loves the Cattle Baron Festival. She loves the cattle show almost as much as she loves the fancy dance afterwards. Holly was always like that. Wanted to be a cowgirl and a fancy psychologist. Wanted to out-ride her big brothers and wanted to keep her nails painted pink. She used to wear lipgloss and hairbows when she cleaned out horse stalls and the barn. Wants the best of both worlds, but she was always willing to work for everything she wanted. I think you can give her both, and the festival is the perfect time to give her a ring. Just don't you ever hurt her, boy, or I'll have plenty to say about it."

"I won't sir. I promise. Thank you."

Holly had never been more thankful of her big brother's overprotective nature than she was standing under the twinkle lights in the rec center flanked by Grant and Austin.

Cheyenne was on the other side of the room. She'd kept a cold glare leveled on Holly since they'd all arrived.

Dec was on stage. The Original Sinners were in the middle of their first set, and the crowd was loving the mix of Country and Classic Rock. Holly and Dec had thanked them profusely for driving all the way out into the Glen. They'd promised to do it regularly so Dec could continue to perform with them. He'd promised to come to Lincoln often to practice.

Camden Ranch had once again won the livestock show that morning, taking first and second place. Third had gone to a smaller ranch nearby. Other than the chill of betrayal housed on the other side of the room, it had been a perfect day.

Holly had no idea what to say to Cheyenne or if she should say anything at all. She wanted no part of Cheyenne's darkness. She didn't have the energy to try to be her light. She never had.

When Dec played the opening chords of *Rebel Yell*, Holly grinned as she recalled the first time she'd heard him play at Duffy's so many months ago.

"He's good. Best band we've had at Cattle Baron's in decades, but kinda makes my skin crawl when I know who he's singing this song about," Grant teased.

"Ah geez, did you have to point that out?" Austin pretended to shudder. "I was just getting to like the guy."

"If you two don' shut it, I'm gonna start describing my *Rebel Yell*."

"You gonna talk to her?" Grant gestured discreetly to Cheyenne.

"Have no idea what to say to her. Little worried I might scalp her if she gets too close."

"I bet that'd get Dec off of the stage," Austin laughed.

A few songs later, the lights darkened. Only the light on center stage remained aglow. Holly's brow furrowed. Dec settled on a stool completely alone.

"What's he doing?" she asked Wyatt who couldn't seem to stop grinning.

"Solo, it looks like."

I want to dance in your light
Affect the chemistry of my longest night
Vanquish the darkness in the heat of your sun
Let your touch give me sight

"Oh my gosh, he's singing it." Unable to stay away, Holly edged to the front of the stage. He winked at her as he continued to sing.

They'd been through hell and had somehow made it back. He'd made several trips all on his own before their souls had found their mate. As he sang her song at the Cattle Baron ball, she knew it had all been worth it. Their future was worth their past, as horrible as his had been.

A shocked gasp wrenched loose from her chest, when he exited the stage and stood before her. "You sure you're ready for this?" he whispered.

"Are you about to. . . .?" She couldn't believe he already had a ring. She couldn't believe he was doing this at her favorite festival. How had he even known?

"Hush," he gave her that sexy-as-sin smirk that she swore would always be her undoing. He fell to his knees and she dammed back tears. "Holly, baby, would you do me the extraordinary honor of being my wife?" He lifted an engagement ring with a diamond that out shined the stars.

"Oh my gosh," she couldn't breathe.

"Is that a yes?" he chuckled.

"Yes, a million billion times yes." He slipped the ring on her finger and stood to catch her as she threw herself into his arms. The crowd broke out in raucous applause. Her brothers filled the hall with wolf-whistles.

The band returned to the stage without their frontman to play *I Need You* by Tim and Faith while Dec spun Holly around the dance floor.

Even Andy seemed happy for them.

Holly was inundated with congratulations and hugs from the town that had raised her. Everyone except the person who'd been her best friend wanted to share their love.

As Holly and Dec made their way around the room, eventually they were upon Cheyenne.

"Guess everything always works out for the Camdens, right? Must be nice to live a charmed life," she sneered.

"Is that really what you think, Chey? You really think our life is charmed? You have no idea. Do you really believe that I deserved what you did?"

"Perfect guy, perfect life, new best friend, looks pretty charmed to me."

"I never had a new best friend. I was unaware I wasn't allowed to have anyone but you, and I was too stupid never to realize that you were never my friend at all." Holly's throat dammed tight, robbing her words of volume.

"You deserve to know how it feels not to get your way."

Dec wrapped his arm around Holly's shoulder, holding her steady in the storm. Breath returned to her lungs.

"I do know what that's like, and I know that life doesn't always work out just the way we want it to. Sometimes you don't get the things you were so sure were for you, but if you'll have a little faith, most of the time you get something so much better."

"I'm not in the mood for your sunshine and roses shit, Holly. You were supposed to help me, and you never would. You were supposed to help me get Grant."

"I could never have done that. Grant saw you for what you were years ago. I never wanted to see it. I wouldn't let myself see it. You made your bed, Cheyenne, and I'm not going to sleep in it. Not anymore."

"So you're Dec, right?" Cheyenne turned her haughty glare on him.

"I would tread very, very carefully if I were you," he warned.

"Or what, my life will somehow be shittier than it is right now?"

"No one said life would always be great, or even fair, or that any of us deserved to have a charmed life. But life did provide you people that could've helped you build a life that wouldn't have been shitty, as you put it, and you chose to throw them on the pyre instead of letting them help you. Nothing Holly or anyone else can do about that. I will say this, though, you are not welcome in our home, on her ranch, or near my fiancée. And if I hear of you doing anything else that upsets her, I won't hesitate to put a stop to it."

"*Our* ranch. She's not welcome on *our* ranch."

"I second that," Grant joined them. "Don't darken the gates of Camden Ranch ever again. Dec's taught me something while he's been around. As long as you're blaming Holly or me or whoever for your problems, you'll never change. The only people who make changes for the better accept their part of the deal. He's done it. Holl's done it, but I don't believe you ever will. Blaming other people's just too easy for you."

"The Camdens and everyone else in this godforsaken town can fuck the hell off," were the last words Holly's best friend ever spoke to her. She stormed out of the rec room.

"Come here, sweetheart," Dec gathered her up in his arms and swayed her to the music right where they were standing. "Toughest lesson you'll ever learn as a psychologist is that you can't save them all. Some people just don't want to be saved, but Holly, baby, you will always be my savior."

CHAPTER FIFTY-FIVE
Christmas Eve

Holly peeked out of the tiny room of the Methodist Church in her hometown to see the pine garlands along the pews and Christmas trees near the altar strung with white lights. The entire town was seated in the pews awaiting her.

Silent snowflakes gathered on the windowpanes, anxious for a front row seat, and cinnamon and cloves permeated the air. Marrying Declan St. James was the most perfect Christmas present ever.

She adjusted her long white gown. Her heart swelled to fill her chest when Beth Kinders came in on the arm of Trevor Singleton Jr. According to Beth, Trev was opening a hiking and whitewater rafting tour company in Colorado in the spring. He'd officially withdrawn from UN and had spent most of Christmas break chasing Beth.

Christmas miracles were everywhere, it seemed.

She'd asked Beth if she still wanted to be her maid-of-honor. They weren't quite there yet, but at least she'd come.

Natalie and her mama had been fussing over her all day. She was ready to get the show on the road.

Most of the members of The Original Sinners were all in suits softly playing guitars in the choir loft. Kade was Dec's best man so they were short two guitarists. Several pews were filled with members of Dec's NA and AA meetings. Matt and his girlfriend Megan had gotten permission to come all the way to Pleasant Glen for the ceremony. Dec still saw Matt every other week in Lincoln, and he'd transitioned him to Dr. Evans, Dec's friend, for treatment. Dr. Evans and his wife had agreed to bring Matt and Megan to Pleasant Glen. Things were going well.

Since Luke and Indie were at home with two healthy twin girls, Grant walked Mrs. Camden to her seat. Natalie made her walk and Holly beamed as the music eased into Savage Garden's *Truly, Madly, Deeply,* when Dec and Kade made their entrance.

"You're sure about this?" Ev asked Holly as he offered her his arm.

She brushed a kiss on his cheek. "I've never been more sure about anything in my entire life, Daddy."

"You know you'll always be my baby girl, right?"

"And you know you'll always be my hero, right?"

Her father blinked back tears, and nodded. "Believe that's our cue."

Dec and Holly vowed to love and care for one another for the rest of their lives. They kissed for several long minutes when prompted and then joined everyone in the church basement for a party where absolutely no alcohol was available. It didn't matter. Everyone had a wonderful time. When Trace wheeled out an entire wedding cake crafted of his doughnuts the crowd cheered.

When Pastor Higgins presented Dec and Holly the marriage certificate to be signed, Dec grinned. "Hang on, I bought something special for this." He pulled a Cross pen from his pocket.

"*You* bought a pen? I'm in shock." Holly beamed.

"Some things are never meant to be undone, and we, my sweet, sexy cowgirl are permanent."

"Promise?" Holly giggled.

"Promise."

EPILOGUE

Stepping out of the shower, Dec scrubbed a towel over his face and hair before he noticed it.

Chuckling, he shook his head as he read the lipstick message on the mirror. 'Working on something in the office. Come find me.' He had no idea what she was up to, but his beautiful wife never ceased to amaze him.

A vase of milkweed she'd rescued before the spring burning last week sat on their counter. A hesitant, sleepy sun peeked through the last of the heavy winter coat of clouds, warming the first of Dec and Holly's calves. Even the birds seemed to believe winter was finally gone. Dec's own personal sun was apparently waiting for him in their home office. He doubted she'd ask for help with her Theories of Personalities Class via a lipstick message, but he never knew with her.

The day before, the St. James Community Counseling Center had opened in what had been an old mercantile a hundred years ago. They'd worked their fingers to the bone, and he'd hoped Holly was in the mood to do a little celebrating. He'd planned to take her to Saddleback's that evening, since that was the only semi-nice restaurant in town.

Accomplishment felt so damn good, and it wasn't even as good as the knowledge that he was giving back.

Shrugging into a pair of Wranglers, he headed towards the office.

"Baby?" he called.

"Shh," she scolded.

Worried he'd misread the message and that she was angry about something, he double-stepped to find out what was wrong.

"Holy fucking hell." His eyes goggled as he took her in. Dressed in nothing but a black vest, grey pencil skirt, black stiletto heels, and glasses, she shot him a smirk that speared through his chest and took up residence in his steel-hard cock.

"Have to be quiet in the library, Dr. St. James," she cooed.

Dec's heart flew. My God, she was perfection. His every fantasy standing before him, wearing his rings and dressed as a naughty librarian.

When she stepped up two rungs on a ladder she must've taken from the barn and had positioned against the bookshelves, a ragged groan wrenched from his gut. The skirt edged upwards, revealing black stockings attached to a lace garter complete with red satin strappings that peeked out.

"I have no idea what I did to deserve this, but tell me so I can keep doing it."

"It was never only supposed to be about my fantasies, sweetheart. We both get to explore, remember?"

"I remember." If only he could breathe.

She eased an old black book from the shelf and gave him another coy grin as she displayed the title, *Fear of Flying* by Erica Jong. Dec swallowed down another round of possessive desire.

"I've never been afraid to fly, but I do enjoy this novel. I think you might like it." He swore the slow bat of her long eyelashes strung his body hard and fast.

"Perhaps you could read it to me."

"Perhaps." She feigned disinterest. "I wouldn't want to get in trouble though."

"Seems if a doctor requests you read, not reading might be what got you in trouble."

"True." She stepped down the ladder. Every cell in his body throbbed. "Where shall I sit for reading?"

"Right here," he took the seat behind his desk and guided her into his lap.

"Mmm, so hard, Dr. St. James."

"All for you, Mrs. St. James. By the way, this is incredible, but I get to live my fantasies every single day because I get to be married to you."

"Promise?"

"Promise."

———

Continue reading in, Un-hitched. Available Spring 2017.

ABOUT THE AUTHOR

Bestselling author Jillian Neal likes her coffee strong and sweet with a shot of sinful spice, the same way she likes her cowboys. In fact, her caffeine addiction is quite possibly considered illicit in several states as are a few of the things her characters do. When she's not writing or reading, you'll find her in the kitchen trying out new recipes or coming up with excuses reasons to purchase yet another handbag or make an additional trip to Sephora. Though she'll always be a Bama girl at heart, Jillian hangs up her hat and kicks up her boots outside of Atlanta with her hunk-of-a-husband and her teenage sons.

For more information...
jillianneal.com
jillian@jillianneal.com

ALSO BY JILLIAN NEAL

www.ingramcontent.com/pod-product-compliance
Lightning Source LLC
Chambersburg PA
CBHW051514250626
47156CB00001B/97